# *Vron*

## Lee Boehm

This book is written in Australian English. The spelling differs from American English.

ISBN: 978-0-6459063-1-8
Paperback

Facebook: Lee Boehm – Author
Instagram: Lee_Boehm_Author

NATIONAL
LIBRARY
OF AUSTRALIA

A catalogue record for this
book is available from the
National Library of Australia

*To Amelia Laing and John Harris.*

*This book is dedicated to you.*

*Thank you for making my children and I who we are today.*


*To my husband, Christopher, who listened to countless
'interesting' things as I discovered them and probably now
knows as much about colonial Australia as I do and is and will be
my faithful companion as I visit all the places that I write about
to research my stories.*

*Thankyou darling.*


*Thank you to all my beautiful friends, who, over the years have
accepted me, validated me and loved me, and allowed me to be
who I am, warts and all. You are my
brothers and sisters of the heart.*

*"And as you can now see, lass,
it's only a matter of time and place,
and circumstances that makes any of us
differ from each other.*

*Under it all we are all the same,
a little good and a little bad,
hopefully more of the good though.*

*But desperate times change how a person reacts,
and sometimes more of the bad has to come out
for them to survive.*

*But never judge a person
on what they had to do to survive,
as that was only them
at that particular time and place."*

Amelia, 1845

*We submit to your humanity*
*as a British fellow subject*
*and to your discretion as a Christian magistrate,*
*the case for this country.*

*In the mutation of human affairs,*
*the arm of oppression which has smitten us with desolation,*
*may strike at your social well-being.*

*Communities allied by blood,*
*language and commerce cannot long suffer alone.*

*We conjure you, therefore, by the unity*
*of colonial interests*
*—as well by the obligations which bind all men*
*to intercede with the strong and unjust*
*on behalf of the feeble and oppressed*
*—to exert your influence to the intent*
*that transportation to V. D. Land may forever cease.*

Letter from the Launceston Association for the Cessation of the Transportation of Convicts, to the chief magistrates, colonial secretaries and legislative councils of the Australian colonies and New Zealand, 1850

# Family Tree

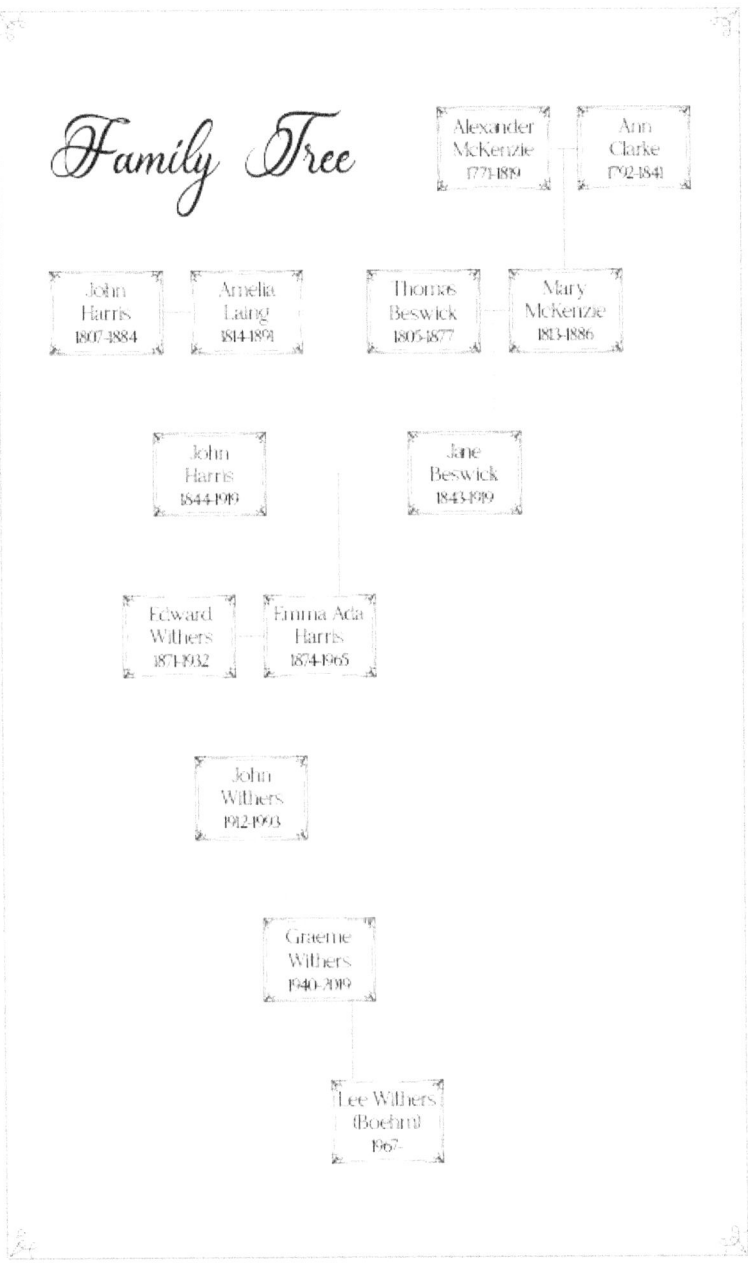

Alexander McKenzie
1771-1819

Ann Clarke
1792-1841

John Harris
1807-1884

Amelia Laing
1814-1891

Thomas Beswick
1805-1877

Mary McKenzie
1813-1886

John Harris
1844-1919

Jane Beswick
1843-1919

Edward Withers
1871-1932

Emma Ada Harris
1874-1965

John Withers
1912-1993

Graeme Withers
1940-2019

Lee Withers (Boehm)
1967-

# Launceston Area Map

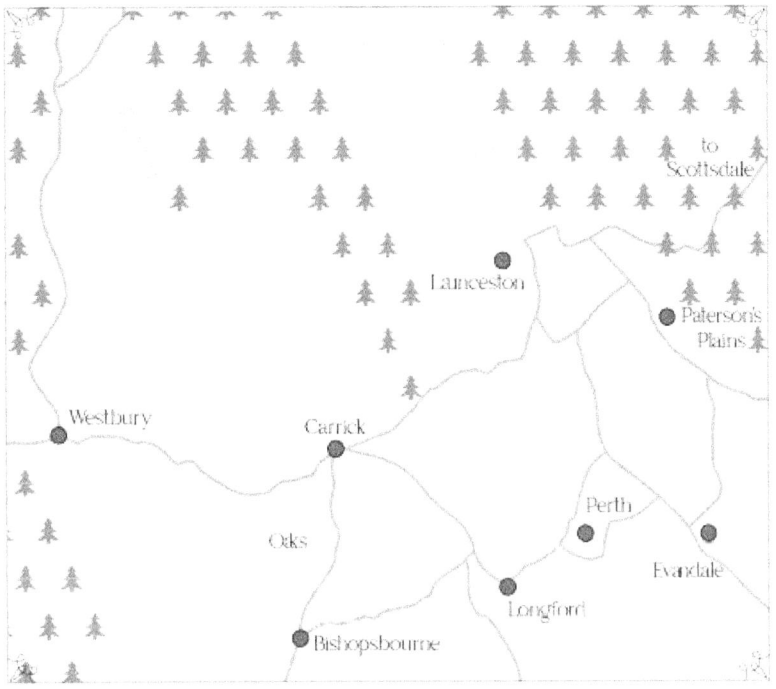

# Chapter One

# *1832 – Lambeth*

*I*t was 1832, and 25-year-old John Harris was sitting in the bowels of the *Leviathan*, a hulk anchored in the Thames River, waiting to be transported to Van Diemen's Land. This was definitely not the plan that he had for his life, and he was more than bitter that his trusting nature had brought him here.

John was born at Lambeth, Surrey, close to the centre of London, on the 1st of April 1807. His family had a good giggle about John and Lizzie's boy being born on April Fool's Day. "He's bound to be a bit of a clown, hey," laughed his grandfather.

John's father was 27 when his son was born and was working as a gardener at the famous Vauxhall Gardens. He had met Lizzie, who worked as a cook at the Gardens, and they had married at St Mary's church, next to Lambeth Palace, on the 27th of May 1800, when John was 20 and Lizzie 25. They had only been blessed with the one child, and while his parents worked, little Johnny was cared for by his grandparents, who all lived in the tiny terrace houses in Horse Ferry Lane, close to Lambeth Palace, where the Archbishop of Canterbury lived.

The Palace of Westminster dominated the opposite bank, and the Vauxhall Bridge provided an easy connection between Lambeth and the Westminster area opposite. At all times of the day and night, ferry's carrying all kinds of goods could be seen coming and going across the river. The population of Lambeth tripled between when John was born and when he was convicted and during that time Lambeth was a busy and thriving area.

When his father was a child most of the area was still farming land, but that soon changed as huge glass and pottery factories were built, including the Doulton factory, the first in England to mass produce artistic pottery and earthenware. The farms soon disappeared and the workers who filled the factories moved into modest dwellings close to the river. John's grandfather, who was a factory worker since being evicted from his farm, had encouraged his son to learn to read and write so that he could get work anywhere except in the factories. He saw men and women get very old and very sick before they should have, standing on their feet all day from before dawn until after dark, in unsanitary buildings that were either freezing cold or stinking hot, and breathing in noxious fumes all day. The hacking coughs from the factory workers could be heard every morning and night as they tramped to and from their homes.

John's grandfather had talked his son into getting a job at the Vauxhall Gardens, which was close to where they lived, and in preparation he sent him to the country from the age of 13 to stay with family that worked on a large country estate owned by a Duke. Young John senior worked for his keep alongside his relatives and learned skills in horticulture, which he found was very different to farming skills; growing and maintaining beautiful flower gardens and lush lawn is very different to growing vegetables and caring for farm animals. While on the estate, John learned how to speak in the refined manner of the upper-class, this being much admired by the gentry and a skill that could lead to acquiring better employment as a footman, waiter or butler. By the time he applied for the job at the Vauxhall Gardens he could speak almost as well as the Lords and Ladies who were regular attendees.

John junior's mother worked as a cook and downstairs maid at Lambeth Castle during the day and at the Vauxhall Gardens at night, sometimes with only hours between each job. Her workmates had been helping her to improve her speech since she started in the kitchen when she was 15, hoping for an upstairs job. When she was at home she would sit with little Johnny and help him to practice his reading, writing, elocution and arithmetic, all skills necessary as a servant in a Palace, and that John would need to know if he too wanted to get a decent job.

Sadly, John's mother died when he was only nine. A tub of boiling fat had tumbled over and burnt her badly on her chest and arms. She succumbed to the shock and infection several days later aged just 41. John was inconsolable and cried and cried for weeks on end. Finally, his father decided to take him to work with him at the Gardens with the permission of the Chief Gardener who saw little John as an extra set of hands for free. The fresh air and the calming work did the boy wonders and he started to smile again.

For a few shillings, John's father paid for him to be tutored in reading, writing and arithmetic by one of the waiters. The waiters employed at the Gardens were prized for their superior literacy as well as their good looks and manners. And now as a single man, which was a prerequisite for the job, John's father with his eloquent speech and handsome face, also picked up night-time work as a waiter.

Vauxhall Gardens was primarily a pleasure gardens set over several acres and easily accessible via the Vauxhall Bridge. The many acres were comprised of spacious gardens intertwined by delightful walks, with high hedges and trees, and paved with gravel. Each garden included collections of the most picturesque and striking objects, pavilions, lodges, groves, grottoes, lawns, temples, and fountains. There were porticoes, colonnades, and rotundas with pillars, statues, and beautiful paintings.

During the day the Gardens were perfect for promenading and taking in the summer weather, but it was at night that the Gardens really came to life. Vauxhall Gardens was most famous for creating a fairytale-like atmosphere with its huge number of lamps, and the dramatic and magical effect produced when these lamps were lit at dusk. By 1822 there were more than 20,000 lamps of many colours, and through a system of linked fuses, the whole Garden could be illuminated in about two minutes. The trail of oil from whale or seal blubber gave the gardens a distinctive smell, that would remind John of the Garden's for the rest of his life.

The Gardens were open for entertainment three nights per week, on Mondays, Wednesdays, and Fridays, from May to September, and were open to anyone who could pay the admission fee. Therefore, the gardens were always overflowing with the most interesting crowd, landed gentry and even royalty mixed with workers and labourers, and all were dressed in their finest attire. Every night, several bands played in the rotundas, and food and drinks were served until early the following morning. It was not unheard of for the cooks and waiters to still be hard at work at 2am in the morning, along with the musicians who played until the crowds finally left. Food was served continuously in supper-boxes to patrons in the rotunda's and at designated tables in the Grove. It was usual for the Gardens to serve around 2,000 meals every night. That required a lot of cooks and a lot of waiters.

The job of a waiter at the Gardens was much sought after. At the time they were called drawers as they 'drew' the corks out of wine bottles. Since the Gardens opened in the mid 1700's, there had been strict requirements for the waiters. They had to be single men, they had to be tall, well built, and handsome, and they had to be able to mix easily with all the patrons, the working class, the upper class, and the gentry. They also needed to know how to read, write and do basic arithmetic. The job was a steppingstone for such men to work for the upper classes in their homes or businesses. For some it was a way to find a rich wife or paramour.

There was a strict uniform code. They wore a frocked overall with tight pants, in blue or brown fabric, over which they wore a blue apron. Each waiter also wore a numbered enamel badge, and the corresponding number would be attached to one of the dining tables. The tables in the Grove were the most highly sought after, as these required bookings and were usually occupied by the wealthiest patrons. There was a pecking order amongst the waiters and those with the most clout got the best tables.

The waiters were not employed by the Gardens but were self-employed. They would take orders from the patrons and then pay for and collect the supper-boxes and wine bottles and other drinks and deliver them to the tables. They would light candles (which cost extra) and uncork and pour the wine. Cigars were not allowed in the Gardens, much to the disgust of many patrons, but necessary due to the highly flammable oil needed to keep the Gardens lit. Having the waiters self-employed took the financial risk away from the owners of the Gardens, the risk being that the patrons would refuse to pay for the waiters' service or that the night would be so slow that a profit could not be made. However, this rarely happened, and in fact it was more common for the waiters to devise ways to rip off the patrons. It was well known that the entry price and the cost of food and drinks were greatly inflated for what was on offer, but it did not stop the crowds from coming due to the magical atmosphere that had been created. It was also not uncommon for the waiters to engage in other paid activities with the patrons during the long periods of time when the Gardens were closed. Many worked as upstairs staff in the exclusive homes throughout London, as salespeople in high class stores, and as paid companions. John's father didn't need to do any of these, being happy with the money he made from his work as a gardener during the warm months and in the glasshouses during the winter.

As soon as John turned 18 his father marched him up to the employment office to sign up as a waiter and a gardener. The overseer eyed him off from top to bottom, although he had already seen the boy working alongside his father for several years. At 18 John was developing into a fine-looking man, tall, with a good physique and a pleasant visage. He could easily have passed for a member of the gentry when dressed well.

"Righto John, let's sign your boy up," the overseer indicated to the far desk where a clerk sat. John's father then took him to the bank that dealt with most of the waiters, where he opened an account. The waiters would generally go directly to the bank with their evening takings to deposit the money before they could fall victim to a pickpocket or other rogues that frequented the area around the Gardens, always on the lookout for drunk, merry patrons with full pockets.

From then on, as his father had before him, John spent his days in the gardens tending to the needs of beautiful flowers and his evenings tending to the needs of beautiful women, and of course, their husbands. He was much in demand for outside work, but he was happy with his jobs at the Gardens. Being so busy with work, and getting so much female attention, he didn't feel the urge to pursue romance in his private life, and he wasn't particularly interested in drinking, gambling, or carousing, like most of his workmates were. He was happy to go home with his father, cook dinner, read, and maybe smoke a pipe and have a glass of port wine on special occasions.

It was a terrible shock when two years after John started as a waiter, his father was gripped with an unknown illness that kept him bedridden for two weeks, during which time he purged all food and drink given to him and failed to rally even with the constant attentions of his son and a local nurse who John contracted to care for his father while he was at work. Although he was able to return to work after three weeks, his energy was greatly depleted, and he had lost a lot of weight.

Then one night as he was collecting a tray of food and drinks, he just keeled over and died. One of his patrons for the night was a doctor and he desperately attempted to revive the poor man, but it was to no avail, his heart, made weak from his illness, had just given out. He was 47 years old.

That night, hearing the commotion, John went meandering across the Grove to see what was happening. When he saw his father lying on the ground, he dropped the food he was carrying and rushed over. But there was nothing that could be done. John's father, and his best and only friend, was gone.

While he was able to maintain his job at the Gardens, John found it more difficult to maintain his job as a waiter. That job required him to be pleasant and upbeat and, on most days, he could barely be bothered getting out of bed. At 20 he was an orphan with no family to care about him. He stuck it out for a couple of years getting increasingly worse tables and falling out with the other waiters. His grief seemed to have no end.

One evening one of the patrons invited John to join him and some of his friends for a night out after the Gardens closed. Being the end of September, it was getting cold and there were less crowds so before midnight it was time to close for the night. John's new friends had a coach which transported the six men over the bridge and through the streets where they ended up at Seven Dials, a notorious part of London where all kinds of scoundrels could be found. But John didn't care, he was too sad to care about anything at all. His new friends pushed him through the door of one of the taverns where a large crowd was gathered listening to bawdy ballads sung by a woman with a very large bust spilling from her dress. Other women of a similar ilk moved around the tavern serving drinks and food and sitting on the patron's laps. It wasn't long before the reason for John's invitation became clear and the group of men were surrounded by women, who had all noticed the tall, handsome stranger arrive.

With drinks being thrust into his hands and being the centre of attention, it wasn't long before John was well and truly drunk. The rest of the night went by in a blur and afterwards he could only remember things in snippets of memory.

He woke the next morning under a lamppost and through blurry eyes saw a bag lady throwing crumbs to the pigeons who were flocked around the post and climbing and defecating all over him. He stood shakily and shoo-ed them away and asked the lady where he was.

"Yer in Dock Street, lad," said the toothless old woman.

John shook himself off and found that he was also penniless, his nights takings from the Gardens gone from his pockets. He felt so bad. A headache was forming in the back of his brain and as he tried to move, his stomach gave way, and he vomited all over the ground in front of him. The birds flew across to see if there was anything worth scavenging but John's stomach had only regurgitated a vile mixture of grog and bile.

Using Westminster as a landmark he staggered down to the river and along the banks, crossing the bridge and making his way back to Lambeth and his home. Once home he went to strip off his filthy clothes. As he lifted his shirt over his head he winced as the fabric stuck to his arm, he then looked down in horror as he saw that the material was soaked in blood on his upper arms.

He wet and peeled the shirt from his skin and was even more horrified when he found a large, ugly tattoo on each of his arms. He must have been unconscious when he was mutilated like this! He went over to the mirror which had been left from before his mother died. She was always very fastidious with her appearance and always checked herself in the mirror before she left the house, particularly as she had been vying for an upstairs job.

On each arm an ugly woman's face was drawn and underneath the right side the letters E.M.J.H.E.M was written and on the left side the letters S.T. He imagined he had been branded for some reason, probably as a joke, by whoever he had been with last night.

Tears of anger and frustration appeared as John realised, he had been robbed and this had been done to him while he was unable to respond.

After sitting in shock for some time John finished cleaning himself up and made a cup of tea, which his stomach desperately needed. He then sat back and took stock of his life.

John understood that he had always been a loner. His only companions growing up had been his parents and grandparents and he didn't seek the company of other children. On the few occasions he had gone to the church school he was bullied for his accent and because he didn't seem to fit in with the other children, who all tried to outdo and compete against each other. John had never had time for conflict, preferring to walk away from it anytime it found him. After his mother and grandparents died John was happy to sit at home with his father and to quietly go about his work. But now, he realised, he had no one to look out for him. No one who even cared a fig about him. And he was obviously gravely naive. Last night was the first time that he had drank more than a small glass of port wine with his father. He didn't like the taste of other liquor or the way it made him feel, and that was now cemented in his mind.

All his life John had been complimented on his looks and his gentlemanly manners and accent, and he mostly brushed it off, having heard it so many times before. There had been plenty of women who flirted with him, at work and around the town, and a few men as well. But John didn't really understand what they wanted or how to talk to them and after a while they gave up.

John wasn't sad that he was a loner, in fact that was how he liked things. His happiest times were when he was working in the garden and tending his plants. He enjoyed walking along the riverbank and through the gardens around London, observing the new buildings and watching the ferries coming and going. He even enjoyed watching the well-dressed ladies and gentlemen promenading around the city and admired their attire and their fashionable clothing and hairstyles. But he never wished to be one of them, or to have a lady on his arm. He was happy with his own thoughts and reading the newspapers and books that he bought with his wages. He enjoyed going to the markets and interacting with the fish mongers and other merchants, choosing fresh produce, and then going home and cooking a delicious meal for himself. He laughed to himself that he ate so well that he needed to go on his long walks every day so that he didn't become portly. That meant instant dismissal for a waiter at the Gardens.

One thing that he realised, was that he no longer enjoyed the frivolity and the waste that he saw at the Gardens at night. So many people superficially laughing gaily and pretending they were enjoying themselves. Spending so much money to make themselves look better than they felt. Some of the people there were positively awful, but he was forced to be polite and fawn all over them. He vowed to go and give his notice that night. The money that he got from his gardening work was almost enough to pay his rent and fund his meagre needs. He would try for a job at The Palace instead. Some of the staff there still remembered his mother and would say hello to him at church on Sundays. Every now and then one of the ladies would bring a loaf of bread or a cake for him to take home, usually introducing their daughters to him at the same time. John happily took the offerings, but his awkwardness prevented much interaction with the daughters.

Yes, thought John, it was time to change things and start living a better life.

Vron

Chapter Two

# *1827 – The Palace*

*W*ith his contacts, looks, manners and experience, John was immediately picked up for a job as a third footman at Lambeth Palace.

He sold his waiter's uniform to one of the new men and with that money and some he had put away he purchased his smart new uniform for the Palace, that included two separate outfits. His morning dress consisted of a smart double-breasted coat, waistcoat, trousers, and a small black tie. After lunch he would change into his livery suit with a striped waistcoat. He also purchased a new garment brush and polishing kit for his leather shoes.

For his first two years John worked in the Palace's extensive library, one of the many footmen who ensured that the books, shelves, and desks were always dust free. He would also put books away when readers had finished with them, and helped to maintain a catalogue of books that were taken out of the library by guests of the Palace. Another job was to track down and gently remind the borrower if the books were not returned in good time. At times when there was an event at the Palace, John worked in the cloak room and would diligently issue a small ticket to the owner and place the coats and bags into the cloak room with matching tickets attached. During the event if any of the garments had dust or mud on them, he would clean them before the owners returned to retrieve them.

John enjoyed his job. Although there were other footmen around in the library or the cloak room, John was able to busy himself with his work and keep out of anyone's way, and that suited him fine. When there were no guests about, he was allowed to read discreetly, and he had been lapping up every book that he could find. He was most interested in books about botany and flora and growing flowers and produce. When it was found that he had grown flowers before, one of the maids showed him how to do simple flower arrangements, and from then on rather than her spending half an hour every day in the library she would simply deliver the flowers to John. She would stop by later to admire his arrangements and tell him what a good job he had done.

He also enjoyed recipe books, although there were none in the library. But the head cook had many of them and, apart from a few of his colleagues, she was the only one at The Palace who he talked to. They enjoyed discussing recipes, what produce was fresh at the time and the best vendors to buy from.

When he was not working, his time was spent much as always. He would walk the riverbanks and across the bridge to Westminster to admire the new architecture and spend time in the parks. He would purchase his supplies and cook himself delicious meals. He kept his small home tidy and clean, and he kept as far away from the ruffians around Southwark as he could. Being so close to the area that was fast becoming one of London's most notorious slums, did not sit well with John. He had never gone near a tavern or ale house again since the night that had left him scarred for life. He winced with painful memories every time he caught a glimpse of the ugly tattoos.

He was often accosted in the street on his way home from work by street harlots looking to make some money. He laughed as he thought what a poor target that he made for them. Although his father had told him about the ways of women and men, he felt no big compulsion to involve himself in the activity. Definitely not like some of the men he worked with who talked about it all the time, making him very uncomfortable. He had even twice been accosted by pimps on the look-out for handsome men who were willing to sell their bodies. Both times he was shocked and horrified. The first told him that many 'men' would like to bed him. He ran off in disgust. The second one told him that ladies would pay him to be their companion for the evening, and that there were a lot of lonely ladies around London apparently. This John could understand as he saw so many men, probably husbands, carousing with harlots and disappearing into gentlemen's clubs late at night. John far preferred his own company and that of a good book, where he would sit by candlelight and dream of faraway places.

In 1831, his 24th year and his third year at the Palace, John was taken under the wing of one of the second footmen and was at first supervised and then allowed to take his turn serving breakfast for the archbishop, his wife, and any visitors. Archbishop Howley was then 64 years old, but had only been in the job since 1828, having previously been the Bishop of London. His morning routine was quite a slow one, but his work never stopped, and he was always in and out of the Palace attending to activities.

As had usually followed in his life John had somehow gained the ire of some of the footmen and other staff who thought him aloof and rude. But it wasn't that at all, it was simply that John didn't know how to make small talk and any attempts were usually terribly awkward and had the other party disengaging quickly.

His quiet manner and good looks also attracted the attention of the female staff who would often sidle up to him for a chat when he was trying to take a five-minute break in the fresh air or having a quick cup of tea in the kitchen between jobs. One time he was highly embarrassed when one of the kitchen girls, having run out of things to try and talk to him about quickly leaned in and kissed him, right on the mouth! She then jumped up, giggled, and called out "I did it! I did it! Youse owe me a penny now!" He turned to see three other kitchen staff laughing at him. He was mortified and from then on kept as far away from the female staff as possible.

Soon he had gained a reputation for not being 'one of the boys' and trying to 'get all the women'. His work was impeccable, and he was always getting compliments in front of his colleagues from the other footmen and even from the Butler himself, which further rankled the other men.

There was much activity at the Palace in 1831, as the archbishop was going to preside over the coronation of the new king. King George IV had died in June 1830, a year after John had started at the Palace and he had needed to purchase another uniform for the mourning period.

The new King William IV was older than the archbishop and the new queen was an old woman of 40. John heard the staff and people in the street giggling that the King would probably keel over at his coronation. It was also a source of entertainment that although the new King had ten living children none of them were legitimate, having been born to his mistress, an Irish actress named Dorothea Bland, better known by her stage name Mrs Jordan. Although he married the soon to be Queen Adelaide in 1818 when she was 26, their marriage had only produced two short-lived daughters. This new king had no heir, leaving the newspapers and town orators to speculate as to who would take the throne after his demise, which could happen at any time, given his age.

For months beforehand, John had heard the archbishop grumble and mutter to his wife that the new king wanted to 'damp down' the whole coronation. He didn't want to spend exorbitant amounts on it like his late brother had done in 1821, which after the expenses of the battle of Waterloo seemed obscene. He also didn't want all the pageantry and boring ceremonial activities. Previous coronation ceremonies had been held for the peerage only, however this time there would be a procession from St James Palace to and from Westminster Abbey and government dignitaries and members of the royal families from other countries would be invited. However, there would not even be a coronation banquet, grumbled the archbishop.

John and all the Palace staff worked the whole evening before the coronation, there being so much to do to prepare the archbishop for his big day. There were also numerous church dignitaries from outside London staying at the Palace who all needed to be attended to and readied for the day.

At 5am a gun salute was fired in Hyde Park which was the signal for the archbishop to leave Lambeth Palace and travel by coach to Westminster Abbey. All the footmen marched along beside the coach as it made its way across the bridge to the Abbey. There were already members of the public lining the streets to ensure the best view of the new King and Queen.

Most of the archbishop's staff, including John, were then allowed to have the day off to watch the procession. John walked around until he found a vendor and bought some hot chestnuts as the morning was cold, and watched on as temporary stands were erected for the spectators. At 9am the royal family started making their way to the Abbey, followed an hour later by the King and Queen in the magnificent Gold State Coach, the first time that it had been used at a coronation.

John, who had fallen asleep against a tree, stood up on his tiptoes to see over the crowd. The beautiful coaches, escorted by cavalry guards, passed along Pall Mall to Charing Cross and then along Whitehall to the abbey. Foot guards lined the route watching for any suspicious activities.

Although the pageantry was wonderful and the day was pleasant with blue skies and warmth in the air, there were way too many people for John's liking. He headed back home and had a well-earned sleep before getting up later in the day and returning to witness the opening of the new avenue, that was now called The Mall, as it was illuminated and opened to the public for the first time.

Life went on as normal for John with not much changing in his small world. After Christmas, having done such a good job over the holiday period John was officially made up to Second footman. His new colleagues welcomed him as he had been helping them for over a year and they had grown to know him well, or as well as John would let anyone know him.

Naturally, John's promotion created a stir amongst the Third footmen who were all jealous of his good fortune. Many of them had been at the Palace a lot longer than John had been. Not many of them stopped to consider their own shortfalls, a little tardiness, a few tart words to the Second footmen, dirt on their shoes, liquor on their breath in the mornings. But not long after Christmas bad fortunes began to befall John of which he could only put down to his disgruntled former colleagues.

One Monday morning as he was preparing for the breakfast service, Nigel his supervisor and one of the First footman, took him to one side and whispered through clenched teeth "Harris, what have you been doing with the gardener's daughter?".

In shock John stuttered "N..nothing Sir, I have not seen the gardener's daughter!"

Everyone knew that the head gardener's daughter, Jenny, was a wild one and spent her days jumping out at the Palace staff and causing mischief. It was said that she had taken several of the male staff into the garden sheds for a tumble and had been seen kissing one of the footmen before, whose service was terminated at once. Fraternisation between staff was not allowed unless sanctioned by the Butler, and he was not of a romantic disposition. The gardener was aware of his daughter's proclivities, she had been sent home from a church school in the country for just this reason. But he would kill any of the staff who he found with her.

"Well Harris, you have been seen fondling with her outside the kitchen."

"No sir, that is not true Sir, I wouldn't do that!" John was exasperated. He didn't even talk to the women, let alone try to fondle them!

The footman stared hard at John looking for any sign of a lie, but seeing none, he dismissed him back to his duties "I've got my eye on you Harris," he spat as he waved his hand for John to leave.

Over the next few months, more and more little incidents occurred. One of the main bullies had also been promoted to second footman. John thought this would be a good opportunity to lose one enemy at least, but James Chambers still seemed to harbour hatred towards him. Several times he tripped John in the breakfast room causing him to spill food and on one occasion break an expensive teacup and saucer. He was clever, and no one saw him do it, so John got the blame each time. Being fearful of confrontation John only glared at his nemesis who smirked back at him.

One afternoon as John was taking a break outside the kitchen Nigel came out and sat next to him.

"Here lad, you know the others don't like you hey?" Said Nigel dropping his posh inside accent, and with a look of concern on his face.

"Yes, I know Sir," said John despondently.

"Listen the lads think you might not like the women, you might like the men better?" John looked at him shocked. "Well, you know, you don't show any interest in any of the girls, and no one has seen you with a woman. Look lad, if that is how you are, that's fine, you can be like that, but if I were you, I'd go pick a better profession, more conducive to my interests if you know what I mean. No one seems to mind the sailors getting up to it, have you thought of that lad? I say this to you now lad because if you get caught doing it here, you'll get flogged and you'll certainly be sacked from the Palace."

By this time John had gone red and was gasping for air like a fish out of water.

"But, Sir, I'm not like that. I do like girls I just don't know what to say to them. I don't know what to say to anyone, Sir. It's always been that way, I like my own company, but NOT the company of other men!"

"Right," said Nigel "Well if it's not that then you've got the men offside for some reason. They don't trust you. You don't talk to them or have a laugh with them or go out to the tavern with them after work. So, you see, they don't understand you and they feel threatened by you."

Nigel then proceeded to explain to John why the men treated him like they did and how it would always be like that if he didn't find a way to build some rapport with others. Learning such a skill would stand him in good stead for his whole life, he said. John knew how to talk to the toffs as he served them or when he saw them in the library or the cloak room, so he just needed to practice the same skills with other people. Small talk it was called. Find a common interest and just talk a little about it. Nothing major, but to build the friendliness.

"But what if I don't have anything to say?" asked John.

"Well then you say, 'Isn't it a nice day,' or 'Oh look at that odd spider there,' or 'say did you hear who won the horses on Saturday,' anything lad to act a bit friendly like." He could see some understanding crossing the young man's face. "Right, you think you can practice that lad, give it a try?"

"Yes Sir," said John slowly "I think so. I'll give it a try anyway."

"Good lad," said Nigel patting John on the back "and it wouldn't hurt to ask the lads where they are off to of a night and tag along, you don't even have to talk to them much, just laugh at what they laugh at. Simple, hey? All right, I'll check in on you next week and see how you are going."

"Thanks, Sir," said John feeling very anxious about pulling this one off. However, he had been able to act before. As a waiter at the Gardens, he had had to act every night like he was interested in the patrons, this would be the same, he thought.

Chapter Three

# *1832 - Sentenced to Life*

*F*or the next month John was a new man, on the outside at

least. He laughed at the bad jokes the men made. He pretended to leer at the women when they did, and even made some rude remarks at young women or those less fortunate, like he heard them doing. Soon they were including him in their inner circle and inviting him to the tavern. He would scurry along with them pretending to have a great time while watering down his ale and drinking it as slowly as he could. All the while he longed to escape back to his sanctuary at home and read his latest book.

He had to admit it made things a lot easier at work. No longer was he the butt of jokes or heard others talking about him in hushed tones. He didn't have to worry about being tripped up or set up. Or so he though.

One afternoon he was leaving after his shift when James Chambers approached him out the back of the kitchen.

"Hey there Johnny boy, I need you to do me a favour." John looked at him curiously. "Look there's an old carpet and a chair in the back of St Mary's there, that the Reverend said I could have. But you see I need it carried out to my uncle's cart, and I can't manage it on my own."

"You want me to help carry them out to a cart?" asked John.

"Yes. You see I'd do it myself, but I have a bad back you know, old army injury," he said rubbing his back. "You're much stronger than me, what with all your gardening work. All the ladies like looking at your strong arms," he winked and made John blush.

John didn't know that he had a bad back or that he'd been in the army, but if he said so. And wanting to remain on Chambers good side was very important to John.

"Show me where it is and where you want it and I'll do my best." Said John.

Chambers led him across to St Mary's church and to a back door, which was open. Just inside the door was a rolled length of cloth and an ornate chair. John didn't see James' pass one of the staff members a coin as they scurried back into the main church area.

"Right, this is it," said Chambers "and just out there by the road can you see a cart, yeah there he is." Chambers waved up to man who stood under a tree with a dark coat on and a hat pulled down over his ears. "That's my uncle, just give it to him and all is well, we can go and have a beer, shouts on me."

John grimaced. He really just wanted to go home and try out a new recipe he had been reading for a soup made from peas and salted ham hock. He'd planned on purchasing some fresh bread on the way home to go with it. But he knew that the easy time he had been having at work came at a price and he needed to pretend he was 'one of the boys.'

John hoisted the linen onto his shoulder and grasped the chair in both arms. They were quite heavy together and he began to plod up the hill. He was almost to the cart when he heard a whistle and saw the cart owner jump up and run off like lightening, leaving the cart behind. He looked behind him to ask Chambers what was going on, but he was gone, and an angry looking vicar was running up the hill behind him followed closely by a policeman.

"Thief," yelled the vicar, "Thief." He was huffing and puffing as he reached John and grabbed hold of him.

"What's going on here then?" said the policeman.

"This young man was taking off with church property! Oh, John Harris how could you?" The vicar said, "I buried your mother and father, and this is how you repay the Church?"

It dawned on John what had happened. Chambers had been trying to steal the items but had got John to do it so that if he got caught, Chambers and his 'uncle' whoever that had been, would be in the clear.

John begged and pleaded with the policeman and told him the story but there he was caught red handed stealing from the Church.

John stood trial at the Surrey Quarter Sessions and was charged with larceny and felony. As it was his first offence, had he stolen something smaller and from anywhere but a church he would probably have only got gaol time, or even just a flogging. But stealing from a church was a felonious (more serious) crime and therefore John was sentenced to Life imprisonment to be served in the colony.

No one came to the court to defend him or speak on his behalf. John found that Nigel had been very correct that being a loner meant really being alone. John had no one on God's earth who cared for him. Until now this had not bothered him, but now, sitting in a Hulk on the Thames, in scratchy garments with dirt up his nails from dragging timber across the dockyards all day, he suddenly felt more alone than he ever had.

Before his conviction, and while he was awaiting his sentencing at Southwark prison, Nigel had come to visit. Nigel knew what had happened, having heard rumours of the sticky-fingered Chambers before, but having no evidence to approach the Butler about it. Knowing what was to happen to John and feeling guilty that he had told John to get in the good books with the other lads, he had arranged to have John's belongings sold and put the money in his account at the bank. Once he was free in the colony, he would be able to access those funds. Nigel gave him some of the money as cash which he had one of the laundry women sew into garments for John to wear, the safest way to keep it from being stolen. When he was on his way to the Hulk, Nigel managed to pass on to him a small trunk that contained some of John's books, writing materials and other precious belongings that he knew John would rather keep than sell.

John was the butt of jokes again when he arrived at the Hulk, amongst a group of men who were all filthy and ragged, some having been on the Hulk for months. Most came from the slums of London or the other big cities such as Liverpool or Glasgow and Edinburgh in Scotland. They laughed at his soft hands with no scars, and they laughed at his toffy accent. But John had learned a bit from Nigel, even though in the end it had brought him undone. He put on his mask again and laughed with the men, instead of getting upset. He even gave out a few of his own insults, which endeared him to them.

As he knew how to read and write, he was put in charge of lessons of an evening. While some of the men were engaged in learning trade skills, all of them were required to spend at least one evening every week learning their letters. This they did with varying degrees of enthusiasm.

John's main job on the hulk was showing the men how to write their letters and sound them out and then as a treat he would read them a story and show them how the letters on the book made the words that he read. After such long, arduous days spent doing manual labour in heavy leg irons, it didn't take much for the men to drift off to sleep, and John's story-time was the best time to do so as they could prop their heads up on their arms or knees and pretend to be awake, the guards watching from behind not able to see their closed eyes. Some, however, became engrossed with the stories and would ask questions at the end until the guards yelled at them to go to bed.

It was a short stay for John as just over a month later he was called up with a large group of other men on the hulk and told to prepare for transportation.

The men were taken in boats to a large ship waiting for them that they could see was called the *York*. On boarding, John was given the number 1463 and went through the motions with the other men. The ship's surgeon inspected each man and either cleared them for the journey or sent them back to the boat. They were measured and weighed and humiliatingly for John the details of his tattoos were recorded after close inspection and smirks from the clerk and the closest men.

Later, after John had found a berth below the decks, surrounded by a motley crew of other ragged men, he heard that the ships to Van Diemen's Land had been busy, with one leaving England every two to three weeks. It was the busiest year so far for transportation, brought about, the men said, by the ever-growing need for more labour, to build the burgeoning economy. The colony was no longer a dreaded prison island that they had heard about as children, but was turning into another Britain, but with better weather. Some said that people were deliberately committing crimes so that they could go to the colony, having heard stories from friends who were there and after serving their sentence had been granted large holdings of land and convicts to help their farms to thrive. Anyone with a trade or other such skill was in hot demand and could make a successful business if they had the talent.

Free settlers had been emigrating to Van Diemen's Land for over twenty years, and not many of them came back. If they did it was to spend the fruits of their success and make contacts to improve their businesses in the colony. The stories that John had heard were mostly of success and happiness. At night the men did tell stories of people they knew who had been flogged to death and ill-treated in the colony while assigned to bad masters, but that happened in England as well. And the men who were bad eggs in Britain often continued to be bad eggs in the colony and kept getting into trouble and having their sentences extended and were imprisoned rather than assigned.

Still the more John heard the more he got the picture of a primitive jungle with lots of farms and not much else. He doubted that there would be any ornate gardens or impressive homes for him to work in.

As the journey commenced John excelled himself as a general hand performing manual labour under the direction of the guards, but his quiet ways were soon noticed, and he was asked what other skills that he had. Soon enough he was put to work on the upper decks serving as an errand boy for the officers, and in the ship's dining room, where he supervised several other convicts. The benefit of this was that when not required for errands he could once again indulge his love of reading, as Captain Spratley kept a small library which John was required to keep clean and tidy, no small feat on a dusty ship with the air filled with humidity. If left open the pages of the books would dampen and curl. John was kept busy constantly wiping mould from the leather covers.

The advantage of working in the dining room was that the cook let the men have whatever food was left on the officer's plates, a nice little supplement to their daily rations. Some would keep the extra food and exchange it for coins below decks. This was then used to purchase items from the sailors, guards and the group of convicts who had formed a mob. While small in comparison to those on other convict ships, the *York's* mob was made up of several notorious criminals including successful forgers, fences, lads-men and a few heavies, those paid by the criminals to rough up people who owed them money or who were otherwise out of favour with them. An illegal gambling and grog ring was thriving below decks as it did on all the ships. However, for the most part the *York* was an orderly ship, with only two convicts needing to be flogged during the journey due to insubordination, and five needing hospitalisations due to exhibiting deranged violence whilst in the tropics. John overheard that the ship's all expected this as it was a common phenomenon amongst the feeble minded and had something to do with the humidity.

The evening routine consisted of dinner at 4pm, followed by exercises on the deck supervised by the surgeon. This usually took the form of jumping jacks, leapfrog or other activities that could be done in small confines. John and the other dining room workers often missed out on the exercises as they were helping the cook to clean up. Then at 5pm on three nights per week services were held by the Missionary Society. The captain attended most of these to ensure that the convicts gave the members of the society the respect they deserved. Some of the convicts took great solace in the sermons and the readings, but others, jaded from years of poor treatment, homelessness, and starvation, did not believe in God so mostly fell asleep. On other evenings lessons were held in reading, writing, arithmetic, or trade work, such as wood turning, sewing and leatherwork. As usual, once it was known what John could do, he was put to work leading reading and writing lessons, as well as a bit of arithmetic which most of the convicts found impossible to grasp. John tried to explain the importance of numbers. Any man who intended to carry out any type or trade or business or own a farm would need to be able to manage money and the numbers were all about money. That got some of them more interested.

The journey of the *York* took 140 days, with 200 male convicts onboard. The surgeon, James McTernan, was pleased that there had been no deaths and few illnesses onboard. Indeed, having left England at the end of summer and arriving at Hobart at the height of summer, there had been pleasant weather for the whole voyage. The only turbulence encountered was as they directly left England and as they crossed the equator, where far off lightning storms had provided evening entertainment for those lucky enough to be allowed on deck.

Soon enough, the sailors were preparing the ship for its arrival in Hobart. By then the convicts were aware of what was going on as the ship had stopped twice to collect provisions during its journey, both times in places where the docks were full of colourful people and trees and birds so different to England. After each stop, the men were treated to delicious fruits rather than their daily lime juice. It was a very welcome treat as they had been subjected to disgusting pickled cabbage once the lime juice had run out. And while in port the men were allowed to have a wash on the deck to scrape off the accumulated sweat and grime of the voyage. The officers went into the town, where music could be heard. One night while in port, fireworks lit up the night for some kind of celebration. The captain allowed the convicts to stay up later on port nights and allowed them to have their own little party with music and singing provided by those who had the talent, and even dancing, which the surgeon said was good for the health. The guards ensured that these little events did not get out of hand and sent the men off to bed as soon as anyone got too rowdy.

The *York* arrived at Hobart four days after Christmas in 1832. From what John could see Hobart appeared to be a thriving little coastal town. The docks were shabby as docks usually were and had the usual kind of people hanging about them, out of work sailors and itinerant men. He even saw a few women lazing around the area. But further along he could see elegant stone buildings and small, neat dwellings where the townsfolk must live.

After the surgeon and the captain had spent the best part of a day over on the shore attending to the formalities of arrival, the men were taken in groups of ten across to the receiving station at the harbour, where once again they were subjected to inspection and interrogation about their previous work and skills. Again, John's tattoos were laughed at as was his accent and his soft hands.

"There ain't much call for a fancy footman here in the colony my lad," said the clerk, "a bit of work on the roads will get them hands all nice and scarred up." He laughed and sent John to a line where other men were waiting.

After a few days in a dark and dinghy prison in Hobart, John's group were put back onto another ship, this time bound for Port Dalrymple to the north of the island. The journey of a few days took them along a coastline and then down a wide river and had them arriving in what seemed to be a thriving farming community. The main town of Launceston was busy with lots of people scurrying about their business. There were impressive looking buildings and churches, and the streets were neatly laid out and full of shopfronts selling all kinds of wares. As they were marched to the gaol John saw several taverns and boarding houses, one that was four storeys high. John was pleased to see that some of the large houses had nice gardens and appeared to have servants coming and going from them.

For the next two months John was housed with a group of 40 other men in the Launceston gaol, sleeping 10 to a room on six dirty flea ridden mattresses. During the day the men were marched by their guard to somewhere in the surrounding area and spent their days breaking rocks and clearing the bush to build roads. The guards were mostly ex- soldier's supplementing their farming income or ticket-of-leave men waiting to be granted their own land. John felt that the convicts were mostly treated fairly.

John didn't mind the work, reminding him of his days at the Gardens, when he was free amongst nature to just get on with his work quietly and let his mind wander to other places, or just to marvel at the plants and birds who came to see what the strange men were doing. They were all so new and different to what he knew in England, so every day was wonderous.

"Where are you from lad?" asked one of the guards over lunch one day. John told him about Lambeth and the next thing he knew he was telling the guard about Vauxhall Gardens and how different the plants in the colony were to the ones that he was used to in London.

"Why lad, that's more than I've heard you speak since ye've been here," laughed the guard in his broad Scottish accent. "And aye, I know the Gardens ye speak of, I went there with a young lady once when the Regiment was in London. Those lights man, I can still see those lights in my head!" he laughed.

"And the way ye speak lad, where did you learn to speak like that?"

Over the next few days John's talks with the guard continued but they were quickly interrupted by the guards need to blow the whistle to get the men back to work. However, by the end of the week the guard had a good idea of what skills that this young man possessed, and he knew that he was wasted on the road gangs.

Not long afterwards John was called into the warden's office where a very well-dressed man sat. John wasn't sure what to do, whether to bow or not!

"Harris, meet Mr Walker. He is a magistrate."

John did bow then and stuttered as well, wondering if he was in trouble "Good morning y..y...y.. Your Honour."

"Young man," said the judge "I am in need of a new man on my estate, and it is difficult to find what I need amongst the damn pickpockets and cut-throats arriving in the colony." Mr Walker stood and walked around the table, standing directly in front of John. They stood around the same height, taller than most.

The judge looked at him from head to toe. He could tell, even in his ragged convict garb that this man had superior looks and build and would be an asset to have at his home. There were now many wealthy men in Van Diemen's Land and finding such a gem to serve in their homes was extremely rare. The quality of one's house servants was as important in the colony as it had been at home in London, France, and Germany where Walker had previously lived before deciding like so many others, to move his interests to the burgeoning new colony where fortunes were being made with ease.

"I hear you have worked at a Palace before?"

"Yes sir, but I was only a Third footman and a Second for only a few months before I came here." The judge waved his hand in the air.

"And you know your letters boy?"

"Yes sir, I can read and write well and know my arithmetic, I needed to know that working at the Gardens and at the Palace."

"Well," said Walker "I currently have a man who is exceptionally good, but he is getting on in age and needs assistance. The estate is thriving and there is too much work now for one man. I will take you on assignment and see how you go, see if my man thinks you will be suitable, and you can also work as a shepherd as I need as many of them as possible, with the thieving blighters out there in the bush."

"Thank you, your honour, thank you." said John, not really knowing what he was thanking him for. He had got used to his routine with the road gang, and although the others were mostly rough and tumble men from the slums of London or impoverished villages, they were mostly good natured and left John alone with his books and his thoughts of an evening. They had started to call him 'Guv" jokingly and some of them asked him questions about different things, so they must think well of him and know that he was worldly in his knowledge. The thought of another change gave John anxiety. He had already been through enough for one year.

The next morning John bid farewell to the other men and the guards and waited by his bed, with his trunk, which now contained a new set of clean convict garb, fresh from the Female Factory in Hobart. He was summoned to the office mid-morning and the prison clerk diligently recorded the details of his new assignment. He was then handed over to what John thought must be Mr Walker's 'man'. The man was tall and distinguished looking with grey hair, neatly cut and a neat moustache. He wore the typical black suit of a butler with highly polished shoes, a white shirt, and a vest and tie.

John gave the man a slight bow. The man was tall enough to look down his nose at John and like Mr Walker looked him up and down. He snorted "I suppose you'll do." He signalled to a man in convict garb to carry John's trunk and ushered John out to a waiting buggy. A new adventure was about to begin for John.

Vron

Chapter Four

# *1839 – Edinburgh*

*A*melia was fed up. Quite literally she did not want to go on.

There she was, like every other day, sat up in the square on High Street, waiting for her turn to fill her bucket with water from the well.

From where she sat, she could see up the road towards Canongate where the genteel inhabitants of Edinburgh lived. But Amelia's life was so far away from theirs that she may as well have been looking up at the moon. Amelia and her acquaintance Margaret were currently staying in an abandoned room in a tenement in the Old Town, not far from The Great Reformer, John Knox's, house. The good thing was that being on the third floor, the room was further away from the stench and squalor of the streets and basements, but the problem was that it was also three flights of stairs to the street then four more flights of stairs down through the streets and down the hill, to get to the well.

Today the queue was long, and the day was cold, the bitter wind cutting through her four thin layers of clothing. She no longer had her coat, having sold it the week before when Margaret had convinced her, after several drams of whisky, to raise more coins to continue their binge. Margaret had told her that she'd get the money to buy it back later that night by entertaining men, something that she had made a career of. But the air had suddenly grown colder with squalls and hail and not even the less fancy men in the street could be convinced to pay for 'one against the wall'.

A very old woman in front of Amelia suddenly fell to the ground. No one moved, unwilling to lose their place in the queue. But then the heavens opened up and rain started to pour down upon all of the poor wretches in the square. Amelia leant down and roused the old woman. Probably fainted from starvation, she thought.

"Come on now, granny, let's get ya to the side over here outta the rain." She gently helped the old woman to the side of one of the buildings under the eves and out of the rain, where they both sat on the cold cobblestones. Most of the people stayed in the queue, not willing to relinquish the hours' long commitment they had already put in. Many of them probably had fires to go back to, to warm their bones and dry their clothes. Amelia didn't have that luxury, and knew that if her clothes got soaked, she risked catching her death from cold. She took her bucket and the old woman's bucket to the edge of the eves to collect some of the rainwater, which might be all that they got that day as the queue had already grown.

"Ey Emma love," she heard a man's voice close by and looked up to see James Ramsey coming towards her with his right hand under his coat. She knew what he had, and she was in no mood to resist.

"All right, come on with ya then."

"I ken ye couldn't resist. Warm ye cockles on this cold wet day." His arm withdrew from his coat and out with it came of bottle of amber liquid. Amelia passed him a coin, grabbed the bottle and took a large swig.

"Ahhhhhh," she said with a smile "that'll make the day seem brighter." She passed him another coin and said gently "and one for granny here."

"Here," she said gently, lifting the bottle to the old woman's mouth, "this will make your worries less, lovey." The old woman thankfully sculled a dram and gave Amelia a gummy smile and squeezed her arm.

"I haven't seen ya at the Chiefs lately Emma, we've been missing your songs, and your company lass."

Amelia's main form of income since she arrived in Edinburgh seven years earlier was her voice. Luckily her Grandma Isabella, her mother's mother, had spent a lot of time with Amelia and her older brother James when they were younger, and she had taught them all the traditional Scottish songs and fables as well as all the new ones she had recently heard. Grandpa Will had taught them how to fiddle which was a source of income for him. The lives of the people in the village were so bleak that anything to brighter their days was welcome, and a bit of song and dance always brought a little happiness to their days. Amelia's talents came in very handy once she arrived in Edinburgh, starving and wretched, having decided that there must be something more than living in abject poverty and starvation.

Amelia was born on the 29th of April 1814 and lived with her parents, John and Catherine and older brother James in a small dwelling in their village of Cults in Fife. Like many people, her mother worked in the cloth industry, from dawn until dark in one of the many large factories looming and weaving cloth. When the children were young, she did some sewing and embroidery at home to bring in some money and had taught Amelia the basics.

Her father worked at the sawmill and was gone every day except Sunday from before the sun came up until well after the sun went down. Amelia and James made some money picking fruit during the harvest season, along with most of the other village children. This endless work allowed them to put food on the table and pay their rent, and nothing more. Like everyone else the whole family were always sick with some kind of illness or pestilence, and there was never enough firewood, so they were also always cold.

Grandma Isabella would often take the children to her own house where their Grandpa Will grew enough vegetables to provide for his family and to sell. As well as his fiddling and songs, he also had a talent for crafting tools and implements from wood. Grandma did a little sewing and embroidery to bring in some funds, and because they were at home and not always at work like their parents, Amelia and James had warmth, food, and love in their home. But sometimes they went hungry and often they went without decent clothing or shoes.

Her Granny Laing, father's mother, told her that it hadn't always been like this. When Granny was young and when her father was a child, the village was lovely, she said. They were able to make a living from farming their small plots of land and paying rents, usually in the form of farm produce, to the local Lairds or the Church. Everyone in the village shared the produce and pooled their resources to help each other out, and the Church and the Lairds provided protections. But that all but ended when the English came and the clearances happened, where all the farmers were 'cleared' from their lands across the country to make way for English sheep pastures. The population of Scotland moved to the big cities to work in the factories, the sawmills, the iron smelters, shipyards, or the fishing towns.

Vron

Granny Laing had told her that their family was descended from the famous Gillespie family, her grandmother was Margaret Gillespie before she had married. The Gillespie family of Scotland were erenaghs, a medieval office. They collected rents and tithes, and oversaw the church owned lands, maintaining the churches and buildings. The family were very prominent in the affairs of the Presbyterian Church started by The Great Reformer John Knox, and were scholars and clergyman, who mixed in circles with famous church and political leaders in Scotland and England. Members of the Gillespie family were some of the most influential people in Scottish politics and in the church in the 17th century. The Reverend George Gillespie who was born in 1613 was very prominent in the Presbyterian Church. Granny told Amelia that his portrait could be seen in a beautiful stained-glass window in the Old Kirk (church) at Kirkcaldy on the coast, to commemorate his church work, but Amelia had never been there to see it.

Grandpa Will died when Amelia was 15, and Grandma Isabella not long afterwards. Granny and Grandpa Laing were still alive, but they lived at Kettle, and they didn't get to see them often. Amelia's life revolved around her small village and the local people who she had grown up with.

The local pimps had been trying to recruit Amelia ever since Grandpa Will died and she had started to look like a woman. There were enough gentry and soldiers around who were willing to pay for a woman's services. It was at this time that Amelia decided that her lot in life would not be one of drunkenness and prostitution. She had seen the results of that lifestyle, and it was not good.

She asked some of the local boys to teach her how to defend herself, and it wasn't long before she was being known as the she-demon of Cults. She would spend her evenings in the taverns or at local gatherings, telling traditional fables and then singing the ballads that Grandpa Will and Grandma Isabella had taught her. She had become adept at changing the tone of her performances to match the mood of the crowd. And her story telling skills had the crowds enthralled. On the rowdier nights she would put a twist on her ballads and make them a little bawdy, much to everyone's delight. In this way Amelia managed to keep herself out of trouble and make enough money to survive without pulling up her skirts. And on the odd occasion when someone in the crowd decided to try and take advantage of her, she beat them up badly and maintained her reputation as the she-demon.

But, as everyone told her, if she wanted a better life she had to go to Edinburgh. The city was full of people and opportunities.

She hung around until 1832 when she turned 18 and had run out of all optimism. The future did not belong there in Fife, surrounded by poverty, sickness, and misery. At the same time as John Harris was being sent to Van Diemen's Land, Amelia, accompanied by a few of the other young men and women, who had also had enough, left Cults on foot.

On their first day they stopped at Kirkcaldy, so that Amelia could view the window that was dedicated to her ancestor. It truly was a beautiful thing to see. It was a beautiful sunny day, for once, and the little group set up a make-shift stage and Amelia started singing. One of her companions accompanied her on the fiddle and a couple of the girls danced a jig in front of them. Within a short time, a crowd had gathered and threw some coins into the hat in front of her. Once a decent crowd had arrived Amelia began to orate some of the fables that she knew were popular and soon had the crowd enthralled.

The townspeople where so appreciative that Amelia's little group dined well that night and slept in a barn at the local tavern. In the morning they were offered a cart ride as far as Stirling, which they were all very glad of after their long walk the day before.

The carter dropped them all near the port area, which was abuzz with people busily hustling and bustling as they went about whatever business they conducted there. There were so many different styles of dress and accents that Amelia didn't recognise. They could see the famous Stirling Castle, high up on a hill behind the city. They asked around about where the best place would be to attract a crowd for entertainment and they were directed to Broad Street, in the Old Town area. They asked around the taverns and found one that was interested in trialling them for the night, which meant they could have a go but wouldn't be paid. The night was such a great success that over the next week the crowds grew, and the publican was extremely happy. In exchange for their services, he gave them two rooms to stay in and two meals per day for the main players, which included Amelia, two girls and two of the men.

Over the next few weeks, the others dwindled off. Some set out for Edinburgh. The girls took up work at the many cloth, or silk making factories, or took up the oldest professional known to man. The English Army was always recruiting, and they had a large permanent recruiting presence at Stirling, designed to snap up the Highlanders who still dwindled into the city, so some of the young men from Amelia's group chose this option, with others joining the factories or signing up for domestic labour.

Amelia's little troupe enjoyed several months of popularity at the tavern in Stirling before there was a severe cholera outbreak which had been endemic in Stirling since the previous year. Both the publican and his wife died, and one of the girls, young Nellie, barely 15, died one morning after suffering for days. It then seemed that no one in the troupe or the town were interested in celebrations and entertainment, with so many grieving their losses.

They decided to finish their journey to Edinburgh.

Once in Edinburgh they sadly found that being in a large town with more people, that was growing every day, meant there was even less work to go around. The men were lucky that they could join the English Army if they could prove they were fit enough, and the men from Amelia's group had just enjoyed months of being well fed, so were quickly snapped up. The girls, apart from Amelia, eventually turned to prostitution as the closest thing to entertaining that they could do and be paid well for.

Luckily Amelia discovered that her specific talent for storytelling and ballad singing could make her even more money in Edinburgh. She started to spend a lot of her time hanging around the local ale houses hoping for an opportunity to perform. She refused to take up whoring, that so many women with few options took.

Sometimes she would pick up work as a domestic in the nicer houses in Edinburgh. She had worked as a dairy maid, a nursery maid (her story telling talents helped her to get those jobs), a scullery maid, and as a cleaner in the taverns during the day and a singer at night. She far preferred the work in the taverns where no airs and graces were necessary.

When things got really tough, she did supplement her income with a less invasive way that a woman could pleasure a man for money, where there was no chance of getting with child or catching the pox. Some men preferred her way rather than rolling around with a smelly strumpet or having a quick skirt lifter in an alleyway.

And then before she knew it, six years had gone by and there she was, still alive, which was something, because three of the girls who she had travelled to Edinburgh with were already dead, one murdered, one who had died in prison and one from fevers. She had lost touch with the men she had travelled with but knew most had joined the Army and gone off to lands far away. Amelia wished every day that she too could go off to lands far far away from cold dreary Edinburgh.

Her acquaintance with Margaret was fairly new. Living in survival mode, as they all did, left little time for friendships and to give your heart to another in friendship or love was to have your heart broken, as one by one people she knew died from illnesses or accidents, or went to prison for crimes committed while trying to stay alive. Between jobs they all slept wherever they were able to find a spot that was dry, if not warm. Amelia was tired, so very tired of it all.

Margaret told her that she was an orphan who was born in Edinburgh and had grown up in a workhouse were all the children worked from dawn until dusk and received little food and daily beatings. After running away from the workhouse when she was about 12, she was taken in by a merchant in the New Town, who had dressed her as a lady and kept her as his plaything, telling others that she was a visiting niece. She was raped continually. She hadn't even started her courses when she found herself pregnant. Her master had punched her in the stomach which got rid of that nuisance, but it kept happening and, reluctant to lose his pet he would arrange for an old crone to attend to Margaret and do something to kill the growing babe inside her, so that for weeks sometimes months, she was out of service. Once she almost died from the blood loss. It was during that episode that he brought home another much younger girl and as soon as Margaret was well enough, he sent her away with only the clothes she was wearing. One good thing from that, said Margaret, was that she now found herself unable to get with child, which was a definite bonus in her profession.

She had been working at the Cock and Trumpet, the famous whorehouse in High Street, but she had been caught stealing food from the kitchen and was banished. Survival now meant frequenting the local ale houses and dockyards in search of customers. That was where Amelia had met her, at the Jinglin' Geordie on Fleshmarket Close, plying her trade with her bosom overflowing from her grubby dress.

Amelia's wandering mind came back to the present and she saw James, kneeling in front of her.

"Aye, I haven't felt much up to performing Jamie. I picked up some work with a local family cleaning but that's ended now. I might be at the Geordie tonight. Try and stir up a crowd for me."

"I will lass, I will. See you there then." James tipped his hat and disappeared back into the crowd.

Amelia got up to retrieve the buckets just as a fat man in a gentleman's suit pushed past and knocked the old lady's bucket over. It had almost been full as well.

"Hey, watch out ya scurvy bloody dog," she yelled after him, but he was gone. Damn, she thought, as she emptied half of her own water into the old woman's bucket. Now she only had half for both her and Margaret.

"Come on granny," she said, helping the old lady to her feet "where are you staying, I'll see you home safely." Amelia helped the old woman up three flights of stairs to a room she was sharing with some relatives. Then she went back down to the street and along to her own dwelling and up the three sets of stairs to her rooms.

Margaret was waiting and had two vegetable pasties that she had bought for their dinner. And they were warm. "Oh Maggie," said Amelia "If this was roast beef and pudding, I bet it would not taste as good." The two girls sat in quiet contemplation as they ate their meal and enjoyed the warmth from the food creeping into their bodies.

"I think I'll go down the Geordie tonight," said Amelia.

"Oh Ems," Emma was Amelia's pet name "You should! It's been ages since you sang. I'll try and knock over my work early and come over to see you. It's always lovely and warm in there, and the crowd are good."

"Ems" said Margaret. "I was talking to this braw lad today after a job and he was telling me about some of his friends who had gone to the colony. Em, he hears from them, and they say it's wonderful. The air is clean and fresh, and the sun shines every day, and you only have to work for a master for a while and then they give the men land, and they are free. And they get to eat a joint every night. A joint of delicious roast meat, or a whole chicken on poor days!!," Margaret was bursting with excitement.

"And there's work for everyone, and not just in whoring neither. And there are so few women that everyone can get a husband, even ugly ones!"

Amelia took in what she was saying. She too had heard talk about people who had gone as convicts or free settlers to Australia and were reported to be having lives much better than they had in Scotland. She also heard of many people who had moved to Canada or America and were similarly enjoying a much better life. There was assisted emigration schemes for people from England and Ireland, that particularly targeted women, but they were not taking women directly from Scotland, so one had to get to London to apply for one of the assisted passages and hope you were accepted. If this was not possible then the only way to get there was as a convict.

That night she was welcomed into the Jinglin' Geordie, the publican coming to greet her personally. He got her a warm bowl of stew and a pint of ale and announced that they had a special guest for the night. Amelia wasn't much in the mood but stumbled through several ballads and a long fable which had even the drunker patrons enthralled. Reading the room, she then finished off with a few bawdy ballads that had the room in an uproar of laughs and back slapping, before handing over to the fiddler for the night who continued the music as the patrons were in the mood by then for a jig, and lots more ale, much to the publican's delight.

She was welcomed to a cosy booth, and as promised Margaret arrived looking pretty, as usual, in her working get-up. Soon the girls were surrounded by men eager to talk to them. At the girls urging, the talk turned to stories of the colony and every man knew someone who had gone to either New South Wales or Van

Diemen's Land either as a convict or a free settler. Either way, it seemed, the journey was rough, but at the end one was rewarded with work that was certainly not as hard as life in Scotland, and the chance to make something of yourself, either as a farmer, or as a merchant or a craftsman. There were so many opportunities, and the weather was glorious. No one had a bad story to tell, although Amelia figured that the convicts who had a bad time didn't get to tell their stories later on.

That night the girls took two sailor's home to their room because the security late at night was always welcome, and they seemed like decent lads. The extra services were on the house that night in exchange for the body warmth and the hot food the men brought up for the girls the next morning before heading back to their ship, which was bound for Norway the following day.

Over the next few days Amelia found herself thinking more and more about getting out of Edinburgh and going to Australia. She talked to lots of people in her networks and they all said that it wasn't as easy as she thought it might be. Unless she was up for committing a really bad crime, the law in Scotland aimed to rehabilitate offenders, so it wasn't unless a heinous crime was committed or multiple crimes, that someone could hope to be transported.

Right, thought Amelia, I'd better start somewhere then.

She decided for her first crime to break into a kitchen of one of the wealthier houses in the High Street, just down from where she and Margaret were staying, and nice and convenient. She spied on the house for a couple of hours and when she saw that the cook had left the scullery unattended, she made her move, jumping the short fence off the laneway and dashing inside. What to take, what to take. It had to be noticeable. She noticed a pretty apron hanging over a chair, obviously belonging to the lady of the house as it was too nice for the cook or maid. She grabbed it and threw it over her head and looked around for something else to take. There in the corner was a large sack full of oats. Ah ha, she thought, no one will miss me staggering around with that. It was heavy, but she managed to lift it and carry it back out to the fence. She made sure that she made a lot of noise while opening and closing the gate and then staggered slowly down the laneway. For a minute she thought that she'd gone un-noticed and started rattling the fences along her route, but then a woman jumped out from one of the yards and yelled out 'Thief, thief, Mr Erskine's being robbed." Soon a crowd of people had gathered around and grabbed Amelia.

Amelia spent a few nights in the city lock-up. She was surrounded by unsavoury types, but they didn't seem to be much different to those who she mixed with in the streets and taverns. She even had a bit of a laugh with one of the old hags who said she was there for her seventh time in three years. She looked to be in her 40's at least and had only one tooth left in her head. Her mind had obviously gone a big stale from the drink, but she was a funny old thing. Amelia hoped that it didn't take her seven goes to score a transportation ticket.

She was finally brought before the Police Court and charged with 'stealing *on 28 May 1839 1 peck of oatmeal and 1 checked apron, value not exceeding £10, from the house of William Erskine at Fountain Close, High Street, Edinburgh'*.

Amelia pleaded not guilty, as she had heard that this would give her a better chance at a higher punishment. The prosecution brought forward their witnesses, Jane Erskine, Margaret Duff

Broker and Leith Wynd, who all gave accounts of finding Amelia in the lane staggering around with the oatmeal, wearing the apron. In a short session, as there were many more prisoners awaiting their trial that day, Amelia was found guilty. But on account of her having lived in the city for seven years with no record of criminal activity, she was only sentenced to 30 days imprisonment at the Edinburgh Gaol.

This is going to take me longer than I thought, thought Amelia despondently.

She was taken to The Bridewell next to the Goal and told to take off her own meagre clothing and those along with her few belongings were taken away in a calico bag marked with her name. Margaret had agreed to take care of her precious fiddle and other small items that she owned such as her bedding and spare clothing.

She was given a set of prison clothes, that were thicker and warmer than her own, and marched into the centre of the circular building where she was allocated a cell. Every prisoner was allocated a shared cell which were set on the outside circumference of the circular building with the openings facing the centre, where an elevated concrete pulpit was placed surrounded by an exercise yard and various tables and chairs. The guards could sit at the tables and have a 360-degree view of all the cells, but it also meant that the prisoners were easily able to see each other and communicate freely.

The pulpit was made good use of every morning and evening for an hour-long sermon in an attempt to reform the prison population into model citizens. Amelia thought their time would be better spent working out how to change the city from a cesspit of poverty so that people didn't need to commit crimes.

The bed in her cell was absolutely plush for someone who had spent many nights sleeping on the cold hard ground or a floor. The mattress was thick and soft, although she did notice a few jumping creatures hopping about when she sat down. And there were thick blankets, three for each prisoner.

She found that all the prisoners were allocated work during the day, which started after morning services and a meal of thick porridge in the communal dining hall, where the male and female prisoners eagerly mixed. The guards tried to stop any interactions but were rarely successful and didn't seem to have any ambition to force the issue.

Amelia was put to work looming and spinning, a task familiar to her from both her granny and her mother. The work was not hard, the buildings were mostly warm, and the other prisoners were in more or less similar situations as her. It was not long before Amelia was asked to perform her stories for her fellow prisoners as they worked over the looms. Some had heard of her talent from the streets.

Amelia chose uplifting fables and tales where the hero of the story had a happy ending. Not all the stories were like that. Many were meant to tell a cautionary tale to the listener. She had to be careful which stories she told as anything about historical battles could potentially offend her jailors, being loyal to the English King. All of Scotland's' wars had been fought against the English!

Before she knew it, and before she had even really settled in, but had started to feel comfortable and at home in The Bridewell, Amelia's 30 days were up, and she was turned out onto the street having given back her warm prison garments and changed back into her own thin clothing.

Damn, she thought, I'll have to cook up something again quickly.

Vron

Vron

Chapter Five

# *1839 - A Grand Plan*

$\mathcal{A}$melia returned to her previous dwelling rooms and found out that not much had changed. Margaret had caught another case of the pox and was out of service until it healed. In the meantime, she had been using her hands and mouth to their best ability and had thrown out her jaw, giving her a bad headache.

"Go an' get me some rum Ems, there's a good girl, I'm in no mood for any customers tonight."

Amelia went down to the street and soon found an acquaintance who filled her small bottle with rum. She gave him the coins that Margaret had given her, and while she was down there, got them both some warm bread, ham, and a boiled egg each. While she was in prison, she had been given a few coins from the guards in exchange for telling them some of her bawdy tales after everyone else was locked in their cells. One took an interest in her, and as she was in no mood for being raped or getting a beating by multiple guards, she gave him her special treatment. In his defence he did make sure that she got an extra helping of stew the next day and an extra blanket.

Jeez, she thought, you're one step away from whoring Amelia! You've got to get out of this mess.

And so it was that two weeks later, on 11 July, she again stood in front of the Police Court charged this time with *'stealing on 9 July 1839 1 check apron and 1 small, blue worsted shawl, value not exceeding £10, from the green behind St Mary's Church, Edinburgh, the property of Margaret Newton, 7 Scotland Street'.*

She pleaded not guilty again, and the prosecutor brought out his witnesses, Catherine Owen a servant, and the friend of Margaret Newton, who she had snatched the items from as the girls walked behind the church after services. John Amos, the day policeman who had arrested her also provided a statement. She was found guilty again and this time sentenced to 60 days imprisonment at the Bridewell. She was rather disappointed because she thought that a crime in the actual church grounds would surely be worthy of transportation this time.

When she arrived back at The Bridewell, Amelia was given a fitting welcome by the prisoners and guards alike and settled back into the daily routine. Aiden, the guard who provided her with the extra blanket was particularly glad of her return and again found her an extra blanket. It became his special treat to visit her cell at the end of a hard week, and a special treat for Amelia in the form of rum and extra rations to enjoy after he had gone. He was happy with the arrangement as there was no chance of him catching the pox, which so many men he knew were often sick with.

Amelia asked Aiden and the other guards and prisoners what she needed to do to get transported. They all hemmed and hawed but concluded that transportation was generally only given for multiple crimes or something more heinous. Bodily harm, highway robbery, assault with a weapon, a crime against a member of the clergy or the gentry, or against a child. None of those were appealing to Amelia, but now at 25 years of age she was not keen to keep putting the effort in to just spend a month or two at the Bridewell. Eventually she would get out and Margaret would have moved on and she'd be homeless.

Her 60 days again went quickly, and she was sad to say goodbye to the new friends she had made at The Bridewell, and she knew that she was going to miss the attentions, and the growing collection of coins, from Aiden. The two had become quite close in their unusual transactional prison relationship. There had been times when she first arrived when some of the other guards had become curious about what made their colleague weak at the knees and willing to put his job in jeopardy, however asking around the town soon gave them their answer and they were all eager to line up for their turn. That was definitely not what Amelia had in mind and luckily Aiden protected her in the prison, as he wanted her all to himself. But on her release, she knew that she had to be extra careful as some of those guards had already been to the Geordie looking for her and she was not sure that they would all be happy with her way of giving a bit of happiness that did not involve any skirt lifting. So there went her best source of income, singing at the Geordie.

She tried her luck at a few other taverns further away from the Geordie and picked up a few nights work here and there but found herself hungry most of the time.

"Aye Ems, just come a-whoring with me love. There's nothing to it. Most of the time it's a quick minute or two and my worries about my supper are gone for a few days. And if I start it off with a little kiss you know where, I can make twice the coin for 30 seconds of that, which then makes the other go even quicker! So easy." She did a little pirouette and showed off the lovely dress with pink and cream frills that one of her customers had paid for. She'd started to accumulate a collection of jewellery and hair combs, made from paste of course, but which further enhanced her marketability on the street. One of her wealthier regulars, a merchant who lived in the New Town, had promised her, in exchange for his weekly visits, a room in one of the nicer buildings closer to his home, so that he could more easily visit her respectably. She had promised that Amelia could join her as she would be too lonely on her own.

As the winter chill started to creep in, Amelia took a job mucking out the pig yard at the home of one of the factory managers in the New Town. How much lower could she stoop, she thought sadly to herself. It was while mucking out the stye one afternoon that the owner's teenage son, who himself greatly resembled one of her charges, with great rolls of fat around his belly and his jowls, decided that her bending over was too much for him and using his bulk to subdue her pushed her against the pig pen, bent her over and raped her from behind.

Strangely enough, and surprisingly, Amelia was not as upset as she thought that she should have been. Once he had finished, after grunting and groaning for a whole 30 seconds, he helped her to stand back up, smiled at her in a guilty bovine looking manner, and gave her his dirty handkerchief to clean up. He then apologised, wiping the drool from his mouth with the back of his dirty hand, smearing dust and mud across his face. He then offered her a ham sandwich, thick with butter, and they sat in companionable silence while Amelia contemplated what had just happened.

Thinking quickly and knowing that as a young lad he'd be ready again, she decided to take advantage of the situation and offered him a look at her breasts and quick rub in exchange for coins. She explained to him what she would do and he nodded his head eagerly in agreement. He quickly counted out what he had, the drool appearing again at his slack jaw as he imagined what was to come. Amelia quickly pocketed the coins as the boy undid his strides, and out popped an appendage well in proportion with the rest of his fat body. Twenty seconds later and it was all over, and she had a pocket of pennies.

The boy gazed at her blankly with a look of awe, but she quickly shooed him away with the promise of another go the next day if he'd bring marmalade sandwiches this time and more coins.

That's it, she thought as she slowly and sadly walked back to the room she shared with Margaret. You are a dirty whore, and you may as well admit it and just get stuck into it like Margaret does. The thought made her weep as that was the very last thing that she wanted her life to turn out as.

Margaret, at twenty-three was still pretty and fresh looking, however she had had the pox for several years now and every now and then she would break out in a rash over her whole body and would be racked with aches and pains. Amelia knew that this could come and go for years and years, but eventually Margaret would be unable to walk and then she would lose her mind.

For the next few months Amelia's lot in life improved thanks to the new room provided by Margaret for a few coins each week, and the lust of the pig owners fat son, who was now stealing from his father and selling the items so that he could continue his daily interludes with Amelia. He was well and truly addicted and thankfully she had convinced him that she would only use her hand and not to try the other again. The only thing worse than what she had found herself doing would be to find herself with child as well.

For the first time in many years, Amelia found herself one day at church. She now had clothes suitable to be seen at services thanks to her wealthy fat friend. As she listened to the sermon, she had a revelation. She would NOT let this be her life. There was more for her than being bent over and used by fat merchants and their pimply progeny. It was time to reinvigorate her transportation dream. But how could she make her crime worse than last time.

The solution came to her as she finished her latest transaction with the fat son. Their sojourns had moved from the pig stye to the boy's room in the big house, and as Amelia walked through the halls and rooms a whole plethora of stealable items were on display for her. Why didn't I think of this before, she thought?

And so it was that on 28 Dec 1839 Amelia was charged with the 'th*eft of a brap or other metal candlestick (2 candlesticks) and a pair of snuffers'.* She had hidden in the foyer of the house after finishing her duties with the pigs of the house, both bovine and human, until she was sure that the house servants were going about their evening duties and would be sure to hear her.

This time she received five months and was described as being *'by habit and repute, a thief'.* Getting closer she thought.

She settled back into her now second home at the Bridewell and into her transactions with Aiden, who was by then married to a shop keeper's daughter. This however did not prevent his visits to Amelia. His marital activities with his wife so far involved her lifting her nightgown and holding her breath until he was finished. With Amelia he could get some pleasure as well as share some conversation as she had been around and had learned things about the world. She always had a story to spin to entertain him, it was like she had a whole library stored up in her head. His wife came from a very sheltered family and was only 15. He felt lucky to now have Ameila for 5 months. But now that he was married his ability to pay was limited, so he took on extra shifts, rather than go without her.

The months flew by for Amelia. She honed her skills on the loom and also took some extra lessons in embroidery. By the end of her sentence, she could embroider quite an acceptable little pattern. She even drew her own designs. She had also been eating like a Queen thanks to gifts from Aiden on the weeks he couldn't pay by coin and had also accumulated a decent nest egg so that she wouldn't have to worry about starving from quite some time after her release. With time on her hands where she wasn't under the constant threat of assault, homelessness, or starvation she had started to make up her own stories and poems, which she tried out on Aiden and her fellow prisoners. Her tales were love stories with damsels in distress and valiant warriors of the Knights Templar, who many Scottish knights went to serve with in France. Woven into her tales were fairies and trolls and seers who could predict the future. Most nights she could see a few of the guards standing in the shadows listening to her stories as well.

But most importantly, she heard more and more stories of Australia and about people who had gone there and sent word back to Scotland. Again, there was not one bad story. Everyone seemed to be a story of success and happiness in a glorious, fresh new land.

However, there was gossip afoot that the King was about to stop the transportation of convicts to Australia, and indeed news soon arrived that convicts would no longer be sent to New South

Wales. It was time to really up-the-ante if she wanted to make her dream come true. Now with her convictions, transportation was her only hope because even if she could make it to London, she would no longer be a candidate for an assisted emigrant passage.

Amelia was released again at the end of May 1840.

Sitting in a tavern one night she heard that several people had recently been transported for crimes against children, and it didn't need to be anything cruel or violent. It was common for young children to wander unattended in the city, to run errands or just to play with the other children. They were easy prey for all kinds of crimes, an easy one being to grab them, strip them of their expensive garments and be gone before they could find anyone to tell.

It took Amelia a while to figure out how best to carry out her crime and days of watching the streets to see the comings and goings of the children and their parents before she chose her targets.

It was about 2 o'clock in the afternoon when Amelia spotted her targets, three little girls about 4 years old. But just as she was about to make her move Margaret turned up dressed in her working finery and carrying a bag of sweets.

"Hello sweeties," she said to the girls, "would you all like a real sweety from Maggie then?" the little girls gathered around Margaret. Margaret didn't notice that as she was talking to two of the little girls who were fussing over her gown that Amelia and the other little girl had gone.

Amelia led the little girl to a nearby stairwell telling her that she had better sweeties. She then stripped the child of her dress and then yelled at her to get back to her friends. Oddly the child failed to cry out as Amelia had wanted. She needed to draw as much attention as she could.

The child scurried off in the direction that Amelia had led her, looking no worse for wear, it being a warm day with the sun shining for once. She then slowly started to walk down the street swinging the dress around her head, hoping that someone would ask her where it came from. But no one did.

Not knowing what to do, short of walking into the Police station and presenting the dress as stolen property, she saw a broker's shop, Bambery's on Blackfriars Wynd and decided to try her luck there. On entering the door there were a few customers standing around the shop. She boldly went up to the counter and presented the dress.

"Sir, I have stolen this dress," she said. The other customers stared at her for a second and then collectively started laughing.

"Lass," said the man behind the counter, "everything in here is stolen," then he also started to laugh.

"Well, well," said Amelia unsure of what to do next.

"Ere, it's a decent dress, I'll give you some coin for it, you look like you could do with a drink to forget your woes."

Sadly, Amelia pawned the dress and wandered despondently back towards the direction of the Geordie, not caring too much anymore what happened to her. There on the corner she met Margaret.

"Where'd you get off to then love," she said. Amelia told her of her plan and how it hadn't worked. Margaret had a laugh and playfully whacked her on the arm. "Look at you then, what sort of criminal are you Emma Laing, can't even get caught when you try," she laughed. "Come on with ya, let's go get a drink."

They walked down to the Geordie where they were greeted by the publican and patrons, who were glad to see Amelia back.

"You going to treat us to a story tonight lass?" asked the publican.

"Nah, I'm paying tonight Ray, and I'm in the mood for some solid drinking." The crowd closest to her let out a whoop and the first glass of rum was passed over to the girls.

Several hours later Amelia and Margaret were quite drunk and having a good time. There had been some singing and some dancing and lots of drinking of both rum and ale.

But suddenly Amelia became melancholy.

"I'm never getting out of here Maggie," a tear ran down her cheek.

"Ah well love, it ain't so bad, you got me ain't ya?" Amelia looked down as Margaret started to scratch her arm vigorously and she could see another of her rashes had appeared.

"Oh Maggie," she said pulling her friend into a hug, "Yes I do."

But Amelia had a new plan, and it was about to happen now. The sun was just setting as Amelia staggered off down towards Canongate, where she knew the nicer people let their children play outside. And sure enough there was a cute little boy dangling a stick into a mud puddle outside one of the nicer buildings. He was with a girl, slightly older than him, but the little boy was dressed like a little gentleman with a black beaver hat, flannel petticoat, cotton, blue and white striped pinafore and leather shoes.

Before she knew what she was doing Amelia had snatched the little boy and run off with him. As she ran, he started to cry and not knowing what best to do in her drunken state she took him back to her room where Margaret sat enjoying a warm pie and more rum.

"Oh lawd Amelia, what have you done now?" she said "Oh my lawd you'll not just get transported if you harm that child, ye'll get hung from the gibbets."

The little boy had stopped crying and accepted some of Margaret's pie.

"Right," said Amelia, "it's all all right then. Now little lad, when you've had your pie, we're just going to take your clothes off and wrap ye in a blanket and take ye back to you ma. And you'll get some sweeties to take with you as well. Is that all right then lovie?"

The little boy wiped his eyes and held his hand out for the sweets.

"Not yet my little gentleman," laughed Amelia, "we've got some work to do first."

"Oh Ems what are you up to?" asked Margaret nervously.

"It's all right Maggie, I'll just take the clothes in tomorrow as if I'm selling them on the street right near where he lives, someone is sure to see me with them and call the police. I'll say I found someone else with them and stole them off them." Her thought process was a little addled by the drink.

As promised, Amelia wrapped the boy in a blanket and accompanied by a not very happy Margaret carried the boy back to where they had found him. By then it was quite dark. "OK then lad, here's your sweetie's." Just as Amelia turned, the boy let out a piercing scream, and people came running from all directions and every house.

Not expecting such a commotion Amelia turned to run, but in the process tripped over her feet and landed flat on her face in the street.

The police were soon on the scene and Amelia was yelled at and harangued by the crowd, the boy's mother landing a square punch on her jaw.

"Ehhh there'll be none of that then," said the constable.

Amelia admitted to stealing the clothes and led the policeman back to her room, where Margaret tried to make a hasty retreat but was not fast enough. As the clothes were found in Margaret's room she was also arrested and taken with Amelia to the watch house.

The next day the two women came before the Court. It took more than a week for the police and the prosecutors to put together their case and to gather witnesses. They had been able to find the parents of the first girl who Amelia stole the dress from and the pawn shop owner who she sold the dress to.

The children said that Margaret Leitch (not Caldwell as Amelia had known her as) only gave them sweets and was not involved, and the children involved in the second theft had not seen her at all.

They all then attested to what Amelia had done.

When it was her turn Amelia pleaded guilty to all charges and gave her account of how the crimes came about.

Margaret Leitch was found not guilty of all charges.

On the 22nd of July 1840, Amelia Laing was found guilty and sentenced to 7 years transportation. Her new adventure was about to begin.

Vron

## Chapter Six
# *1840 – London bound*

*A*melia arrived back at her second home at The Bridewell and received her package of clothes and bedding. She didn't know how long it would be until she could be sent to Australia or how long that it would be before she left The Bridewell. She was pleased when she discovered that Scottish prisoners awaiting transportation were kept in Scottish prisons rather than being sent to London and kept at the dreaded Newgate or Millbank Prisons or one of the Prison hulks on the Thames.

She settled back into the life of The Bridewell. Aiden visited not long after she arrived but told her that he could no longer pay for her company. They struck a deal, her company in exchange for writing lessons. While Amelia could read, she had never learned to write and she realised that she would dearly love to write down some of her new stories, as sometimes she forgot the details when she was next telling them.

Not long after she arrived Margaret visited with her fiddle and a parcel of her belongings.

"I've sewed your coins into your drawers pet," she whispered.

"Oh, thank you Maggie," said Amelia "I'm going to miss you. I wish you were coming with me."

"Nah Ems that's too much adventure for me," she laughed. "Besides I've got my fancy man now and my nice rooms. I don't even have to go out on the street much now neither." Which was good thought Amelia, because she had started to limp, and the rashes were coming more and more frequently.

Amelia knew that she would never see her friend again.

"I'll write you Maggie, I can write now!" she said proudly. The two friends who had been through so much together looked into each other's eyes searching. They knew it would be for the last time. Margaret stood abruptly and hugged her friend "Right, I'll be seeing ya then Ems." She turned quickly and rushed out the door, leaving Amelia with a tear running down her cheek.

In her small parcel of belongings there was several books that she had been given or bought over the years which she referred to for some of her stories. She had her bibles, but her favourites were Gulliver's Travels and Pride and Prejudice which was where she got some of the inspiration for her love stories from.

Time went by and more girls arrived who were set to be transported to Australia. When there was a group of six, they were moved from The Bridewell to the Calton prison, where the longer-term prisoners were kept for punishment rather than for rehabilitation. Luckily there were rooms and an exercise yard set aside just for the women being transported. A matron was put in charge of them. She told them that the Scottish girls sentenced to transportation were kept at Edinburgh until there were enough to make it worthwhile moving them all to London, and then they were kept at Newgate, the dreaded main prison in London. Everyone had heard terrible tales of Newgate, where people starved or were bashed to death.

When they expressed their concerns, she assured them that it was usual for the Scottish girls to arrive at Newgate very soon before their journey, and they were kept in an area separate to the main population of the gaol. She told them that Newgate followed the teachings of Mrs Fry, as did the gaols in Scotland, which taught that rehabilitation was better than punishment and the best way to rehabilitate felons was to give them something to do and a good grounding in his Lord's teachings, the aim being to turn them into useful and compliant servants on their release. It was in their very best interests, she said, to spend their time in Edinburgh learning as many skills as they could in preparation for their arrival in the colony, so that they could be assured of a good assignment.

Amelia came to a deal with another female prisoner, in exchange for fiddling lessons she offered to continue Amelia's writing lessons, and she eagerly threw herself into her lessons. Her embroidery skills were also getting much better.

Amelia found the bible studies and the scriptures boring, but she had to admit that there were some interesting stories in both the Old and New Testaments. Matron frowned at Amelia's fiddling but when she turned some of her stories and songs into bible-based ones Matron found that acceptable and even asked Amelia to read some of the scriptures during their twice daily bible studies.

The days turned into weeks, which turned into months and there was no word yet about when they would travel to Australia but week by week more women arrived.

By the time that the Hogmanay celebrations were over, which for the prisoners only meant more religious studies and the sounds of revelry from outside the prison, there were 14 women awaiting transportation.

Christina 'Chrissie' McLeod was originally from Ireland and was tried along with Janet Paterson. Christina and Janet, along with Margaret 'Maggie' Speirs had been 'on the town' in Edinburgh and knew Amelia's friend Margaret. They were rough around the edges, greatly missed their rum and ale and were always good for a laugh. None of them were very interested in learning new skills, laughing that they'd earn their keep on their backs which they were all good at.

There were three older women. Izzy Clapperton, a widow, was about 10 years older that Amelia and was an excellent seamstress and embroiderer. Old Sarah Woodhouse barely spoke and was simple minded, but she eventually told them that she was 53 and a dressmaker. She said that some bad people had made her steal from her master, and then she wept uncontrollably until someone gave her a hug. Christian Stevenson was 43, and along with her husband was an umbrella maker and had a business that did very well. She was leaving her husband and three young children behind. She said that they had been involved in a fencing ring, but it was only Christian who had been caught with stolen goods, which was a good thing because at least their father was left behind to care for the children. Maybe they might join her one day in Australia.

Young Eliza Deans was as dark as the night sky, and originally from New York. She proudly told them that she was the daughter of freed slaves and was a hat maker by trade. She had been convinced to go to Scotland by a fancy man she had met in New York, who had promptly abandoned her on arrival. She had been arrested stealing food to survive.

There were two Jane's, black Jane and white Jane. They were both named Jane Johnson. Jane 1 was born to a black father from

Africa and a Scottish mother. She'd been a house servant and washer woman. Jane 2 had worked as a house servant, washer woman and a milk maid. They were both of a similar nature, quiet and obedient. Amelia figured that they would both get good assignments.

Charlotte Dundas, only 22, was a housemaid and dressmaker by trade; Margaret Miller had many skills, she could milk, make butter and cheese and bake. And there was Ann Muir who was from Spain, had very dark hair and eyes, and spoke with a thick accent; and Margaret Williams who was 25.

Amelia knew that something was finally about to happen when a group of 16 more women arrived from Glasgow. The Edinburgh women were told to be quiet and go to one side of the room while Matron told the Glasgow girls the same story that she had told the others on their arrival. Then they were all allowed to mix and get to know each other. As happens when a group of women get together, before long the room was filled with a cacophony of voices and laughter, the voices getting louder and louder, as everyone tried to talk over the top of each other.

Having not seen anyone from outside of their room and yard for months the Edinburgh girls were keen to hear any news from outside but most of the Glasgow girls had similarly been kept in isolation and only those most recently sentenced had any news from the outside.

Soon it was time for the afternoon bible study during which several of the Glasgow girls, tired from their travel, fell asleep, causing Matron to scurry over to them and flick them with the switch that she kept handy for such transgressions.

Over the past few weeks Amelia had somehow fallen in with the more gregarious girls; Christina, known as Chrissie, Janet, Margaret, known as Mags and black Eliza. That night, Jane McLaughlan, who had been a prostitute in Glasgow for years, sensing kindred spirits, joined them in their merriment and introduced them to three of the other Glasgow girls, all young women who had only been on the town for a few months before their convictions. Lizzie Harrigan was very loud and a lot of fun. Mary Girdwood and Maggie Neillis were quieter but took in everything and giggled a lot.

When things had quietened down, and the girls were supposed to be reading their bibles or other literature approved by Matron, Eliza gave Amelia a long side eye and then dug her in the ribs with her elbow. "Ere, what's that for."

"Got a secret" said Eliza in her American drawl and with a wink of her eye. "Well spit it out then lassie," said Amelia with a laugh.

Eliza then drew out a tin flask from inside her skirts. Amelia's eyes widened and she let out a giggle.

"Where'd you get that from then?"

"Well, you know that Matron's been letting me down to the laundry room to learn the ironing, well let's just say that several of the guards ain't never been with a black woman," she gave Amelia another wink.

"Oh Eliza, you didn't?"

"No, no nothing like that. I'm not stupid and the last thing I want is to arrive in the colony with some prison guard's brat! I used mah hands didn't I. I can do two at once that way and make twice the prize!" Amelia broke into giggles and then told her about the fat pig owner's son. They both dissolved into giggles which brought the others over to find out what was so funny.

Eliza ushered them all into forming an enclosed circle so that what they were doing couldn't be seen by the others. "Okay you'all I'm going to pass the flask around and you can take a slug, but then you have to say a bible passage out loud, any passage, that will keep Matron away if she thinks we are doing bible study."

And so, the flask, and then another that miraculously emerged from Eliza's skirts was passed around quietly, and bible passages were quietly uttered, in amongst giggles that got more regular and louder the more the flask was passed around. The bible passages soon turned into singing as Amelia led them in one of her songs that included crowd participation. Ordinarily, the verses were a bit rude and meant for the taverns but knowing that she'd be pushing her luck Amelia kept the song sweet.

Soon the rest of the women gathered around and as they all appeared in good spirits and not up to mischief, Matron let them have their fun for an hour before calling bedtime and an end to their enjoyment. Matron sat up sewing for an hour longer, as she did every night, to make sure that there were no nighttime shenanigans.

Soon enough the women were told that it was time to get ready to travel to London. The journey by five large stagecoaches took five days. Six prison guards came with the women who were put in ankle irons for the duration. At night they slept around a fire on the side of the road with only bread, butter, and water with lime juice for rations.

For the first two days Amelia and the rowdy girls had a great time looking out at the countryside, laughing with each other and being cheeky to the guards and the coach drivers. But by day three they all had sores on their ankles and were hungry and sick of the constant bumping around from the rough roads. Poor old Sarah started crying on day three and could not be consoled. The girls tried hugging her and singing to her, but the old woman just kept crying, until she would fall asleep exhausted, but start again as soon as she woke and remembered where she was.

They finally arrived in London which looked like a larger version of Edinburgh with the same kinds of buildings and the same kind of people.

Their reception at Newgate was scary. They could hear constant howls and screams from behind the walls, and the most awful stench permeated the air even outside the walls. Once inside they were quickly ushered down dark foreboding hallways and into a large, whitewashed room that contained several tables and chairs.

There they met Matron Kezia Hayter.

Miss Hayter was a small, young woman with quite a pretty face, who was dressed like a lady. As the group of Scotswomen stood in the middle of the large room, she advised them in a refined accent that she would be accompanying them to Van Diemen's Land and would ensure their health and safety on the voyage.

"Miss la de da thinks she can look after us!" Chrissie whispered with a smirk. Miss Hayter overheard and quickly said "Of course the ship will also have the full complement of guards and sailors, who will also ensure the safety of the ship's cargo, that is, you women!"

"And now to meet your shipmates," said Miss Hayter. One of the guards opened a door and there was an influx of around 20 women and several children. Some carried large carpet bags and a few dragged trunks along behind them. Soon the air was filled with multiple female accents as they greeted each other. The English girls marvelled at the thick clothing of the Scottish girls, theirs being much thinner and poorer quality.

Miss Hayter clapped her hands loudly to bring them all to silence. "Services will be held at 5 o'clock followed by supper. You will then have an early night as tomorrow we have a lot to do before we board the ship in three days' time. You will have to make do for the next few nights with sharing the mattresses, but I'm sure that many of you have had to do that before." With that she turned abruptly and left the room.

The nights at Newgate were not pleasant as the women were forced to sleep four to a mattress and with limited washing facilities the smells from body odour and body gases were nauseating. That, along with the snoring and nightmares of some, and the screaming and howling from the rest of the prison, meant that not much sleep was had. The women were also full of excitement and anxiety awaiting their sea voyage. Most of them had already travelled further in the past weeks than they had done in their whole lives. Amelia found that she was one of the most travelled of the group, having gone from her hometown to Edinburgh all those years ago. Some of the women were convicted in London and had never left the few square miles from where they were born.

Early on the morning of the 23rd of March 1841, Miss Hayter woke the women, and they were quietly led out of Newgate before the sun rose and shuffled along dark corridors to the exit where there were guards waiting to rivet them into leg irons. Amelia winced as they were put on as she still had sores from their journey from Scotland.

The women were then shuffled into covered carriages. "Oi," said one of the women "We ain't dead yet", realising that the carriages were hearses. Miss Hayter explained that prisoners being transported were once taken to Woolwich in open carts which caused a huge ruckus every time with hecklers and people throwing things at them, along with weeping family members running along next to the carts. It was decided to move the convicts in covered carriages, and the easiest and cheapest to get were hearses.

As they arrived at the docks the girls saw what she meant as a huge crowd had gathered which included hecklers, protestors against transportation and a few people weeping and calling out, who Amelia imagined must be family members.

As she looked out to the river Miss Hayter pointed out a large ship which she said was their ship, the *Rajah*. The girls all stood in fear and awe.

They were rowed in small boats out to the ship where they scrabbled up the ladder holding their meagre belongings close. An officer then welcomed Miss Hayter onboard and ordered another sailor to take her to her rooms, and then yelled at the convicts to line up along the deck. Each woman was then made to sit on a small stool while her leg irons were removed and they then joined another line which led to a table where a clerk and a man who they were told was the Ship's Surgeon, Doctor James Donovan, waited.

Each woman was inspected, weighed, and measured and her details written down. Amelia peeked at what the clerk was writing "Ere lad I do not have a small turned up nose!" she said, to which he scowled at her and growled at her to move on. Surgeon Donovan gave Amelia a wooden bowl, spoon, a blanket, and a long, thick bag filled with straw that was to serve as a mattress. They were then directed to a bucket of water where a cake of soap and sponge had been left by the previous woman, and told to wash, fully clothed. At least Amelia was able to wash some of the accumulated grime from her face, in her ears and around her neck. She also took her shoes off and washed her feet and bathed the sores on her ankles.

Once there were ten girls ready a guard directed them down two hatchways and into the bowels of the ship where it was very dark, stuffy, and claustrophobic. He told them that this was where they would sleep and to choose a berth closest to the hatch, "Less fumes from the bilge," he said touching his cap and waving his hand in front of his nose.

Once the girls had chosen their berths with a lot of giggling and carry-on, the guard took them back up the hatches to where a large group of women were scrubbing the deck. "You're a lot more lively than this poor lot," said the guard. Amelia glanced around and saw what looked like an army of clones. The women all had bald, or almost bald heads, and none of them were making any noise, and they all looked forlorn and without hope.

"Right then," said the guard, "get to work, no slacking around on this ship," and he left to go and collect his next group of women.

None of the bald women looked at the new arrivals, dedicated to their chore at hand.

"Ermmm, excuse me lass," said Janet "should we just start scrubbing then?" The girl looked up startled then her eyes darted around her looking for something. She looked at Janet with a look of desperate fear and put her finger to her lips and quietly, in a whisper said, "Shoosh", and pointed out where the brushes were.

The Newgate group looked at each other uneasily. Something had obviously traumatised these women terribly.

Later in the day the Newgate women were summoned by Miss Hayter and told to divide into 'Messes'- groups of twelve. Miss Hayter told them that the women in their mess would be responsible for each other during the journey and would be tasked by mess. Each Mess was told to choose the woman from their group who was best at cooking, as that woman would be responsible for collecting and protecting their rations and providing meals for them. Ann Muir, the Spanish girl, was chosen as the Mess woman for Amelia's group.

Along with Ann, Amelia's Mess mates included two girls from Yorkshire, Elizabeth Archer and Ann Wright who had been sentenced together for the same crime; Eliza, Chrissie and Mags from Edinburgh (although they sent Janet to another Mess to break up that duo), Jane and Lizzie from Glasgow, old Sarah, and the two Janes.

As the women were being sent off to bed after prayers that night, Amelia asked if she could talk to Miss Hayter.

"Pardon me Ma'am," she said, "but what is wrong with those women, the bald ones?" Miss Hayter explained that the bald women has been imprisoned at Millbank, which followed strict punishment rules that included solitary confinement for the first six months, the shaving of hair and silence to be observed at all times. If any rule was broken the women were severely beaten. The only time they were allowed to talk was to Mrs Fry's ladies when they visited and only in relation to their needlework.

Miss Hayter told Amelia that Mrs Fry and her ladies belonged to the Quakers, or the Religious Society of Friends, which was why they all spoke old fashioned English, which made the girls giggle. Mrs Fry had been diligently working for prisoner rights and wellbeing for over twenty years and was the reason why the women had enjoyed such good treatment in the prisons. The young Queen Victoria and the British government listened to Mrs Fry and had implemented a lot of her recommendations, including about transportation conditions. Mrs Fry was the reason why Miss Hayter was sent with them on the journey and in Hobart it was hoped that Miss Hayter could influence Lady Franklin and the Governor to adopt some of the recommendations for prison reform in Van Diemen's Land.

Over the next few days several of the Millbank women went mad and showed violent symptoms of derangement with loud howling, wailing, and flailing of arms and legs. Eventually five of them were disembarked.

It was with much excitement that the women watched a few days later as a boat full of ladies wearing the white bonnets that marked them as Mrs Fry's ladies, approached the ship. There was a busy bustle around the ship as the guards got the women ready for the visit.

The ladies set up on the deck and for four days received each prisoner with grace and humbleness. When it was Amelia's turn, she stepped up to the table and took a seat opposite the actual Mrs Fry. After hearing the stories of what this woman had done for women prisoners Amelia was in awe, but in front of her sat a kind, gentle looking old lady.

Mrs Fry asked Amelia about her hometown and her thoughts about her imprisonment in Scotland and at Newgate, and about her hopes for the future. She then talked to her about what to expect onboard the ship and once she arrived in Van Diemen's Land. The main things that she emphasised was to remain pious and trust the Lord, devote yourself to religious studies and be industrious, useful in whatever way you could be, and remain quiet and compliant. In this way, said Mrs Fry, a convict could bide out their term until they again gained their freedom.

While Amelia understood what she was saying and could probably try to be like that if she concentrated on it, she was very certain that some of her fellow shipmates would not be able to live that way even for one day. They were all in for an interesting time.

Mrs Fry then handed her a large hessian sack full of items for the journey. Each convict received a new bible, two aprons, one hessian and one black, a black cotton cap, a comb, a knife and fork, and a small bag containing various sewing notions, including a pair of scissors and two pounds of patchwork pieces. If needed, they were also issued with new spectacles.

Amelia watched as two children at another table with their mother, laughed with glee as they were given gifts, the girl a doll and the boy a toy boat.

Finally, Mrs Fry stood, grasped Amelia's hands, and gave her a warm smile and then placed a red cord with a tin ticket around her neck with the number 229 stamped on it.

Later Miss Hayter came to visit Amelia's Mess and handed each girl a white dress which she told them not to wear but to save for best, and a supply of napkins for their courses. She explained that the last passengers, the Reverend Davies with his wife and small son, would be arriving that afternoon and the final preparations to leave England would begin.

Amelia's much longed for journey was about to begin.

Vron

Chapter Seven
# *1841 – The High Seas*

*K*ezia Hayter was very glad that the Reverend Davies was soon to join her with his wife Maria and three-year-old son Rowland. Reverend Davies had already lived in Van Diemen's Land and Maria's uncle's owned thriving properties to the north of the island near a town called Longford. It was at the Reverend Davies' sermon, in England in March 1841, that Kezia decided that her calling lay with furthering the teachings of Mrs Fry in the colonies.

There was nothing for Kezia in England. At only 22 she was living with an elderly Great Aunt, having been sent from her parents to live with distant family as a young girl. As she blossomed, she was subjected to cruel treatment by her cousins, whose parents failed to protect her. She had turned to the Lord to try and understand her life and where she fit into the great scheme of things, coming from such a terrible beginning. While both Amelia and Kezia were both escaping England, the two young women were from very different social spectrums. Kezia's family where wealthy and she had never wanted for a roof over her head or food in her stomach. It was only love that she was starved of.

The Reverend Davies had previously been in the colony for 11 years and led the congregation at Longford, where he had met Maria, the daughter of Launceston's Police Magistrate, Captain Lyttleton. He and Maria had returned to England in 1840 due to Maria's poor health, but the young woman rallied, and the couple were returning to Longford with a loan of 1,000 pounds to build a new church, and they were both very excited.

Kezia at 22, Maria at 26 and the Reverend at 37 still had the exuberance of youth, and it was their jubilation and hopefulness that they passed on to the 180 convict women and 10 children on board the *Rajah*.

The ship was not long out of the harbour when the Davies' set about putting together a makeshift church on the main deck. Seats were made of planks and tubs and the sailors helped to rig up a canvas awning, which provided a beautiful place of contemplation out of the sun's harsh rays and gave the setting an air of reverence and peace during the Reverend's nightly sermons, which happened every evening at 5pm, weather permitting.

Amelia was not a religious girl, a trait that she shared with many of the female convicts. Most of them had grown up in similar circumstances to her and found it tiresome to be preached at that some divine being was looking out for them. Many showed the scars, inside and outside, to prove that in their short lives nobody had been looking out for them. However, Amelia had to admit that some of the things that the Reverend talked about were relevant to her. Both the Reverend and Miss Hayter preached about being good and pious and nice and compliant. Amelia had to admit that it would seem that at least in her current situation, and while in prison, this had rung true. Those who bucked the system and caused trouble, just ended up in more trouble.

It was harder for some than for others to obey the teachings in the sermons. With the Reverend, Mrs Davies, and the Matron onboard, the Captain, Charles Ferguson, was able to keep a firm control over his crew as well as the convicts. Charles had been at the helm of the *Rajah* since 1838 so was very familiar with the ship and the crew. He knew how to keep his crew happy and content, but it was far easier to keep them out of trouble when the female crew was peaceable and not unruly. However, he was aware that there were several women keeping company with members of the crew, voluntarily thank goodness as this was not always the case on other ships, and that treats of extra rations and liquor were being exchanged for this company. There was also a gambling ring happening amongst the convicts that he was aware of and that the guards turned a blind eye to in exchange for some of the takings. These things he kept from the Reverend and Miss Kezia, as he knew that they would never be able to stamp out the practices and to try would only earn the ire of the crew and the convicts. And everything was so far, so peaceful.

As well as participating in shipboard chores, the women were soon to regularly partake of Miss Hayter's sewing groups. Every day Miss Hayter would supervise morning and afternoon groups of four messes at a time, as they practiced their sewing, embroidery, reading, writing and other skills that would be in demand in the colony. Chrissie, Mags, Jane 3 (from Glasgow) and Lizzie all laughed that they would only need to remember how to spread their legs to make do, so when not engaged in Miss Hayter's classes, she relegated them to laundry and stateroom duties where they washed bedding and cleaned the rooms of the passengers and crew. "That way you will know how to make up the bed as well as lay in it," she said with a flick of her curls.

As soon as it was found that Amelia had a talent for singing and storytelling and could also read and write, she was put to work schooling the 10 children onboard, so that their mothers could get on with their duties.

At first Amelia found the children tedious, not having been around any before. But gradually they grew on her, especially when the little ones sidled up for a cuddle and told her how pretty she was. She found that she actually seemed to have a talent for teaching and even the smallest of the children were starting to form their letters and sound them out. Some of them had never heard stories before so Amelia didn't have to dig too far into her repertoire to have them enthralled. After a few weeks Amelia was in high demand at the 'school' which she worked at every second day.

The women working with the children were ably supervised by Mary Smith who had been a school mistress and set schedules of what the children would do each day. She would even arrange little 'field exercises' where the children would visit the ships hospital or watch as the crew went about their many tasks, the young officers eager to explain what was happening, to both the children and of course to the pretty young school mistresses. One particularly exciting lesson was about celestial navigation. The ship's navigator took the children onto the deck at night while they were still in the northern hemisphere and showed them the stars and explained some of the constellations. He did this a few times just to show them that he was not tricking them when a month later he excitedly led them up the steps onto the deck and the stars had changed! He explained that the stars that they could see were different in the northern and the southern hemispheres. The children were enchanted, as were the convict women with them. Of course, Amelia and the others couldn't wait to tell the other women and for the next couple of weeks dark figures could be seen creeping up onto the deck to look at the stars and then scuttling back inside when they heard the guards.

A rumour began circulating that some of the women and children had seen Miss Hayter with the Captain up on the top deck on the nights they were all watching the stars. And they were alone!

On the days in between schoolwork, Amelia would help the convict women with their reading and writing and work on her own sewing and embroidery skills. Miss Hayter was keen for the women to produce quilts with the squares that they had been given. "This will provide thee with a tangible reminder of just what even the lowliest person can achieve with the love of God behind thee," she said in her calming manner. It was certainly true that even the most hardened of the convict women had started to soften during their days and nights on the *Rajah*. The tender care from the Reverend, his wife and Miss Hayter, along with the respectful treatment from Captain Ferguson and his crew and Surgeon Donovan was the best treatment that most of the women had ever had. Even the rough weather, of which there was little during the journey thankfully, was nothing, some said, compared to sleeping rough during a British winter and almost freezing to death, and the fear of having to be watchful every second in case you were attacked by evil forces.

After hearing her lovely voice with the children, the Reverend engaged Amelia to lead the hymns at his nightly services. Amelia was not very familiar with any of them, but Mrs Davies and Miss Hayter helped her out until she knew all the tunes off by heart. Sadly, there was not much call for her more interesting, bawdy verses, although sometimes at night she would quietly regale the women with her tunes and loved hearing them all giggle, especially the Millgate women who had started coming out of their shells and interacting more with the others. She was particularly popular when the gambling group were at work, her tunes muffling their voices as they played.

Ann Muir was busy learning all there was to being a decent cook, and the rest of her mess had to admit the food that she produced looked much better than some of the other messes. "Is some of zee tings I remember from the old country," she said in her strong accent. No one was arguing, the food was good, and plentiful. In fact, Amelia had started to get a little tight in the waist since her time in gaol and on the ship. For once, with good nutrition and exercise, her skin glowed and she felt strong and fit. "I knew this would be a good idea," she thought, thinking back to her days starving and freezing in Edinburgh.

"You know what Ems?" said Jane 2 one night to Amelia. "I have not felt starving once since we got on the ship!" She had a good laugh at this, but it was true. Most of the women knew the savage pangs of hunger that crept into your stomach and took over your body with cravings until you would suck on leaves or pieces or leather to try and quell the pains. There had been none of that on the ship, with three square meals for day, at least one with meat, a little milk everyday thanks to the ships cow and goat, and of course the Surgeon's lime juice ration, or when they ran out, the cabbage. Most turned their nose up at the pickled cabbage, but they all ate it, the crew having told them stories of scurvy ships where men became ill with aches and pains, spots, and bleeding gums. Many sailors died from scurvy before the citrus juice treatment was found, half a century earlier.

Apart from a little sea sickness, no one from Amelia's mess became ill during the journey. However, as the Surgeon had predicted, when the ship was becalmed for several days once they had crossed into the tropics, several of the feeble-minded women became upset. Old Sarah was probably the worst. The women had all been warned that the ship may be stuck for some time until the trade winds picked up the sails and hurled it again towards Van Diemen's Land, but some of the women got very scared in a ship that was not moving. Sarah howled and screamed and had to be restrained at times by the other women in her mess. Amelia crooned stories and songs to her and the other massaged her hands and feet, but the terror did not pass until the ship was once again under sail and racing through the waves.

One day at the morning muster, the women all stood on the deck wearily shaking off sleep before morning prayers and then the breakfast ritual began. Miss Hayter, who some were now calling Miss Kezia, told the women that the Surgeon was going to vaccinate them all against smallpox, something each ship tried to do before they reached Van Diemen's Land. Each mess was to report to the Surgeon over the next few days.

When Amelia's mess arrived at their allocated time, they found the Surgeon in a bit of a fluster. Eliza Dean was the nurse assistant for the day (having had previous nursing experience in New York, she said) and told the girls that one of the Irish women, a girl called Louisa, had tried to kill herself overnight and had ended up with serious bruising to her neck that was preventing her from swallowing. The Surgeon had been busy tending to her. Eliza did a quick check of all the women from her mess who, like most of the others on the ship, had all been previously vaccinated. If not done by one of the poor societies, they had received vaccinations in the many prisons they had come from.

Over the past couple of months, the astute observations of the convict children and their night-time caregivers proved correct. The Reverend and Mrs Davies took their meals each day along with the Surgeon, the few senior officers, Captain Ferguson, and Miss Hayter. It soon became obvious that both the Captain and Miss Hayter had eyes for each other and whenever there was an opportunity to spend time together, they did. However, the only time that it was slightly appropriate for them to be alone was on the top deck at night under the ruse of star gazing. Suddenly they both became very interested in celestial navigation and spent hours together talking at first of the stars, and then of their journey and then about anything and everything. They found themselves falling in love.

By June Charles had had enough and had made up his mind. On bended knee one evening he asked Kezia to be his wife. By this time Kezia knew that she too wanted to be Charles' wife, but she still made him wait for six whole days before giving him her answer, six whole days where the poor officers were subjected to a most cranky Captain.

After morning prayers in June, the Reverend told the women that they were all to finish work early that afternoon as there was to be a small celebration after services. They were told to all wear their new white dresses and to have a wash if possible. Having not long left their latest port the crew brought up large tubs of water and soap for the women to use, and as soon as they were knocked off work the women all clambered to the decks to begin their much-appreciated ablutions.

Dinner followed and then the women all made a fuss or getting out and donning their soft white dresses and doing what they could to arrange their hair, pinching their cheeks and lips to bring the colour of youth back into them. Those less conscious of their appearance were just happy to have clean necks and ears and to feel new fabric against their skin.

At 5pm the women ascended the steps and ladders and arrived at the 'chapel' looking like a tribe of angels all in white. Seeing them all so calm and happy, on such a beautiful night with calm seas, a blue sky and a soft breeze blowing gently and just stirring the calico canopy, the Reverend felt a tear run down his cheek. "Oh, what bliss," he thought whimsically, "can come from such sorrow and deprivation."

After the service the women were told to remain seated, and Mrs Davies rose to the makeshift pulpit.

"I have something important to announce." She decreed. "I have been asked by the betrothed to let you all know that Miss Kezia Hayter has agreed to marry our Captain Charles Ferguson."

The ship erupted into celebratory whoops and clapping as the newly engaged couple stepped up to the pulpit. After thanking the massed crowd, the captain announced that the ship's cook was bringing up some treats and that the whole ship, less those required to work for Its safety, could partake in a small celebration. He urged any of the musically talented onboard to bring their instruments and provide some entertainments.

That was all Amelia needed to rush down to grab her fiddle and back up to the deck. Two of the sailors also had fiddles and soon the trio had started to sing uplifting songs that they all knew. Most happened to be church songs, but there were also some folk tunes thrown in.

Miraculously a few bottles of wine began to circulate towards the back of the crowd and soon there was a lot of merriment going on. As the bottle was being chugged by one of the English girls, Surgeon Donovan appeared from nowhere. Luckily, he just tipped his hat and said, "It's just a bit of grape juice you know, good for the health!" Knowing that there was not nearly enough to get the women or crew drunk, he was happy to keep their secret, and in that quantity, it probably was a good nutritional supplement.

Chapter Eight
# *1841 - Van Diemen's Land*

*A*s the ship began its final preparations before arriving in Hobart, Captain Ferguson thought of how lucky the ship had been. There had been few illnesses, the weather and the seas had been calm and clear most days, and the convicts and crew had mostly been very well behaved. He wished that all his journeys could be so blessed. And then of course there was his engagement to the beautiful Kezia who he fondly called Lizzie. As a career naval man Charles had despaired of having a family of his own, and there were long talks had with Kezia on the quarterdeck about their future. Kezia understood that Charles would be required to stay as a ship's captain, and she said that she was happy to live their lives around his career. Indeed, it seemed that a long engagement was on the cards as it would be hard to even find times when they could be together at the same time and in the same place. And Kezia had her work to be done in Van Diemen's Land. She hadn't forgotten about that in the excitement of the engagement. The Reverend, with his daily sermons had only stirred up her resolve to bring Mrs Fry's teaching to the colony, and to help these poor convict women, who on this journey had proved to be all that Mrs Fry said that they could be.

The end of the journey was marked with great sadness when one of the poor simple older women succumbed to an illness that she had been concealing for weeks on the ship and was finally hospitalised on 29 June. Sadly, Sarah Parfitt died of her illness the day before the *Rajah* arrived in Hobart. On their last evening at sea the service included prayers for her eternal rest with the Lord.

It was the very middle of winter as the *Rajah* skimmed the coastline of Van Diemen's Land towards its ultimate destination. The sailors all sprang into action preparing for their arrival. Rations were running low, so everyone was looking forward to landfall.

The ship turned northwards and passed Bruny Island. Rugged dolomite cliffs rose over 600 foot into the sky and caves that dotted the coastline could be distinguished by the gushing of water in and the exploding of water out. Amelia and the rest of her Mess were lucky enough to be on deck-scrubbing duty in the bitter cold to view these amazing sights. Great, fat, brown creatures that looked like huge slugs with hairy whiskers lazed around on rock ledges. Tiny, winged penguins spluttered out of the surf and waddled up the edges of the cliffs. And so many different types of sea birds were flying around in the sky. Ones that the girls had never seen before. One of the guards, who had been to Van Diemen's Land several times before came over and pointed out the fast mutton birds who sat on floating logs between diving for fish. Huge birds that he called albatrosses were miraculously graceful as they flew over the tops of the spindly coastal tress that lined the edges. And then there were sleek black faced cormorants darting in and out of the ocean with their beaks full of fish.

As the ship turned into the River Derwent, they encountered whaling ships with their bloody catches hanging on the decks, and merchant ships loaded with goods.

As they approached Hobart, Captain Ferguson alerted the town to their arrival and the crew hoisted a square flag, half red and half white to signal that women prisoners were its cargo.

Finally, the ship anchored off Hunter Island in Sullivans Cove. Their journey of 105 days had come to its end.

Captain Ferguson was immediately rowed ashore to meet the local officials, along with the chief guard, and the body of poor Sara Parfitt that was to be taken to the Hobart hospital and from their buried in the convict graveyard.

The next few days went by boringly for everyone onboard as they waited for the mechanisms of government to turn so that they would be allowed off the ship. The ship was scrubbed from top to bottom. Fresh rations arrived by boat included a rum ration for the crew, which was gratefully received, going by the loud singing and deck thumping jigs that were heard from below decks that night.

The women anxiously waited to find out what their next fate might be. Miss Kezia and the Davies' tried to prepare them as best they could, gently explaining the types of assignment that they might be given and what to expect from their master's and the general population. They explained that a strange caste system had developed in the colony. Having few titled gentries, the military had assumed that social position along with wealthy merchants and farmers, most who had come as free settlers, but some, the Reverend noted, had come out as convicts in the earlier days and in time had become very successful indeed. There was a definite distinction, though, between the free settlers who called themselves the exclusives and the freed convicts who were known as the emancipists. Most of the exclusives held themselves in high esteem and looked down on emancipists, even if the emancipists were much wealthier and more successful. The convict stain this was called. The Reverend told the women to be aware of this but not to feel disheartened by it because many of the most successful and happiest families in the colony had arrived as convicts. Trust in the Lord and live in accordance with the teachings of his Son and all would be well.

During their time in the harbour the ship was visited by the Chief Superintendent of Convicts who, with Surgeon Donovan, again interviewed each of the prisoners, the Chief Superintendent checking that the health of each was as Donovan said, and noting their skills and the type of work that they might be suitable for. After the interview the women were each told where they would be going on disembarkation. Amelia was told that she was to go to the settlement of Launceston in the north. She was a bit distraught thinking that it might be a wilderness, but Mrs Davies quickly told the north bound women that the north was where her family lived, and it was beautiful with a lovely town and many prosperous farms and businesses.

On 23 July the women all donned their white dresses and bonnets again and were paraded onto the main deck for the arrival of Sir John Franklin, the Lieutenant Governor of Van Dieman's Land and his wife Lady Jane Franklin. They were escorted by Captain Ferguson and first met with Miss Kezia who had refused to leave her charges in the days after their arrival.

Next, Lady Franklin was presented with a large and beautiful quilt which had been made by the women during the journey especially for this moment. It took six women to hold the quilt out so that it could be properly inspected. Amelia noticed a few small blood stains on the back, obviously where someone had accidentally pricked her finger during her work. She giggled.

The inscription on the quilt which all of the women now intoned for Lady Franklin on Miss Kezia's signal said:


*TO THE LADIES*
*of the*
*Convict Ship Committee*
*This quilt worked by the Convicts*
*Of the ship Rajah during their voyage*
*To Van Diemen's Land is presented as a*
*testimony of the gratitude with which*
*they remember their exertions for their*
*welfare while in England and during*
*their passage and also as proof that*
*they have not neglected the Ladies*
*kind admonitions of being industrious*
*June 1841.*


A short service was then held by the Reverend, and Amelia then led the women in a hymn. The dignitaries stayed on board for a short period of time and after they left there was a short speech by Captain Ferguson where he thanked the women for their exemplary behaviour onboard. The Reverend and Miss Kezia then gave their final farewells.

The following day the women started being moved to the shore. The first were a small group of young women with various ailments bound for the hospital, including Anne Screech who had a sickly 9-month-old baby. The next were the women deemed unassignable who were bound for the Cascades Female Factory and included dear Sarah Woodhouse. She cried and cried and hugged her mess mates and then had to be pried from Ann, who she had become close to, helping her with the cooking.

Amelia was hustled into a large contingent of women, over a third of the shipload, who were ferried not to shore but straight to another ship that was bound for Launceston.

Boarding another ship was the last thing that Amelia wanted to do, but she diligently followed the group. The journey was not too bad. The ship, although smaller than the *Rajah,* had much better accommodations for the travellers, and the food was also good and plentiful. However, they did not have the protections afforded by the Reverend Davies and Miss Kezia, so several of the women were accosted by rude sailors and even one intoxicated passenger. But the journey was only for four days so it was tolerable, and several of the women who had been 'on the town' and knew how to look after themselves and others, including Amelia, sorted out the amorous fools. After almost four months on the high seas none of the women were interested in physical contact, not even for money or favours.

The first part of the journey was again in open ocean although the coast was visible on the port side of the ship. Eventually they came to the opening of a wide river. The sailors told the women that it was the Tamar River and was deep enough for ships to sail in. On either side of the ship was dense forests with strange plants, and when the forests opened to plains Amelia could see strange bouncing animals with faces like dogs and other creatures that looked like hairy rocks, that moved ever so slowly. What a strange, grand land, she thought, and giggled at her life and what it had become.

Vron

The women were settled into the Launceston Female Factory, which was terribly overcrowded. Mattresses were shared by three or four others, and as it was the middle of a bitter winter, the sharing was not such a hardship, so long as you didn't get stuck with a stinky bed mate. It was obvious that some of the women's constitutions struggled to cope with the diet that they had been on since leaving England. And since arriving in Hobart every night they had been stuffed with lamb stew or roast meat and potatoes, with dumplings or thick slices of bread. Some of the women had only ever previously had meat on the odd occasions. The diet changed in the prison, though, as every meal was some kind of tasteless gruel.

There was no gift bag given out at the Launceston Female Factory, no Mrs Fry or Miss Kezia to say calming words to them, and when the women showed the matron the squares of cloth and sewing implements that they had been provided by Mrs Fry's society, she laughed and scoffed at them and said they'd have little chance to do their fancy needlepoint here in Van Diemen's Land.

Once again, the women went through the rigmarole of telling more wardens and government officials what work they had done before. Margaret and Christina laughing raucously while telling them they were good on their back or their front and even on their side if needed. Amelia shooshed them but those two were incorrigible. Amelia hadn't even known that it was possible to do it on one's side but as the girls told her, "Sometimes with them fat bastards that's the only way ya can do it, there old codger is stuck in all that fat down there an' ya have to turn 'em on the side and back up onto them, like a bitch on heat."

The women were then sent to various work rooms to start their chores, and in amongst the chores, of course, were church services. Amelia was allocated to the sewing room, where she was set to work sewing together work outfits. One of the other women told her that the clothing that they were working on had previously been convict attire provided for free by the government but in the past year the masters were now required to pay for any of the clothing made at the Female Factory, so now the garments had to go through rigorous quality checks before they could be sent to the shop for sale. After finishing each garment Amelia took it to a woman who sat at the front of the room, who marked the garment with chalk with Amelia's convict number. If a garment was found to be deficient the convict who had sewn it would lose rations or be demoted to hard labour, which meant the laundry or cleaning duties.

Over the next couple of weeks women were called out during their duties and never seen again. They had been assigned to employers, said the other women. "Lucky buggers to get outta here."

The women were told that it was expected that they would work at the Female Factory for six months after which time they would be granted Probation and then be allowed to work in town for wages. The old system where convicts were assigned, and their upkeep paid for by the government, was over. Citizens wishing to employ one of the women would come to the Factory with their list of requirements, and it was not unheard of for women to go before their six months was up if they had skills that were in demand in the town. Some of the women had been in the gaol for a long time. Generally, they were the ones who had been 'on the town' in England and had no other skills, those who were simple or physically weak, and those of unsound mind. There was also a large group of women who had committed crimes again, after they had been let out of the Factory. They went to Third class first, where the hard labour happened.

There were so many ways that a woman could get into trouble again, Amelia was told. If you talked back to your master or his wife, if you were lazy or tardy in your work, if you didn't report for your chores on time. Those women might get three or six months back in the Factory. Of course, there were the usual more serious crimes such as drunkenness, stealing and assault that could attract years back in the Factory and an extension of their original sentences. And there was the crime of pregnancy. As women under sentence were considered to be owned by the government, it was a crime for them to get pregnant while under sentence. This was in stark contrast to the early days of the colony when partnerships and breeding was encouraged, to expand the colony, and could earn both the parents their conditional pardons and land grants.

Under the new system there were few masters who would be happy to provide for a convict woman with child. They were sent to the magistrate and charged when they could no longer do their work adequately and stayed until the baby was weaned. They then had to serve six months in hard labour before being released back to their master, if he still wanted her. The baby would remain in the nursery at the Factory until it's third birthday and if it had not been collected by then it would be sent to the Orphan's School. But many children didn't make it that far and died before their third birthday.

The gaol was so overcrowded it was difficult for the women from the *Rajah* to keep in touch with each other, but they tried as much as possible. As had happened in the prisons in England, Amelia found that there was a black market going on with grog being brought in, gambling being rife, and a group of women, which soon included Maggie and Chrissie, were bribing the guards to let them out at night to undertake their famous trade, and there was no shortage of customers, they were proud to advise the others.

Chistian, who had left her husband and children behind in England was one of the first to disappear. Being older and with skills, it was no surprise to the others. Black Jane and White Jane left next, on the same day.

And then the days just all rolled into one as the rhythm of prison life chugged along slowly.

# Chapter Nine

# *1833 - Vron*

*A*fter John left the Launceston goal in early 1833, it took about
two and a half hours for the buggy to arrive at the Walker house,
which was named *Vron* after a family farm in Wales. The journey
took the travellers through the villages and farming communities
of Breadalbane, Perth, and Longford, which John could see were
all thriving, though still small. On the way through Perth Mr Jarvis
pointed out a charming double storey home surrounded by lovely
gardens full of native plants.

"That is *Kerry Lodge*," said Jarvis "the family lived there for their
first three years in the colony. *Vron* is much larger." He noted
with his nose pointing higher into the air.

John's lack of social skills did not concern Jarvis, who prattled on
to John throughout the journey. He told John that the estate was
considered to be one of the finest in the north and was managed
by a Mr Dryden who came to Van Diemen's Land with Mr Walker
in 1825, having previously worked for him in London, France and
Germany.

When Mr Walker left England, he brought 15 prize Merino ewes
and two rams from Wiltshire and arrived with seven new lambs
as well. Since then, the flock had grown to several hundred and
Walker supplied the government with wool, meat, wheat, and
corn. There were over 200 head of cattle, including the dairy
cows, an impressive stable with around 30 horses used for

various purposes, a blacksmith, a cider mill, a cheese cave, and an impressive orchard.

The family consisted of Mr Walker who was 47, his wife Jane who was 38 and their children Marianne 16, Henry 15, George 8, Edwin 5, Alfred 3, and the baby Adelaide. Mrs Walker's parents, the Fletcher's had arrived in Van Diemen's Land before the Walkers and had a substantial farm called *The Moat* at Carrick, about seven miles from *Vron*. Mrs Fletcher was currently living with the Walker's due to ill health.

The estate had many workers made up of convicts, Ticket-of-leave holders, and free settlers. As well as Dryden and Jarvis, there was a cook and maids, a nanny, a governess and a lady's maid and around 60 farm workers who carried out a variety of jobs including shepherding, maintaining the crops, taking care of the horses and other animals, maintaining the vehicles and farm equipment, and maintaining the home. There was even a barrel maker who also managed the small cider mill that Mr Walker took pride in.

Walker also maintained a double storey home in Launceston which he used when his work as a magistrate required him to stay in the town, and the family used when attending events.

Eventually they rounded a curve in the road and in front of them stood a most impressive house. There was a large double storey frontage with a single storey covered, arched entrance where carriages and buggies could drive, undercover, right up to the double front doors, along a circular pathway. Coming in from the side, John could see that behind the double storey main building was a very large and sprawling single storey addition surrounded by wrap around verandas. Behind this were several other single storey buildings, and he could see a vegetable garden and pens for farm animals.

John was sent with the convict who had accompanied them from Launceston to settle into the workers quarters. The men were all out working, but the man, Richard Sparks "Sparky to all!" he said jovially, showed John to a spare bed which had a bedside table and a closet with a lock which Sparky said that Jarvis would give him a key for. He showed him where the water closet and the washing facilities were and told him that Walker and Dryden were fastidious about cleanliness. That was good, thought John, because so was he. There was also a large communal room that had an outdoor oven and benches for the men to use and tables and chairs inside for their use. Sparky said that there were often card nights held on Saturdays when the men received a ration of ale, and on special occasions rum.

Sparky then pointed out a small building that was close to the main house and made a throat cutting motion. "That place is OFF limits. That's where the women live, and we are NOT allowed anywhere near there, got it?"

"Yes, yes of course," said John rather flustered. Did he look like a man who stalked women? How little this Sparky knew about him, he thought having a little chuckle to himself.

He wasn't sure what work was meant for him, so John spent the afternoon unpacking his meagre belongings and cleaning his kit as well as he could. If he was to serve indoors, he would need a better outfit than any of the convict garb that he owned. Luckily, he had sturdy boots, that Nigel had brought with him in his trunk, having acquired them with money from the sale of some of his other belongings, "You're bound to need these, lad." He had said and that had been very true, seeing the terrible state of some of the men's footwear on the ship.

That evening the other men trickled back from their duties and those who were on shepherding duty overnight woke to ready themselves for their shift. Sparky introduced John to some of them and they all gave a cursory nod or a good-natured greeting. While most of the men were English, most with cockney accents, there were a few Scots and Irishmen.

A wonderful meal was later brought in by two kitchen maids and the cook who was a pudding faced woman well past her youth with a plump body to match her face, and a broad Scottish accent. Good, thought John, that is the sign of a good cook. Cook bantered cheekily with the men as she served up a delicious chicken stew with fat dumplings. The men all chatted away amongst themselves and after the stew was finished, cook brought in an apricot pudding with thick custard. The men all whooped with joy, this obviously being one of their favourites.

"Aye, youse are lucky, laddies, it's the last of the fresh apricots that you be having tonight." They made mock sobbing noises and Cook laughed. "Righto, best get meself up to the Big House and finish off the meal for the family." And she was off back to the house.

John looked around and realised that far from being the poor, abused wretches that he had expected, these men seemed very content, happy even. He knew that he'd find out more as he settled in. It was not in John's nature to ask questions or to make small talk.

John helped with the cleaning up and as he was drying the plates, he saw Jarvis coming from the house. The evening meal at the main house must be finished.

Jarvis enquired how John was settling in and he replied in the affirmative.

"Right lad, the master had wanted you to start in the house as soon as possible but it seems that Mrs Walker has reservations. She prefers that I spend some time getting to know you first and that you be put to other tasks for a while until we can all be sure of you."

John thought this was most sensible.

"I hear you know a bit about gardening, lad?"

John told him about his work at The Gardens.

"That's perfect then, the master wishes to have a garden to rival those in England, but" he waved his hand out across the sparse front garden, "this is all that anyone has managed to come up with so far."

John looked out over the garden and thought about the many books he had read about plants and gardens and thought that first he would need to find out what could actually grow in this climate.

"Also, lad, like everyone else out of doors, you are going to have to take your turn with the shepherding. You know much about sheep?"

John admitted that he had never even seen one up close.

"Well lad there isn't much to learn, dumb creature they are, but they are worth a fortune here, to sell, or as breeding stock and the bushrangers and the blacks often steal them for meat. Do you know how to use a rifle?"

John had to admit again that he did not, having never had need of one.

"Well, you're going to get a quick lesson tomorrow then, on sheep and rifles!" laughed Jarvis. "There's not many blacks around anymore, they all got rounded up a few years ago, but the odd one still appears, poor starving mites they are. We just take them in to the gaol. But there's still damned bushrangers out there, and there's always bloody poachers around too, so you've got to keep your wits about you. You'll be under Dryden out here and I will take you over to him next, but I will be keeping an eye on you lad because I need you in the house as soon as possible."

"Yes sir," said John.

Dryden had an office off the veranda at the back of the Big House where he also had a room to sleep in, as did Jarvis. Dryden sized John up and then gave Jarvis a long side eye.

"What are you sending me here Mr Jarvis?" Jarvis explained that the master's idea was for Harris to work in the house, but Mrs Walker wanted him vetted first. "Well, he's just going to be a burden to me until he understands the work." He said tersely.

"All right lad, well you seem sturdy enough anyway and apparently even with your inside mannerisms you received a good report from the constables at the gaol, so we'll give you the benefit of the doubt. You'll find Vron an easy place to work, if you do the right thing by the master, and by me. If not well that's a very different story and I'm not adverse to a little flogging if the magistrate, that is Mr Walker, agrees to it." He glared at John for dramatic effect, but John knew that there was probably no way that he would be putting himself into a position to be flogged. He enjoyed an easy life as well.

Over the next week John was introduced to the sheep and their interesting ways. He went out during the day and the night with one of the other men. There was a lot of walking involved getting to and from where the sheep were, which John enjoyed a lot, reminding him of his days meandering through London. He learned how to use a rifle and practiced shooting apples off a fence. While he was not great at it, he figured out the basics quickly.

He was shown the garden and introduced to old Sammy. The men told John that old Sammy Cox lived in a small wooden cottage that he had built himself, at *The Moat*, the property of Mrs Walkers parents, and had done so for many years. He spent his time between *The Moat* and *Vron* and various other estates, attending to the gardens.

Legend had it that old Sammy had been shipwrecked somehow as a young man and had lived with the natives for 20 years, before ending up at *The Moat*. Old Sammy was at least 50, maybe older, and as John found out, he knew everything about the native plants. He was a man of few words which suited John just fine, and communicated mostly with grunts and hand gestures, although he was capable of full speech if needed.

"The missus," he said quietly to John "she wants the flowers from England, but I told the master, 'Master they don't grow here,' but she keeps going on and on about it," he gave an exacerbated sigh.

John was told that he would be on both day and night shifts with the sheep. One night shift, followed by three hours in the garden for six days and then one day off to attend to his kit and to attend services or read the bible, followed by the next six days where he would be three hours in the garden from before dawn and then the day shift.

John settled into his routine very happily. Once he was allowed to go out shepherding alone, he found that he thoroughly relished the time that he could sit amongst nature and watch the trees blowing in the breeze and the clouds floating by above him. The sheep were easy to manage and so far, he hadn't encountered anybody other than his relieving shepherd while on his duties. He spent the time examining the plants and animals and just thinking about life.

The main things that John had to worry about while our shepherding was the hyena's, often called tigers as they had stripey coats, and other creatures that were called devils, and very aptly named. Both would sneak in if they were able to and slaughter any stray lambs.

John thought that the devils were possibly the most ugly of all of animals he knew of, having seen quite a few animals in the zoos in London. They were about as large as a middle-sized dog with a head that resembled an otter but was out of proportion with the rest of the body. They were sable in colour, had three rows of sharp teeth and short legs that were covered with a tough skin free from hair and a short, thick tail.

While the devils kept to the bush and the hills, the tigers were a constant threat around the house as they tried to attack the chickens and other small animals, and steal food if left out.

Vron

During his garden shifts he also thoroughly enjoyed spending time with old Sammy who would come and go and meander about. He showed John all the plants in the garden and told him what their names were, both in the native language and what the English called them. He explained when they flowered and how much sun and water that they needed. It was a constant battle to keep other native plants from encroaching on the well set out gardens that Sammy had established in the way that Mrs Walker wanted them to look. He shook his head and grumbled and said that these plants were meant to grow wild, not be harnessed into patches like the convicts that the King had sent out here as slave labour, also to be harnessed and kept prisoner.

A month or so went by and on one of John's days off Jarvis came to visit while John sat in the dining hall writing in his journal, another of the gifts that Nigel had left in his trunk.

"You like writing Harris?" asked Jarvis.

"Well, I like reading more sir, but I only have a few books and have read them all many times." He then told Jarvis about his time working in the library. Jarvis rattled off a few popular books, all of which John had read.

"How would you like it if I brought you the newspapers? There's a local one in Launceston now, the owner is courting young Marianne, and the master gets the papers from Hobart, Sydney, and London. It would be good if you are to serve the family to be abreast of current affairs."

John's eye lit up "Oh yes, Sir, I would like that very much Sir, thank you Sir so very much."

"One thing though lad, while not many of the men can read, some of them can, and sometimes there are reports about convict unrest. I'd rather that the men still under sentence don't know about that sort of thing, you understand?" John nodded that he did.

"But I don't think that the master would be upset if you were to read some of the other news to the men, particularly the farming news from Launceston. Some of the men already have their Tickets- of-leave, and others soon will, and they might be considering taking up their own land. We have had a few leave over the years, but by and by most of the workers here at *Vron* seem happy to stay on, even as free men, and the master pays a decent wage. The only ones who leave really are those who have found a farmer's daughter at services of a Sunday, or other such occasion. The ones who wish to start their own family. But now that land grants have stopped, the men have to save up to buy their own farms. Makes it harder for them. The horse racing attracts the ladies," he said whimsically. "But that's not something that you need to be thinking about for a long time Harris. But serve your time here well and a good life will come to you."

"Thank you, Sir, thank you," said John and he genuinely meant it. Being able to read was one of John's greatest joys and the newspapers were like a million books in one.

And so, Jarvis would present a stack of newspapers to John every month which John would devour while on shepherd duty during the day or before he slept at night. Then on his days off after dinner, he would regale the men with snippets that he had found in various papers. He would always include something about England and what was happening there as well as light-hearted stories from around the colony and the local news about events and happenings. Launceston was growing by the day and all kinds of sporting events such as cricket and horse racing were being held around the area, as well as fairs and other entertainments. The men got particularly excited when finding out about these, checking if it was their day off when they were on.

Not all the workers where on shepherd duties and some worked day jobs only with the farm animals and the wheat and corn crops. There was a blacksmith and a coachman who also maintained the workshop and carried out household and farm maintenance. There were stable-men and dairy girls. Some of the men were out mending fences and checking dams and outposts. There were convict women in the kitchen, the dairy, the house garden, chicken coop and the pig stye. There were many jobs to be done to keep *Vron* prosperous.

Although he had not met them yet, John had seen Mrs Walker and the children around the house and in the gardens. Mrs Walker often led her mother around the veranda. The poor woman looked weaker and weaker every time John saw her. The eldest daughter, Marianne, who was 16, could often be seen walking through the gardens or sitting reading or doing her tapestries on the veranda with her mother. Marianne was often visited by Mr Jackson who was the editor of the Launceston Advertiser, as they were engaged to be married. Mr Jackson had a very impressive carriage and dressed like a member of the landed gentry in England.

Henry, the heir to *Vron*, was currently studying in England and expected to be away for several years. Then there was George 9, Edwin 5, and Alfred who was 3. George could often be seen wandering around the yard and he would chat with old Sammy, although not to John yet. He would catch insects in jars and sit watching them for a long time and then release them writing notes in a small journal that he'd brought with him. Every now and then he was seen with the two younger boys, obviously vested with entertaining them which John noted that he found to be a chore, the little ones running amok about the garden and George yelling at them to stop pulling out the flowers.

Mrs Walker had a lady's maid who she had brought out from France where they had previously lived. Miss Lemaire looked a bit older than Mrs Walker and also served as a governess to the children. Sparky told John that in his whole time at *Vron*, and he had also been at Kerry Lodge beforehand, he had never seen Miss Lemaire talk to any men except Jarvis, nor had he known her to go into Launceston, except to accompany Mrs Walker. Miss Lemaire lived in the main house in a room next to Mrs Walker, not in the women's quarters.

There was also a young nanny who was with the Walker's when they arrived in Van Diemen's Land. George was only a baby when they arrived, so Nanny Elizabeth had raised all the young Walker's and was now 25 years old. Sparky said that she had previously been friendly with one of the free men who worked at *Vron*, but that had petered out when he received a land grant over near Breadalbane and Nanny did not want to leave the family. Nanny was young and fair and gave off an air of happiness as she pushed baby Adelaide around in her pram and led little Freddy about by the hand. George and Edwin were mostly in the schoolroom with Miss Lemaire now. Nanny did go into Launceston every now and then for purchases and to meet some of her lady friends who she had met through church services.

Vron

There was no church nearby in 1833, so Mr Walker offered up *Vron* as a place of worship for the local Church of England community. There were several lay preachers who conducted the services and a group of ladies who supplied refreshments after the service. Sundays saw a small mass of buggies arrive and the groom wrangled the extra workers for the morning to help with the horses. Once the vehicles had left there was a lot of muck to remove from the normally pristine pathways. John thought it was nice to see all the locals dressed up and intermingling.

Although the Walker's welcomed all landowners and businesspeople and their families, some of whom were emancipists, and even some Ticket-of-leave men who had already become successful in the community, they did not welcome convicts or farm workers into their home. They would have to wait until they could get into town for services or bid for a lay preacher to attend them at their places of work.

Mr Walker allowed Miss Lemaire, Nanny, Jarvis, and Dryden (who also brought his family) to attend the weekly services in the house, and he arranged for a preacher to provide a service for his workers in the communal room after the main service at the house. A belief in the Lord, following the church's rulings and an understanding of moral and spiritual responsibilities was instrumental in developing the culture that was wanted in the colony, so services were very important.

The family would attend services at the very impressive St John's in Launceston every two or three months, or to coincide with some other event in the town. Jarvis told John that St John's was only built a few years before and was very beautiful. He liked to accompany the family when he could.

In the middle of winter, a sad thing happened when Mrs Walker's mother passed away. The doctor attended to do the official paperwork, but her death had been expected. The family all left for several days to attend the funeral which was held in Launceston. There was talk amongst the men that Mr Fletcher was in grave financial difficulty, and he hadn't been seen at *Vron* for some time despite his wife's ill health.

The master was not often at *Vron*, being very busy with his duties as a magistrate in Launceston. He mostly stayed in his town house where he kept a cook and a valet who doubled as a carriage driver when he travelled around the area. When he was at home at *Vron* he liked to entertain other wealthy landowners from around the area, and dignitaries from all over the colony.

This, Jarvis said, was why he needed John in the Big House. He needed other men to help as footmen in the dining room when the master entertained and so far, none of the other men could fit the bill, often being an embarrassment to the master and to Jarvis; and in the colony, just as in England, to wealthy men, impressions were everything and could make or break a career.

Over the winter months there was little call for John in the garden and old Sammy stayed away at his cottage most of the time, the rain, hail, and snow creating too much of a danger for travel. The men were kept busy hand feeding the sheep and tending to the lambs that were kept in a large barn when the frosts crept in. John spent a lot of that time mucking out the barn, but at least the men were warm most nights being closer to the house. It could get very cold with the sheep at night out on the plains.

The food changed from mostly fresh produce to a lot of pickled and preserved vegetables. There was still a lot of meat, and milk was plentiful from the house cows. Best of all there was an abundance of milk pudding which John loved, as well as delicious fruit cakes, some with a little fire from the rum that was added to aid preservation. A steaming hot cup of tea and a slice of fruitcake made any day a better day, thought John. And if he had new newspapers as well, then he was as happy as he ever thought he could be.

Many months went by, and winter came and went. As spring crept in Jarvis approached John one afternoon.

"Harris, it will soon be Ball season again and I need you to get into Launceston and get fitted out for a uniform as you will be helping me inside this year."

Jarvis gave him a set of instructions of who was to take him and where to go. Once he had ordered the items on the list, he was to go to see Mr Walker at his house in Launceston and he would stay there for two nights. This would be the first time that John had spoken to Mr Walker in person, and he was quite anxious. All his time with the sheep and the rough men may have worn off his smooth edges and he was concerned now about appearing unrefined and unworthy of inside work.

John asked anxiously if he was allowed to be in the town unsupervised, still being under sentence.

"Lad, here is a letter from Mr Walker himself authorising you to go about his business in the town. Now do you think anyone will argue with the magistrate himself?" he laughed as he handed John the letter and then walked away.

Vron

## Chapter Ten
# *1833 - Launceston*

*T*he next day John climbed into the buggy with a sense of excitement and a little trepidation. This would be his first unsupervised outing since he was arrested over a year ago. He felt like he was off to explore the moon on his own.

On the way into Launceston John took note of the gardens in some of the more substantial homes. He noted vast orchards, especially with apples, which were also plentiful at *Vron*, as well as peaches, plums, and other familiar stone fruit. There were huge bushes overladen with berries. But apart from native flowering shrubs, nicely arranged as they were at *Vron*, there were no English flowers.

Dryden had recently given John a pamphlet from a horticulturalist from England called Daniel Bunce who had published a list of plants available at his nursery near Hobart, as well as Bunce's manual of practical gardening in Van Diemen's Land. John read the pamphlet several times and had discussed it with old Sammy who just waved his arm and muttered something about 'that woman trying to make this bush into an English country garden,' and shook his head. He also found out that old Sammy had many packets of flower seeds in the small garden shed, that had been purchased by Mr Dryden from a man called Frank Lipscombe who ran a nursery called 'Pineapple Nursery" near Hobart. The packets had not even been opened.

Vron

On the way to Launceston, they passed several gangs of convicts working on the roads, some in leg irons and others without. John asked the buggy driver what the difference was. Young Stevens worked as a stable hand when he was not shepherding with the other men. He was from Yorkshire and had been at *Vron* for over three years and had been on a hulk for almost a year in London.

"Well Harry, old man," John had acquired this monicker from the men "them's the difference between ones who arrived here from home and have not done nothing wrong since then. But maybe they's just not smart enough to be assigned, you know what I mean? They don't need leg irons."

John nodded his understanding. The men who he had met in the Launceston gaol where all nice enough but none of them seemed to have too many smarts about them. John often preferred that kind of man, though, less likely to cause him trouble.

"Then there's them what can't keep outta trouble! To be honest though not everyone is lucky enough to get a master like old Walker and Dryden's a fair man as well. I have talked to men who were treated so badly by their master's that they ran off. Some were beaten badly for small mistakes that Dryden would just cut ya rations for a day for. Some men prefer to get into trouble to be sent back to prison, as it's easier there than with their masters."

John raised his eyebrows, but then understood that not everyone here in the colony was having such a good time of it obviously.

"I had a right bastard for my first master, look!" Stevens lifted the back of his shirt and twisted towards John, revealing a back criss-crossed with red, raised, scars. John winced.

"I'm so sorry," said John softly.

"You know what that was for? The horse kicked over its bucket of water as I was shoeing it, and the water went over the master's jacket that he'd left on the floor of the barn. Twenty-five he gave me, the rotten coot! But I seen him give another man fifty and he barely lived. And for something equally as stupid."

John just looked at the man with quiet compassion.

"I thought to meself, 'self you ain't gunna stay around here and get thrashed to death,' so I ran away. Got taken back to the gaol and charged and spent some time on the chain gangs again. In leg irons! But even that was an easier life than working for that old bastard had been. I was so worried that I'd have to go back to 'im and he'd kill me the next time. But then one day Dryden came into the gaol, and someone had told him that I knew horses, and I could ride and drive a buggy and even a carriage. And he needed someone at *Vron*. So that's how I got there. And I've been happy as a pig in muck ever since."

John realised just how lucky he had been.

"So, Dryden told me, he's recommending me for a Ticket-of-leave and then I will be as free as a bird, well almost! But you know what, apart from thinking I might like to find me a young lady one day and maybe have my own little farm, I think I'm just going to stay on with Walker. I like it where I am, and he pays a good wage, so I can start saving for me own place one day."

"How old are you, Stevens?" asked John.

"I'll be 22 years old soon Harry."

So young thought John for the life he has already lived, but with so much life yet to be lived. John hoped that Stevens would get the life he wished for.

The closer they got to Launceston the denser the houses got. They passed small lots with gardens full of fruit trees and vegetable gardens, chickens running around the fenced plots. Then soon they were in the town with smaller houses closer together and whitewashed with pots of geraniums on their front patios. John commented about them to Stevens.

"Oh, those are everywhere," said Stevens "I guess they grow all right here then, maybe you can get some of them in the missus' garden?"

They then passed the area that John was already familiar with along lower Paterson Street where he saw the gaol, the gallows, the Female House of Correction, the treadmill, police offices and the courthouse. Nearby were the commissariat store, convict barracks on the corner of William and George Streets, military barracks and officers' quarters, male and female hiring depots, a police watchhouse and the stocks in Cameron Street.

As they turned into the town proper, they passed numerous large and impressive buildings. John could see hotels, boarding houses, merchant's warehouses, and every type of shop including tailors, hatters, mercers, dressmakers, dyers, staymakers, wigmakers and bootmakers. There was a large bank and the offices of Mr Jackson's Launceston Advertiser and many buildings with large, impressive frontages. There were large market gardens interspersed around the town with small carts where the produce could be purchased from.

There were numerous carts, buggies, and a few carriages, along with many riders on beautiful horses and many horses tethered along the street. People filled the streets in all kinds of garb. There were ladies and gentlemen dressed in their finery, workers in their cotton and calico working outfits, policemen and soldiers in their uniforms, a few sailors, and even a few people who looked of Asian or African decent, who he had frequently seen around London. It was certainly a colourful mix of people and reminded him on a very small scale of London.

"That's the Walker's town house," said Stevens as he pointed out a double storey stone house with ornate entrance features. "I'll drop you off outside the tailor's and you can make your way back to Walker's when you're finished."

The tailor shop was much like any in London. The tailor appeared competent enough and measured John up for the items that Jarvis had left on his list. There were several outfits ordered including a basic footmen's uniform as well as a black suit suitable for a butler which John was surprised at, but maybe this was in case Jarvis was unwell, thought John. Also on the list were two day-outfits in the style that he had seen the Ticket-of-leave and emancipist worker's wear. John was told to come back in two days to collect his purchases.

He then wandered along the street very aware of his convict attire, but there were other men in similar clothing, and he didn't seem to attract any unwanted attention.

Next, he came to the shoemaker's shop on Jarvis' list. *Beswick Bootmaker* said the sign in large red letters with a cream outline. In the front window sat several decent looking pairs of work boots as well as gentlemen's boots and black and brown leather shoes. There were even small versions obviously made for children. He smiled at the cute pair of cream leather slippers with a white ribbon.

A bell tinkled as John opened the door.

"Hello Sir, what can I do for you," John was greeted by a cheery young man about the same age as him. On the counter he had magazines spread out with pictures of fashions, including shoes. The man noticed John looking at them.

"I have a friend who gets these for me, her mother has a dress making business over at Paterson's Plains." John nodded his head.

"Thomas Beswick at your service Sir," he made a mock bow. "What can I do for you today, and I'm Thomas to you if you are to be a customer," he held his hand out to shake which surprised John, but he took the handshake gratefully and smiled at the man.

John gave him the list from Jarvis and Thomas whistled under his breathe. "Ah, Judge Walker, he likes his men to look sharp that's for sure."

As he was measured up for the new boots and shoes the two men started talking. John strangely found himself able to talk easily to this man. It wasn't the usual small talk or pointless banter that he despised. This man seemed genuinely interested in him and he immediately felt at ease. John told him about where he came from in London and his previous jobs.

"Ah, that's why the Judge wants you in the Big House then," nodded Thomas knowingly, "you don't find many with your skills over here. I only started to learn my skills once I was stuck in the hulk, can you believe it!" He laughed and told Thomas that he was from Seven Dials, but his father was a successful publican. "Can you believe it, I'd never done anything stupid like that in my life, but here I am, and to be honest, I'm not so sad that I am here."

As John had already heard several times, a lot of people who had come out as convicts considered their lives to be better off here than they could have expected in England. John was not too sure because he really did miss his cozy house and his job at Lambeth Palace, and access to all the books that he could devour.

Thomas told him that he too had been lucky to get an excellent master when he had arrived in 1823, aged all of 18 years old. Launceston was a very different place back then he said. He waved his arm around.

"All of these building have gone up since then."

After Thomas had arrive in the colony, he had spent some time, with the other convicts assigned with him, building the house and all the other buildings on his master's land grant. Once that was done and Thomas felt comfortable enough to ask, he had told his master that he had a passion for boot-making. His master, Anthony Cottrell, was now a constable in Launceston and had recently returned from helping a man appointed by Governor Arthur to convince the last of the natives to surrender and move to Flinders Island where they would be safe. Thomas related a recent story that Cottrell had told him about an amazing native woman who had accompanied the group as guides and advisors, called Truganini, and her husband Woraddy.

John found the story very interesting as he had still not seen a native person, although he had seen some women and young children this morning with darker than English skin, and who were dressed like everyone else in the town. Where they natives he wondered?

Thomas told him that Cottrell also still maintained his farming interests and had helped Thomas to get into his shop, first setting him up in a workshop outside of town and arranging for him to be mentored by another bootmaker in Launceston. Now he had his Ticket-of -leave and was recommended for a pardon.

"There's enough work for all of us, and more." He noted. "So, if your master has taken a liking to you, you will be fine young Sir, your life here can be anything you want it to be."

John left Mr Beswick's shop feeling much enlightened in his head and in his heart.

It took John a while to walk to Mr Walker's residence and along the way he stopped at the produce stall and purchased a large red apple with coins that Jarvis had given him for expenses. As he had hoped, the apple was sweet and juicy, and John had to wipe his mouth before the juice dripped down onto his shirt.

It was mid-afternoon by the time John arrived at Mr Walker's. He wandered down the narrow pathway between the Walker's house and the one next door until he found a gate in the six-foot-high fence. As he opened the gate the sound of a dog of unknown size but sounding to him like a lion in full roar, assaulted his senses. He quickly closed the gate shut and was about to run off up the pathway back to the street when he heard a man's voice cajoling the dog and then the gate opening again.

"Hey up man," laughed Stevens, "I forgot to tell you to use the front door. Lucky I was here, or old Brutus here may have had your leg for supper," he laughed again out loud. "Come on in then, he'll no hurt you while I'm here."

Old Brutus as it turned out was an ancient looking bulldog, who could still hear exceedingly well and still had a bark that could scare off burglars.

"Mr Walker leaves Brutus here to look after the house when he's not around, provides a bit of safety for Cookie too when there's no man in the house." Stevens led Walker through the back yard which was dense with vegetable gardens and wandering chickens. A cow grazed on a hay bale in a small paddock towards the back of the yard. A small milking shed, and larger chicken coop, completed the yard. This was a useful, not an ornamental, yard.

Once inside, Stevens led him through to the kitchen which was separate but attached to the back of the main house. As they entered the kitchen a tall woman who looked to be around 40 came through the opposite door rubbing her hands down her apron.

"Here he is then," she said with a big smile, "he what's worked at the Vauxhall Gardens and all." John looked surprised.

"I worked there and all!" she said, "Ah the stories we can share about that place aye?" John smiled not sure what to say but he was glad of having someone who knew and could relate to where he came from. The woman explained that she was known as Cookie to differentiate between Cook at *Vron*.

"Ere, you must be hungry then young laddie, Harry isn't it?" John answered her in the affirmative. "Well, I just got some scones out of the oven so I say we sit here and have one each and a nice cuppa tea and then you and Stevens here can help me prepare the veggies for the master's dinner. I've got us a nice mutton stew been cooking all day and some damper to go with it for our dinner. The master has his roast beef."

"Mr Walker won't be home until dark," said Stevens to John.

Later, after the men had helped with the food, Stevens took John to leave his bag where he would sleep that night, in a cozy room off the kitchen and next to where the horse was stabled for the night and the buggy kept. Mr Walker's fine carriage was also still in Launceston and John could see it through the open gates of the shed where it was kept.

About an hour after John, Stevens and Cookie had had their dinner and cleaned up, John heard Mr Walker arrive home which signalled for both Stevens and Cookie to leap to work and attend to his needs including his dinner. John noted that Stevens, as unprepared as he was, served as footman and took the courses in to Mr Walker and poured his wine.

Then an hour or so after that when John was growing weary but had spruced himself up ready to jump into action, Stevens summoned him and said that Mr Walker was ready to see him.

John put on his best professional walk and bearing as he knocked at the door and then waited straight as a rod as he had been taught by Nigel.

"Ah, Harris, come in young man." Walker sat in a large leather couch, a pipe in one hand and a glass of amber liquor in a small glass on the table next to him. John let his eyes quickly glance around the room and he saw walls full of books and interesting ornaments.

Vron

John stood to attention in front of Mr Walker's chair.

"Ah, relax young man, relax. Jarvis has already sung your praises and I can see from your bearing that you are wasted out on the plains with my sheep when I need you in the house with the family and I have been told about your past work and the reason why you are here. Don't worry lad I won't ask you to explain why you did it, you have proven trustworthy so far and that, along with Jarvis' expert opinion is enough for me. Right, it will soon be Ball season and we will be entertaining again, so I need you to start as soon as you get back to *Vron*. You will stay in the men's quarters as you have been and you will still help old Sammy in the garden a few mornings per week, but the rest of the time you are now Jarvis' man. You understand?"

"Yes Sir, thank you sir." Said John.

"Well, for the next few days while you are here you can busy yourself helping Cookie, and I hear that you worked in the library at Lambeth Palace?" John nodded. "Well, this mess here needs to be catalogued," he waved his arms around the room at the multitude of books, "so you can busy yourself starting that work. I don't expect you to finish but you can make a start and keep working on it when you visit here, which may be quite frequently. Oh, and while you are here, get Stevens to take you around the town and see if you can't find out what darned flowers they grow and how you can buy them and grow them at *Vron*. Mrs Walker will not let up on that situation."

John went to sleep that night feeling elated. He had met new people today, and he felt that he and Thomas Beswick could be friends. His master was pleased with him. And he would get to work around his beloved books again. Sweet thoughts filled his dreams.

The next few days were a flurry of excitement. Cookie was a dream to be around, always having a kind word and delicious food for the two men. John and Stevens travelled all over the area stopping when they found homes that had anything that resembled English gardens. They would then try to find someone who knew about the flowers. Several kind people gave them cuttings of their plants. All the herbs grew, they were happy to tell John but none of the more delicate flowers. However, roses did seem to grow well, so perhaps Mrs Walker would be happy with that, even though they only bloomed for a short time. Several gardeners told John that if he got a chance, to go past the Archer's *Woolmers* and *Brickendon* estates near Longford as they had the best gardens in the colony.

John set about cataloguing Walker's library. He could still remember most of the categories from the archbishop's library. This kept him very busy, and he got to read a few of the books in between. Mr Walker sent him to visit the Tasmanian Society for the Diffusion of Useful Knowledge which John Pascoe Fawkner, who was the owner of The Launceston Advertiser, as well as many other business interests in Launceston, had created several years before to 'soften otherwise barbarous manners.' He took note of how the books were catalogued as well as writing down a few titles he thought would be useful for Mr Walker to procure.

On day three, he wandered back down to the tailor and picked up his new outfits. His boots and shoes would not be ready for a month or so, Mr Beswick would notify Mr Walker when they were ready.

He and Stevens then began the journey back to *Vron*. As recommended, they called past the impressive *Woolmers* and *Brickendon* estates and they marvelled at the beautiful gardens. When they explained what they were doing there, they were kindly given several cuttings.

Vron

Chapter Eleven
# *1833 - History*

*J*ohn settled into his new routine at *Vron*. While he still lived in the men's quarter's he was at the big house every morning as the sun rose to help Jarvis prepare the house for the day. In summer there were windows to throw open and curtains to sash. In winter it was curtains to open and fires to start. All the verandas had to be swept daily as so much dust got in. The candles all needed their wicks trimmed and wax cleaned. The fireplaces had to be cleaned and polished. When Mr Walker was home, Jarvis took him his morning cup of tea, and Miss Lemaire took Mrs Walker hers, while John hurried around taking food into the breakfast room for the family. Usually, Miss Lemaire and Nanny would bring the children in first, after which John cleaned up, and the Walker's followed later.

After breakfast John was kept busy helping Cook to clean up and then he was out in the garden with old Sammy. He had convinced the old man to start a rose garden and so far, the cuttings were growing well. On cold days and in winter, he was inside cleaning and dusting and polishing the silver. Mr Walker also kept a library at *Vron* that included text and picture books for the children, and John started to catalogue those as well as the ones at the Launceston house.

Nanny and Miss Lemaire organised lunch for the children but John and Jarvis served the Walker's and any guests they might have.

Afternoons were busy with more tidying and cleaning and helping Cook in the kitchen. John would often take a brisk walk out past the main house along the route he used to travel to get to the sheep, to keep his constitution healthy, especially with all the good food that Cook provided. He had asked Jarvis to accompany him, to be polite, but he had declined which John was thankful for as he preferred his own company.

If Mr Walker was home Mr Dryden would visit him and brief him in the afternoons. Mr Dryden kept a room at *Vron*, but he had his own small farm and family nearby so spent most nights at his own house. This left John to wrangle any mishaps with the men, but this rarely happened as they all knew how good they had it at *Vron*. As Stevens had said, not all masters were fair or kind.

The evening meal in the house was always busy as the Walker's liked their children to dine with them in the evening. All but baby Adelaide would eat in the main dining room and sometimes there was a bit of chaos, which Mrs Walker or Miss Lemaire always jumped on immediately. This made John smile to himself. It was good to see happy children. He thought sadly about the poor starving wretches who he saw daily around his home at Lambeth.

The busiest time was after the evening meal. Cook needed help and the Walker's often wanted after-dinner tea or port or supper. Then there were the candles to snuff and more cleaning to do. It was usually around 10pm before John could think about heading off to bed.

The Sunday services continued, and John assisted with the visiting horses and took care of cloaks, coats, and umbrellas, then spent the afternoon taking care of his kit. He also continued to spend time with the men, reading them the news from the papers and helping some of them to read and write. He had even convinced them that learning their numbers was important and, after he mentioned it to Miss Lemaire, she presented him with a small box full of coloured blocks that he could use to teach arithmetic. She also kept him stocked with paper, ink, and quill pens.

Every now and then the Walker's would entertain either at *Vron* or at the house in Launceston. If they went to town, Jarvis and John would go as well, and they could see that the Walkers were proud to have two such experienced servants.

While in Launceston John would pop in for a quick visit to his friend Thomas Beswick, whose company he enjoyed greatly. It was with great happiness that John learned that Thomas was to marry a young widow, the daughter of the woman who he was now in business with, out at Paterson's Plains. He might not always be in the Launceston Shop, he told John, as he would now have a very large farm to run as well, because the farm at Paterson's Plains had been inherited by Mary after her father died.

"Luckily though, her stepfather runs it all very well and intends to keep doing so after we wed, and I will keep on with my business." said Thomas.

All in all, thought John, it was a good life at *Vron*. In fact, John had almost forgotten that he was a convict.

The wedding of Marianne, now 18 and Mr John Alexander Jackson was held at *Vron* on 24 March 1834 with everyone who was anyone in Launceston, as well as many from Hobart and some even from the mainland, attending the wedding. The Walker's hired many extra workers for the event which went until the early hours of the next morning. The food, drinks, decorations, and entertainment were extravagant as befitted a family such as the Walker's.

After the wedding and early the next morning after Jarvis and John had finished the last of the cleaning up and sent the men to bed, Jarvis poured a port for John and gestured for him to join him on the veranda.

Jarvis had had a few ports while cleaning up, not something that he often did but the night had been a great success, and a celebration for the whole family, including the workers, was warranted. He waxed lyrical with John about his time with the family in France, Germany, London, and the early days in Van Diemen's Land, and then he told him two stories that quite shocked John.

Poor Mrs Walker had lost three children before they came to Van Diemen's Land. While they were in France, a baby boy was born very prematurely five months after Henry was born and died the same night. Then 18 months later little Jane was born and was such a joy with bouncing blonde curls. Two years later, after they had moved to Germany, little Jane was followed by a boy named after his father. There were two boys and two girls, and the family was gloriously happy.

But the family were then devastated when little Jane died aged two and a half from an illness that consumed her almost overnight. Mrs Walker was in despair and struggled to care for herself, let alone her three surviving children; Marianne was 7, Henry 6 and little William just three months old. That was when Miss Lemaire had stepped in and cared not just for the children but for Mrs Walker as well. And this was much needed because only 10 months later baby William also died just two days after his first birthday.

There was a time, said Jarvis, after the children died, when Miss Lemaire felt it a triumph if she got Mrs Walker to have just two spoonsful of soup for her dinner.

Mr Walker, despairing for his wife, moved the family briefly back to London. He had heard that great wealth was to be made in the colony, so after collecting his prized merinos he whisked his wife and two grieving children off to a new land on the other side of the world, in the hopes that things would brighten for them all.

The family travelled out to Van Diemen's Land and young George was born in October, during the journey. They arrived in January 1825, but, Jarvis said, Mrs Walker was still not right in the head and then in 1826, she attracted the attentions of someone else, who Jarvis said, was not right in his head.

Colonel William Balfour had arrived in Van Diemen's Land the same month as the Walker's and took up the position of Commandant in Launceston. Balfour was a military man in his early forties and soon won popular acclaim for his hospitality, upright impartiality, and prompt attention to duty. He sought out similar successful men and was quick to appoint William Walker as a magistrate and befriend his family as they had wives and children of a similar age.

In a terrible tragedy, Balfour's wife Charlotte died of the fever in August 1825, aged just 33, leaving him a widower with four small children. Balfour was obviously bereft, and over the next month's became rather erratic. Jane Walker stepped in to help with the children as much as she could, having them stay at *Vron* and visiting the commandant's home with her own children when in Launceston.

It was a warm summer at the end of 1825, and Balfour asked Jane if she would take his children for a seaside holiday to George Town, which she had already planned with her own two older children, Marianne, and Henry, leaving baby George at home with Nanny Elizabeth. George Town had become a seaside resort for the wealthy people of northern Van Diemen's Land. Everyone at *Vron* thought it was a wonderful idea and a chance for Mrs Walker to maybe get back to herself again. Mrs Walker was accompanied by Miss Lemaire, Balfour's governess, and by two of Balfour's soldiers as there was a constant threat from bushrangers on the journey which would take two days by ship and carriage. Miss Lemaire later told Jarvis that the children had a wonderful time at the seaside, rambling along the beach and filling their buckets with shells and sponges and paddling in the shallows. Young Henry, who had learnt to swim well in the south of France, was allowed to go out further and everyone watched him catch the waves and swim into shore.

However, there was a terrible threat hanging over the area as the notorious bushranger Matthew Brady and his gang were on the rampage in the north during that Christmas period and several settlers and travellers had been robbed and assaulted. It was deemed to be too much of a risk for the women and children to remain on their own at remote George Town and Balfour quickly raced up the river to rescue them all. It was then that he spent several evenings, including the journey back, with Jane Walker. Nobody thought anything of it as they were accompanied by many others, but something obviously happened over those days because the relationship between Jane and Balfour had changed.

Both Mrs Walker and Balfour suddenly had a spring in their step and a smile of their faces where before there was only sadness.

Balfour, being renowned for his Ball's in the months before Charlotte's death, finally threw one while the weather was still warmish. The Walkers were one of the most important couples invited and it was a most pleasant night, until Mr Walker shockingly found Colonel Balfour trying to kiss his wife in the gardens. Mr Walker was incensed and challenged Balfour to a duel which Balfour declined. With both being magistrates and their fellow magistrates and other leading citizens becoming most concerned about the situation that had caused obvious discord in the community, they took up the matter with Governor Arthur. The Governor took swift action and within days Colonel Balfour was transferred from his post and out of the colony.

That was certainly enough gossip and scandal for John to take in. His mind was full of dark emotions thinking about both the issues that the poor Walker's had faced. And here he was just thinking that they were a lucky, wealthy family with no problems.

Later that year Mr Walker and Mr Jackson went into business together to form the Cornwall Insurance Company and from discussions that John overheard, it went very well for them.

Later that year John was shocked to report to the men that the houses of parliament at the Palace at Westminster, the same Palace that he had seen almost every day of his life and were such a huge landmark on the Thames, had burned to the ground. John couldn't believe they were gone.

Vron

Chapter Twelve

# *1835 – Love blossoms*

*I*n 1835 Mrs Walker welcomed a new baby. Little Rhoda Walker joined the family in April when Adelaide was almost four. Nanny Elizabeth was very busy again with both her new charge and a toddler to chase after. Marianne's first son, John was also born in 1835 and she would often visit, and the two new mothers and their babies were often seen on large picnic blankets in the garden with a feast that Cook had brought out for them.

The days and months and years went by with not much changing in John's life at *Vron*. Life was punctuated by the seasons and by the major events of the year such as Easter and Christmas and the harvest and shearing seasons when *Vron* saw an influx of temporary workers and was busy and full of people. There were Ball's and dinners to be had at *Vron* and in Launceston. At one point there were over 100 permanent workers at *Vron*.

When John first arrived at *Vron*, more or less straight off the ship from England, he was intrigued to find that Mr Walker and his friends didn't seem to treat the convicts, Ticket-of-leave and free men differently. He had heard mixed reports while on the hulk about what it was like for the convicts once they got to the colonies. Before he was arrested John had never once thought about the colonies. His world revolved around Lambeth Palace and his small home. At times, as he saw the rabble from Southwark encroaching on his local area, he thought of moving somewhere else to live, maybe across the river. But never once had he contemplated the colonies, because his life was good in England, or so he thought. But, as he heard on the hulk, some of those men who he called the rabble, were just not as lucky as him and were living horrible lives in England, and they heard from others who had gone to New South Wales or Van Diemen's Land and had gone from poverty to riches that they could never have imagined. No wonder, they said, that people were committing crimes purely to get out of England and to Australia. There were very few hardened criminals who came out to Australia as they were kept in England, and some put to death. In general, the majority of convicts were a bunch of unfortunate citizens who had been duped, as John had been, or had stolen to try to improve their lives a bit.

How they turned out once they were in the colony was often dependant on who they were assigned to. Men who stayed on the chain gangs, doing roadworks and building, often absconded, and got into more trouble. Their life wasn't pleasant, long days of hard labour and then being locked in the gaol every night. And some were assigned to terrible masters who treated them very poorly, cruelly even. Surprisingly enough, some of these master's had themselves been convicts. The men and women assigned to bad master's often ran away or were charged with insubordination or refusing to obey orders. Some became bushrangers or turned to other criminal activities to survive. Those poor wretches ended up on Sarah Island, a very isolated island off the west coast, or since 1833 at Port Arthur down near Hobart.

John found that some of the gentlemen who came to Mr Walker's house for dinners and Ball's had been convicts. Richard Dry was a very successful Launceston businessman. In 1835 he owned about 12,000 acres, most of which he had bought, because after his original grant his other applications had been refused as he was deemed too successful and wealthy to need to have land granted to him. In 1828 he was one of the founders of the Cornwall Bank and in 1832 of the Tamar Steam Navigation Co. He lived at his farm, *Elphin*, near Launceston, but he also owned two other estates, *Adelphi* and *Quamby*. Mr Dry had come to New South Wales as a political prisoner from Ireland in 1800 and after spending some time on Norfolk Island, he married a free woman which at that time made him free as well. He then became a clerk for Governor Macquarie until 1818 when the Governor granted him land in Van Diemen's Land.

Another frequent visitor, Thomas Reibey, was born free in New South Wales, but his mother Mary had come to New South Wales as a convict in 1792 and worked as a nursery maid for Lieutenant Governor Grose before marrying a naval officer who was granted land on the Hawkesbury River. They owned several very successful businesses and when he died in 1811, Mary took over the running of them all, as well as raising her seven children. Her children Thomas, James, George, and Jane, all moved to Van Diemen's Land. Thomas built the impressive *Entally House* near Carrick on 2,500 acres of land. Thomas had also helped to establish the Cornwall Bank, with Richard Dry.

Other notable visitors were the Archer brothers, William, Edward, Joseph, and Thomas. They had come to Van Diemen's Land as free settlers and in 1835 owned large tracts of land and many businesses. The brothers had all built beautiful and substantial estates in the area. William owned the beautiful *Brickendon* estate and Thomas the *Woolmers* estate. In 1835 William had just become a magistrate with Mr Walker.

As well as seeing the wealthy landowners, who had convict roots, John had met lots of successful businessmen and merchants, like his friend Thomas Beswick, who had come out as convicts or who were the children of convicts. John also met lots of men who worked for Mr Walker, or the other landowners and they were all a very mixed bag. Englishmen of the middle classes mixed equally with those from the poorest areas of Britain, along with Scotsmen and Irish, and every now and then someone with an American accent was found in the mix, even a couple of black American's who had moved to England to change their fortunes only to find themselves as convicts in Van Diemen's Land.

There were landowners who had children who were half native but were being raised as British citizens. Often, they were the landowner's own children, and there were also some native children who had been adopted by landowners, often after their parents had died, either from white man's diseases that seemed to affect them so much worse, or they had been killed during the Black Wars. The official government stance was to take any native person to the local gaol to be sent to Flinders Island, where a mission had been set up for their protection, but some of the landowners kept them and raised them as their own, or sadly kept them as maids or labourers. This was against the law, but the government turned a blind eye if it appeared they were being cared for appropriately, which meant, being raised as white children.

John had heard about the 'convict stain' and how it would taint anybody who had been a convict, and they would be looked down upon forever. That may be the case in stuffy old England, he thought, but nobody seemed to care much here in Van

Diemen's Land, and John was starting to enjoy that aspect of the colony.

Mrs Walker loved to come out and cut fresh roses and she marvelled at how old Sammy and John had been able to raise them, and in so many colours and varieties. It warmed her heart she told them one afternoon. That made them both smile. She was also growing fonder of the native flowers and wattles that also had beautiful blooms, just more muted and subtle than what Europeans were used to.

It was with great excitement that in March 1836, the first stone of a new church was laid at Westbury by the Lieutenant-Governor, Colonel George Arthur. The building was expected to take a while to finish so in the meantime Mr Thomas Cole, the Police Clerk who had been preaching at *Vron*, decided to conduct his services from the Police Office so that the community could see the progress of the church that was just across the road. From then on everyone who was able to, travelled to the service at Westbury. In good weather it would take an hour by buggy or horse or two hours walking. John would walk as often as possible, sometimes accompanied by other men, but often on his own. Sometimes he would be offered a ride back which he would accept depending on how he was feeling.

Many of the workers at *Vron* were already Ticket-of-leave men which meant that they could go about the town on their own, purchase land, and could apply to be married if they wanted. Being a Lifer, it would take John a lot longer to get a Ticket-of-leave but even if he got one, he had no intention of doing any of those things. He was very happy where he was with Mr Walker, who had a few times mentioned that he would offer him a handsome wage to stay on once he did get a Ticket-of -leave.

John was often bailed up by other wealthy landowners offering him work once he was able to leave *Vron*. Everyone wanted a Palace trained footman.

There was a gaggle of farmer's and merchant's daughters to fight off every time he went to church. It seemed that every mother wanted the tall, handsome John Harris as their son-in-law. It didn't even seem to matter that he had nothing to offer in the way of land or money, as the fathers offered him work as well. Everyone who wished to be anyone in Launceston wanted their daughter to marry a man who could easily pass himself off as gentry with his speech and bearing.

Even when they realised how awkward he was, the girls still fawned over him and brought him cakes and cups of tea and offered him a walk around the churchyard or around the town.

John felt a bit flattered by all the attention, but he had no idea what he would do with a girl, or a woman, or a wife. Everything he needed was provided at *Vron* and when he wanted to be alone, he could be. If he had a wife, he supposed that he would have to try and keep her happy and he wasn't sure that he knew how to do that.

Of course, he had all the normal urgings of a man, and the men in the shed could be very crude when they wanted to be. John had heard several retellings of the activities that some of them got up to at the bawdy houses in town. And he had to admit that some of the lasses at church or the ones who came to help Cook at shearing and harvest time, were very nice to look at and made him feel a bit weak at the knees. But if he felt any urgings he would just wait until he was alone and get that over and done with.

Vron

John turned 30 in 1837 and quietly had a small port by himself in the library after everyone had gone to bed and thought about his mother and his father. It was only the second time that he had touched liquor since the incident in Seven Dials, and a small port was all that he would indulge in. He still missed both of his parents greatly.

At the end of October, the papers announced that King William IV had died in June aged 72. Having no legitimate children, the crown was passed to his niece the young Princess Victoria who was just 18. John could imagine the mixed feelings in London. On the one hand the people would have to pretend to be in mourning for the old King but on the other hand they would be jubilant beyond compare, to have a lovely new Queen to brighten England.

The church at Westbury was going at a very slow pace and Mr Walker tossed up whether to have services back at *Vron*. But on Mrs Walkers recommendation, he instead decided to donate one hundred pounds to move things on a little. He had already donated a similar amount to the Reverend Davies' Christ Church at Longford, and wondered which would be finished first.

In November 1838 John was finally able to read in the papers about the coronation of Queen Victoria that was held on 28 June. He revelled in reading the description of the event to the workers as reported in the Cornwall Chronicle. He could picture it all in his head and would have loved to have been there, although to be honest he wasn't sure how Archbishop Howley had got through the big day again, being now 72 years of age.

The same month, it was with much fanfare that young Henry Walker arrived home from England all freshly educated and with a tight British accent. He turned 21 the following month, three days before Christmas, so *Vron* was thrown into chaos for several weeks beforehand. The Walker's had hired 30 extra workers for the 21$^{st}$, Christmas and the New Years celebrations, that were all to be extravagant. A tent city had opened at the back of the house and the kitchen had been expanded to four times its usual size. It had taken Mr Walker months to find enough men who could adequately fulfil the job of footman/waiter for the cocktail event that was planned for Henry's birthday party. When they all arrived five days before the event, Jarvis and John put them through a rigorous training regime to make sure that they were up to the job. Of the 10 who arrived, two didn't last until the event. One was found having 'relations' with the latest convict maid in the bushes behind the dairy/pigsty. That threw the house into scandal, and Mrs Walker even cried and ran to her room when she found out. Of course, the maid had to be sent back to the Female Factory so now Mrs Walker was down a maid at such an important time. And another was found in his cups and unable to be roused at 2pm when it was time for the afternoon training session. He was sent away on foot as Walker would not even waste the horse and buggy on him.

Despite the extravagance of the end of year celebrations, these events followed a few months of disquiet in the household. There were rumours starting that Mr Walker might be in financial difficulty. The investments that he had made in the activities of the new colony at Port Phillip, like a lot of wealthy men in Van Diemen's Land had, were not showing the kind of profits that they had imagined, in fact they were getting no returns on their investments at all yet. Wool prices were at an all-time low, and the market for wool, wheat, and livestock on the mainland, which had been the mainstay of the wealth creation in Van Diemen's

Land, collapsed as land was settled and stock and crops thrived at Port Phillip Bay in the area now named Melbourne, after the British Prime Minister.

There was a huge surplus of sheep, and the family, and the workers were enjoying roast lamb and lamb stew almost every night. But they had noticed less sugar being provided, the tea was of a lower quality and the boots that Mr Walker ordered for the men no longer came from Mr Beswick and were of a much poorer quality.

Mr Walker had put off a number of men and also cut the wages of the Free and Ticket-of-leave men, but his wages were still better than most, so none left. But John noticed that Mrs Brennan and Mr Beswick visited less often nowadays to measure Mrs Walker and the children for new clothes and shoes, and Jarvis told John only to light half the usual candles at night.

There had been an incident of insubordination with one of the men over winter. At that time of year, the men were always more restless than usual, being cooped up inside more often. Walker usually let Mr Dryden handle such things, which were very rare occurrences at *Vron* anyway, but this time there was something going on with Mr Walker and he imposed a punishment of flogging on the man. And it was Walker who delivered the punishment, which was even more unusual. He was definitely not himself.

Another sign that there were difficulties came when it was decided that rather than sending 15-year-old George to England, like his brother had, he would be schooled by a man who the Walker's had procured. The man, an emancipist, had been a school master in England at a rather prestigious school. The man was only available for one day per week, being much in demand attending other private residences on the other days of the week. But he set young George plenty of assignments to go on with. At the time, many wealthy young men were being sent to a private school, the Norfolk Plains Academy, owned by the Reibey's, which cost 10 pounds per year, however it seemed that perhaps Mr Walker could not even afford that now.

But despite all of that, Henry's 21st celebrations were elaborate to say the least. It seemed that every son and daughter of every successful landowner, merchant or businessman in the colony was invited to Henry's 21st birthday party, along with their parents. It also appeared that every dignitary in the colony was also invited. Mr Jackson sent a reporter along to record the proceedings for the next edition of the Launceston Advertiser. It was said later that many a marriage had its fledgling beginnings at Henry Walker's 21st birthday party.

In fact, a very unusual thing happened to John Harris in amongst the chaos of the events at the end of 1838. Nanny Elizabeth had always kept to herself and mixed only with Miss Lemaire, the family and the maids who came and went from the house. In Launceston the only other person she spoke to was Cookie.

By the end of 1838 Nanny's job had become far less busy because all the older children were now with Miss Lemaire most of the time and Nanny only had little Rhoda who was 3 and only required a little supervision. During the celebratory events at the end of 1838, Nanny started to talk to John.

The first time he almost tripped over his feet. They were passing each other on the way to and from the kitchen when Elizabeth looked John right in the eye, which she had never done before, and said "Hello, Mr Harris." John was so surprised he stopped in his tracks and could only nod in acknowledgement, his voice failing him. But Elizabeth then gave him a most beautiful smile and he couldn't help but smile back.

Over the next few months Elizabeth started to sit next to him in the kitchen as they took their meals and ask him about his day. John found that he delighted in finding things during his daily tasks that he thought Elizabeth might be interested in, and even though they were very normal things, such as a new bloom in the garden or something he had read in the paper, she always looked enthralled with what he had to say.

Jarvis noticed the change in their relationship and quietly commented to John to remember that he was still waiting for his Ticket-of-leave and to be careful mixing with a free woman. Miss Lemaire had already given him a few glares.

But in their newfound bliss neither John, nor Elizabeth cared about the opinions of their colleagues. Mr and Mrs Walker had quietly nodded their approval when they had caught the pair conversing, so that was good enough for them both.

And so, over the next two years their friendship blossomed into something more and they sought each other's company whenever possible. As John was still under sentence their ability to be alone was limited, although on Sundays when the weather was fine, they enjoyed the walk to Westbury together, where the church that had been named St Andrew's was slowly being built. John didn't know where his voice had come from, having never before felt like chatting with another person for extended periods of time. But suddenly he wanted to know everything he could about the beautiful fair-haired Elizabeth. And, even more oddly, he wanted to tell her things as well.

John discovered that Elizabeth had met the Walker's in London in 1825 just before they were due to sail out to Van Diemen's Land. Elizabeth was 16 at the time and was living with her two Aunt's in London since her parents had died in a carriage accident when she was 12. When her parents died it was found that her father had been living well above his means and died penniless after his debts were paid. Her father's two sisters, a widow, and a spinster, took her in, but it was known that she would have to go out sooner or later and make her own living. They provided her with opportunities to learn how to be a nanny or a governess, and so it was, that having nothing to keep her in London she agreed to the Walker's proposal to travel with them to Van Diemen's Land.

"There was only Marianne and Henry then, and they were old enough to take care of themselves," Elizabeth confided in John "and Miss Lemaire did their schoolwork. But Madam was pregnant and had just lost three little ones not long before. She was sad all the time. George was born onboard the ship and luckily the Ships Surgeon was very good and helped her through it as I don't think she even wanted to have the child, having lost the last three."

John listened carefully as Elizabeth described her early life in London, which it seemed was spent with a rather cold nanny while her parents were usually out at parties or sleeping the day away.

"I don't think that I have ever felt love, John," she told him "Well not towards me anyway. I have seen love. I have seen how Mr

Walker and Mrs Walker look at each other. I have seen the way some of the couples at church look at each other. It seems a wondrous thing."

They were sitting together on a picnic blanket under a tree, having stopped for refreshments on their long walk back to *Vron* after church.

John looked at Elizabeth's face, slightly flushed from the walk and with a whisp of hair escaping from her bonnet and floating across her face. Her deep blue eyes and long lashes making him feel like falling into the depths of her and never climbing out. Suddenly as if something he did not recognise took over him, John reached across gently and brushed the hair from her face and then leaned in to kiss her plump, pretty lips. Elizabeth did not shun him as he may have feared, if he had been able to think, but thinking was beyond him. All that John could do was to feel. To feel an overwhelming joy that he didn't think he had ever felt before.

The kiss was over all too soon. Neither wanted it to end. But equally neither wanted to overstep any boundaries.

They looked shyly up at each other and then Elizabeth smiled, a beautiful, fulfilled smile, and John smiled back.

The rest of the walk was made hand in hand until they got closer to *Vron*. Although they knew that the evolution of their friendship was not a secret, they also did not wish to have any ungracious gossip spread about them.

From then on, they found as many opportunities as possible to spend time together, although they both agreed that their kisses, as delicious as they were, would have to be kept to a minimum if they did not want to tempt human nature. And they could not risk things going any further as that could end in disgrace for them both. John was soon to be eligible for a Ticket-of-leave and then he would be free to apply to marry Elizabeth if that's what they wanted to do. And more and more, that was what they wanted to do. They discussed what they would do once they married, and John said that he would like to stay on with the Walker's but find a house nearby, which Elizabeth thought was an excellent idea. Mrs Walker was amazingly pregnant again and Elizabeth would be needed more again once the new baby arrived.

Chapter Thirteen
# *1839 – The Beginning of the end*

*T*hroughout 1839 things became more and more difficult at Vron.

Marianne and her husband John Jackson now had three children. John's public life and abilities had attracted the attention of Governor George Gawler of South Australia who sent him an invitation to join the public service there. John and Marianne left for Adelaide in August and by October, John had been appointed colonial treasurer and accountant general.

They left at a time when Mr Walker was increasingly relying on advice from his son-in-law about his own business interests and the ones that they had entered into together. Mr Jackson still had two large farms as well as his impressive home called *Rosetta* on the Esk river. Having not made a profit for a while he put off the workers and closed down his interests, leaving only a skeleton staff at *Rosetta* to ensure that it didn't fall into disrepair.

The Cornwall Insurance Company which Walker and Jackson owned together had provided insurance for many of the farmers and merchants in the area and as they started to fall into difficulty and then fold, the Company had to pay out what they had promised. Funds began to deplete quickly.

Amongst all this worry there was much happiness, although mixed with some trepidation, when Mrs Walker gave birth to little Rebecca in February 1840 when she thought she was well past her breeding cycle at 46. Miss Lemaire was kept very busy with the four children in her care as well as taking care of Mrs Walker who was quite unwell throughout the pregnancy. After little Rebecca was born Elizabeth was once again busy caring for the tiny baby, although with this one Mrs Walker had wanted to keep her closer and would even often keep her in her room overnight. Maybe she thought the baby could stop the turning tide of misfortune that seemed to be descending on the Walker's.

Mr Walker became increasingly irritable, more so when he was told to take leave from his work as a magistrate to get his affairs in order. The house in Launceston was sold and Cookie finished up with the family. She had recently become engaged to an emancipist farmer from Breadalbane so was intending on leaving the Walker's anyway. Still, she had been with the family for over ten years and the whole family would be sorry to see her move on, but happy for her new life and marriage.

Most of the furniture and other effects from the Launceston house were sold but the contents of the library, and several expensive paintings arrived at *Vron* in large crates. Organising and cataloguing them consumed John's spare time for several months.

Henry Walker had been learning how to manage the farm from Mr Dryden, who also left the family in early 1840, after being with the Walkers for over 20 years. With the farm turning only a meagre profit, and the Cornwall Insurance Company threatening to bankrupt both Mr Walker and Mr Jackson, Mr Walker asked for his job as magistrate back and was granted it as no-one knew yet the extent of his predicament. He took a room at The Cornwall Hotel, which was one of the respectable hotels in Launceston, built in the early days by John Pascoe Fawkner who was now busy helping to form the new town of Melbourne.

Several events happened in 1840 that started a great depression in Van Diemen's Land. It was decreed that New South Wales was to stop taking convicts, but England was still sending lots of them to Australia. From 1840 they all arrived in Van Diemen's Land, and soon there was a surplus of convicts and not enough work. On top of this the government had been promoting free settlers to the colony and they continued to arrive in steady numbers. Land grants had stopped so anyone wanting to start farming needed to purchase their own land. But farm work and the ability to make a profit from it was again much worsened when a massive drought, which had been building up for some time, hit the colony.

Mr Walker and poor Henry, just 24 and with little farming or business experience, were doing all they could to keep *Vron* afloat. Although there was no longer a lucrative market on the mainland for their wheat, corn and wool, the products were still needed by the government stores for the hundreds of convicts now employed on the chain gangs building roads and government infrastructure. And there was a small local market still to sell to other farmers who were engaged in other crops and livestock. But it was certainly not the kind of money that the Walker's, or any of the farmers, had been used to in the 1820's and early 1830's.

Before long it was obvious that the government could no longer afford the surplus of convicts with not enough government work to keep them employed and not enough funds for their upkeep.

Vron

The government declared that convicts would no longer be assigned 'on stores' which had been happening since the colony was settled. Under that system, landowners and businessmen could be assigned convicts by the government, and until their received their Tickets-of-leave, the master's did not have to pay them, and were, in fact, paid money from the government for their upkeep. The government also supplied their clothing and tools.

This stopped in 1840 and the masters were then expected to pay a wage to convicts who had passed their probationary period on the public works gangs if they wanted them to work on their farms or businesses. And the government no longer paid for their upkeep.

At *Vron*, with Mr Dryden gone, the discipline amongst the workers had deteriorated. Mr Walker had already put many of them off, to get the paid workers to a bare minimum. Poor Henry suddenly found himself having to dole out punishments to insolent and lazy workers. One was even sent back to gaol for being absent, after leaving on a drunken bender and not reporting until four days later. Several were put on reduced rations for insubordination. And while Henry dealt with all of that, the bushranger threat had increased as convicts found this to be an easier life than being imprisoned or indentured, even if on minimum pay. He was having to spend more on rifles and ammunition to ensure the safety of his shepherds and the men now slept with rifles under their beds.

Jarvis, Nanny Elizabeth, Miss Lemaire and John found that they had to do tasks that had previously been done by other workers and maids, so their list of jobs now included the cleaning and the laundry. Luckily Cook took care of the farm animals, getting up before dawn to milk the cows and collect the eggs before her never-ending job of feeding everyone started. Lessons for the children now included learning household and farming skills, the boys going out with the workers to learn how to care for the crops and the sheep, and the girls spending time in the kitchen and helping to pick veggies for the meals. This was something that the children of well to do families would never have done previously, but John thought that the Walker's saw the writing on the wall, and that they were coming to the understanding that due to recent events, their children's futures may be very different to what they had imagined for them.

Towards the end of winter John and Elizabeth were at church with the family on a Sunday. It had been a very cold winter and several of the older parishioners were notably absent once the weather was good enough to travel. On this particular day Elizabeth had travelled with Mrs Walker and the children in the carriage, leaving baby Beccy with Miss Lemaire for the morning. John travelled with Jarvis, Mr Walker, Henry, and George in the buggy.

Once they were inside the church the sound of coughs and sneezes rang out across the room. There had been a lot of people sick with colds and flu, but everyone had to get on with it as times were hard for everyone.

But by the following day Elizabeth was very ill, along with Rhoda who was five and Adelaide, nine. When their fevers worsened through the day Mrs Walker, who was distraught and convinced she was going to lose another two children, sent for the doctor from Longford. He arrived in the Walker's carriage several hours later and examined the patients. The girls had already started to rally and were asking for food, but Elizabeth remained bedridden and dropped in and out of consciousness. The doctor patted her hand and advised of the usual treatment, cold compresses and water or broth to be forced, if necessary, but said that she "Was now at the will of God."

John was not overly concerned. People became sick all the time but after a few days they came around and were fine again. With the excellent diet that they all enjoyed in the colony, even while under economic strain, John was sure that anyone could survive illnesses. Far more than the starving wretches in England, who died in the streets with no concern shown by anyone. Although he had seen a man die from lockjaw from a splinter and another from eating poisoned mushrooms, there had been no major outbreaks of diseases since John had been in the colony.

But then, before anyone could think too much about it, Elizabeth failed to wake on the fourth morning of her illness. Her body had been unable to shake of whatever was attacking it and beautiful, fair-haired, blue-eyed Elizabeth, aged just 31, was dead.

Miss Lemaire screamed when she discovered her and then the house was thrown into a terrible uproar. Mr Walker sprang into action and sent for the doctor and the undertaker, while Cook suspended her duties and attended to the poor, sweet body so it wouldn't deteriorate.

It was impossible to keep the news secret and before long the children and Mrs Walker were in fits of tears.

Jarvis and John found out quickly what had happened. Jarvis stood ramrod straight and looked at John. John, for an instant looked into Jarvis' eyes and then past his right ear into the distance. "I think I shall go for a walk, Sir," said John.

Jarvis nodded and placed his hand on John's shoulder.

"You do that son, you do that." Jarvis had never before called John son, but John found it comforting. John had an overwhelming need to escape the confines of the house. He walked out of the back door, down past the workers quarters, past the dairy and pig stye, past the kitchen garden and out onto the path that he used to take to tend the sheep. And then in his good shoes John found himself running. Running and running and running. He didn't know how far or how long he ran for, he just kept going. Then suddenly as quickly as he'd started, he stopped. But as soon as he stopped his body was wrenched with spasms of grief and he fell to his knees and howled to the heavens. He howled and howled until there was nothing left in him. His beautiful, sweet Elizabeth, the only person since his father who understood him, who loved him, was gone.

John didn't know how long he'd been on the ground, but finally he dragged himself up and trudged the distance back to the house. When he arrived back, he was dirty and bedraggled, his shoes scuffed beyond repair. He staggered into the kitchen and Cook yelled out for Jarvis, something she would never normally do. Jarvis led John into his room, helped him to undress and clean himself up, and then sat next to him and made him drink several large mouthfuls of whisky. John blearily realised that it was the Scotch whisky that Mr Walker kept for special occasions. "Well,'" he thought "it is the special occasion of my world ending," he thought as he collapsed into an exhausted sleep made deeper by the whisky.

The rest of the year went by in a blur for John. It was like he had also died when Elizabeth died. He vaguely remembered the funeral at St Andrews, helping to carry the coffin into the Police

Office that still doubled as a church, hearing the sermon, watching as her body was committed to the earth. Hearing that Mr Walker had commissioned a headstone for the grave.

Then it was just work, sleep, work, sleep, work, sleep. John did not even feel like reading, and he ate little. Cook started to bring in cake and hot milk with cocoa to his room at night to try and get extra nourishment into him.

"He's such a handsome lad and all, but he's fading away." She heard him say to Jarvis one afternoon.

Jarvis tapped on John's door one night as he was lying there by candlelight staring into nothingness, willing himself to sleep so that he could at least have some reprieve from the constant grief. Jarvis came in with John's nightly treats from Cook and placed them on the table next to his bed. John didn't move but said a quiet thank you. Jarvis then sat on the bed and patted John on the leg.

"You know, son, this too will pass," he said gently. John nodded. He knew that it would, but he also knew that it had taken him a long time to grieve after both of his parents died so he was not expecting to get better any time soon.

"Work helps, son," said Jarvis. John nodded; he knew this too. When he was working, he stopped thinking.

"When I lost my Ada and our two youngsters, I thought my world had ended." John slowly sat up. Jarvis had never talked about his private life before the Walkers.

"I was working in Oxford at the time in a grand house, for a grand family, the Taunton's, the master was a lawyer. We had a little house nearby in the village. One afternoon Ada thought that she'd surprise me after my shift had ended and brought the two little ones, James who was five and Clarence, just a baby. It was quite busy near the house. James saw me coming and dashed out into the road in front of a full carriage, and then Ada, carrying baby Clarence, ran to pull him from harm's way. But they were all killed. Mangled under the horse's hooves and the carriage wheels." Jarvis paused and took a deep breath.

"I think I was much like you for some time afterwards. I lost my job in the end as I could no longer muster the strength to rise and was late too often. For a time, I worked as a street sweeper, which suited me well as there was no need to talk to anyone. Then one day I just rallied. I went to Mr Taunton and asked him for a reference, which he was happy to give, and took myself off to London. Which was where I met Mr Walker. He saved me. I had nothing to keep me in England and wished to be far away from the place of my grief, so when he decided to move to France, I was happy to go as well."

John looked at the man sitting next to him. A sadness had befallen him that John had never seen before. Jarvis must now be in his 50's and had never found love again. He lived with such a deep sadness but still he went on.

"Since then, John, I find solace and happiness in small things, in the tasks that I do well during the day. In making life easier for others. In the sermons on Sunday and in the books I read. That has been enough for me. But, son, there is much life in you yet. There are so many more things to conquer. Remember when you are at your saddest, that this too shall pass." He again patted John on the leg and then wearily rose from the bed and left the room, closing the door softly behind him.

Elizabeth wasn't replaced. John assumed that Mr Walker couldn't afford to find a new nanny. But Mrs Walker had been very hands on with little Beccy anyway, more so than with any of her other children. The children all mourned Elizabeth who had been their second mother for so long, but especially the little girls, Adelaide and Rhoda, who were almost as morose as John.

The 1840 Christmas season was very different from those before. There were no new dresses and no extravagant parties. In fact, John wondered if the Walkers were still invited to the society parties and Balls in Launceston. He knew that they still happened despite the economic downturn, as he read about them in the papers, although it seemed they were on a much smaller scale. The only papers that came to *Vron* now were The Launceston Advertiser, which John knew Mr Walker got for free, and The Cornwall Chronicle.

Christmas was a quiet celebration for just the family and the workers. John was relieved. He didn't have the energy for entertaining or training extra staff.

John did not even work up any excitement when he was called into the dining room one evening after the family had finished their evening meal. He wasn't sure what to make of it when Jarvis and Miss Lemaire followed him and stood to one side as the Walker family all rose and Mr Walker cheerily announced that John had been approved for his Ticket-of-leave. As a Lifer he had had to wait eight years to get one, but the time was finally here. Mr Walker made a big show of shaking his hand and handing the document to him and then everyone clapped and little Rhoda ran over and hugged his leg. He looked down and smiled. This is nice he thought. These people have become almost like family to me.

Mr Walker even invited John and Jarvis to join him in the library for port and cigars. John accepted the port but didn't indulge in a cigar as he had previously been very ill after smoking one. That night Mr Walker confessed to the men that the family were in grave financial difficulty. He told them that he intended to hold out and keep *Vron* for as long as possible and hoped that he could ride out the worst of it until the tide turned and they could enjoy prosperity again.

John didn't much care what happened. He was so deep into depression that he was only just getting by step by step every day.

One afternoon at the end of January, John was out tending the roses with old Sammy when there was a commotion at the house. Mr Walker was in Launceston and Henry was out in the fields with the men. There was only Miss Lemaire, Jarvis, and John to care for the family. John heard shouting and crying from the house, it sounded like Mrs Walker, and then the children all set in as well.

John ran at double speed to find Miss Lemaire collapsed on the floor of the schoolroom. Cook arrived at the room at the same time as John and she quickly lifted Miss Lemaire's head and tried to get her to wake. Miss Lemaire came around but when she did, she tried to speak but one side of her mouth was turned down and she could only groan and stare wildly at them all as if in some kind of terrible shock.

John raced off at double speed and took the buggy to Longford to summon the doctor. When John and the doctor arrived back at *Vron*, several hours later, Miss Lemaire was still on the floor where she had collapsed but had a soft pillow under her head and blankets keeping her warm. The children were all snuggled next to her as she drifted in and out of consciousness.

The doctor examined her and advised Mrs Walker that Miss Lemaire had been struck down by apoplexy, and that she may or may not recover, but there was not more than rest that could be done for her. If she did recover, she may be permanently impaired.

The doctor and John carried Miss Lemaire to her room and Cook became her nursemaid, along with Mrs Walker, the roles suddenly reversed.

Over the next few months, the house was thrown into chaos. The Walker's suddenly realised just how much the peace and tranquillity of the house had been dependant on Miss Lemaire and Elizabeth controlling the children. Henry and even George, now 16 tried to instil some disciple in the others when their father was in Launceston, but Eddy 13, Alfie 11, Adelaide 9, and Rhoda 5, demanded attention all day and night, grieving both their nanny and governess. Mrs Walker, overwhelmed with the situation, spent her time in her room with baby Beccy or sat by Miss Lemaire's bed, mostly crying.

John and Cook were left to wrangle the children and try to keep them occupied. Eddie could sometimes join in with George's lessons, but the rest were too young. Old Sammy would shake his fists at the group as they rampaged through his gardens, and Cook would yell at the little girls who got into the chicken yard to chase the fowls around giggling their heads off.

John tried his best when his other tasks allowed him, to try and set some lessons for the children. But they didn't think of John as a disciplinarian and ran rings around him, refusing to do as he asked. The girls would draw pictures if he allowed them, and at least that kept them quiet for a while. And one of the men showed John how to make paper planes and he taught that to the boys, who enjoyed it for a while.

When Mr Walker was in Launceston, Mrs Walker begged Cook and John to sit with her and the children at dinner to help her to wrangle them all. This made things very busy for John and Cook who had to prepare and serve the meal and then try to entertain the children. Cook also had to spoon feed Miss Lemaire who had lost the use of her left hand and was shaky with her right.

It was a slow recovery for Miss Lemaire. Mr Walker obtained a chair on wheels from somewhere which allowed Mrs Walker to wheel her out onto the veranda if the weather was fine and slowly but surely her speech returned although she had a distinct slur. She was unable to walk but could bear weight on her legs if supported, which allowed John, Henry, or George to help her to swing into her chair.

By the end of June, it was apparent that Miss Lemaire was not going to return to her old self, and that despite Mr Walker's ill fortunes something desperate was needed at his house. Miss Lemaire was able to set lessons for the children but could not write anything down nor supervise them outdoors or without someone else with her to assist. Mr Walker advised his wife that the only option was to try and find someone suitable from the newly arrived convict women. Mrs Walker cried loudly at this. Of all the convict women she had seen, they were only good as cooks and basic maids, most of them being of intolerable manners. Most of them cussed and swore worse than the men and drank themselves back into gaol if given the chance. Or worse they would put the devil's temptation in front of even the most pious of men and try to wangle their freedom by trying to marry any man who would have them.

But at this point, what choice was there?

Vron

Chapter Fourteen
# *1841 – New beginnings*

*A*melia was in the middle of sewing a pair of men's pants, and had pricked herself several times, cursing and sucking the drop of blood each time, when she was called out one afternoon. She was taken down the corridors into a room that she figured must be a type of employment office. Women prisoners sat at tables in front of men who appeared to be questioning them.

The guard led Amelia to a table at which a gentleman stood awaiting her.

"Sir, this is prisoner 229, Laing."

"Thank you, son, thank you," said the man, and motioned for Amelia to sit. He was wearing a fine tailored outfit and was quite broad of shoulder and beam. As he sat, he spread his legs a little and pulled at the knees of his trousers, as some men did, so as not to split them. Amelia thought he must have been in his 50's and must have been someone quite important, as his dress and bearing was very different from the other 'employers' that she could see around the room, who appeared to be wearing the garb of farmers, such as she had seen growing up.

"Young lady," said the man "my name is William Walker, and I am a magistrate here in Launceston," he heard Amelia draw breath "Ah nothing to be fearful of I assure you. I also have a large estate, a couple of hours from here." Mr Walker paused and grimaced a little as if it pained him to say what he had to say next. "Our nanny died last year, and our governess has been struck down by apoplexy. I have four children that need a tutor as my wife also has a new baby and is unable to tend to them all. The governess is now able to make herself known and set lessons, but the children have grown rather wild and need someone who is physically capable of keeping them in line and making sure that they do their lessons and don't get into mischief."

Amelia nodded, starting to understand what he was after.

He went on "You would live at my estate near Longford and help my wife and Miss Lemaire to manage the children. You will have your own room and your keep, and I will pay you a small wage in line with current expectations. Now! You can read and write can you girl? The warden told me that you can and that you helped teach the children onboard the ship. He also told me that you are recommended by the Reverend Davies who is revered around here and is about to build a magnificent new church at Longford."

"Yes," said Amelia quietly, "it is all true."

"You're Scots?" cried Mr Walker in alarm.

"Aye, that I am Sir," said Amelia, understanding that Mr Walker would probably have preferred a nice upper class English girl to care for his children, but either they were very difficult to come by, or Mr Walker was unable to get one for other reasons.

"Oh dash," said Mr Walker, shaking his head. "Stand won't you girl, let me get a look at you." Amelia stood as commanded and paraded in a circle like a prize cow. She then stood in front of Mr Walker and put what she hoped was a pleasant smile on her lips.

Walker was obviously a wealthy man and owned an 'estate' he had called it. Amelia would far rather work as a nursemaid or governess on an 'estate' than milk cows and shovel pig dung, or clean workers sheds or plant crops, or any of the other menial tasks that she had heard were on offer for the convict women outside the gaol. If she was honest, working as a governess or even a nanny was something that she had never even dreamed of in Scotland. The likes of her would never get that type of work, being reserved for the unmarried daughters of wealthy men who had found themselves in financial trouble and no longer able to keep their unmarried children. Or for penniless spinsters or widows from good families.

"Ah, you have a good look about you." Amelia almost rolled her eyes at that. She hoped that wasn't to be part of her duties. Amelia knew that she had a pleasant appearance. Since she had been eating such a rich diet, her hair, that was brown but shone a little auburn in the sun, had grown long and shiny and her skin, thankfully, was still clear, as were her light green eyes. She was told that she had developed a small smattering of freckles during the journey on the *Rajah*, thanks to the sunshine that they had enjoyed, and her figure had blossomed into curves which she felt, as her garments seemed to shrink against her skin. But she knew that if she had to, she'd just as quickly kick this Mr Walker in the cods as she'd had to do plenty of times before on the streets and in her village.

"Ah, I'm going to take a chance on you, my girl," said Mr Walker again shaking his head "I hope you don't make me regret it. As it is, Mrs Walker will have kittens when she finds out you're a Scot, but you fit all the other bills, and we are quite desperate I must tell you." Amelia raised her eyes at this, but with so many children and no nanny or governess she was sure that the lady of the estate was struggling. The upper-class didn't cope well raising their own children, she thought, not like the mothers she saw in her village raising a dozen children and taking in work to make ends meet. Although Amelia had to admit that those children did raise themselves mostly.

The warden brought over the paperwork and started to complete it with Mr Walker as Amelia was led back to her cell block to collect her things. The other women were all at work so like the others she didn't have a chance to say goodbye.

Prisoner 229 walked out of the Launceston Female Factory in August 1841, lugging her small trunk and large calico bag containing everything that she owned in the world. She saw a fancy carriage waiting with Mr Walker inside. He beckoned her to approach. As she climbed into the carriage, she saw that it was packed full of items of all descriptions, obviously meant to be taken to the 'estate'. The carriage was so packed that Amelia sitting on one side of the carriage was unable to see Mr Walker on the other side. Mr Walker kindly passed her a thick woollen blanket which was most appreciated as it was bitterly cold. They passed a pleasant journey, mostly in silence, travelling through beautiful countryside, smattered with small farmhouses, medium houses built from stone with lovely verandas, workers cottages and barns, and every now and then, large elaborate homes surrounded by beautiful gardens.

About an hour had passed by, when the carriage turned off from the main road and towards a house that Amelia could see in the distance. As they approached, Amelia could see that the house was made from stone with a large wrap around veranda. A huge tree sat opposite the house and there were several smaller dwellings around the property. Being winter there was no one around and Amelia wondered why they were at this house. While it was a large and attractive homestead it was not what she would describe as an 'estate'.

A heavily pregnant woman who looked to be around the same age as Amelia, opened the heavy wooden front door. She was dressed all in black.

Mr Walker climbed out of the carriage and indicated for Amelia to do the same, giving her a steadying hand. They approached the door as the woman didn't seem to be coming out further to greet them. Mr Walker had with him a large bunch of flowers and a rolled bundle of something.

"Mrs Beswick, a very good day to you my dear," said Mr Walker.

"Thank you, Mr Walker." Said the young woman despondently.

"I'm Mary." She said to Amelia. Amelia nodded, not sure what this was all about.

"Well, I have these for you Mrs Beswick," said Mr Walker handing her the flowers "and this for young Thomas, it's a length of black leather that he's been after for a while, straight off the boat, I made sure I got in fast to purchase it."

Mary smiled sadly at Mr Walker. "Thank you, Mr Walker but Thomas is currently at The Springs with Mr Brennan, there is much to be arranged now that mother has died so unexpectedly."

"Yes, yes, I understand," he said quietly. "Are you still able to help me here with this young woman, though? It is fine if you are not," he winced as he spoke.

"Yes Mr Walker. If you'd like to take a seat here, Maisie will be out shortly to fetch you a refreshment and I shall take the young lady and see if there is something suitable. Come…" she said beckoning Amelia to follow her.

They walked outside through a back door and down the veranda to a large room that was full of fabrics and notions, comfortable chairs and cutting tables.

"Ah, you be a seamstress mistress?" said Amelia.

"Oh, yes I suppose," said Mary. "My mother was the seamstress. She was so very good at it, and she had me and many of the local women working for her in here. But she died, just three weeks ago, 'twas a fire in the store house at my stepfather's farm, and it took her quickly, thank the Lord." Mary drew a long deep breath.

"Oh no, I'm so sorry" said Amelia slowly, and then tentatively held the women in a gentle hug as tears started to run down her face.

Eventually the tears subsided, and Mary looked at Amelia.

"You're from Scotland," she stated, rubbing the tears from her face, "My father was from Scotland, but he died when I was only six, but I do remember how he sounded, and we have many Scottish friends here." She paused and then looked Amelia up and down, "Now to get you sorted, what is your name?"

"Oh, I'm Amelia but everyone calls me Emma. What are we getting sorted?" she asked tentatively.

"Oh, hasn't he told you? Well Mr Walker, we have known him for many years. My mother would outfit his entire household every year, suits for him, gowns for Mrs Walker, outfits for the children and the paid staff. He sent me a note to say that he is employing you as a nursemaid and to assist the governess who has become poorly, but that he didn't want you wearing convict garb."

The situation dawned on Amelia. This man who appeared to be wealthy and successful was going to try and pass her off as a proper governess, not a convict.

Mary leaned in and whispered to Amelia as she ran a tape measure around her hips. "There is talk that Mr Walker may be in some trouble, money trouble, which would be why he has picked you up from the Factory and not imported a governess from beyond Van Dieman's Land. There are plenty of unmarried daughters of landowners here and on the mainland, looking for work such as that, but we think maybe Mr Walker can't afford it." Mary suddenly looked alarmed at what she had said, "Oh, please Emma, please don't mention what I have told you to anyone else, I feel terrible being a gossip."

"Oh no mistress," said Amelia with a slight bow, "I'll no tell anyone I swear."

"And none of that mistress business either, I am simply Mary or Mrs Beswick if you please. Happy to be Mary to you. The footman at *Vron*, Mr Harris, John, is friends with my husband Thomas. They both think very highly of each other. In fact, he will be out there in a day or two to drop off your new uniforms, so you'll get to meet him. Now to find something to tide you over," she scurried over to a huge cupboard and when she opened it Amelia saw that it contained shelves full of clothing, neatly folded.

"My mother preferred to make the clothing for our workers, sturdier than that from The Factory, so these are all the items that we have been issued over the years. Don't worry it will go to good use as we need it. I'm not sure that this room will be putting out as much product as we had been under Mother's guidance. No one can bear to be in here yet. Except me if I need to," she grabbed several items from the cupboard and came across to Amelia.

"Now this should do, you can try them on behind that curtain?"

Mary handed Amelia a long white cotton shift, and a black pinafore apron to go over the top, along with a woollen chemise, pantaloons and a black bonnet, the clothing in soft cotton. The convict garb was made of drill, a harsh scratchy fabric, apart from the one white dress from Mrs Fry's supplies. The garments all fit Amelia perfectly once she had tied the apron at the back. There was also room to expand, which Amelia thought was a good idea if she was to be back on three proper meals per day.

"Now your boots," said Mary. She looked them over, "hmmmm they don't seem to be too bad. I'll ask Thomas to have a look at them when he drops off your uniforms in a few days. Oh, Thomas is a bootmaker, I forgot to say, he has a shop in Launceston, but for how long I don't know. My stepfather runs most of the farming business, but he is very old now, and so sad since Mother died. Thomas has had to be at home since she died."

Oh dear, thought Amelia, people have their problems no matter where they are in this big old world. Her heart ached for this poor lovely woman who she had just met.

As the women went back into the main room, Mr Walker was chatting along with one of the maids, who was giggling at what he had to say. Maybe this man is going to be a good master. She hoped so, anyway.

Their next stop was at the most impressive house that Amelia had so far seen. A sign at the entrance from the road said *Woolmers*. Amelia marvelled at the many buildings and gardens in the estate as they drove in.

"Right, you'll stay here this time Laing, um Miss Laing," Walker corrected himself. If he wanted to pass her off as a proper governess, he would have to address her as such.

Walker disappeared around a corner and returned a few minutes later with another well-dressed man and several workers. A lot of conversation went on between Walker and the other man as the workers opened the carriage door, giving her a "Hello ma'am" and a tilt of their caps, as they wrestled out two huge trunks and three large but obviously heavy boxes. These they loaded onto a small cart led by a donkey and off they went towards the main buildings.

"Once again I'm much obliged to you William," said the man as Mr Walker climbed back into the now much emptier carriage. He also tipped his hat to Amelia, oddly enough, and soon they were on their way again.

"That Miss Laing was Mr Archer, one of the wealthiest men in the colony, self-made he is too, like me." They were able to converse now that most of the clutter was gone.

"I have eight children Miss Laing," Amelia's eyes widened, that was a lot of children to wrangle. "Oh no, not all of them need tending to. My eldest Henry, he's running the farm while I'm in Launceston, and Marianne, she's married and lives in the new colony of South Australia with her husband who is the colonial treasurer." His chest puffed out a little as he said that. "At home there is George who is 17, Edwin 14 and Alfred 12. They are all being schooled by a school master who visits the house every week," he rolled his eyes, "the rest of the time at present they are up to mischief. It is too cold for farm work as all the crops are dormant, so I can't keep them occupied that way, and they don't listen to Henry or either of my men Jarvis or Harris." He sighed and wiped his brow with a white handkerchief that he produced from his pocket, even though it was quite bitter cold outside. This was a man under severe stress, Amelia could tell.

"There is also young Adelaide 10 and Rhoda who is six. Those girls are better than the boys but oh they fight. Too much competition between them! They will be your main charges. There is also baby Rebecca, but she will be with her mother for some time yet. Miss Lemaire, the governess, is getting much better!" he announced with a touch of desperation "But," he announced "she can no longer walk, and her speech is slurred. She can set lessons, but she cannot wrangle my tribe, and their mother is impossibly upset by the whole situation!"

Amelia stopped short of asking him why he hadn't just brought a proper governess out from England, but she thought she might have a good idea why.

"Anyway," said Mr Walker waving his hand as if to dismiss his thoughts, "the staff can tell you more when we get to *Vron*."

That ended the conversation and Amelia spent a pleasant hour or so looking out at the countryside.

There was a soft drizzle as they arrived at *Vron*, and quite a thick fog. Still, Amelia looked in amazement as the huge building came into view. *Vron* was a substantial estate, and the main house was extravagant, with a double storey frontage, with the rest of the building being single storey with verandas that seemed to go on forever. Amelia could see more buildings out the back. There was an impressive garden in front of the circular pathway at the front of the house. She could see a large array of rose bushes that were bare for winter, just as in England.

There was a greeting party as they arrived, and Amelia tidied her hair and brushed down her new apron.

There was a tall, handsome, older man in full butler's uniform, and next to him a tall, handsome, younger man who Amelia thought was about the same age as her. Next to them stood the caricature of a household cook. She was an older, stout, and short woman with a brown dress with a white calico apron and mop cap.

As Amelia climbed out of the carriage an elegant looking woman in a lovely day dress of deep burgundy velvet, with a high lace neck and tight waistline, came out of the door and stood opposite the servants. This must be the lady of the house, though Amelia. And then in a rush, out of the door, sprang a tangle of arms and legs, giggling and yelling as they ran out onto the front veranda. This must be the wild tribe, thought Amelia, with not a lot of enthusiasm.

Amelia had not minded some of the children onboard the *Rajah*, the smaller ones were quite cute when they snuggled in for a cuddle, particularly little Rowland Davies who came with his mother every few days to play with the other children, but she couldn't abide them when they became bored or rowdy. But at least the children on the *Rajah* had a reason to be untoward, coming mostly from poverty. These lot had obviously enjoyed a privileged life and she saw no reason that they should be bad mannered or poorly behaved.

Amelia was introduced to Mrs Walker who actually took her hand, gently, and said "We are so glad that you are here, my dear," which shocked Amelia a bit. She wasn't too sure what Mrs Walker had been led to think that she was. Perhaps Mr Walker had told her that she was a real a governess come free to the colony?

Mr Walker then handed her over to the tall butler and the family went inside to much excited chatter from the children.

"I am Jarvis, young lady," said the butler, "and this is Harris and Cook," the other two nodded at Amelia but did not smile. She gave them a small curtsey. "What name do you go by?"

"Emma, sir. I'm Amelia, but everyone calls me Emma."

"No, no, no. Here you will be known by your last name."

"Oh, it's Laing, sir."

"Right Miss Laing it is, the miss is only due to the master wishing to portray the air that you are not a convict, so we may address you as Miss Laing, or just as Laing." Amelia nodded her understanding.

"Now," said Jarvis, "we know you're a convict lass and you are probably wondering why you are not out in the yard milking the cow or scrubbing the floors? Well, there'll be some of that in store for you as well, but at present Mrs Walker needs you too manage the children. You do know how to do that don't you?"

Amelia gave a small, uncertain nod. "To be honest, sir, the only time I have cared for children was on the ship coming over."

Jarvis gave a quick intake of breath, "So what can you do then?"

"Well, I can do most anything. I can read and write, and I write songs and poems and I can sing. I led the hymns on the ship." Amellia hoped that this information would put her in higher regard. She did notice that the man Harris gave a small nod and a half smile, but quickly snapped back into a professional stance.

"Well let's just hope that you can do something to calm the current chaos in this house! Cook will take you to your rooms now. There are few men left here at present, being winter and err, for other reasons, so you won't be bothered by them. They are all out tending what's left of the herd," said Jarvis. "You will share the women's quarters with Cook, so you will have plenty of room. Cook can explain your other duties and then I will take you to meet Miss Lemaire. You will report dually to both myself, and to Miss Lemaire. Miss Lemaire for the children's tasks and me for the household tasks."

Amelia saw a pleasant smile appear on the face of the man Harris, and then Cook took her by the hand and led her up the hallway towards the back of the house.

"Now lass, don't be all concerned, things here at *Vron* are very good, and so long as you do your chores as expected and dinna cause any problems, your sentence will go quickly here. You can expect to get a Ticket-of-leave in four years if you stay out of trouble, or if you find a husband to marry, then he will become your master while you bide out your sentence. That's what most of the women do."

"Not yourself then, Cook? Do you have another name?" asked Amelia. She was happy to hear Cook's Scottish accent.

"Aye, lass I did have another name, but I've been just Cook for so long now I barely remember it. Alice I was. I've been here with the Walker's now for 16 years, since they arrived, and I arrived at around the same time, straight off the ship. I was older than most then and I'm much older now. I've had husbands, two of the blighters, and children, God bless their souls. But I stopped thinking of them years ago."

"Are, are your children still alive, Cook?" Amelia knew she was prying but was a little intrigued.

"I believe one may still be lassie. He would be about your age now, I guess. I never heard anything about him after I left England. My darling girl had died the year before I was caught. I had two of them husbands who was good for nothing and liked to beat me when they were in their cups. I was caught stealing a loaf of bread, can you believe it, a loaf of bread to feed my starving son! Every day here I make three or four loaves. It used to be twenty or more, but since the men have left..." she let her words trail off without explanation. "I daresay my young Jimmy was sent to the workhouse, poor lad, he could even be out here as far as I know."

They had walked down the long corridor to the back of the house and along an undercover walkway into a huge kitchen with two large ovens and three huge preparation benches in the middle of the room. Amelia could see a storeroom off to the side with rows and rows of jars full of preserves. Large chunks of meat, some with legs attached lay across one of the benches. A very young girl in convict garb jumped to attention as they entered "Tilly this is Miss Laing, Miss Laing, Tilly." Said Cook as they breezed through the kitchen.

They went through another back door and along another covered walkway to what Amelia imagined was a worker's cottage. It was much larger than her parent's cottage had been back in Scotland. At the end of a walkway, going in the opposite direction was a huge building. "That's where the men workers live." Between the two buildings was a kitchen garden, with a chicken coop and a pig stye a bit further away. A woman was bent over collecting vegetables in a basket. "And that's Jane. Jane," called out Cook, "this is Miss Laing, the new governess." Jane looked up shading her eyes with her hand. She gave a cheery wave and Amelia waved back. New governess! Amelia gave a little chuckle inside. Well, she never thought she'd ever be called that!

Down at the front of the building Amelia could see Jarvis, Harris and two other men in convict garb unloading the carriage.

They entered the cottage and Amelia gasped at how lovely it was. A large central room contained a hearth with a fire that was warming the whole building. Pleasant lace curtains hung from the windows and a rug of some kind of animal skin lay across the floor. There were six comfortable looking chairs with side tables, two that had newspapers on them and one with a bowl of some kind of native flowers. There were six doors leading off the room.

"That there is my room," said Cook pointing to the one closest to the kitchen end, "and this here will be yours," she took Amelia across the other side of the room. We used to be two to a room except for me but not anymore."

The bedroom was lovely. A patchwork quilt in pink tones lay over the top of a steel framed bed with what looked like a thick mattress, with two pillows. There was another fur rug on the floor, a side table, and a wardrobe with a mirror on the front of it! Amelia had not seen her reflection in years other than in store windows or in a pool of water. She slowly moved in front of the wardrobe and even more slowly looked up. Then she burst into tears.

"Oh lassie, lass, oh, come now," said Cook as she came over to give Amelia a hug. At that Amelia stiffened, not used to human touch, and quickly brushed the tears from her eyes. Then she looked back up again. What she saw was not the young, innocent girl that she had once been, fighting her way through life to stop from starving or freezing to death, but a grown woman hardened by life, but with a look of hope and wonder on her pleasant looking features.

"You'll be fine here lassie," said Cook, "you'll see. The Walkers are a kindly family, even those wild children. They weren't always like that. Miss Lemaire had them all in hand at one time, but…." Her words trailed off again.

Amelia put her meagre sack of belongings on the bed. The men were bringing her trunk.

"If you need anything lovey just ask old Cook hey, I can get pretty much everything you need. Get yourself sorted and have a freshen up and come back in and Harris will take you to meet Miss Lemaire."

Amelia watched as Cook started to walk out the door.

"Cook," she said stopping her in her tracks, "are there many other workers here on the estate?"

Cook turned to face her, "Well, ah, lovey, it's usually quieter in the winter anyways, the ground freezes so there's no crops to tend and the animals are herded to the one area, so we don't need as many shepherds. But ah yes, this year be different. We think Mr Walker is having some troubles, the money kind you know. Lots of farmers have been doing it tough lately, but yes, a lot of men and most of the maids were put off a while ago now. I've just got me two kitchen girls now, I used to have half a dozen and some maids."

So, Amelia's suspicions were correct then, the Walkers were in trouble. Darn it, she thought, so much for a cushy work assignment, she'd probably be back at the Factory before long.

That afternoon she met Miss Lemaire. Amelia was quite taken aback at just how bad she was. She was confined to a chair on wheels that the men or older boys pushed her around in. She could not use her left arm and only had limited use of her right arm. She could still write but Amelia could see how difficult and laborious it was for her. When she spoke in her French accent, only one side of her mouth worked and on the other side a slow stream of saliva ran down her chin. Mrs Walker paid constant attention and wiped the spit away diligently. As Miss Lemaire tried to explain what she wanted of Amelia, with her halting, dribbly speech, Mrs Walker hovered over them both with a hopeful and desperate look on her face.

"I won't always be here," said Mrs Walker, "I am only here now because I cannot trust those girls to help Miss Lemaire, they have gone wild since Nanny went and Miss Lemaire fell ill." She took a shuddering deep breath and looked as if she was about to cry, "and I have Beccy to care for now, with no nanny, and she has the cholic."

Amelia figured that she had a good understanding of the issues at hand. Mrs Walker was not a young woman. She looked a lot older than most women who had a new baby, so raising one on her own must be difficult for someone used to such an easy life with servants to attend to her every need. There was lots of work to do.

Amelia's first job was to meet the children over dinner. The children's dining room was far down the main hallway and close to the kitchen. Amelia helped Cook to prepare the meal and was then quite astounded when the children, Rhoda, Adelaide, Alfred, and Edwin all arrived to collect their plates and cutlery. It was then Amelia's job to sit with them in the dining room while they ate and to make sure that they used their manners and didn't squabble. Amelia didn't think she was quite the one to teach table manners, but she could certainly stop squabbling.

"You talk funny," said 6-year-old Rhoda.

"She does not silly, she's Scottish," said Adelaide, 10, "don't worry Miss Laing, she's just rude," Adelaide poked her tongue out at Rhoda who poked her own tongue out in turn, causing Amelia to have to hush them and remind them of their table manners.

"It doesn't matter anymore, anyway," said Adelaide, "we'll all be poor farmers children soon anyway, stupid father, I hate him!" She burst into tears. Alfred 12, and Edwin 14 then growled at her, forgetting their own manners.

"Don't you say anything about father, Addy," said Alfred, "anyway a job as a maid would suit you well, you already look like a scrubber." At this Adelaide jumped up and went over and hit Alfred over the head several times causing Edwin to get involved to hold her back and then both girls were in tears and the boys just glared at them, and then at Amelia.

Great start thought Amelia. She gave Rhoda a hug and made Adelaide apologise to Alfred and then they finished off their meals in sullen silence. This was obviously not a harmonious home.

"Now what happens?" said Amelia to Edwin, not having been given further directions.

"Now we go and clean up in the kitchen and then we go to bed and read. Sometimes mother lets us sit with her in the parlour. We used to have music nights, but that doesn't happen anymore. Sometimes our older brothers take Alfie and I to discuss farm matters, as we all must know now."

"Nanny and then Miss Lemaire used to tell us bedtime stories," said Rhoda quietly, a tear escaping again.

"Well," said Amelia, "that I can do."

As Edwin had said, the children all piled into the kitchen and washed and dried their own plates. Cook was busy preparing the meal for their parents and older brothers. Then the boys went off to their rooms, Amelia presumed, and the girls led her to the main house and up a flight of curved stairs to their rooms.

On the way they passed the Walker's and Amelia presumed the eldest Henry and George, on their way to the main dining room.

"Ah Miss Laing," said Mr Walker, "I see you have the children in hand already, well done." Mrs Walker also nodded appreciatively. Lucky you didn't see them half an hour ago thought Amelia.

The girl's rooms were huge, both with large four poster beds with beautiful canopies and quilts in pinks for Rhoda and green and lilac for Adelaide. Their rooms were full of toys and wardrobes spilling over with beautiful clothes and tiny white, pink, and cream slippers, and leather boots. The walls were painted in elegant tones to match the bedding and a mural of a princess adorned Rhoda's room. The floors were covered with rugs in colours to complement the rest of the room. Each room had a bookshelf full of picture books that Amelia had never seen before.

The little girls changed into nightgowns. As they were doing this Amelia heard an odd sound. It sounded like a man cooing a lullaby. As the girls were busy, she snuck out of the room and heard the sound coming from the next room. As she looked in, she saw Harris, sitting in a comfortable chair by the fire gently rocking a baby in his arms and singing quietly to her. The baby looked to be deep in sleep.

Amelia saw Harris look up and he pressed a finger to his lips but smiled at her. She smiled back and scurried back to her charges.

Rhoda and Adelaide both climbed up into Adelaide's bed ready for their story.

"Which story would you like?" asked Amelia looking across to the full bookshelf.

"None of those, we know them all," said Adelaide.

"Yes, we've heard them over and over and over," said Rhoda dramatically rolling her eyes. I like this little one, thought Amelia, she's got spirit.

"Well," said Amelia, "do you want to hear one of my stories?"

"Oh yes please!" they both squealed happily.

Amelia ended up telling them three or four stories, ones that she had written for the children on the ship, and she wasn't sure how long she had been with the girls until she noticed both of their eyes starting to close. "Ok, back to your room Rhoda," said Amelia gently shaking the girl awake. "No, no," said Adelaide sleepily, "she sleeps in here now, since Nanny died."

"OK then. Sweet dreams then little girls," said Amelia, and the girls were asleep before she blew out the candles and left the room.

Amelia made her way back to the kitchen. On her way out of the main building she could see a light in one of the rooms and could hear low male voices. At one point the voices seemed raised but then they died down again. Walker and his older sons she imagined.

Cook and Harris were sitting at one of the benches in the kitchen, and it looked like all the chores had been completed for the night. Cook jumped up when she saw Amelia arrive and put the kettle back on to boil. John also jumped up as she entered the room. What a gentleman she thought. He nodded an acknowledgement to her and didn't sit again until she had taken a seat near him.

"How's your first day been then pet? Those children didn't run rings around you I hope?"

Amelia smiled, suddenly feeling quite exhausted but also quite happy. "No Cook, they are all a bit funny but also a bit charming," she ran her hand across her brow as if to wipe away the day. Suddenly she thought that tonight would be the first night is such a very, very long time that she would be sleeping alone. She wondered if she'd be able to sleep or if her mind would still be in constant turmoil and on the lookout for danger.

Cook brought her over a mug of tea and a slice of fruitcake, with white icing on it. Amelia could get very used to this fancy kind of lifestyle, she thought to herself.

"I saw you with the babe, Mr Harris," she said taking a bite of her cake. John went bright red from his neck to the top of his head, and he quickly diverted his eyes from hers.

"Ere, don't be so shy Mr Harris," said Cook, "He's got the touch with the young'uns does Mr Harris. And thankfully for that. After Nanny died, bless her soul, 'twas the only way we could get Mrs Walker to eat her dinner by Mr Harris 'ere rocking young Beccy to sleep. No one else mind you. Only Mr Harris. So that's become his nightly task now so that Mrs Walker can have a couple of hours to herself."

Amelia nodded at him appreciatively. "Tis a wonderful talent to be able to sooth an unsettled babe." She had learned that on the ship, some had the talent, but many didn't. John looked up and smiled shyly at Amelia and for a tiny moment her heart skipped.

This day just gets better and better she thought. Perhaps this is exactly where I am meant to be after all those months of trying to get out of dismal Scotland. She smiled as her thoughts turned into dreams in her warm, soft bed in this warm, safe place.

Chapter Fifteen
# *1841 – Work to do*

*A*melia woke the next morning feeling the freshest that she ever had. For the first time in forever she slept alone, in a warm, soft bed with no fear of attack by anything. Even though the house was unfamiliar she felt so much safer than she had felt for so long.

Cook came and fetched her before the sun came up, but she was already awake and dressed. Her days fell into a familiar pattern. She would meet Cook, Tilly, and Jane in the kitchen where they would have a cup of tea and toast and then start the bread for the next day and do any other meal preparations that needed to start early. Jane had already been out milking the cows. Often Jarvis and Harris would join them, they had already been upstairs to stoke the fires and check the breakfast rooms were in order.

Cook would then leave Amelia to prepare the breakfast trays while she took trays up for Mrs Walker and Miss Lemaire, and Tilly and Jane took supplies to the men's quarters. Cook would be gone for a while as she had to help Miss Lemaire with her food and tea and help Mrs Walker to prepare herself for the day, she didn't trust the other girls.

"Ere, never thought the likes of me would be a lady's maid, and a nursemaid." laughed Cook, "Never thought I'd be doing five people's jobs neither!" She scratched her head and gave a frustrated shake, looking at Amelia. "You know at one time we had over 100 workers here. And more in the party season," she shook her head again sadly, "I'd 'ave five kitchen maids and two dairy maids thank you very much, and we was always busy, and that's just 'ere in the kitchen. We always had three maids just for the house too."

Henry and George, who was 17, would arrive next at the kitchen and collect breakfast to go, before they went to join the farm workers to prepare for whatever work they had for the day. George had already been in helping Jarvis to lift Miss Lemaire from her bed to her chair ready for her breakfast.

Amelia awakened the children, helped the younger ones to dress and the girls to do their hair and then organised and supervised their breakfast. The girls then spent an hour with Cook and the maids, collecting eggs and vegetables in the fine weather, and the boys spent an hour with the men out the back, while Amelia scurried around making the beds and tidying up. Jarvis and Harris were busy cleaning and polishing and doing any maintenance jobs that needed doing.

This was all very new, Cook told Amelia. It wasn't long ago when none of the children were expected to do anything to help or any type of chores. Their mother was being quite stoic in preparing them for the changes that were on the wind. "Oh, they bucked and kicked for a while," said Cook, "but then Miss Lemaire fell ill and most of the workers were put off and there was just no one else to get things done. So, they all just settled into the new routine."

Mr Walker left in the fine carriage two days after Amelia's arrival. The carriage was full of boxes and trunks filled with household valuables and farming equipment.

"Well," said Jarvis, "that's the end of the silver, no more for you to polish hey Harris?" He said this good naturedly, but Amelia could sense the tension amongst the trio in the kitchen.

The morning was filled with lessons which Miss Lemaire set for the children and Amelia did her best to deliver. It was easier in the afternoons when the lessons were of a practical nature and often involved getting outside for some adventuring to learn about the flora and fauna, the seasons, and so many other things of a scientific nature that Amelia really knew little about. Often Harris would come and help her with the lessons. She discovered that he had become a bit of a school master himself to the many workers who had come through *Vron* over the years. He was excellent at reading, writing and arithmetic, which Amelia knew very little about, and he also seemed to know so much about so many other things.

By the time they had finished afternoon lessons the children were all too tired, mentally, and physically, to get up to the mischief that Cook told her that had been up to before her arrival. "They's were just bored is all, they're all good children really."

Amelia had to agree. So long as they had things to do, and their minds were being fed with interesting information the children were easy company. And Amelia was also learning so many interesting things from Harris, who took her one afternoon to see the library, which so far had not been stripped of its treasures.

After a while, the task of setting lessons seemed to naturally fall to Amelia and Harris, and Miss Lemaire was only consulted about the format and contents. She would offer them some advice or suggestions but soon was happy to sit quietly in the corner while the two younger tutors took care of her charges. Adelaide was tasked with helping Miss Lemaire with her cup of tea and biscuits and her sandwiches at lunch.

There was a loud disagreement one week when Mr Walker was home from Launceston, this time being dropped off in a buggy. From what they could hear from the kitchen it seemed that Mr Walker needed to put off George's school master, the one who visited each week. The man was a pompous fool, thought Amelia and barely deigned to acknowledge her or Harris. And the work that he set for George was barely sufficient for a boy Alfred's age, said Harris. And so, it came about that Harris became less of a footman, because really there was little footman work to do, and more of a full-time tutor to all the boys.

But for all his knowledge, Amelia saw that Harris had a very sad expression and demeanour. There as an underlying feeling that he was in pain deep down in his heart and that to him the world was grey and sad, not colourful, and joyous as it now was for Amelia.

By this time Amelia and Harris had become quite friendly with each other, as they needed to be, working on the same assignment. They spent time of a night reading together in companionable silence and Harris taught her to play backgammon, which was all the rage, and that he had learned while at the Palace, to pass the rare quiet times with Nigel and some of the others. This game could be a source of fun and frustration but gave them a common activity that they could both enjoy.

As the seasons changed the flowers began to bloom again and it became a new lesson for both the children and Amelia, to learn all about how the flowers grew and what type they were, and to cut them and learn how to arrange them. That was one thing that couldn't be taken away from them, their beautiful flowers that grew for free, thanks to Mrs Walkers urging and the skills of Harris and old Sammy.

There was one day that Harris had arranged for old Sammy to visit the school room and give a lesson on growing roses and about some of the local flowers. It was a much-anticipated visit and everyone, even Mrs Walker seemed excited by the diversion from her long, troubled days. Old Sammy arrived in his work outfit, having walked from his cottage on a neighbouring estate, and removed his boots before he climbed the veranda.

"In all these years I've been here," he said in a slow, quiet voice "I have never stepped onto this veranda." He spent a good few hours regaling everyone with his extensive knowledge and it was Mrs Walker who asked the most questions. She appeared somewhat lightened in the presence of this man who seemed part tramp, part flower wizard.

One night after everyone had gone to bed Amelia approached Cook as they arrived at their cottage.

"Can I ask you something please Cook, of a personal nature?"

"Yes, you can lass," said Cook tentatively.

"Why is Mr Harris so sad." It was a direct question, but she couldn't think of any other way of putting it.

"Well lass, Mr Harris, John be his name, he's a bit of what you call a loner like. You know, for many years he never spoke to anyone much. Oh, he'd read the papers to the men, and he'd do his lessons with them, but ye never could get much talk out of him. He kept to himself like, you know?" Amelia nodded. "All we's knew was 'e came from a Palace in London and 'e had the manners and looks for it and all, but he never spoke much," she drew a breath then looked at Amelia like she was thinking about whether to continue. "So, we'd had Nanny Elizabeth with us since before I came along, she met the Walker's in London. She were a beautiful lass. And beautiful soul too, Emma, she were one of the good ones she was. Took all of the bossing from the Missus, oh yes Mrs Walker might be a bit 'umbled now but she were a tyrant back in the early days. But Elizabeth took it all with a smile." She took a breath and then went across to sit in one of the chairs beckoning Amelia to do so as well.

"Well, it were after Master Henry's 21st birthday, Oh what a hullabaloo that was, everyone in Van Diemen's land was here I was sure of it. So, something happened that weekend and after that John and Elizabeth were sweet on each other. We would see them talking together and sitting together and taking walks together. But John was still under sentence so there was nothing for it, but I think they were planning. But then Elizabeth died," she stopped short, and a tear slowly ran down her cheek. She must have loved Elizabeth.

"John, Mr Harris, well he's never been the same. He was quiet before, but he had a sense of contentment, now I see him and he's only sad, all the time. It's been over a year since we lost Elizabeth, and John got his Ticket-of-leave in January just past, a few months too late for them..." her sad voice trailed off.

"Oh," said Amelia sadly, "that explains it then. Thank you for sharing that with me Cook."

"Aye I think ye needed to know, girl. I see you and him getting closer these days, well there's not many of us around nowadays so we only have each other now. It's good that you talk to him. I do notice he seems less glum when he's with you," she smiled at Amelia then groaned as she lifted herself back out of the chair. She touched Amelia briefly on her knee and looked her in the eye, "you're doing good here lass, you'll do well here."

Vron

## Chapter Sixteen
# *1841 - Love*

$J$ohn knew something big was about to happen. He could feel it. Although he had to admit he did not have the best senses as far as danger was concerned, as evidenced from his past. However, ever since Elizabeth died and then Mr Walker sent most of the workers away, he had felt a sense of foreboding.

He had very much enjoyed all his years with the Walker's. In a lot of ways, it had been better than his time in London. He had been able to indulge in his love of gardening, dress in his smart uniform and care for the family and he was able to take the long walks that he so loved. But best of all, he had unlimited access to books, so many amazing books. He had felt useful and needed and even a little bit loved, maybe, by Jarvis and by Cook.

Since the last of Cook's maids had gone, he had even got to do some cooking, which he dearly missed. Even Tilly and Jane had been sent back to be re-assigned. And he didn't just get to do the mundane jobs of peeling and chopping the vegetables or kneading the dough for the bread, but he had made some delicious sauces and cakes that had been much appreciated by the household.

He had been a naïve boy when he arrived. And if he was honest, he was now just a naïve man probably, but he had many more skills. He had honed his skills at teaching. Who would have thought? But it was something that the waiters at the Gardens would often do to supplement their incomes, so he came a little prepared.

And he had been in love. Oh yes, he had been, fully and openly in love, and now he understood what the big deal was about. Elizabeth was everything that a woman could be, she was pure and beautiful and to think of her made his heart both happy that he had known her, happy that he had kissed her, happy that he had found another human who he could talk to and share his thoughts with and who was actually interested in the same things that he was. And he was also so very, very sad. Sad that such a beautiful person as Elizabeth would not get to have a life that she should have had, to live long and raise babies and be happy. And sad to think that he had lost her and lost the life that they were planning to have.

After Elizabeth died John had settled into knowing that he would be in unimaginable pain for a long time, the same as he was after both of his parents died. And it happened. The mundane day to day chores had helped him to forget for a while and sleep was a blessing, but it wasn't until Miss Laing arrived that John even took any notice of what day it was or what time of day, he had been going through life on automation.

But two things shook him out of his misery. Not completely, but a little. First was the shock of understanding that Mr Walker was going broke. Mr Walker had been one of the wealthiest and most successful men in the area, as well as a respected magistrate. *Vron* had once been teeming with people, workers, both men and women, so many accents and so much life in the place! There were carts coming and going every day dropping off supplies or collecting the farm produce to sell. The family had lived like gentry, oblivious to the day-to-day motions on the estate, and Mr

Dryden and Mr Jarvis had run it all like a well-oiled clock. Everyone had felt secure and happy at *Vron*. And then they weren't.

And then Miss Laing, Emma as he now knew her, had arrived. She seemed so timid that first day, her eyes so wide not knowing what to expect. He must have looked the same when he arrived, he thought.

But since she had shown such an affinity with the children and the tutoring she had come out of her shell and was a fun and spirited woman, with a smart and enquiring mind. She would make him laugh at some of the things that she would ask him, they would be talking about types of fish and suddenly she would tell him that she had seen a big lizard in the garden and ask if he had books about lizards for her to read. Yesterday he had found her quietly sitting with the children as they practiced their handwriting and then suddenly, she leapt up and told them that their bones had been settled for too long and it was time to jump up and pretend to be elephants along the veranda. The children loved Miss Laing, she was young and fun and spontaneous, and she had that lovely sing song Scottish accent. The children all tried to copy her, which made Miss Lemaire stamp her walking stick on the ground and scowl at them. Heaven forbid, her charges ended up sounding like Scotsmen.

And she had such a beautiful singing voice. Every day she sang something to the children and taught them to sing it too. She told John that she was composing them herself at night as a way for the children to remember parts of their lessons, and it worked because when they were being questioned John could hear them quietly singing the song that gave them the answer under their breath. How clever she was, he thought.

Neither of them talked of their past. It hadn't come up yet and it was probable that Emma may not wish to relive that part of her life. But now they were all fresh and washed clean of their past in this new land. And John was now almost free as well. He was recommended for a Conditional Pardon that could come through at any time. That meant that he couldn't go back to England, but there was nothing there for him anyway. He had even met people who he considered to be friends. Thomas and Mary Beswick and her stepfather, Thomas Brennan. Mary Beswick's two brothers William and John. The two Reverend's, Reverend Bishton from Westbury and Reverend Davies from Longford. And there were several workers at *Vron* and the other estates who he had become friendly with. He had spent long hours with workers from other estates when the Walker's had thrown their parties and dinners, and he would see them at church or in town.

No one had spoken the forbidden words; what would happen to the last workers if *Vron* had to be sold and the Walker's had to move. Henry and now also George, took care of the farm workers, tending what was left of the crops and livestock. The cider mill had long been locked up and the stables and carriage house were almost empty. Most of the workers left were still under sentence so would just go back to be re-assigned, or to work on the road gangs.

John knew that he, along with Jarvis and Cook would be highly prized in all the homes and estates in Van Diemen's Land, and could probably fetch a higher wage as well, but he really didn't want to be separated from them. They had become like his parents in a way.

Those thoughts now kept him awake at night.

But now that Miss Laing was here, his days were filled with, if not exactly joyfulness, then definitely a happiness he had not known since Elizabeth died.

One evening, the family were away from *Vron* for the night. This used to be a very normal thing as they would all pile into Mr Walker's elaborate carriages and attend dinners and parties at other wealthy landowner's homes. And they were often away at their house in Launceston too. On those visits John would accompany the family, and if they were staying at the Launceston house, Jarvis as well. But this time it was one of the landowners who sent their carriage to collect Mrs Walker with baby Beccy and all the boys. The two girls stayed at home with Amelia and Miss Lemaire.

Amelia had made a fun night of it with the little girls and made a picnic in Miss Lemaire's room. Even Miss Lemaire was cheerful and giggled at the funny stories Amelia told and the songs that she got the girls to sing about animals complete with animal noises. Amelia took the girls off to bed and John who came to help Miss Lemaire from her chair, waited while Amelia helped her to change to her nightgown, and then lifted her bony body into bed. Miss Lemaire had become bird like and was as light as a feather. She also now slept a lot.

After their shared dinner Jarvis surprised them all by bringing out a bottle of whisky. None of them drank often, but every now and then would have a small port, but not a whisky! That was something special.

"Here everyone." Said Jarvis formally, "Real Scottish whisky. This was given me as a gift by one of the men down near Breadalbane. You may remember I helped at a wake down there a while ago."

"Not Mr Brennan?" said John, "But he's Irish."

"Yes Harris, he is Irish, but he kindly gave me one of the bottles still left from Mr Sandy McKenzie's stock," he gave a slight superior smile.

"No!" said Cook, "but that's got to be over 20 years old!"

"22, my dear Cook," said Jarvis, "and tonight we are all going to indulge in a small dram. I think we all deserve it after the year that we have all had. And I'm sure that Miss Laing will appreciate a little of the old country, that is if you indulge my dear?"

Amelia's eyes lit up. Real Scottish whisky, and 22-years-old as well. Oh Lordy, this is like dining with the Queen, she thought.

"Oh, you bet I do, Mr Jarvis. I feel like the Queen already."

They all enjoyed a couple of drams and their spirits seemed to lift and conversation came easily.

"Do any of you play card games?" asked Amelia shyly, wondering if they might think she was a bit of a wench knowing tavern games.

"Oh well," said Jarvis, "I used to love to have a game of cards but that was a long time ago."

"Oh, I did lassie, I used to love me cards." Said Cook.

"I think there are a few packs in the library," offered John.

"Well off you go man, go find one for us." laughed Jarvis, now in high spirits, of the liquid and the emotional kind.

Amelia took the cards from John and removed all but 36 of them.

"We only use the sixes and above and Jack is the highest card."

They all picked up the game quickly and spent a wonderful couple of hours playing and laughing.

It was quite late when Cook said that she needed to go to bed or there'd be no bread made in the morning. Jarvis also decided it was time for him to head off to bed.

Over the game of Scottish whist Mr Harris became John and Miss Laing became Emma but Cook said she preferred just Cook as she'd never remember to answer to her real name, and Jarvis agreed, he would remain just Jarvis.

That just left John and Amelia, who shyly looked up at each other after the others left.

"Would you mind if I called you Amelia, you seem more like an Amelia to me?" said John shyly.

Amelia was flattered, Emma was her street name, but she herself had always felt like she was really Amelia inside.

John then asked if she would like to see something wonderful. Of course she did, but she giggled nervously, as she was suddenly a bit anxious about what John wanted to show her.

"It's a bit of a walk I'm afraid," he said, "but if what I think is there it will be worth it." As she had on her sturdy boots Amelia agreed, what an adventure!

"You see," said John as they climbed the steep hill behind the main buildings, "the spring equinox will be next Wednesday, and we should be able to see an amazing sight."

As they got higher up the hill, they saw that the sky was glowing a faint bright green. Amelia scurried further up the hill. At the top she looked down and across the plains at the green sky with what looked like read streamers glowing up into the sky.

She turned to John with her eyes wide with wonder.

"You see," said John, his arms pointing out across the great expanse, "this hill points south, and it's almost the spring equinox, and as the sky is so clear tonight, I thought we might just have a very good chance of seeing this. Captain Cook named it Aurora Australis. Fascinating really. It's so very interesting..." John's words were cut off because Amelia had thrown her arms around his neck and kissed him square on his lips.

"Oh," said John a little shocked.

"Oh yes, or oh no?" said Amelia, and without any thought on the matter he gently placed his own arms around Amelia and took her into a warm embrace and kissed her lips like he had never kissed before.

Before they knew it and as if some kind of force beyond their control had taken over, they were both half undressed and caressing each other with both gentleness and then passion as they lay on the soft grass. There were no words spoken as neither of them wanted to jinx the moment that just felt too good to stop.

They lay there caressing each other for what seemed like hours but suddenly they were startled by the sound of a door opening down below. It was either the workers moving about or Cook looking for Amelia, probably concerned for her safety. They quickly dressed and, hand in hand and giggling, they scurried back down the hill.

John gave her a soft kiss goodnight and watched as she entered the cottage.

They both slept the sleep of happy lovers that night, a little confused but very happy and content and excited to see what the future would hold for them.

Vron

Vron

## Chapter Seventeen
# *1841 – Shocking news*

*T*hings went along as normal for the next two weeks, except that once everyone was in bed and she thought they were asleep, Amelia would sneak into John's room in the big house and they would resume their lessons in getting to know each other, both physically and emotionally. Once they had started atop the hill overlooking the southern lights it was like a tap had been turned on and could not be turned off.

Amelia had seen his ugly tattoo's. He had at first tried to lie at angles to prevent her from seeing them, but in the heat of their passion it became impossible. He quickly told her an abbreviated story about how he got them at which she giggled and then climbed on top of him and kissed him so deeply his breath was taken away.

John knew that he was using Amelia to replace Elizabeth, but it had been over a year that he had been mourning, and Amelia was very different to Elizabeth. Amelia was intellectual and sassy, where Elizabeth was only gentle and calm. Amelia was very forward where Elizabeth was very chaste. John had dreamt for three years of having a life with Elizabeth, being a husband and a father, and having his own home and family to love him again like he once had with his parents. And then that dream had been destroyed so suddenly. Maybe there was still time for him to have it after all, but with Amelia.

Things were changing fast at *Vron* and none of the staff knew what the future or even the near present may hold for them. John knew that if worst came to worst, he could get a position anywhere with a good household, probably on one of the prestigious estates, and he was now able to apply to be married, and if that happened, Amelia would be assigned to him. They could then purchase a small home and start a family.

Amelia had similar thoughts. As much as she was enjoying her time at *Vron*, she could see that things were changing and there was such an underlying tension amongst the staff and the family. Amelia with her good nature knew that she was the only thing stopping the children from getting very upset at what they could see happening, their beautiful home, slowly dying and closing up around them. Amelia knew that if she married that she would be assigned to her husband and she had to admit John was a pretty good catch. He was very different from any of the men she had ever known before. He reminded her of some of the toffy nose customers that Margaret would have around her. But he didn't have the same pretension and pompousness that wealthy men had. Neither did Jarvis. They were just two very nice working men who happened to look very nice and speak very well.

She enjoyed the fact that she could have an intelligent conversation with John, and he didn't talk down to her, like most men did, but he seemed interested and intrigued with her thoughts and ideas. She loved the way that he would give her cute little smiles or side eyes and laugh when she did or said something silly or funny.

She liked that he was so tall and so handsome. She liked that he was always such a gentleman, and so nice and kind, but when they were alone at night in his room, he showed her such a strong, manly passion that almost made her lose her senses.

They both knew that it would not be a good idea for her to get pregnant, so they could only go so far with their nighttime escapades. A convict getting pregnant was considered to be a crime and she would be sent back to the Female Factory until the birth and until the baby was weaned. It would also be a misdemeanour that could hurt their chances of being approved to marry, which as a convict, Amelia also had to apply for.

One afternoon Mr Walker was dropped off in a buggy. He came inside with his head down and his face drawn. He went straight to see Mrs Walker, and Amelia was told to take Beccy, and John was told to wheel Miss Lemaire around the veranda.

Henry and George were called in next, and Mrs Walker did not emerge.

The dinner routine went on as usual, Amelia wrangling the children and Jarvis, John and Cook attending to the older Walker's and Miss Lemaire. As the meal was finishing Mr Walker said, "Jarvis, could you arrange for the staff, just Laing, Harris, Cook and yourself, to meet with me in the parlour at 8pm." He didn't say why, but it was already 7pm so Jarvis, John and Cook snapped to it to get all their chores done. John went up to let Amelia know that she was required at 8pm.

At 8pm Jarvis, John, Amelia and Cook all diligently filed into the parlour where they found Mr Walker standing in front of the large window that looked out across the front of *Vron.*

"Gentlemen, and ladies," he said with an air of formality, "it is with great sadness that I inform you that *Vron*, as part of the

Walker family, is no more." No one was surprised by this revelation.

"It has come to the point where I am required to pass the property into the hands of trustees. They will take over the operation of the estate until such time as it can be sold. They have kindly allowed me to use credit to purchase a timber farm at Frogmore, up near the coast. Mrs Walker likes the sea air, and it will be good for Miss Lemaire as well. Miss Lemaire, now my ward, and Miss Laing will accompany us. I will be taking a new convict as a cook and maid, she arrives tomorrow. Cook I will leave you to teach her all that you can before we leave." He looked at the ceiling despondently. "Jarvis, I have found you a position at *Brickendon* with Mr Archer, if you would be interested. He jumped at the chance for you to join the household. You would not be butler as you have been here, but rather an under butler, the property is so big they need two or three anyway. And…" said Mr Walker grandly, "Archer will be increasing your salary, which is something I should have done years ago," he shook his head sadly.

"Cook, you will be needed here to feed the workers which may increase now that the trustee's will be managing everything, and Harris, I put you forward to take care of the house, does that suit you?"

"Yes, sir," said John tentatively.

"Of course, you are free at any time to find other employment, but I think that the trustee's main interest will be in the farm and what it can produce for a profit, and to make sure that this house does not fall into disrepair, so your job will be more of a caretaker and maintenance man. Henry will be staying here to manage the estate as he has been doing since Mr Dryden left us."

John looked around at the others not really knowing what to say.

"Henry and the lads will look after themselves, so no need for you to go kow-towing to Henry. He will maintain his room in the house, but he will just be another employee of the trustees the same as you both, do you understand?" John and Cook both nodded.

"But you'll need to keep the house in order so that potential buyers can see it in a good state. I want it kept as it is now, you understand?" He sounded very sad, but he suddenly looked up with a sparkle in his eye.

"I bet those young ladies at the church will fall over themselves to bring you cakes and the like once they know you're here on your own, Harris!" Walker chuckled, obviously unaware of the new developments in the household.

"Right," said Mr Walker, "so that's settled then. You can spend the rest of this week getting things ready and the carriages will arrive on Monday to take us to Frogmore. Jarvis, you can leave anytime you wish, just let me know when you prefer, and Henry will arrange a buggy and driver to take you. You can even stay on here for a while to help Harris if you wish, but I can no longer pay your wage."

Later that evening, after they had all finished the late chores, they met in the kitchen. Cook suggested that they all take tea in the women's quarters. Jarvis raised his eyes at that, but Cook scoffed at him, "I reckon all bets are off now Mr Jarvis, come on with ya, we've got a nice cosy room in there, we can take tea and discuss this terrible situation," she brushed a tear from her eye and put the kettle on to boil.

Over tea and gingerbread biscuits, the group had a chat.

"I'll of course stay with you here for a bit John," said Jarvis.

"Thank you, Mr Jarvis," said John.

"And you'll be all good won't you, lassie," said Cook to Amelia, "you's off for an adventure hey. The Walker's love you Emma and they will look after you well...." her voice trailed off. Amelia was not feeling loved or wonderful about a new adventure. Things had changed with the family dynamic and the children had started to act up again and were not as easy to manage as they had been.

"And" said Jarvis, "I think that you have successfully kept the change in your 'friendship' a secret from the family," he raised his eyebrows and looked at both John and then Amelia.

John blushed and Amelia looked down at her hands.

"You're going to have to figure all of that out in the next few days," he said gently.

The next day was spent in a bustle as Amelia learned that she was in charge of organising the children's possessions for the move as well as packing up the school room and helping with Miss Lemaire and Miss Walker's packing. School work was off as the preparations for the move took centre stage. The children, without supervision and tasks to keep them occupied, ran wild. Amelia tried to keep them quiet, but it was impossible.

"Oh, for goodness sakes Laing, let them outside," said an exasperated Mrs Walker, "I cannot stand the noise of them all."

It was October and the sun was shining. It was a good day for children to be out playing.

"But I can't watch them, Mrs Walker, I have to keep packing in here," said Amelia.

"Oh, that's fine," said Mrs Walker, "from now on they are going to have to get used to being bush children," she then burst into tears. Then Miss Lemaire burst into tears. Amelia just looked at them, rolled her eyes and walked into the next room to keep packing. Seriously, they know nothing about hardship, she thought.

With less than a week to be together, John and Amelia knew that they had to make the most of their time together and the more time they spent together the more they wanted each other, in the worst but the best possible way. They managed for the first few days to keep the bottom half of their clothing on, but with three days to go it became impossible and all they both wanted was to feel each other's skin pressed as close against each other as possible. And then, suddenly one night, and without much thought, at the age of thirty-four, John finally felt what it was like to truly be with a woman.

The first time lasted for only a few minutes and John was very embarrassed and blushed profusely. But Amelia kissed away his embarrassment and before long he was ready to try again. Within three days they had it down to a fine art and consummated their love at least two or three times every night, before falling asleep in each other's arms. They didn't even care anymore who knew, so Amelia didn't bother to return to her own room until they both awoke for their chores in the morning.

The day finally came when the family were to leave for Frogmore. Six, large, covered carts had already left in the days prior carrying all the goods and chattels that the family were taking. John and Jarvis noted that much of the expensive items were being left, including most of the paintings and nearly all the library. Mr Walker took John aside at sometime during the activities and told him that he could choose as many books as he wanted to keep for himself, and to do it soon before anyone came to inspect the house for sale.

"The library will eventually be sold, along with everything else left in this house, so I'd rather someone I know get some advantage from these books that took me so long to collect. You've been a good man, Harris, a good man, please help yourself." He gave John a pat on his shoulder in a fatherly way.

Amelia never left John's side the whole night before they left, and they didn't get much sleep either. Cook came and fetched her before the sun rose and chastised her.

"Emma! You are putting both yours and Mr Harris's futures in jeopardy! The Walker's would see Mr Harris in a poor light if they knew what you two have been doing, and they'd most probably send you back to the Factory."

Amelia gave her a distasteful look and then turned to go and collect her meagre belongings to take to the new house. She couldn't give a tuppeny fig what the Walker's thought about her and John. She especially didn't care what they thought about her and although she had been enjoying her time with the children this whole new arrangement sounded very different. Amelia was not scared of hard work, or offensive work, Lord she'd mucked out enough pig stye's to not be too fussy about what she did to survive. She didn't even care if she had to go back to the Factory. She'd done fine in prisons before.

She was worried about John's reputation, he was a good man, and he had worked hard to develop it and could get a job at any of the big houses, but being with a convict girl might tarnish that, or so said Cook. But Cook had been holed up at *Vron* for 15 years and Amelia wasn't so sure that she knew what contemporary thoughts were on such relationships. She did know that just in the short time she had been at *Vron* she had seen several wealthy couples where one or both had been convicts and many of the local citizens, where both had been convicts or convicts who had married people who were free born (usually the children of emancipists). The line between the so-called exclusives and ex-convicts, emancipists, was getting thinner than ever in 1841.

Amelia was very busy getting the four youngest children organised, although only the two little girls and baby Beccy really needed help. Beccy was now starting to toddle around, and didn't like to be carried, which added an extra complexity to Amelia's day, as Mrs Walker expected her to be the one chasing Beccy and keeping her safe. George was going with the family and the plan seemed to be that he and Mr Walker would manage the farm, with Henry and the convict men joining them as soon as the house was sold. Mr Walker had said quietly to John that if all went well, he might be sending for him again as butler.

The family and Amelia left mid-morning. The journey to Frogmore would take two days in the carriages, and they would stop overnight at an inn that Mr Walker had already scoped out on his visits to the new house.

Jarvis, John, and Cook waved sadly as they left. Henry had stayed away. He was becoming increasingly belligerent and could often be heard shouting at the men. Poor fellow, thought John, after his years in England learning to be an educated gentleman, he had expected to live his life in privilege and either get work like his father as a magistrate or another higher-level public service role, or to inherit *Vron* as a thriving and successful estate. Instead, he would now be lucky to afford a small subsistence farm, if his father wasn't able to make this new farm a success. But Henry knew the extent of his father's debt's and they were substantial, thanks to the folding of the insurance company.

Jarvis stayed at *Vron* for about two weeks. Mr Walker had sold off small parcels of land on the boundary of *Vron* to try to stay afloat financially, and a small village had started to form, with a hotel, a butcher, and several grocers. During the weeks before Jarvis left, he, John and Cook used the horse and buggy to visit the local vendors and closest land holders to let them know about the changes at *Vron*. They also visited Westbury and Longford and saw the church communities. Everyone was extremely sympathetic to the situation and gave them all kinds of foodstuffs to take back to sustain them. In exchange they gave gifts of fresh fruits and flowers, that were again flourishing at *Vron*, thanks to John and old Sammy's endeavours over the years. Old Sammy still visited *Vron* but not in any set pattern. John would just find him out there some days, working on the gardens. He was no longer being paid, and John discovered that he had basically been working for nothing for years, but he didn't care, he said, as he had his cottage and everything he needed. The gardens that he worked on at the many local estates were his hobby he said, not his work.

The trustees, a Mr Swanston and a Mr Gleadow, came to inspect the estate the week after the family left. They talked to John about their expectations, which were as Mr Walker had said, just to basically take care of the house. They told both John and Cook that they both worked for them and not for Henry and any requests or complaints should be addressed with them directly.

They then spent a great deal of time with Henry and travelled around inspecting the livestock and the pastures.

Henry came in later and told Cook to expect an influx of workers in the next month as the trustees were keen to ramp up profits on the estate. That was good, thought John, as the trees were now laden with fruit and there had been no one to pick them. Cook was also to get two kitchen maids, which pleased her immensely.

Before Jarvis left, he and John put dust covers over all the furnishings and closed all the curtains and doors to the rooms that were not being used. Then it would just a matter of keeping any dust and tarnish at bay.

John stayed in his workers garb all the time now and had carefully cleaned, ironed, and stored away his footmen's uniforms.

In the afternoon's Henry and the men were out working, and after he had helped Cook with anything that she needed, John would usually go for his regular walk after lunch for about an hour, and then come back and spend the afternoon reading. The library still had many books that he hadn't got through yet. He also started to write lesson plans on all kinds of topics, with pictures and diagrams and a list of resources that he would need for each lesson. He would also write poetry. It wasn't very good, but it made him feel happy as he only wrote about happy things.

He often sang songs that he had learned from church and songs he had learned from Amelia.

And he sat and missed Amelia.

He missed Jarvis as well. But mostly he missed Amelia. Her voice, her laugh, her conversation, her sass. And the feel of her skin against his.

At night he wrote her letters and sometimes poems. By the end of each week, when he would take the buggy to Longford to post and collect the mail, he had a dozen letters for her. He also collected the newspapers that were still being sent to *Vron*. That gave him something to read for the next day or so.

On Sundays he made a trip for church services. He would usually now go to Longford, where the Reverend Davies, who had been on the convict ship with Amelia was now building a magnificent place of worship. He would still go to Westbury where St Andrew's had finally finished being built, and the Reverend Bishton always liked to have a chat with him about gardening. Old Sammy looked after the church garden there as well.

Henry and the men didn't go to church services. Some of the free and Ticket-of-leave men, including Henry, took the buggy on Friday afternoons and didn't get back until Saturday afternoons or Sunday mornings. John could tell they had been drinking and up to no good, probably in Launceston. Henry and his men had gone a bit wild in the past year and now they had a group of new men from all kinds of backgrounds and most of them quite rough. Henry didn't even try to tame them very much. John had a bit of an understanding of why. Often Henry would sleep in the men's quarters which was excellent for John, as his room didn't need any attention then.

One Sunday morning they were back late, and John had been concerned because if they didn't get back in time, he'd be late for services. He could have walked but it was too late to start. On arrival Henry sensed his frustration.

"I don't know why you bother with that tripe Harris, if there was any God he sure as hell wouldn't have ruined my father and our family like he has." Another time Henry said to him, "Harris, you know you are better off than me, who would have thought? You could get a good job anywhere or run your own small farm, you have skills. What have I got? An upper crust English accent and basic farm knowledge! So much for that expensive education, what?"

Henry laughingly told John to take the pick of any of the rooms that he wanted because there were, "Only ghosts in there now!" Henry told him to choose one of the rooms for himself, but John preferred his cosy room near the kitchen. It now reminded him of his time with Amelia.

Bushrangers were still an ever-present danger and John always kept a rifle on him or near him. So far, though, the only intruder had been a crazy possum one night that had somehow got into the house and had John leaping around in his breeches in the middle of the night, rifle in hand. He screamed when the possum flew at him which brought Henry and some of the men running, then they all had a great time laughing at him, "You better bloody stick to your women's chores, eh Harris," said Henry, not unkindly.

John realised that his life was very good, and with no one to answer to daily, he was his own man. His life was not too dissimilar to what it had been in London. There was of course the constant foreboding about the future, but even that wasn't much to worry about. Every time he went into one of the villages several of the wealthy landowners asked if he would be interested in a position. The trustees were putting his wage into the bank and John checked it on occasion. Within a year or so he would have enough to purchase his own small farm if that was what he wanted to do.

But he did miss Amelia, he certainly did miss Amelia.

## Chapter Eighteen

# *1841 – the Frogmore adventure*

*I*t was about five weeks since the Walker's had left *Vron*, and towards the end of October. John was sitting on the side veranda, in the middle of a warm day, when he thought that he saw dust being kicked up by someone on foot. This was quite unusual as even old Sammy rode his horse to *Vron* now that he was getting on in age. Perhaps it was one of the men coming back from an odd direction from out at the paddocks. Fairly unlikely though. Bushrangers! John had stupidly left his rifle on the kitchen bench. He raced inside to get it and made sure that he had enough shot in case he needed to use it.

He went back out to the veranda and hid behind the chairs and watched the figure as it ambled along the road and then up the driveway. Suddenly he realised that it was a woman. Well, there were woman criminals, but it was very rare here in Van Diemen's Land. The poor woman had a limp and was carrying a bag over her shoulder. Her bonnet had once been white but was now stained with brown dirt.

As she got closer to the house the woman lifted her bonnet, to see how close she was. Oh My God, thought John, it's Amelia!

He ran down the steps and down the path to greet her, as she collapsed into his arms.

"Oh, my dear, Oh, my sweet, what has happened to you Amelia?"

"Water," was all that she could say.

He carried her into the house and down to his room, where he placed her gently on his bed. He wasn't sure what was going on, but his senses told him that Henry probably shouldn't know that she was here. He raced back into the kitchen and grabbed a jug of water and a glass and took it into Amelia. Cook was off having her afternoon break and the girls were busy in the garden, so no-one saw them. He lifted Amelia's head and helped her to drink. At first, she tried to gulp it but then almost threw up, so he slowed her and only allowed her tiny sips. After she had drank her fill, her head fell back, and her eyes closed. John sat with her holding her hand while she slept. What on earth had happened to her? She was supposed to be safe with the Walker's.

Henry and the others arrived back at the men's quarters as the sun was setting and Amelia was still asleep. John had been checking on her every hour, but she was sleeping peacefully. When dinner time came around and John sat down to eat with Cook and the girls, he couldn't keep it secret any longer and quietly took Cook to his room.

Cook gasped when she saw Amelia. She was still sleeping but it was obvious that she was worse for wear. Cook told John to be quiet because until they knew what had happened it was best to keep the girls and Henry out of it. After the girls had left the kitchen, Cook made soft vanilla rice pudding, the same as she had made for Miss Lemaire after her seizure.

The stars were out by the time Amelia woke. John quickly told her that they would have to whisper as they couldn't risk Henry hearing them. If what he suspected was true, Henry would be obliged to take Amelia into the Factory.

Slowly Amelia's story came out. They had arrived at the new house, which was made of mud bricks and had only eight rooms. It had been built by a farmer who had gone broke, and Mr Walker had got it at a good price. There was a cow and some chickens, but the kitchen garden was all dead and the block was heavily treed making everything feel enclosed and eerie. A small stream was the only place to get fresh water from, and none of their furniture fit into the rooms of the small farmhouse.

There were no towns around, and they only passed through two small villages on their way over two days. Mr Walker said there was a small village on the coast a few hours away. There were also few farmers, the ones that had been there had left recently as the land was found unsuitable for livestock or crops.

Miss Lemaire and Mrs Walker started crying as soon as they saw the house and had barely stopped. Both Mr and Mrs Walker quickly became short tempered and mean as the days went on and their new circumstances became apparent. The children were no better, refusing to listen to Amelia or their parents. If pushed, they would run off into the bushes and cuss from the trees.

Miss Lemaire suddenly became much worse and could no longer use the toilet, and it fell to Amelia to change her napkins and clean and feed her. Mrs Walker stopped eating for a while and Mr Walker begged and yelled at her and then yelled at the new convict girl and Amelia to do something.

All of that was fine by Amelia, she was used to bad tempers, but then Miss Lemaire started to bite, pinch and hit her when she was trying to help her, and then Mrs Walker did the same when she lost her temper about something one day. That was it. Amelia was damned if she was going to hang around in the middle of nowhere with that bunch of ill-tempered wild things and let herself be beaten. She'd rather be looming and sewing back at The Factory. She only felt regret at leaving the other poor girl there with them.

Amelia knew that she'd be found by Henry sooner or later and that she would have to go to the Factory, but she asked for a few days of peace to recover from the journey. Mr Walker would take longer than that to get back to *Vron* if he cared to chase her down. With everything going on at the new house he was more likely to just send a letter to Henry and the Factory. Before that, Amelia said, she would be much obliged if John would drive her into Launceston to give herself up.

Amelia arrived at the Launceston police watchhouse two days later. John went in with her to vouch for her character, but the constable was not interested. As far as he was concerned, she was just a plain convict absent from her master, and that was a heinous offence. All John could do was wave to her as she disappeared into the gaol with her new captors. She was charged the next day, sentenced to six weeks of hard labour, and marched across to the Factory. She had left her belongings with John so had little on her which meant less to be stolen.

She had only been away from the Factory for less than three months so many of the faces were familiar. This time instead of being in with the main population she was sent straight to Third Class, the group sentenced to hard labour, and down to the laundry. Her days were filled with picking apart old tar-laden ropes and washing them in tubs, to be passed onto the girls on the looms. Her hands were soon red raw as the spikey rope cut into her flesh.

Each group of women were strictly segregated but could see each other during the seemingly never-ending church services and communicate using facial expressions and lip reading. Sometimes notes could be passed at church if the women were smart enough, but getting caught meant a flogging or a demotion to one of the lower classes or down to the laundry where Amelia now worked. There were no male prison guards, and the female guards were mean, most had only recently moved from the Factory as prisoners, to their present work having no skills to make them assignable and revelled in being cruel to the women. There was no Mrs Fry here, thought Amelia, no Miss Kezia either.

The women were keen for news from the outside, but Amelia had nothing much to tell them, apart from the fact that it seemed that some of the wealthy landowners were going broke due to the depression. Most of the women who she arrived with from the *Rajah* seemed to be gone now.

The week after her arrival Amelia was overjoyed to see Maggie Speirs from the *Rajah*, arrive in the laundry. They both saw each other and gave each other a huge smile. That was all that was possible because silence was observed at the gaol. Amelia remembered the women on the ship who had come from Millbank and how forlorn they appeared, like they had lost all hope. They even shaved the heads of the women in Third Class who were in for longer terms, but lucky for her she wasn't one of them. But the silence drove her mad. The women would take the opportunity to quickly pass on news during hymns at church services, and at night after the matron had gone to her room it was possible to quietly whisper to each other.

Misconduct was met swiftly with harsh punishment. Some women were even flogged. Maggie told Amelia that her master had flogged her like a man but hadn't used the cat-o-nine tails which ripped flesh apart. Amelia was shocked to hear this was going on, as she had really had a fairly easy time, and the bad temper exhibited by the Walker's in her later days with them was understandable. She just wasn't going to stay around and be a punching bag. She wondered how the little convict girl Jane, was going, poor thing. Maggie told Amelia that she had quickly become popular with the men at her new assignment and was greatly welcomed in their quarters on Sundays when most of the household were at church. Her Sunday 'work' gained her sly grog which helped her days to go by more easily while she worked in the pig stye and dairy.

Six weeks went by. Christmas came and went with the additional church services and Christmas hymns and just a bit of plum pudding and custard in the days ration of tasteless gruel to mark it as Christmas day.

Amelia with her sore, swollen hands, found herself escorted to the assignment office on the day after her sentence expired. She wasn't sure what to expect. She was still assigned to Mr Walker, but he may have decided to hand her back and get someone else, or worse he might want her back at Frogmore. However, she let her breath out with relief when, as she walked into the office, there were John and Cook, waiting for her. It took everything for her not to run over and hug them, but instead she just gave them a smile and diverted her eyes to the ground to stop herself looking too excited which might gain the ire of the guards.

John completed the paperwork and then led Amelia out to the buggy that was waiting on the street. Then they all had a hug. Cook had tears in her eyes.

"Oh, I never slept one wink, knowing youse was in 'ere my girl." She clutched Amelia who eventually had to wriggle out of the tight embrace so that she could take a breath.

As they drove back to *Vron,* John explained what had happened. Mr Walker had told the trustees that he didn't want Amelia back and had procured another convict girl from The Factory who was now up at Frogmore. The trustee's, however, knew that Amelia was already familiar with *Vron* and were happy to have her back, but assigned to them.

"They told me to speak very bluntly with you about not running away again, mind you." Said John with a glint in his eye and a half smile.

"Oh John! Cook! I'm so very happy, you cannot ken how happy that makes me!" her Scottish came out in her relief.

It was starting to get dark as they pulled onto the pathway at *Vron*.

"We've got a little surprise for you Emma," said Cook trying to contain her excitement.

Amelia could hear music and smell delicious cooking smells. Suddenly she recognised the music and remembered what day it was. Hogmanay!

John stopped the buggy at the stables, not the front of the house, and as they got out, they could see a big bonfire out the back of the men's quarters. There must have been a hundred people down there dancing and singing Scottish tunes that Amelia knew well. There was a long table set out that was covered in food of all kinds, but not the fancy food that the Walker's would have served, but simple meats and vegetables, pies and trifles, the likes of which Amelia had known growing up at village celebrations. And all along the table were bottles of what Amelia thought must be whisky, especially by the atmosphere at the party.

"You know," said John, "that many of the men are Scottish? And there are a number here from the other farms around as well. Over there are the McTyre's from the village and there are the Fraser's from Westbury, they come and help at harvest time."

Soon several attendees came over to meet and greet Amelia and handed her a mug of whisky which she gratefully sipped. What a difference 24 hours makes she thought. And how kind of John to arrange this for her. He must know that she missed some of the Scottish traditions, although that was about all she missed. She didn't have rosy memories of her past like it seemed John did. From the limited talks that they had had about their backgrounds, John waxed lyrical about his time in London, while Amelia usually changed the subject.

Cook noticed her hands and went inside and brought back a jar of wool fat and sat in front of Amelia and gentle rubbed the gooey mass into her sore hands, "There lass, that'll make you feel a bit more comfortable, and they will be good as new before you know it. I've had several girls here over the years who've been on the rope at The Factory. A cruel job 'tis."

The whisky and the hand massage had made Amelia feel quite lightheaded and when the musicians started up one of her favourite ballads, she couldn't help but go and stand with them and sing the song that they were playing. It was a low and slow ballad about hard times, and everyone stopped their partying to listen to the words. Whether they had come free or as convicts it seemed that everyone had a memory that they could relate the song to and they all swayed soberly raising their mugs every now and then until the ballad finished. Then the band struck up some dancing tunes and everyone was back into it, whooping and hollering, dancing their jigs and singing along.

Both Amelia and John were kept busy chatting to the attendee's, some who worked at *Vron* but who they had never spoken to, being men from the workers quarters. They could see that some of the men had obviously invited young ladies to the celebration and as well as some elderly parents that were also there, the mix was quite an interesting one, and it was a lot of fun. No one had any airs or graces on. Amelia wondered what John made of it all, but he seemed to be just as happy as her, catching her eye every now and then smiling. He was busy making sure the tables were full of food and the bottles refreshed with new ones. A good footman, thought Amelia, giggling. But he was also chatting with the guests, which was good.

Later on, things started to slow down, and some of the guests began to leave in their buggies, or retreated to canvas tents that Amelia imagined some of them must have brought so that they could stay the night.

John appeared behind her and for a moment startled her. He had a bottle of something and a rug under his arm, and he gently took her by the hand. He gestured to the hill behind the house, the hill where they had their first kiss. Amelia nodded her head with excitement, of course she wanted to go up there with him again!

They trekked half-way up in silence listening to the fading music and voices, and just enjoying the peace and the smell of the bush.

"I'm afraid that the lights won't be here this time," said John.

"Oh, that's all right John Harris," Amelia winked at him, "there'll be other things I haven't seen for a while that I'm sure you won't mind showing me again," she laughed and ran a little way up the hill, with John hot on her tail.

At the top they fell to the ground puffing and laughing.

And then they kissed. A long, deep lingering kiss that felt as if they were expelling all the pent-up worry and emotions of the past couple of months. They finally surfaced for air but only long enough for John to lay the rug on the ground and stand, silhouetted by the moonlight as he removed his clothing until he stood naked and vulnerable in front of her. She stood in front of him and let him gently remove her clothes as well and then they sunk into a deep embrace on the rug, where their bodies and minds became one for the next hour and no words were necessary.

Later, they lay on the rug, half dressed and watched everyone packing up and going off to bed. They noticed a few other couples paired up as well.

"Where's Master Walker?" said Amelia suddenly, surely Henry wouldn't stand for this behaviour.

"Oh Henry," said John using his first name, "well for a start he's up with his parents at Frogmore for Christmas, should be back here soon. And Henry," he made sure that he enunciated the first name, "couldn't give a fig anymore to be honest. The trustees are paying him to oversee the men and the farm operations, what happens in the house, they leave to me, and to Cook as far as feeding everyone goes. It's very different around here now." Amelia nodded her head in appreciation of the new situation.

"The new girl Amy is now with young Oliver from the quarters, they are both still under sentence but they are in love so there isn't much can be done other than to give them the usual warnings. He only has a year to go until his Ticket-of-Leave, so hopefully they can marry after that." He looked at her with a strange look in his eyes. "I let them use Jarvis' old room," he looked searchingly for any hint of reproval, but he saw none. Amelia thought it was great how things had turned out. No more stuffiness.

"The trustee's do expect a high level of output though, so when it's worktime everyone knuckles down to do their best. We all know how good we have it. They doubled my salary! I guess they know how many other landowners have been vying for me to work for them!" John gave a rare chuckle.

"I guess I've ruined any chance we had to marry then?" Said Amelia forlornly.

"Well, I wouldn't say that exactly. I guess now they probably wouldn't be too open to approve you to marry but do well by the trustees for a few months and then let's see what happens. Maybe you can apply around Easter, and we can set the date for September. A beautiful Spring wedding!"

Amelia threw her arms around John. He had been thinking about their future, and a future together! Amelia could see all her hopes and dreams for her future, all the dreams that she had dreamt while sleeping on the streets in Edinburgh, were coming to fruition. Her plan for a better life had worked!

"We just need to be careful for now Amelia," said John seriously, "the men have told me about what happens to convict women if they get with child and it's not good at all. You'd be sent back to

The Factory, forced to give birth there, and to stay until the child is weaned and then do six months of hard labour, and nothing can stop that from happening. The law has become very strict with that now," he looked at her suddenly with concern, "you haven't fallen already, have you?"

"No!" said Amelia shocked, "I'm sure that I'd know if I had, although it weren't for want of trying before I left last time!" She winked at him, and he blushed, smiling.

Serious again he said "Well this time we will have to stop, to make sure that nothing gets in the way of us marrying. Once we are married there will be plenty of time for that, and for babies and for our life together," he leaned over and kissed her passionately, feeling his body rise to betray the words he had just spoken.

"John Harris?" said Amelia cheekily.

"Yes," he gasped, struggling for control.

"There be other ways to have pleasure without the worry of getting with child," she cooed and gently pushed him back onto the rug. "Close your eyes, man, and let me show you just one of those ways."

Within seconds John's body exploded with such strong feelings of passion and pleasure like nothing he had ever known and as he fell into a blissful trance, feelings and sensations that he never thought possible exploded in his mind, his stomach, his legs, in every part of his being. And in amongst this trance and this passion, he had sense enough to think that his life was better, oh so much better than he had ever imagined it could be.

Chapter Nineteen
# *1842 – Consequences*

$\mathcal{A}$melia moved back into her room in the women's quarters

with Cook and the two new maids, Amy and Jessica. Amy had only just turned 16 and was the one being courted by one of the workers, Oliver Johnson. Amelia made a note to talk to her about ways to not make a baby.

Amy came from London. Her father was a printer with a penchant for gambling. When he died in a bar fight during a card game, her mother found herself penniless and forced to collect dog droppings for the tanners, the lowest of the low work possible. Poor Amy was caught pick-pocketing a handkerchief to buy food for their dinner. Amy liked to talk. About anything and about everything. She loved it when John read out the papers, lapping up the gossip from London especially. She made Amelia laugh but made Cook pull her hair out. She preferred a bit of peace and quiet in her kitchen.

Jessica was in her mid-twenties and was the opposite of Amy. Jess was plain and quiet as a church mouse. She would cringe if anyone brushed past her accidentally. Amelia sensed that she had had a hard life, but so far had been unable to find out why. As soon as her work was done for the day she escaped into the women's quarters. She liked to knit and crochet, and John had been buying needles and yarn for her with her meagre earnings, secretly supplemented by him. He said that she could take the items that she made, mainly baby clothes and doilies, to the village and one of the store owners might purchase them from her.

John had started his lessons again in the men's quarters. Things were much more relaxed now. Jess attended the lessons and so far, was the best student in his class. Some of the men scoffed at the lessons but all of them gathered around when John read out the weekly newspapers each week. John told Amelia that she would be very welcome to come along and help him with the lessons.

The women undertook most of the domestic chores, tending the vegetable garden, looking after the dairy and the chicken coop and the endless laundry. But Cook had put her foot down with the trustees and said that her girls would no longer be mucking out the pig stye. If the men wanted bacon, ham, and pork, one of them could be put in charge of caring for the stinky pigs, AND the stye was to be moved further away from the quarters. Cook said she was just as happy to make lamb or chicken every night. Henry had soon capitulated to her request and moved the pig stye and assigned one of the men to take care of it. When Amelia arrived, the latest pig had just been slaughtered and was currently in the smoking shed being turned into delicious bacon and ham. Roast and pickled pork had featured heavily on the menu since she arrived.

Mealtimes were now very different. Everyone congregated in the big room in the men's quarters where four large tables were set up seating ten people at each. Everyone was responsible for their own crockery and cutlery and would form a line and follow each other into the kitchen where Cook and the girls, now including Amelia, had put all the food into large pots and platters for them all to serve themselves.

Henry, or John in his absence, made sure that the men had all washed before they came into the kitchen, and inspected them at the door, and also made sure that Grace was said before anyone started eating. After the meal the men washed their own implements in the basin in the big room, before settling in for reading or board games or whatever entertained them. The women were welcome to join in as well if they wished. After they had cleaned up the kitchen, Amy usually went to the big room for a while and spent time with Oliver and his workmates. Cook would also usually go for a while before retiring for the night. But Jess went straight to the women's quarters unless it was lesson night. The only things banned during the working week were gambling and drinking.

The weekend after Hogmanay, John said that he had another surprise for Amelia and also for Cook. He told them to put on their best dresses, which, for Amelia happened to be the one that Mary Beswick had given her to dress as a governess when she first arrived. Cook came out of her room on the morning of their adventure wearing a most beautiful dress in the shade of a lavender flower with cream lace accents and a matching bonnet. Amelia gasped. Cook rarely came to church and Amelia had never seen her dressed in such an outfit. John donned his suit, and they left in the finest buggy early in the morning.

On the way, Amelia tried to guess where he was taking her. Her first thought was that they were going to the Beswick's house. Amelia had not spent much time with them, but she knew that John considered Thomas to be a good friend, and they were heading in that direction. It was a fine day, and the horse was travelling well. Within an hour Amelia gasped as they turned into a most beautiful estate. There was an impressive sign out the front of the estate, similar to the one she had seen when visiting the other estate with Mr Walker when she first arrived. This one said *Brickendon.*

"Oh, my goodness, we are visiting Mr Jarvis!" said Amelia. "But are we allowed to?" she asked. Cook too was excited, they hadn't seen Jarvis since he'd left *Vron* over two months before.

Cook and Amelia all but leapt out of the buggy and then raced to the other side when Amelia saw, to her disbelief not only Jarvis but Miss Hayter and Maggie Miller, one of the girls from Edinburgh, who had also come out on the *Rajah*, as well as another girl who she recognised from the *Rajah*, she thought her name was Elizabeth. Amelia rushed over to Miss Hayter and curtseyed, looking up into her eyes.

"Oh, none of that Amelia, what has happened to thee?" Miss Hayter laughed.

"Oh, I'm so sorry Miss Kezia, I am just so happy to see you, I have had a horrible time."

Kezia Hayter gave a withering look to John and Cook.

"No!" said Amelia quickly, "not by them". She realised that everyone was around them and now was not the right time.

Jarvis came forward and gave her a hug and then she saw the Reverend and Mrs Davies approaching as well.

Introductions were quickly made, and Jarvis then led them all to a beautiful rotunda in the grounds outside of the main house.

"Mr Archer has made this available to us for the morning," he said, "tea and cake will soon be served."

It turned out that Mrs Davies was the niece of the Mr Archer who owned *Brickendon* and as Miss Kezia was not having a wonderful time with Lady Jane Franklin in Hobart, the Reverend had invited her to join them for Christmas in the north.

Everyone settled in to catching up and sharing news. Cook, John and Jarvis gathered together to talk about the happenings at *Vron* and Miss Kezia and the Davies' were eager to find out about how Amelia had fared.

She told them about how happy she was at first at *Vron* and of course how wonderful, John, Jarvis and Cook had been to her. And then she told them about the Walker's downturn in fortune, the episode in Frogmore and her recent time at The Factory.

"Oh, my dear, do not let this dishearten you," said Miss Kezia, "the Lord has a few more trials for you I can see, but Amelia you are strong with The Spirit, and you will overcome this trouble with the help of our Lord. Let us pray." Miss Hayter then led the small group in a short prayer for Amelia. Amelia was not too fussed by it but was glad to unburden herself of her story. And Miss Kezia and the Davies' seemed sympathetic.

Amelia had been happy to know that Maggie and Elizabeth were doing well at *Brickendon* and the Archer's didn't seem to be troubled by the depression, luckily. They told her that another of their shipmates, Georgiana Gatehouse was assigned to one of the other Archer brothers estates called *Woolmers*. Amelia told them that she had been to *Woolmers* when she first arrived. Georgiana was one of the most industrious workers on the *Rajah* so Amelia wasn't surprised that she had received a good assignment. There had been two Elizabeth Slater's on the *Rajah,* funnily enough, and Elizabeth told her that the other was at *Woolmers,* and it could get a bit confusing! Sarah Turton who was envied for her amazing cooking skills on the *Rajah*, was also at *Woolmers* cooking up treats for the Archers now. Maria Feans was also at *Brickendon* but had sadly been too busy with her duties to join the tea party.

Miss Kezia confessed to the girls that it sadly appeared that the good work of Mrs Fry was not being embraced very well in Van Diemen's Land, despite her arrival and discussions with the Franklin's and others in authority. While they seemed to acknowledge the benefits of the policies that Mrs Fry was able to get implemented in Britain, there was not much of an appetite to help the women once in the colony.

The tea and cake were lovely, and a wonderful time was had by all for a couple of hours. They were even treated to a walk around the grounds with Jarvis explaining all the sights. The garden really was impressive, thought John, even more so than *Woolmers*, Mr Archer's brother's estate. All too soon it was time to go and there were hugs all around.

As they drove off down the road, and were out of sight from the others, Amelia turned and gave John a big hug and a big kiss.

"Ere you two, enough of that with old Cook here around." They all laughed and had a lovely trip back to *Vron*. The Reverend Davies had made John promise that he would encourage the workers at *Vron* to come and attend his services at Longford, hoping to expand his new congregation. They had talked for a considerable length of time and Amelia could see that the Reverend was impressed by John with his genteel manners and intelligent conversation. The Reverend was a keen horticulturist and had brought a collection of plants with him on the *Rajah*. He was a member of the Launceston Horticultural Society and was very interested to learn about the work at *Vron* of John and old Sammy. He told John that he would be very pleased to visit *Vron* soon and see the gardens.

The weeks marched on with the same routine that became easy and familiar. While Amelia slept in her room in the women's quarters, she often spent time with John in the library of an evening and then in his bed for a couple of hours before retiring to her own.

One night Amelia had just finished pleasuring John and he was lying back on the pillow catching his breath when he said, "Amelia, is there some way that I could give you pleasure too?" Amelia giggled, "Well of course there is silly, we all have parts that work in a similar way."

"But you don't have a part like I do." Said John in a confused manner.

"Oh no," said Amelia, "mine is inside." John looked more confused.

"Look, I'll explain it to you. My friend Maggie, in Edinburgh, used to work at the most popular brothel in the city and she told me all kinds of tricks. The girls would do it to each other in front of the men, who seemed to enjoy watching it as much as the girls enjoyed having it done to them. I can't say that I have actually had it done to me and there are a few ways to do it, so this will be a new adventure."

After Amelia explained the different ways, John threw himself into the tasks at hand with gusto, and from then on was equally happy to pleasure Amelia as she was happy to pleasure him. The nights could sometimes be exhausting, but in such a delicious way.

But as the months passed Amelia began to get more and more concerned. She realised that she had not had her courses since before the first night on the hill. She had brushed it off as being related to the changes in her life; her courses often stopped for a while when she was in difficult situations. But this time she also had very tender breasts and she was expanding at an alarming rate. Her waist had all but disappeared. Wearing the work garb, it was easy to disguise it, she just tied her belt more loosely. And at night she told John that she wanted to keep her garments on, except her britches, due to the cold. But by early May she felt what she knew must be the baby moving inside her, and once it started it didn't want to stop, hopping and jumping in there like it was dancing a Highland Jig.

It was the end of April before Amelia knew that she had to tell John, and Cook too, she would know how to help her.

Amelia waited until one night when they were alone in John's room and she shyly said to him, "John, there is something I need to show you," and started to remove her clothes. She hadn't done so for at least two months and John's eyes lit up with anticipation. But as her garments fell to the floor his lust turned to confusion as Amelia revealed her bulging stomach. He looked at her for answers.

"It's a babe John!"

"Oh," said John looking again at the bulging belly against her otherwise lean figure. Everything else looked the same, although her breasts looked enormous. He quickly stopped himself thinking of such thoughts and brought his mind back to the situation at hand.

"What are we going to do? Why didn't you tell me?"

"I don't know," said Amelia bursting into tears, "I didn't want it to be real, this is everything that we didn't want to happen. This will ruin everything."

John put his arms and a blanket around her thin shoulders. It seemed that the pregnancy had overly expanded both her breasts and her belly but the rest of her was still as lean as ever.

"Cook will know what to do," said John grasping at straws, "she's a woman, I think she's had babies. She will know what to do. The main thing is not to let anyone else know. If the authorities find out they will arrest you and take you to the Factory."

He stopped and tried to think, "Tomorrow we will go to Launceston and you will submit a request to marry. I will go and talk to the trustee's first to get their approval and then we can go to the magistrate. I won't tell them about the situation though. Once we are married and you are assigned to me there's nothing they can do to you without my permission, and I would never let you be taken to that God forsaken place!"

Amelia nodded through sobs. They then dressed and as it was still quite early they went to find Cook.

She was still in the kitchen tidying up but the other girls had retired for the night. They told Cook about the situation to which she remained calm and although she gave Amelia a quick hug she quickly went into action mode. "Right you two, this is a secret, ya hear, no one else is to know about this or you risk it all, you understand." They both nodded, they understood all too well.

"Once you've got that marriage licence, then you'll both be fine, and we can look towards taking care of the mother here to make sure that all goes well with the birthing. I know a few of the women around who do the birthing work, but I won't even enquire yet until you get that licence."

There was not much sleep between the three of them that night.

The next morning John dressed in his suit and Amelia in her most modest convict attire. After a hearty breakfast to sustain them, they hopped into the buggy for the long ride to Launceston.

Chapter Twenty
# *1842 – The Factory*

*W*hen they arrived in Launceston, John went straight to the offices of Mr Swanston and Mr Gleadow. He explained to them that he dearly wished to marry Miss Laing and requested their support and a letter of recommendation for Amelia to take to the magistrate. He assured them that after their marriage Amelia would stay on and work for them but without pay as John would provide for her keep.

"Well son," said Mr Gleadow soberly, "I'm surprised that you're so quick to make this decision, but you are a man after all." He rubbed his forehead and looked over at Mr Swanston.

"Look here Harris," said Mr Swanston, "Miss Laing does not have a good track record, and we were hesitant to keep her on at *Vron* after her episode with the Walkers at Frogmore. However, if she is able to secure approval to marry you, I trust that you will be able to keep her in check?"

"Oh yes Sir," said John, "of course Sir."

"Well, there will be no setting up house in the big house, do you understand me?" asked Mr Gleadow, "you can remain living in the servants quarters or you can purchase your own house near the property, I know that Walker sold many small blocks on the boundary, and there are more available through us if that's what you want to do."

"Oh no Sir, I think we would stay at *Vron*, if that suits you, I will just take up the two rooms that Mr Jarvis and I have been using for all of these years."

"All right fine!" Said Mr Gleadow quickly writing his letter of support. He then passed it to Mr Swanston to sign as well.

"Good luck to you John." Said Mr Gleadow kindly, handing him the letter.

John saw them both shaking their heads out of the corner of his eye as he left their office.

It was then a quick trip to the magistrate's office. There were already a lot of people waiting with their own petitions, so John and Amelia took a seat and waited.

Several hours later Amelia was led into the magistrate's office. A quarter hour went by, and Amelia came back out, rubbing her eyes with tears streaming out.

"I was denied John, denied! He said that I need to show better conduct before I would be considered for a marriage licence!"

John threw his arm around her and hastened her towards the door. As he opened the door a big gust of wind blew in and pushed them almost back inside, at the same time blowing Amelia's light convict skirts against her body.

"Ere," called out one of the clerks, "that convict there be with child!" He blew his whistle, and John knew it was no use running. A constable came running in through the main door to see what the problem was.

The clerk explained what he had seen. The constable questioned Amelia and John and confirmed that she was a convict under assignment. The constable then grabbed her arm roughly and led her off into a side room. All she could do was cry out to John who was helpless to be able to do anything. The law was the law.

Amelia was shackled in leg irons and told to wait in a gloomy hallway, sitting on a hard wood chair that looked like a church pew.

She again waited for several hours but on her own now, with plenty of time to contemplate the fate that awaited her. Finally, a middle-aged man wearing a suit arrived and motioned her to enter a room with him. She shuffled in as best she could with her leg irons on.

The man motioned for her to stand in front of him and he then proceeded to lift her skirts. She tried not to flinch or to cry.

He felt around her belly and then dropped her skirts.

"Yes," he said, not unkindly, "definitely with child young lady. Due in a couple of months I'd say. Sadly, for you those months will be spent stitching garments next door," he nodded in the direction of the Factory.

He rang a bell on his desk and a constable came in. The doctor wrote a quick note and gave it to the constable, "Take this to the magistrate, constable." He turned to Amelia, "I'll be seeing more of you over the coming months young lady."

Amelia spent a night in a holding cell at the watchhouse with several very drunken women and two who had been arrested that day for other petty crimes. One of them had been caught after running away from a cruel master.

"He were a right bastard," said the girl who wouldn't be any older than 14, "old as the hills, and his wife were an old woman who could barely walk, and the old bastard would follow me into the dairy and try to have his way with me, I fought the old coot but he got to me several times. He might be old but he were strong still and still had a rod on him, may he burn in hell. His old lady, she'd be calling out for him as he were doing it to me. And then I just couldn't take it no more." A tear ran down her unblemished face. Amelia patted her on the leg.

"At least I 'ope he ain't got me with child!" She said sadly, then turned to Amelia, "Oh, sorry missus, I didn't mean to offend."

"No offence taken," she patted the girl on the leg again, "my situation is very different. This baby was made with love."

"Oh, that be good then," said the young girl, "I 'ope you get outta here soon then." Sadly, Amelia knew that probably wasn't going to happen.

Amelia was charged the next day and sentenced to six months of hard labour, to be served after her child was weaned, and she was to be retained at the Factory until then.

She was marched across to the Factory with the other poor wretches and went through the humiliating process of induction. During her last stay which was only for six weeks she didn't have to go through the full induction, and she saw her little cell mate from the night before, being led off with the others who had received short sentences. But Amelia was off to Third Class.

The women were all lined up and had their hair cut off. This was the terrible punishment meted out to the poor women who were from Millbank, and it took them months on the *Rajah* to heal from their trauma and come out of their shells. Oh, what torment, thought Amelia. Although personally she didn't care very much about the hair issue, hair grew back after all, many of the women were in severe distress, which was obviously the reaction the authorities meant it to have.

The guards again were all women, although most looked like men, and they appeared to all be permanently angry and mean. There'd be no opportunities for favours here, she realised.

The Third Class area where she was to live and sleep, was worse than where she had been last time, with four women to a mattress. The latrine and washroom was disgusting, the latrine was full and often overflowing and stank badly. Green furry moss and black mould grew on the walls where the water dripped. Everything was damp and cold and horrible.

As Amelia settled in and claimed her area she looked around and saw that there were several women who were noticeably with child. Even as far along as Amelia apparently was, it was easy to disguise the fact in the baggy convict garb. But she noticed one girl coming towards her who she vaguely recognised from the *Rajah*.

"Emma!" said the woman, "Emma with the angel's voice, how is ya then? Hannah, it's Hannah, remember me?"

"Oh yes, Hannah how are you?" said Amelia, not really remembering much about her at all. She seemed to recall that she had been convicted with another girl of stealing mugs from a tavern of all things, but it wasn't their first offence and in England, that meant transportation.

"Well, I'm not that great am I, look at me?" she held her skirts down against her body to show off her enormous belly.

"Oh," laughed Amelia, "so am I!" and held her own skirt against her not so huge belly.

"Hahahaha," laughed Hannah, her red hair sticking up in spikes all over her head, "looks like we've both had a good time! But to be honest I thought I was more likely to see Chrissie or Mags or Jane or Lizzie or one of the other naughty girls, rather than you."

"Yes, well," said Amelia, "apparently when ye play with fire ye going to get burnt eventually."

The women shared their stories. Hannah's story was similar to Amelia's. She had met a young man at her assignment, and they had played with fire as well. He was still in his first year of his sentence so there was no chance of them being allowed to marry. And Hannah had been charged twice early on with drunkenness – the men shared their sly grog with the women, so what was a girl to do? Hannah got found out early in the piece and had been in the Factory for four months already.

"Doctor says I'm fit ta burst very soon," she laughed, "and look at me!" she pulled her dress across her belly again. They both laughed.

Hannah told Amelia that until it was time for the baby to come she would be working as a seamstress in Second Class. This was fine by Amelia, as she'd done that plenty of times before now. The work was long and hard, but you got to sit down, said Hannah. The food was terrible, worse than it had been at Newgate she told Amelia, but Amelia already knew this from her last little visit. She actually thought it was better, as they always got a decent meat ration whereas at Newgate if you did get any meat, it was fatty scraps. The services were long and boring as usual, and the only thing they were allowed to read was the bible. They were allowed to write if they had paper and ink, but the Matron read all the letters before they were sealed, and it was hit or miss if they ever got to who they were being sent to.

But the worst, Hannah said, was the silence rule. The only time the women were able to talk freely was this hour before services and dinner, after that and at all times they were not allowed to talk, and if they were caught, would have their heads shaved again and be put on bread and water rations, "Except not us, they can't risk being seen to starve unborn babies."

Amelia settled into the prison routine again, but this time, much like when she was in Edinburgh, she knew that it would be for a long time. Babies wean around six to nine months the others told her, but then she'd have to serve her six months of hard labour in Third Class after that, and that would be back in the laundry washing or doing the ropes again. For six months! She was looking at being in here for over a year!

About two weeks later Hannah was struck by the pains around midday and was escorted out of the workroom and off to the nursery. The nursery was in a different part of the prison and the women were usually never seen again in Second class which was where the sewing was done. Months later they would appear in Third Class and start their six months sentence. Some of the women had already been through this process, some more than once. How terrible, thought Amelia.

And once the mothers had left the Factory she was told, the babies were left in the nursery until their third birthday, and then they would then be sent to the Orphan's school. A lot of them didn't get there though, as so many died at the nursery. It was rare for a mother to actually get to collect a live, healthy child after their convict sentence had expired.

Three more years at worst case, thought Amelia. Hopefully by then she could get her Ticket of Leave if she stayed out of trouble, or if she was lucky enough to get a marriage licence, they could pick the child up then. She had already started to bond with and feel emotions for the squirming creature in her belly.

Letters were given out after the Sunday service and before dinner. The women had to open the letters and parcels in front of the snarling guards, and any contraband was taken from them. The guards also read the letters before they were given to the women in case there were any plots being made.

Every Sunday since she'd arrived Amelia received a package and a letter from John. He told her that when he got back to *Vron*, Cook and the others were desolate. However, they had been spending their time turning Jarvis' old room into a lovely nursery for the child when they could finally be brought 'home.' Jess was busy as a bee knitting baby clothes and even Cook had started to learn so that she could also make some gifts for the baby. In each package was a baby blanket, some booties, or a little jacket, as well as new paper, ink, and quills for Amelia to write back with. The baby was going to need these warm clothes, she thought, as it was due to be born in mid-winter, and she didn't expect that the nursery would be a warm and cosy place.

Towards the end of July Amelia was preparing for bed when she felt a warm wet sensation running down her leg. She looked down and there was a puddle of liquid on the floor below her. A few of the women squealed and jumped away from her, but one of the older women came and put her arm around her and called out for the Matron. She sat Amelia on the bed as a huge pain gripped her around the belly.

Matron came over and shushed all the women, who had started making comments and encouragements to Amelia. It was silent time. She told Amelia to grab her belongings and follow her. Amelia's meagre belongings were already stashed in her prison issued bag, which she grabbed and followed the guard. They left the Third Class dormitory through a door that she had never been through before and entered a long wide corridor. As they got towards the end, she could hear children crying and calling out. The noise got much louder as they opened the door. The door opened to a large room. It had concrete floors and plain walls with small windows on the outer wall side. Several lanterns lit the room and made eery shadows on the walls and ceiling. Matron's desk sat near the door and to her left there were several beds with what looked like curtains on low free standing curtain rails.

Off to the right against the wall were about a dozen beds with small tables next to them, and prison bags neatly tucked under them. She hoped this meant that she would have her own bed. One woman sat on a bed feeding a small baby, and Amelia was very happy to see that it was Hannah. She resisted rushing over as the guard was talking to Matron about her. In the centre and around the room set out in rows were multiple cribs, with multiple babies in them. They ranged from tiny newborns to toddlers standing on the side trying to get out or just crying. The women who Amelia assumed were the mothers were going from crib to crib trying to soothe and settle them. There were a lot more babies than there were mothers.

"Nurse," called the stout Matron, "got one for you." The guard left and a small, pretty woman in a nurse's uniform came to greet Amelia.

"Ah, here you are then lassie," she took Amelia gently by the arm and led her to one of the beds that had the curtains, "now dinna fash yeself lovey, we'll have that baby outta you in no time." Amelia was comforted to hear her Scottish accent.

Amelia could hear a distant scream coming from beyond another door behind the examination beds. She looked worriedly in that direction. "Now dinna worry, lass, there's only one other girlie having a baby tonight, that is just her getting ready to birth it. Is this your first babe lass?" She looked at Amelia questioningly, and Amelia nodded. She guessed it was unusual to have your first baby at 28.

"Right let's have a look at you then." The nurse, who told Amelia that her name was Annie, helped her up onto the bed and closed the curtains. She felt around Amelia's belly, "That's good, lamb, baby is lying headfirst, ready for a quick escape." She gave Amelia a long, steady look. "Well, it dinna seem like things be happening quickly, lass, and it could be hours and hours being a first birth, so why don't you settle in over there, matron will allocate you a bed, and we will keep an eye on things."

Matron actually seemed quite kindly as well, certainly more so than the matrons and guards in the other areas. She led Amelia over to the bed next to Hannah, who on seeing Amelia leapt up, with baby attached, and gave her a big hug.

"Seems ye know each other already," said Matron with a half smile, and in an Irish accent, "Hannah here will show ye all ye need to know, Amelia."

Vron

"Oh, it's Emma Ma'am, people call me Emma."

"Righto, Emma it is," she turned and went back to whatever she was doing at her desk.

"Oh Emma, it's right good to see ya," said Hannah, "look here's me little Johnny." She passed the plump baby across to Amelia.

Amelia looked at the floppy baby and felt at a loss as to how to hold him properly, but Hannah showed her how to hold his little head and nestle him into the crook of her arm, and soon little Johnny was gazing up into her eyes and coo-ing softly. Amelia looked on in amazement. The tiny but perfect little face! The rose bud lips blowing little milk bubbles as he coo-ed. He was adorable.

Suddenly she was gripped with another pain and winced, gripping onto Johnny tightly. He didn't seem to care and snuggled in closer.

"Another one, ay pet? That's good hey, it means your babe is on its way, but I got to warn ya, them pains are gunna get closer together and a lot worse before the babe is ready to be born."

Amelia looked at her with a look of horror realising that this was it. She was actually going to have a baby, and very soon. Either that or she was living her last few hours on this earth. Either way she knew that she was in for a rough time in the next hours.

She looked around the room. The other women all seemed to be going from crib to crib trying to settle the babies. But there were definitely not enough women for all the babies. One woman sat against a wall on a rug with about a dozen small children gathered around her. She was singing some kind of poem, and the children were making hand motions. At least they were quiet, she thought.

In the opposite corner sat two women, one with a toddler on her lap, the other telling a story to another group of about a dozen toddlers.

The other women went from crib to crib patting the babies on the back or picking them up to try and rock them to sleep.

There was one stout woman sitting in a low chair near Matron's desk, nursing a small baby, but her heart didn't seem to be in it, she looked half asleep, and Amelia saw Matron nudge her as the baby almost fell from her arms.

Hannah saw Amelia looking. "That's old Madge, her baby died a few months ago, failed to thrive sadly, and she had such a supply of milk that she opted to stay here as a wet nurse rather than serve out her sentence in Third Class."

"Oh, so that's not her baby then?" asked Amelia.

"No love, that baby there, she belonged to young Ann, only 14 when she come in here with her huge belly. We heard her screaming for two days, and then the doctor came and the screaming stopped. The baby survived but poor Ann, she were too small to birth a babe. We had a little service for her the next day."

Amelia was horrified and sad at the same time. Of course she knew this happened, it was just confronting to see it in real life.

"How many mothers die, Hannah?"

"Oh not many, lovey, there's only three ere what's mother died birthing them, two more whose mothers have died since then, the bloody flux you know, it runs through the whole nursery when one person gets it, takes the babes and the mothers!" This was not helping Amelia to feel any better.

"Why are there so many babies and so few mothers?"

"Well, pet, once the babies can suck the milk out of the bread and chew on a bit of meat, they's considered weaned and the matron sends for the guards to take their mother away to the prison again, but to the hard labour this time. The children stay here until their third birthday, and at that time the Orphan school takes them, unless their mothers have been back since to collect them. It does happen you know, the mothers finish their sentence and come and get their child. The ones who live close and have good masters who allow them, can visit their children on Sundays. Sundays are always busier in here than normal."

That gave Amelia a bit of hope. Another pain gripped her.

"So's, for the rest of us still here, we earn our keep by caring for all the other babies that's mothers have left. Some of them babies weren't ready to wean or have their mother taken away and they just cry and cry. We usually just shove them onto old Madge's udders if they won't stop. That soothes them. They go through the teething here as well, and that's not a good time for the poor mites, some get the fever and the runs and all."

Amelia could detect the distinct aroma of vomit, urine, and excrement in the closed-up room. Similar to the taverns of a morning, she thought in disgust. There were two fires going at either end of the room, which took the edge off the bitter cold, but the further away one was the colder it grew.

She was pleased to see some toys against the back wall, neatly stacked on shelves. And some books as well.

Little Johnny had settled and nodded off to sleep. Hannah took him and placed him in the centre of her bed with two rolled up blankets on either side of him. "Better go earn our keep," she winked at Amelia and led her off into the jungle of cribs.

It was getter later and Amelia was having to stop and catch her breath every 5 to 10 minutes. The length of the pains was also getting longer. Every time that she had a pain it was accompanied by an emission of warm fluid again, but not as much as the first time. She had to keep going back to the nurse for a new towel to place in her britches.

The baby soothing job certainly wasn't onerous, and Amelia felt a bit of joy in her heart as the little ones stopped crying and slowly drifted off to sleep in her arms or as she patted their backs. Slowly but surely the noise in the room started to calm until only the story tellers could be heard. Their charges were a bit older and easier to settle.

Suddenly Amelia realised that she could no longer hear the woman screaming either, she went quickly over to Hannah. "Is she all right do you think?"

"Hush lovey, we'll find out soon enough."

The children were all popped into their cribs and the exhausted looking women all drifted slowly over to the mother's area. Hannah introduced them to Amelia as they arrived, but they all looked too tired to talk.

And just when they thought the babies were all asleep one would wake and start crying again. Someone had rescued the last baby, who was sleeping soundly, from old Madge's ample bosom, and put them into a crib. The woman closest to the crying baby went over to it and tried patting it, then when it didn't work, and the crying got louder she picked it up roughly and brought it briskly over to Madge.

"Wake up ye old hoyden," she whispered poking Madge in the arm, Madge stirred and grasped the new baby to her breast. It latched on eagerly, but Madge's head dropped back, and she started to snore. "Damn you," whispered the other woman, "I'll have to sit here now so ye don't suffocate the poor babe." Some of the other women who had seen the exchange chuckled. "Don't you be laughing Annie Myers, it be you next gotta sit with this lump o' lard."

Hannah quietly told Amelia that old Madge was simple in the head, "Not much smarter than one o' these kiddies here," she pointed towards the older children's cribs, "she's been in here four times they say. Her master be a brute and he let the men have their way wit' her. Over and over the poor thing. No sooner is she out o' prison then she's back in with another brat cooking. One o' the other women we had in here who was from the same place said the master knew she kept getting with child, but he kept her there until she was almost due to drop every time, to keep the men happy. 'E were letting six o' them a night at her, apparently."

Amelia shook her head, but she knew the ways of some men, and was not shocked, just saddened.

An hour or so later, the nurse, Annie, came out to check on Amelia and saw that she was bending over the bed with Hannah rubbing her back.

"Not long now then lassie, just let me get young Polly out here and settled and I'll take you in to get this baby out ey?"

She scurried off back through the door behind the curtains. Soon she came out again leading a young girl who held a wrapped bundle to her chest. Annie led her gently over to one of the vacant beds and all the women who were awake let out little cheers and 'Well done love', 'what did you have deary?' "Ah it's a bonnie wee lassie, girls.'

The nurse settled Polly into bed and tucked a towel under her bottom. She scurried back behind the curtains and came back with a fresh jug of water, a mug of hot tea with a biscuit of all things! And it looked like shortbread! This pain will be worth it if I get a decent shortbread, thought Amelia with a giggle.

The nurse then brought something wrapped in a towel which Hannah told Amelia was a stone heated in the coals, to help with the after pains. Hannah then explained those to Amelia. Amelia wrinkled her nose in distaste.

The women who were still awake gathered around Polly and her new baby girl and coo-ed and clucked away.

Amelia was suddenly struck with a pain much more severe that the others and her knees crumbled under her.

"That was good timing," said Annie. She scrambled up from where she had been helping Polly to get the tiny new baby to latch on for a feed and hurried over to Amelia.

"You better come with me now Emma, say goodbye to the ladies, you'll see them all again soon enough." Amelia waved limply to the woman who whispered encouragements too her as she walked off with Annie. This better not be my last walk, she thought with a sudden pang of fear. That pang was quickly replaced by a very sharp gripping pain at the base of her belly.

Annie led her through the door into another large room. This room had one tall window at the end and then on one side were multiple washing troughs against the wall, and several clean beds against the opposite wall. There were many closets and a few tables containing lotions and potions and towels and whatever else a nurse needed. There was also a desk with some books and papers stacked on it. The doctors desk Annie explained.

"Have ye seen the doctors much?" she asked.

"No," said Amelia, "only that once at the watch-house, when he sentenced me to here," she rolled her eyes.

Over the next couple of hours Amelia filled Annie in on her story, somehow it all seemed to come out easily when she was in excruciating pain.

"Oh lass, if only you'd been able to keep it a secret, a lot of girls do you know. Mostly the ones who get pregnant to their masters. The magistrate seems to turn a blind eye and give out marriage licences quickly to them what's got money," this time Annie rolled her eyes.

"But it's all good pet, you'll have a nice 6 months in 'ere and it's not all that bad, cuddling babies all day, there's worse work you could have!" They both laughed until the humour was taken away by Amelia having a deep and sudden urge to push, like she had been gripped with the flux and her insides wanted to turn inside out.

"Right, up on the bed then lovey. We'll get this gear all off yay, you'll feel free-er without it." Annie proceeded to strip Amelia of her clothes, to which she didn't give a hoot, being in such agony. When she got onto the bed she had an urge to get up on all fours for some reason; a reason that was beyond reason and was more of an animal instinct.

"That's right lass, I can see from that direction as well, so I can."

Amelia let out a howl like a wounded beast, incapable of stopping the noise from escaping her lips. Ah, she thought, this is what poor Polly was howling about.

"Well done my girl," said Annie, "I can see the wee ones 'ead so I can, it's got a thatch of lovely dark hair lassie."

Amelia let out another unearthly scream and pushed with all of her might feeling an overwhelming sensation to get this child out of her body. She no longer heard Annie, just the sound in her head of her own rapid heartbeat and the unearthly howls that she screamed.

"All right lassie, baby is popping its wee head in and out and in and out but what we need is for you to push extra extra hard to get that little wee head out. That's the last big pain you'll have lass, so this time you go for it, you 'ere?"

Exhausted, all Amelia wanted to do was to collapse onto the bed and cry but feeling another contraction coming on she mustered all of the strength that she had ever had and pushed with all of her might. Suddenly she felt the pain go away and a very, very odd sensation like her insides were slithering out of her body. She looked back behind her and saw Annie holding what looked like a skinned rabbit up by its legs and then realised it was over and that was her baby. Annie worked quickly and shook the tiny body gently, coo-ing encouraging words. She then gave the baby a quick tap on its bottom at which time it came to life, started to squirm and then let out a long mewling noise, that quickly turned into a full-blown baby cry, as Annie quickly handed it to Amelia who had rolled onto her front. Annie quickly went and grabbed a knife and a length of twine and came back to Amelia and the baby.

Amelia gazed down at the thing in her arms. It had now stopped crying and was gazing up at her, its eyes slowly opening and closing against the offending light, its tiny arms making clutching movements, and its little mouth opening and closing as if practicing for its first meal. Amelia noticed that it was a girl. She smiled down at her newborn daughter and a name came into her head.

"She's going to be Emily," Amelia said to Annie, "John and I never got to discuss it. I think I'd like her to be named after me, but not Amelia, which is my real name, or Emma which is my street name, but Emily, that's kind of a twist on my names."

"Emily it is then lass," Annie patted her on the arm after covering her in a warm blanket that had been heating by the fire. She opened the blanket and took Emily, who was still lying quietly taking everything in, from her mother, and placed her naked on the bed next to Amelia. She then proceeded to examine the baby, and prodded and poked her, looked in her mouth, turned her over and checked her spine. Emily did not like this very much and started to howl. Amelia felt a pang of anxiety.

"It's all right mother, this will give Emily a good appetite," she then expertly tied a clout around tiny Emily and then wrapped her tightly in a swaddling cloth. Emily stopped her howling and settled down again, her tiny eyes darting around looking at everything.

Annie lifted her up to Amelia who had now settled back onto the mountain of cushions at the head of the bed. Annie placed Emily near Amelia's bare breast, and the baby, sensing food, opened her mouth wide and started throwing her head from side to side, looking for the food source. Annie showed Amelia how to grab her tiny head and hold it still and lead her to her breast. Within a minute Emily was happily suckling, and Amelia had a sigh of relief that it was all over, and they were both still alive.

Chapter Twenty One
# *1842 – The Nursery*

*A*melia and Emily settled into life in the nursery. It was July and it was bitterly cold, so no-one missed going outside very much, although Annie and the other nurses grumbled that the fresh air would help the babies and mothers thrive and may prevent some of the many illnesses that ran rampant through the crowded, stuffy room.

Emily progressed and took to breast-feeding well. She had settled into a nice four hourly routine, which Annie said was ideal. Amelia heard the nurses arguing with the matrons about the quality and quantity of food being provided to the mothers and the children, saying that the mother's rations were not enough to sustain a small woman, let alone one who was feeding another.

1842 was the peak of the depression and everyone was feeling the pinch, not just those in the prison. Meat, eggs, and milk rations had been cut and meals consisted mainly of bread and gruel, sometimes with a few vegetables and a bit of chicken mixed in, or on really good mornings, some honey drizzled on the top for breakfast. There were no rich joints of meat with gravy and baked root vegetables that had become Amelia's staple meals at *Vron,* as well as delicious cakes that both Cook and sometimes John made with love. Oh, she missed good food! But she had certainly lived on less, and at least her clothes had loosened!

Vron

Every week at least one or two new women arrived to give birth and one or two left to serve their sentences in Third Class, as the doctor deemed their babies to be weaned. It broke Amelia's heart every time to see the absolute devastation of both the mothers and the babies when they were parted. The babies knew and they just cried for days and days. There was a lot of cuddling to be done by the mothers left behind. As Hannah had told her, many of those babies then regressed and went into a type of baby melancholia. Some of them got sick, almost overnight. From being happy thriving babes with their mothers, it was like they just lost hope.

Amelia witnessed the first baby's death within the first month. It was one of the babies recently parted from its mother. Little Albert had been a happy, thriving child and was pulling himself up onto the cribs and a few times had almost let go to try to walk but had thought better of it and dropped onto his bottom. His mother, Agnes, had named him after the Prince, Queen Victoria's husband, hoping to invest him with good fortune.

His mother had left to serve her time in Third Class the week after Amelia arrived. Little Albie just regressed terribly almost overnight. No matter how many cuddles the women tried to give him he remained desolate and refused food. The women took him over to the older children who loved playing with the babies, but even then, he remained terribly sad and refused to play. Even when the children sang funny songs to him, he could only muster a small smile, before sighing deeply and looking sad again. He started to lose weight rapidly and the nurses were concerned, tempting him with toast with honey or jam. He would sometimes lick the honey or jam but refused the bread. The nurses were too busy with all the other babies who were teething or had coughs and runny noses or had developed opthalmia with red, sore eyes that made then howl in pain.

The doctors came regularly to check the mothers and the babies, but other than recommending different foods, warm baths, and cuddles there was not much that they could do in the cramped conditions. With so many babies teething, the scent of oil of cloves hung in the air, almost stifling the smell of rancid milk, vomit, and poop, but not quite. For mothers and children who were very restless from pain or sadness, the doctors would sometimes prescribe milk of poppy, which at least made them quiet, although Amelia worried that they might not wake up again, and she was told this had happened before.

Finally in desperation Annie told the matron that little Albie would have to be put on old Madge to try and get some sustenance into him. But even though poor old Madge tickled and coo-ed at him, he refused to feed and just looked up at her sadly.

One morning Albie just didn't wake, and when alerted by one of the mothers, Matron went over and examined him, then wrapped him in a bundle, with his little face covered and disappeared into the nurse's room with him.

"Awww poor little mite," said Hannah sadly.

"Is he dead?" asked Amelia rubbing the sleep from her eyes and preparing to position Emily for her first feed of the day.

"Yes, he is lovey, you'll get used to it. Just hope that ye aren't here when one of the epidemics runs through this joint. In my first few weeks the flux went through, and we lost eight babies in one week, and one of the mothers. I was near beside meself with fear, I didn't want to touch none of those other children, fearing that Johnny and I would be next."

Amelia realised that she and Emily were sitting in a literal room of death. With no way to escape to the outside for fresh air or to get away from everyone else, everyone in the nursery was just trapped and waiting for the diseases to get them! Still, what could she do? Nothing! So best to try not to think about it and to just get on with the work at hand, trying to stay healthy and keep these children alive.

Mary Johnson from the *Rajah* came in a few weeks after Amelia and gave birth to a little boy, and then in early October two other women, Sarah Esp and Sarah Wetherell from the *Rajah* came in, two days apart from each other. Sarah Esp named her little girl Amelia and laughed when she found out that it was Amelia's real name as everyone was used to calling her Emma. Sadly, Sarah Wetherell's baby didn't survive its birth and dear Sarah was also very unwell, from both fever and melancholia, in the days after the tragedy.

With nowhere else to put the mothers who were grieving, Sarah was put in a bed at the end of the row of mothers, seeing them cuddling and nursing their babies. She cried and cried and Amelia, Hannah and the others went over frequently to sit with her. Amelia had started to put her voice and story-telling skills to good use and would sit and massage Sarah's hands and sing her pretty songs in Gaelic. Nurse Annie was the only one of the staff who knew Gaelic, but several of the mothers did, and Amelia would often add a few funny verses with naughty words to her songs which lifted the spirits of those who understood. When the laughing peaked the English girls would ask the others what she had said and then they too would share in the laughter.

Laughter was good in the nursery, because the women's laughter would transfer to the children who would also laugh, even if they didn't know what was being said. Laughter was a universal medicine, thought Amelia, and you didn't even need words to spread it.

Poor Sarah had just gotten over the fevers when Matron sent for a guard and she was hastened out the door, off to Third Class to work off her 6-month sentence.

"It wasn't always like this ye know," said nurse Annie one night as she was sitting with the women after most of the babies had drifted off to sleep. The nurses would come around at night if there were no babies to be birthed and check that the mothers were well, and that their babies were feeding properly.

"Twenty years or so ago, when the colony first started here in Van Diemen's Land, the Governor wanted people to have lots of babies. And there were so few women at the time, even if you were a new convict, if you took up with a free or a ticket-of-leave man, or even better, a soldier, the Governor would not only assign you straight to him, but would usually grant you both a conditional pardon within the year, and he would also give a land grant to the man, as well as convicts 'on stores' to help him to build and maintain the farm. The government would then buy the produce to feed the soldiers and convicts. That is how a lot of our successful farms and families came about. Back then it was a joy and a blessing for a woman to get with child in the colony. And look what they've done to ye all now!"

The women shook their heads. It was hard enough for the women like Amelia and Hannah who had known what they were doing and played with fire, but for the other women who had been raped, especially the ones not long out of their own childhoods or worse still children themselves, the current system seemed to be harsh in the extreme. But when they considered what some of the men went through for petty indiscretions such as insubordination or tardiness it didn't seem to be so bad, they guessed. The men were put in the stocks or the evil treadmill in the main street in Launceston, where people threw rotten eggs and tomatoes at them while they toiled all day in all weather, for days on end. They were also lashed, sometimes with the cat-o-nine tails, an evil whip with sharp metal on the tips to slash open flesh. Many men didn't survive these thrashings.

There were, of course, the usual church services, brought into the nursery for the women. However rather than every day, the services only happened on Sundays. On Sundays the mothers would gather the children around and try to keep them from crying or running off, as the Reverend gave a very concise and summarised sermon, often trying to make it into a story that the little ones could relate to. It didn't work very well, and services usually terminated when the din from the crying children became too much for the Reverend, who left quickly, covering his nose in a failed attempt to stop his disgust at the foul smell of the nursery.

In October, not long after poor Sarah had left the nursery, a huge commotion was heard one night. There was screaming and howling coming from the main prison. It sounded like a group of women, and it sounded like they were outside of the main concrete walls, as usually they couldn't be heard from the nursery. Everyone stopped to listen and try and figure out what was going on, even the children were silent for a time, listening to the odd commotion. Soon the sound of the constable's whistles rang out and the threats and the swearing of the women was joined by threats from the constables.

Matron put the bolt across the nursery door as a precaution and told everyone to get on with their usual routines. As the commotion went on for hour after hour Matron finally got up and told the nurse on duty that she was going to investigate but to bolt the door behind her and only to open the door for her when she returned and no one else.

The women waited in eager anticipation to see what had happened.

Matron came back about an hour later and told them that "some of the silly hoydens," where unhappy about something, so had decided to protest and then tried to escape. "Don't worry, it will all be over soon, get back to your work. We'll keep the door bolted for a bit longer though."

The 'protest' went on for two nights. Later, after she was free, Amelia read a report on the incident in a local newspaper:

> *The Launceston Examiner, 22 October 1842:*
>
> *FEMALE FACTORY - "The Revolt of the Harem" was played for two consecutive nights during the week, not on the boards of a theatre, but in the female penitentiary. In imitation of the cast bales, whose harps by transmutation became lances, the "factory ladies" armed themselves with the spindles of their spinning wheels, and nobly defied both superintendents and constables, " It seems one of the fair sisters was placed in "solitary," and this excited the others to rebellion. On Thursday night, the officers in charge were afraid of an escape, and constables*

*surrounded the onside of the building at every point, but the eighty females, however well acquainted with other branches of military warfare, could not succeed in scaling the walls, and they consequently reunited in the citadel like bees, inclined to swarm, but forcibly detained in durance. According to one of the theories of "Scriblerns," the soul of a woman resides in her tongue, and these amazons would have furnished him with sufficient proof to sustain his views: the noise of their yells and hootings and execrations disturbed the neighbourhood and were distinctly heard at a considerable distance. Several strange stories are afloat in connection with the "revolt." One respected gentleman, it is said, endeavored to quell the tumult by his presence, but he was hastily snatched up by some half decent viragos, and amidst the plaudits of the whole party, was forcibly borne on their shoulders round the inner building, and safely deposited at the place where he was taken up: from which he made a speedy retreat. We understand the solitary cells have been filled with the recusant females, and a number have been lodged in the goal, and quietness has in a measure been restored.*

Every now and then a parcel would arrive for Amelia. John and Cook, with the help and support of the Reverend Davies and Miss Kezia, would send items that Amelia said in her letters that she needed. Food, the only thing that they really needed, was banned, as were books, newspapers, and anything sharp. But baby clothes and blankets, toys and children's books were allowed. Fresh towels and clouts and soap and combs were also a welcome addition. All the women, as well as the matrons and the nurses were all very grateful to Amelia and her supporters on the outside.

Amelia and the other women from the *Rajah* told the others about the work of Mrs Fry, and that Miss Kezia was hoping to bring such reform to the colony. They all knew of Mrs Fry, having come from English prisons, and most fondly remembered her little packs and the tickets on red ribbons that they all still kept as proof of their identity. But many of them who had come out earlier were not lucky enough to have had a matron such as Miss Kezia onboard with them and certainly not a kindly Reverend and his wife. They laughed that it sounded like the *Rajah* was a pleasure cruise, next to what they went through on ships captained by cruel masters and crueller guards and sailors. Amelia and the others realised how good they had had it. But it didn't seem like Mrs Fry's work was being embraced here. Far from providing the women with useful lessons that could help their future prospects, the women here were just treated as slave labour. While in the nursery, the nurses, and even the matrons, were quite kindly, the rest of the prison was not like that at all, and the women were treated very poorly.

In December several other *Rajah* women arrived and had their babies, and then over half of the mothers were *Rajah* women. The parcels from Miss Kezia increased, along with a letter from her to the women, to try to instil hope in them, and small bibles with words of hope and support that Miss Kezia had written herself.

The nursery had a continuous turnover of women, and they were traumatised by the continuous onslaught of innocent deaths. Amelia stopped trying to befriend every woman who came in and also stopped trying to care so much for the little children because it was too painful when the women died or left to go to Third Class, and the children left to go to the cemetery or the orphanage.

Deaths were not even acknowledged as they happened but were summarised in a list at the Sunday services. A short mention by a Reverend and an unmarked grave was all that marked the lives and deaths of all these beautiful women and children, made to go through this awful tragedy.

As much as the frequent tragedies upset everyone there were also happy times. The third birthday of one of the children was celebrated with the others old enough to understand, and the birthday child was given an apple and a piece of shortbread as a treat. The children had all grown up knowing that their third birthday would mark the end of their time in the nursery and that they would be going to some mysterious place called the Orphan School where they would be taught lessons and how to behave so that one day, they could be useful in society. It was a right of passage for these poor mites who longed for a mother who most of them didn't remember and wondered with fear and trepidation what the Orphan School would be like, and if they would even see their little friends again.

As Emily grew and began to engage with those around her, Amelia started to run the little reading, singing and play groups for the older children. It helped Amelia to keep her mind active and not dwell so much on her awful situation and kept Emily happy as she sat laughing at the children who in turn made funny faces at her and brought toys over for her to grasp and chew on. There was a little dance group that Amelia had arranged, and Matron was happy so long as it didn't get too out of hand. The group had so much fun that often the other mothers would also come over and join in.

Sometimes the children played by themselves and Amelia or the other mothers just sat to supervise them. She was constantly accosted with questions about the Orphan School and life outside the nursery. She tried to give them answers that would please them and not make them more concerned, but she realised that many of the children had never seen grass, never seen plants, never seen trees or streams or horses or coaches, and once they were taken out of the nursery it was going to be a big, confusing, and scary thing for them. She tried to prepare them as best she could by describing all the things outside of the prison. The children listened to her wide eyed and marvelled at the things they would see once they left these four walls where they had been born.

Some of the older children were lucky and their mothers were able to visit them on Sundays, a joyful and then sorrowful thing to watch, but that was few and far between. It seemed that for many, the women who had birthed them had either died or had abandoned them, seeing their future as being easier without a child to raise.

But every now and then, on rare occasions, perhaps six times since July when Amelia had arrived in the nursery, a child would be summoned by Matron, and one of the mothers was told to prepare them for their release. On these joyous occasions their mother had been granted her Ticket-of-leave or had been assigned to or approved to marry a man who allowed them to have their child with them, or even rarer a family member had petitioned to adopt the child and been approved. Due to the huge number of convicts that made up the population, there were not many with extended families yet in the colony.

The children were not reunited with their mother in the nursery but taken by the nurse out through the main door never to be seen again. These happy occasions provided some degree of hope for the mothers left behind.

Not long before Christmas the matron told the women that old Madge's time was due to end and her master wanted her back so she would be leaving before Christmas. That would leave the nursery without a wet nurse, which wasn't ideal and if one wasn't found it would mean that all the mothers may need to share the job of feeding other people's babies. Some of them didn't mind and had been doing so already, but it was an opportunity for someone to stay in the nursery rather than go and slave away in Third Class, washing endless laundry or pulling apart ropes.

One of the older women put her hand up. "I've birthed me 21 babies, so feeding more won't be a problem." It turned out that of the 21 children that she had birthed only four had survived past their second birthday in Cornwall, and she had left those four behind with her sister when she was convicted of stealing a belt buckle from a house where she was employed as a scullery maid, two years ago. This latest child was the product of a relationship with another convict at her assignment, who she hoped to join up with again once she was released. "But I'm no spring chicken and standing on me feet all day is unbearable nowadays, easier to sit here and suckle poor babes."

There were 44 children in the nursery over Christmas 1842, which was marked with the singing of Christmas hymns and stories from the bible about Jesus' birth, and then on Christmas day each person, mothers, and children alike, were given an apple and a gingerbread cookie as well as a small meal of real meat and vegetables rather than the usual gruel. The mothers even got a tiny plum pudding to cut into portions between them. Each got at least a mouthful of the delicious delicacy.

In January Hannah's time was up, even though she had tried very hard not to let Johnny eat any food so that she could stay for longer. But the doctor caught onto her and popped the sturdy baby into a chair and handed him bread soaked in broth, which he grabbed and munched down then put his chubby hand out for more with a very cute 'Ta?" to the doctor. Nothing Hannah could say could stop him from signing her documents to say that she was ready for start her sentence in Third Class.

Johnny was chubby and healthy and at almost nine months had started to say a few words and was crawling all over the place. He was a happy child and loved playing with the older children who all adored him as well, with his cute chubby face and charming mannerisms.

"Please, please Emma, I begs of ya, please take care of my Johnny! I'll be back here as soon as I can to get 'im back, I promise I will."

She looked pleadingly at Amelia who could see the desperation in her face, "Dinna you worry Hannah, I'll take good care of your boy." But she worried about whether she would be able to.

It broke Amelia's heart the day that Hannah left. There were the usual hugs and tears and then screams and hollers from Johnny after she left the room with her prison bundle. Amelia went straight over and grabbed Johnny from his crib and brought him over to her bed with Emily to try to distract him. They started doing some finger shapes singing to a little song, and then Amelia made some shadow puppets on the wall for them, but within a few minutes Johnny would just look over towards the door and reach towards it crying "Mumma, mumma," and start sobbing again.

Over the next few days Amelia tried to distract him as often as she could, and he didn't seem to be suffering the melancholia as badly as some of the children did. He seemed happy for one of the other mothers to pick him up and take him to the table for his meals and take him over for the activities.

It was stiflingly hot in the nursery coming up to February and even with all the small windows open the heat could be oppressive. The babies broke out in all kinds of rashes and the heat made the fevers from the teething a lot worse. It was terribly hard to settle them all to sleep in the thick, steamy air that stank of everything bad.

And then the bloody flux broke out. Before long the entire room was full of sick and dying mothers and children. Hannah had warned Amelia about such a situation, but she had so far not witnessed it en masse. The doctors were run off their feet trying to think of ways to stop the disease from spreading, but it was too late, everyone had it, even the nurses and matrons. The sick mothers had to raise their ailing bodies to go and change numerous clouts and try to force the children to drink some water or breast feed as many of the babies who still could be.

The doctor finally made the unprecedented decision to allow the mothers who were well enough, along with any children who were well enough, out of the building and into one of the exercise yards during the day while the other convicts were at work. Sadly, there were few who were well enough to take up the offer, although most of the mothers who could do, including Amelia, dragged their sick bodies outside just to gaze up at the sky for the first time in months.

But by the end of the week two mothers and nine babies had died just as the disease turned a corner and the others started to rally.

One of the babies who died was little Johnny Perry. When Amelia found him dead in his crib she fell to the ground, half mad with her own sickness and by the devastating loss. She wrapped him in a blanket and took him back to her bed where little Emily lay recovering from her own bout of the illness.

There Amelia sat rocking the dead baby for hours before the matron could make her hand him over. Amelia cried and cried and coo-ed over the little body, his eyes closed as if in a peaceful sleep, the long dark lashes lying across his chubby red cheeks. He was only 10 months old.

On Sunday as the service was said for the ten dead people from the nursery, Amelia wondered if Hannah knew. Had she been told yet? And if she had been told, how was she holding up? How could they expect grieving mothers to keep up the relentless work in Third Class!

Letters came regularly from John and from the Reverend and Mrs Davies. The Reverend had been to *Vron* and held a service for the workers, John said, to try and tempt them to his church. John wrote that many of the new men and the ones who Dryden bought were rough and ready older men who had come from hard lives and didn't have much faith in the church. But the Reverend was also there to look at *Vron* for other reasons that

John didn't know yet. So far there were no buyers and life went on as usual.

During Sunday services one steamy day in February 1843, a fire broke out at the Factory, later attributed to a lump of burning soot falling from the chimney of the kitchen onto the shingle roof of the surgery. But while the women in the nursery could smell the smoke and hear the shouts and whistles it was all over very quickly and didn't affect them.

John's letters told her that Miss Kezia and Captain Ferguson had set a date for their wedding which was to be held in Hobart in July and that she might be leaving Van Diemen's Land with him shortly after that, having become disillusioned by her inability to convince the authorities of the merit of Mrs Frys' methods. Amelia was very sad about that. She had seen how kind treatment and having productive work to do could change a group of rag tag street women into interesting and resilient women with hopes for the future. And equally here at the Factory she had seen the same women turned into desperate and hopeless wretches with dreams only of hatred and revenge towards their captors. She worried about what would become of these mothers once they finally left the Factory. She knew that for herself, the hard years in Edinburgh hadn't broken her, but seeing so much innocent loss and grief here in the nursery had definitely changed her, and she might never come back from that.

By April it was obvious that no matter how hard Amelia tried to hide the fact that Emily was growing up, her daughter kept thwarting her. Not only was Emily already saying all the usual baby babble, but the children had taught her all the animal noises, that they had been taught by the mothers, and she revelled in making the noises at all times of the day and night to make the children giggle and play with her. She was pulling herself up to standing already and it was hilarious watching her during dance sessions wobbling her bottom, made huge from the clouts she was wearing, and shaking her top half as she held tightly to a chair leg, or the arm of one of the older children. She would clap her hands and laugh in delight when the singing started and eagerly tried to join in.

But worse than that she had started to grab at the food that the children were eating and would find any scrap of food that had been dropped on the floor and put it straight into her mouth.

Amelia was terrified of what would happen to Emily one she was forced to leave her, and the day was quickly approaching. She wouldn't be able to hide her advancement for much longer.

She wrote to John to let him know that she was again going to apply to the magistrate for a marriage licence. John needed to take the application in on her behalf and to certify that he was a willing party to the marriage and had the means to support her. If the licence was granted Amelia would be allowed to take Emily with her when she left The Factory after her sentence was completed. At least that would be something to look forward to.

Amelia waiting eagerly for advice of the outcome of her request.

She was still waiting on the outcome when Doctor Maddox came around one day for his rounds and, after checking all the newborns and the sick children, his eye caught Emily being held by the hands by one of the older children as she stood and wiggled her bottom again to a song sung by the girl holding her.

"That's the Laing child isn't it?" he asked Matron.

"Yes Sir, that is correct," said Matron.

"It's mother is still here, isn't she?" he looked around the room and caught sight of Amelia trying to hide in amongst the cribs full of sick children.

"Well, that child is much too old to need its mother anymore. It's time for Laing to go and serve out her sentence. The sooner she gets that over with, the sooner she can try and get the child back."

Matron gave Amelia a sad look and motioned for her to come over and join them at her desk. Amelia knew that this was coming but was by no means ready to be parted from Emily. Tears sprung to her eyes but what could she do?

She trudged over to Matron's desk as if walking to the hangman's noose and stood quietly with tears streaming down her face as the paperwork was completed.

"Chin up woman," said the doctor, "Keep your nose clean and keep out of trouble and you'll have little, er…" he struggled to remember Emily's name.

"Emily," said Matron with a degree of irritation. Yes, it was true that there was a constant stream of babies both in and out of the nursery, but there was less than 40 at any one time and you'd think that the doctors could at least remember their names. Or maybe like her, he was so jaded from signing death certificates for so many of them, that he preferred not to name them and make them real.

"Yes, little Emily, you'll have her back with you before you know it."

Vron

That afternoon it was Amelia's time to say goodbye to her daughter. She was so distraught, but she didn't want to pass that onto little Emily who was still happily playing with the older children. Lunch was served and Amelia didn't try to stop Emily eating the food this time, getting a bowl full for her which she eagerly devoured, grasping each item in her chubby hands. It was then nap time and Amelia breast fed her daughter for the last time, watching her pretty little face as she gazed up into her mother's eyes for the last time in God knew how long. Emily's hair had grown into a beautiful mass of baby fine chestnut curls which Amelia stroked trying to embed the memory of her soft skin and her delicious baby smell into her subconscious so that she would always remember it while toiling away in Third Class.

Emily dropped off to sleep in her crib just as the guard arrived to take Amelia off to the Third Class dormitory. There were quiet but tearful goodbyes all around and then finally Amelia stepped through the door and away from her baby, her love, a piece of her own self that she was leaving to the will of God. She knew right then that she would never, ever get over the feeling of this day.

Vron

## Chapter Twenty Two
# *1842 – A Tragic Loss*

*A*fter John had left Amelia at the magistrate's office, he knew that there was nothing that he could do. He was completely bereft, but the law was the law and although John now knew some high-profile people in Launceston and surrounds, not even any of them could help him. Only last week one of the wealthier landowner's sons had caused a commotion at one of the taverns in town and had assaulted a constable who had come to stop the affray. He was sentenced to two days in the stocks, and there he was with egg running down his face, John saw, as he slowly walked down the main street to collect the buggy.

Back at *Vron*, Cook was eagerly waiting to greet a newly engaged couple and was distraught when John told her the news. It was very sad around the house for several weeks. But then Cook rallied and spoke to Jess and Amy and told them that while they waited for Emma and the baby to come home again, they could all spend their time making up care packs for her. Jess was excited that her talent was to be put to good use. Her baby items had been selling well in the village, and she was sure they would be welcomed by the mothers at the Factory.

Everyone had heard terrible stories about the poor mothers and babies at the Factory. They knew that the chances of bringing a baby home from there was slim, and that many of them died beforehand. But they had to maintain hope, for John's sake and their own. Still, just to make sure, John and the women diligently attended Sunday services, much to the Reverend Davies delight, either at Longford where he was based or sometimes at Cressy where he went after the Longford service every week. A few times he had even called into *Vron* and delivered a service for the workers in the big room. He was a busy man.

At *Vron*, things were again changing. Henry Walker had been offered employment as an overseer with Mr James Robertson who had extensive farming interests adjoining the *Vron* estate, but on the other side of the ever-expanding village. Unlike *Vron*, Mr Robertsons' farms were thriving as he had been pouring money into improvements and had gained several government contracts to supply crops and meat. He needed a good, experienced man to manage his interests. Henry left, taking several of the free and Ticket-of-leave men with him, not long after Amelia was incarcerated.

John was very happy to see Mr Dryden and several new men arrive the day after Henry left. He hadn't had very much to do with Mr Dryden previously but knew that he was a fair and competent manager and if anyone could be trusted with *Vron*, it was him. John knew that the trustee's didn't care very much if the property was profitable, they only wanted to maintain it in a saleable state to enable the best price when it sold. Maintenance, not expansion was the task for everyone left at *Vron*.

When they first met again John wasn't sure how to approach and speak to Mr Dryden. Last time he was just Harris the footman and servant, and in those days, John rarely spoke to anyone.

But Mr Dryden was very kind, greeting him warmly and shaking his hand. The trustees and Henry had appraised him of the situation at *Vron* and he told John that his agreement was to do what he could to competently manage the estate until such time as it was sold. The trustees were actively seeking buyers at present. Mr Dryden said that he understood that the farm was his domain, and the house was John's, and he didn't intend to meddle in John's business.

Mr Dryden took his bundle into his old room but was quick to tell John and Cook that he would rarely be staying the night. He told them that with the new arrangements he felt it would be better for him to have a separation from the men, and living and working with them would not provide that separation. Plus, he dearly wanted to go home to his wife every night if possible. He had been enjoying his retirement and it had taken a lot for the trustees to cajole him out of it.

John and Cook kept a close association with Jarvis and others from the *Brickendon* and *Woolmers* estates, seeing them at Sunday services. Invitations were often extended to John to attend events and activities at the homes of families around the area. He was still known as a very eligible bachelor, although his close friends knew this not to be the case. Jarvis had talked of John far and wide; of his talents and of his genteel manners and this was backed up by the Reverend Davies. Invitations to events held by the Reverend where some of the few that John accepted.

In early 1843 John received a letter to say that he had been recommended by the Reverend for membership of the Mechanic's Institute in Launceston. Jarvis had vouched for his skill in reading, writing, and teaching in all manners of literature, and his skill at cataloguing the library at *Vron* and the Walker's Launceston house.

Mechanics' Institutes had originated in Edinburgh, Scotland in 1821 and had soon spread to the rest of the British Isles and throughout the world. They sought to give skilled working men further education for life and work, providing lectures, classes, libraries and even museums. The Launceston Institute was conceived from other similar pursuits that had opened earlier with varying success, such as John Pascoe Fawkner's reading room, which he said was designed to 'soften otherwise barbarous manners.' This was followed by the Tasmanian Society for the Diffusion of Useful Knowledge which opened not long before John had arrived in the colony, and James Hill's Circulating Library that had opened in 1835.

John advised the trustees of *Vron* of his new membership, and they were very supportive. He knew that it would be good for them to have a member of the Institute as the caretaker at *Vron* and make it more saleable to good people with money. They told him that they were happy for him to attend meetings so long as they fit in around his duties at *Vron*, and that a buggy would be available for his use for the outings, as it was for other activities such as attending services and going to purchase supplies, although most of the time the household and farming supplies were delivered to *Vron*.

John attended his first meeting with trepidation but was warmly welcomed by other members who knew of his talents and of the influential acquaintances who he had made over the years.

He stayed the night at Mary Beswick's brother John McKenzie's hotel, the Scottish Chiefs, on the corner of Wellington and Canning Streets. The hotel was one of the more respectable establishments in the town. John was a confirmed bachelor and had a strong interest in horse racing, which was becoming more and more popular in the area. He was very different to his brother-in-law Thomas who was much more interested in the arts and intellectual pursuits, but he was always very welcoming to John, and he knew of John's situation with Amelia and cast no aspersions.

One family that John always accepted invitations from was the Beswick's. Although it was a long drive over the Paterson's Plains, John was always welcome and if there was a dinner or evening event there was always a bed available for him. The Beswick's also knew about John's situation with Amelia and the birth of his first daughter, which was of course celebrated in the Scottish tradition with a few drams of Mr McKenzie's now very old and rare whisky. The women who still sewed in the Beswick workroom always had a bundle of beautiful outfits for the new baby and Amelia whenever John visited.

John was visiting the Beswick's in April 1843 and told them that he had just taken in a petition for a marriage licence for Amelia on his latest visit to the Institute. He always stopped in at the Factory every time he was in Launceston and hand delivered the letters and parcels for Amelia, sadly gazing up at the high concrete walls, knowing that the two most important people in his life were stuck in there.

Mary Beswick excitedly told him that they were expecting again, probably around spring, which would just about coincide with Amelia's release from prison. They already had 11-year-old Mary Ann from Mary's first marriage, Tommy, named after his father, who was four, and Margaret aged two. Tragically in May 1840, their first child together, four-year-old daughter Margaret had died from tonsillitis, so they had named their youngest in honour of their beautiful, spirited first child.

John's visits to the Beswick's were always enhanced by his interesting chats with the two elderly members of the family, Thomas' mother Mrs Beswick who was 71 and Mr Brennan, Mary's stepfather who was 78. He loved hearing their stories of the olden days both in the colony and back in England. He so wished that his parents were still alive so that he could have these chats with them.

John, Cook and the girls were hoping and praying with all their might that Amelia would get her marriage licence so that on her release, she and John could bring little Emily home with them. One of the other mothers at the Factory who was an amateur portrait artist, had made a beautiful charcoal likeness of baby Emily and one of Amelia holding Emily. It was John's most prized possession and although he wanted to keep it all to himself, he found an old frame in one of the storerooms and placed the picture of Amelia with Emily in the kitchen for Cook to also admire.

John was devastated to learn in late April that Amelia's petition had again been denied. However, he was not surprised. It had been a long shot for a convict in prison for a secondary offence to be permitted a marriage licence. Even after pulling in all the recommendations that John could find, including one from the Reverend Davies and his wife and one from Miss Kezia Hayter, who kindly gave up her time to write a beautiful recommendation in amongst the preparations for her wedding, as well as separate letters from the trustee's this time.

In May 1843 John heard that the Jackson's, Mr Walker's daughter Marianne and her husband John Jackson, had returned to Launceston and moved back into their home *Rosetta*. Rumours circulated that Mr Jackson had been sacked at the colonial treasurer in Adelaide over some kind of misconduct, but it was all shrouded in secrecy.

John was sitting on the veranda one morning in the first week of June. It was probably going to be one of the last mornings where he could sit outside as the air was starting to get bitterly cold again. He had been sweeping the interminable dust from the veranda and enjoying a hot cup of tea when he saw an impressive carriage coming up the path towards the house. He knew whose carriage it was as he had seen it many times. He quickly ran inside and washed his hands and face and dusted off his pants as best as he could, while calling out to Cook at the same time to prepare some refreshments.

He rushed out the side door to greet the Reverend who knew now not to come to the front door as that part of the house was now closed up.

The carriage driver gave John a nod to which he responded, and he saw the Reverend slowly climbing out of the carriage, giving a hand to Mrs Davies who was with him.

The Davies' came around the carriage and John noticed that the Reverend had his hat in his hand.

"John," said the Reverend in a very low and sombre tone, "I am so very sorry."

No! Thought John. Not his Amelia. No! He could not bear it. He had already lost everyone in his life who he cared for most. He went to church every week when he was able to! Why would God punish him so much?

"It's not Amelia," said Mrs Davies quickly, holding her hand out towards him.

"It's Emily John, your daughter, she has been taken into the Lord's care John, she is peaceful now in heaven."

John did not know how to react. First, he was very thankful that it was not Amelia, but then the devastation of losing his first child, his first daughter, a daughter he had never gotten to meet, hit him. He almost collapsed and the Reverend grabbed him as his legs buckled and the Davies' helped him up onto the veranda and into one of the chairs.

Cook came out with a tray of tea and cakes just as they had settled John.

"Here you are then dearies, Oh, it's always such a pleasure and an honour to have you both here." Cook looked at the faces in front of her and, realising that something very bad had happened, took a deep breath, and gently placed her tray on the table so that she didn't drop it, before standing to her full height and clutching her hands in front of her.

"It's the baby, dear Cook," said Mrs Davies sadly, placing a hand on Cook's arm. Cook took a step back, blinking back tears as her own losses came back to her. As she thought of baby Emily a flash of memory that seemed so real brought a picture of her own beautiful young daughter into her head.

Cook went over to sit next to John who was in shock and had gone a shade of grey. She took his hand in hers and patted it slowly. There was nothing that could be said. How could you explain why the Lord would take a tiny baby. John had never even got to meet her.

Cook knew that it was very normal for the babies to die at the Factory not long after their mothers left them to serve their sentence. They died from broken hearts it was said, and that made Cook even sadder. Who breaks a baby's heart!

The Reverend did what he knew best to do, he pulled out his bible and led them all in prayer. He hoped that his kind words would give them all a tiny bit of comfort. They didn't.

The rest of that day went by for John on automation. At some stage old Sammy turned up at the kitchen door and was shushed away by the girls, after telling him what had happened. The Reverend went and spoke to Mr Dryden when he came in for the day, and he came inside and gave his condolences to John, who sat in a chair in the kitchen like a stunned mullet, unable to muster the strength to talk, even to the Reverend, who kept attempting to recite verses from the bible that he thought may be of comfort. It wasn't.

Before he left, the Reverend said that if John wanted, he would hold a service for Emily, either private or as part of his Sunday services, here or at either of his churches. He was unable to inter her, he said, shaking his head, as she had already been buried at the Factory in the convict's graveyard, and outside services were not allowed there.

Amelia still had five months left to serve of her sentence. How must she be feeling, thought John! His heart ached so badly as he thought of her slogging away in the damp, cold laundry in utter devastation at losing her child.

John went to bed that night and didn't come out of his room for two days. Every now and then Cook would tap on his door and call out to make sure that he was still alive, and after two nights had gone by, she took in a large jug of water and some toast with honey but found him lying on his side with his face to the wall.

"It's all right lovey," she said patting him on the shoulder, "you gets them sad's out. There ain't nothing out here that needs you right now. You take your time."

Jarvis arrived in a buggy on the third night. He greeted Cook and told her that the Reverend had been to *Brickendon* to tell him the news, knowing that John was like a son to him. He then disappeared into John's room. When Cook went to bed later that night they were still in there.

The next morning the two men emerged, went to wash, and came into the kitchen for breakfast freshly washed and in clean clothes. Cook was glad to see that John had shaved and the shade of grey had all but disappeared. Jarvis left not long afterwards, "Damn this place, it's such a common thing for a child to die, it's not seen as something that's devastating, just a fact of life. I was lucky that Mr Archer let me take the buggy and have the day off. I'll see you on Sunday at Longford?" Cook said that she would and saw him out.

She came inside, and John told her that he was going for a walk. Every day he went for a walk for about an hour, but he hadn't been for one of his long walks for a long time. Cook saw that he had his work boots on, so didn't expect him to be back for a while. She packed extra water and some hard cakes for him as well as a small jar or honey to give him energy, honey being the only sweetener still easy to procure, thanks to old Sammy setting up and maintaining the hives near the village.

As the weeks went by, John kept finding himself constantly dwelling on Amelia and Emily. It became an obsession and consumed his every thought. The work that he was doing meant that he was usually on his own and this gave his mind plenty of time to wander. And his mind was full of sadness and worry. What would Emily have looked like? Who would she have grown up to be? Would she have been spirited like her mother, or shy like her father? Oh Emily, he thought, if only I had been able to meet you, to cuddle you, to comfort you when your mother was cruelly ripped away from you.

And Amelia, such a funny, energetic, and stoic woman. How was she holding up? Would this tragedy have changed her? Would she ever recover from it? Would it steal away her spirit?

Cook made sure that John always came out to the big room to share his meal with the others and encouraged him to keep up his lessons and weekly newspaper readings.

"You might be sad, John Harris, but your lessons and readings be the one thing some of them men look forward to as well you know. You've known love at least, some of those poor beggars might never find a wife or find love, there ain't enough women here in the colony for them all."

John perked up before too long and was back to his old self, which was still quiet but not as sad as he had been. He commenced his lessons again. The men had suddenly become very interested in learning their numbers. He had heard that some of them had been ripped off in town because they didn't know how to add and subtract to make sure that they were paying the right prices. And with everything so tight it was important not to waste any money. He pulled out the coloured blocks that Miss Lemaire had given him and set about teaching the men who were interested, how to manage their money. This kept him busy and filled his mind with something other than his grief.

Not long after the bad news, a buggy arrived full of fresh produce, flowers, cakes, and linen, as well as several bottles of cider and Irish Whiskey this time, obviously the calling card of the Beswick household. A card passed on their sincere condolences and their hopes to see both John and Amelia soon after her return towards the end of the year. John didn't see the Beswick's at church as they preferred to attend St John's in Launceston, being closer for them. But he knew that every time that they made it to church, which was infrequently, neither of them being very religious, they would drop off letters and parcels for Amelia.

Winter dragged on and it was getting closer to Amelia's release date at the end of October. The nursery items were hastily packed away in a storeroom, and Jarvis' old room was turned into a cosy sitting room. Although John thought that Amelia might prefer some time in her old room in the women's quarters at first, he was hoping that they could be a couple on her return. It would be almost 18 months that they had been apart. John had to admit that he felt rather shy about being with Amelia again. Before they found out she was pregnant their relationship was hot and steamy with no care for repercussions, but now they had both been burnt and suffered the most terrible consequences, and doing it again almost scared him.

## Chapter Twenty Three
# *1843 - The Journey Home*

*F*inally, the day came for John to go and collect Amelia from the Factory. He was so nervous he could barely eat. Along with things for her comfort on the return journey, such as a warm rug, a basket of goodies from Cook, and fresh clothing so that she could get out of her prison garb, he also took copies of the letters from the trustees as well as his own, so that Amelia could petition the magistrate again for them to wed. He didn't want Amelia to think that now there was no baby that he no longer wished to marry her, as he wished that with all his might.

On the day, John sat patiently with the others who had come to collect prisoners in the quadrangle outside the prison gates and across from the magistrate's office. The prisoners came out in dribs and drabs and then finally he heard what he'd been waiting for.

"229, Laing." John jumped up and rushed over to the desk with his letter from the trustee's, who Amelia was officially assigned to, that noted that he was their representative to collect her.

He hastily signed the documents and looked up as she came through the door.

This was not the same woman who he had said goodbye to all those long months ago in the magistrate's office. This was a ghost of a woman, thin as a rake, her skin grey and dry, her hair hanging in thin strings from under her convict mop cap. She looked up and saw John, a tear running down her cheek, and raised her arm towards him. John quickly reached out to support her. They both looked searchingly into each other's eyes and then John quickly hastened her out of the prison area and across the street. John helped her into the buggy but realised that she was too weak and distraught to travel. She could barely speak.

Thinking quickly, he drove the buggy around to John McKenzie's hotel and stopped out the back, rapping on the back door, where he knew John's office and sitting area was located.

The door was opened by John McKenzie, a broad man about the same age as John. He only had on his shirt and no jacket and as he came outside, he stretched as if he'd just woken from a long slumber. But seeing John, and an obviously distressed Amelia, he sprang into action.

"What do you need man?" he quickly said, realising that they must have come straight from the Factory, as John helped Amelia out of the carriage and carried her in his arms to the door.

"If you don't mind, John, I think Miss Laing here needs a rest in a soft, warm bed and some good food to warm her up before we start our journey back to *Vron*."

"Of course, of course," said John McKenzie, "we can do better than that." He called out to someone inside the hotel as he ushered them in. He offered them seats in his office and then dashed off saying he'd be back shortly.

A short while later John came back to collect the couple and handed them over to a maid who ushered them up a set of narrow stairs. She opened an unassuming door and indicated for them to step inside.

"Johhny Mac be calling this one the 'Kings suite', "she said with a wink.

John looked around the expansive room, that must have taken up half of the top floor of the hotel. The room was exquisite. A giant four poster bed, made up with luxurious looking linens and multiple soft looking pillows was the centrepiece of the room, that also included a sitting area with two comfortable looking chairs and a low table with windows on either side to look out across the town, and a charming fireplace in the middle. But the thing that drew both of their eyes the most was the deep tin bath that sat on a low block of stone to protect the floorboards. And there was a constant stream of ladies coming in and out of the room now with steaming jugs of water.

"Now there, lassie, old Annie 'ere will take care of you. Wash away all the dirt from that evil place, ey?" old Annie must have been the head maid for the hotel, and she had a Scottish accent broader than Amelia had ever had. John looked at the activity in a bit of shock, but Amelia gave Annie a small smile and then all but fell into one of the chairs.

"And you laddie, you have some fresh clothes for your lass?" John quickly said that he had and delved into his bag to get them out.

"Right then lad, you go and see Johnny Mac now and he'll look after you while we look after your beautiful lassie here," she started to shoo him out the door, and he was a bit put out until he looked over at poor Amelia sitting there all wretched. She gave him a small smile and a wave as if to say, 'off you go, these women will take care of me."

As John closed the door behind him Amelia looked up at the women. Annie and two maids were busy preparing her bath and had even sprinkled crushed rose petals into it, which she could smell even from over by the window. A soft towel stood waiting for her. She was ashamed of how she looked, and how she smelt, but she knew that the best way to feel better would be to do exactly what these women said. She could sense that they had done this before.

Satisfied that everything was ready one of the maids left and Annie and the other woman came over to her and quietly and gently helped her out of her clothing.

Amelia knew that she stunk. She had only been able to change her clothes once a month, and slept in the same clothes as she worked in. As Annie removed her mop cap she wondered if the lice she could feel biting her, would all run out at once, or wait for the best moment, or just stay put. Her hair tumbled to her shoulders. At least it had grown back to a decent length in the 18 months since they had shorn her like a sheep. Having been of good behaviour, she had not been shorn again, like so many of the other women had been. After Emily had died there seemed to be no reason to protest about anything or get worked up about anything or feel anything. It was easier to stay numb and not think.

"Dinna ye worry girl, we'll get rid of all of them beasties. Now Sinead and I will pop some vinegar and lemon juice on ye this time and comb what beasties out that we find, but when ye get home you mix up some kerosene and vinegar and sit with that on for a few hours, that will kill any what's left. Do you have a fine-tooth comb at home?" Amelia said that she did. "Well then, you just need someone to comb all the beasties wee bodies out once they is all dead then. We'll do what best we can today," she paused, "Ye got any down below then?" she said indicating her groin area.

"I don't think so," said Amelia, but who could tell. Everything itched, she was sore and red all over her body.

As Sinead and Annie helped her out of her prison garments, she could suddenly smell the extra foul smell that they must also be smelling. In prison the women could only wash the towels from their courses infrequently, so they wrapped them in oil cloth and kept them in pockets inside their britches until they could wash them. Amelia had some waiting to be washed. The smell coming from everything about her was so bad that she retched at her own smell. The other two did not, bless them.

Amelia started to apologise profusely and almost started to cry.

"Nay, ye dinna lassie!" said Annie abruptly, "Ye only going through the same trial that many of us have been through before, mine was many years ago now, but Sinead only came in here nine months ago straight from the prison. Johnny Mac heard that one of his Irish friend's relatives were about to be released, so he went and picked up young Sinead here. She works here now, as a maid and in the kitchen. And we've had many men bring their women here straight after release. Johnny Mac puts out that he's a safe place to recover."

Sinead smiled lovingly at Amelia, who managed a small smile in return. Amelia knew that she looked like a scraggly skeleton, her bones poking out all over, far from the curvaceous bonnie girl who had disembarked from the *Rajah* only two years before. The skin on her hands was red raw from the work in the laundry, with weeping cracks that ached constantly. And her drooping breasts and belly covered in stretch marks, revealed the extent of her trauma.

Sinead looked at Amelia's belly and then up at her face, a question in her expression. Amelia quickly shook her head as a tear ran down her cheek. No other words were necessary. The women all knew the score.

The women indicated for her to step into the bath. It was the most glorious feeling that Amelia had ever had, and she immediately immersed herself and ducked her whole head into the water. As she emerged the women were laughing.

"Eye, that's the way to do it lovey, but duck yer head out now before the beasties ruin ye bath. We'll get you all cleaned up first."

She stood as they lathered her up with tallow soap and then scrubbed her all over with a soft cloth. The water turned a nasty brown colour. She heard the door open, and Sinead filled a large jug with water from the bath and then replaced it with a fresh jug of clean hot water from the other maid, passing the cloths over to be washed as well. What luxury, though Amelia. She let herself fall back against the edge of the bath, and closed her eyes, feeling sleepy and blissful.

"Sorry lass, now be the hard part," said Annie as she and Sinead took stools on either side of Amelia's head and started to slowly comb out her hair. With each stroke a number of black specs fell into the water to drown. It took over an hour for them to be satisfied, with Sinead regularly swapping jugs of cooler water for jugs of hot water.

Annie indicated for Amelia to stand up and step out of the bath, that was quite offensive now, filled with dead lice and fleas. She wrapped her in a big towel and told her to dry herself while they took the water down to tip out in the garden.

Amelia dried herself and fell into one of the armchairs with the towel still around her.

The women returned soon after. "Right, over here with you, time for the best part." Amelia cautiously approached them. "Now, this here be a most luxurious potion lassie, and you deserve it after your ordeal. It's almond oil, rose oil and beeswax. Now, we is going to leave you but you take some time rubbing this all over your poor dear skin, all right, especially on them hands of yours? Then you get that nightgown there on and hop into that bed. We'll keep Mr Harris down with us for a bit then send him up with something to fill your belly. But ye may just like to sleep, lass, so don't feel like you need to let him stay. Johnny Mac has set him up in one of the other rooms. But if ye need some comfort, lass, you have 'im in your bed, ain't no one going to judge you here."

Amelia looked at Annie in amazement. Where had this angel come from?

"Now, a word of caution. You've been eating only the gruel for a while I bet?" Amelia nodded, "well your poor belly won't be used to decent food. I'm sending up some chicken soup, which is quite bland but full of goodness, but dinna be surprised if yer belly rebels, if ye know what I mean?" Amelia nodded that she did. Sadly, after being in the Factory and especially in the nursery, explosive diarrhoea was quite familiar. "There's a chamber pot under ye bed, just ring for one of us if ye need and we'll take it out for ye." Annie showed her where there was a small lever next to the bed attached to a cord that disappeared into a tiny hole in the floor. It must be attached to a bell downstairs. Just like a Queen, thought Amelia.

After she had coated herself with the delicious smelling oil that Annie had given her which calmed her dry, sore skin, she donned the light nightgown that had been left on the bed and climbed under the plush quilt. Her mind and body had gone from hyper-vigilance and survival mode to complete relaxation in a short couple of hours. She felt like she was floating on a cloud in a dream. She was almost about to drift off to sleep when there was a soft knock on the door.

"Yes?" said Amelia sleepily.

"It's just me, John," he cleared his throat and Amelia could hear the trepidation in his voice.

"Come in," she said dreamily, she still felt like this was all a dream.

John entered quietly with a bowl of steaming soup that smelled incredible. Suddenly Amelia was ravenous. John helped her to have a few mouthfuls and as her belly grumbled, she remembered what Annie had said and waved the bowl away. She had already had more that she usually had for most meals.

Amelia and John looked at each other.

"I thought you might like to hear some poetry, my love?"

Amelia giggled. "There is nothing that I could want more."

"May I sit next to you on the bed?"

"You may."

John climbed up onto the bed and opened the book that he had brought, poems by William Cowper, a fairly new writer. Amelia snuggled under his arm and as he spoke the words of the poet Amelia drifted off into another world. John hoped that her dreams were sweet.

Amelia woke the next morning after sleeping from mid-afternoon and all through the night. She had had the most blissful night that she thought she had ever had. She looked over and saw John sound asleep in one of the armchairs. She went over and kissed him on his lips to wake him. He woke dreamily and looking up into her face gave her a beautiful smile, which she returned.

John went to get tea and toast and, on his return discussed with Amelia submitting another petition for their marriage that morning if she was up to it. After her luxurious pampering the day before Amelia said that she was up to tackle anything.

So it was that they were sitting back at the magistrate's office that morning. The wait was longer this time, over three hours, but finally Amelia was called in. She came out about a quarter hour later but this time with a huge smile on her thin face and holding a document above her head in glee. She rushed over to John.

"They approved it John, we can marry!" The newly engaged couple embraced and several calls of 'bravo', 'congratulations', broke out amongst the other people waiting.

They went over to the counter to complete the paperwork to sign Amelia over to John, and then there was a quick visit to the trustee's office to let them know, and a visit to *The Scottish Chiefs* where the real Scottish whisky was broken out again. They then started the journey back to *Vron*.

The trip took longer than usual, as they also stopped into the Beswick's to let them know the good news. Mary Beswick, knowing about their loss, didn't at first bring her new daughter Jane out, but when Amelia heard her stirring, she insisted that she meet the newest baby. Little Jane was just over a month old and still had the newborn floppiness and opened and closed her eyes as she tried to focus on the new faces around her. Amelia sat and cuddled her as they had a cup of tea.

Mary scheduled a visit to *Vron* to measure Amelia up for her wedding dress. John and Amelia had decided to have the wedding as soon as possible, and their next stop was to see the Reverend Davies at Longford so that he could arrange the formalities. Mrs Davies, who they saw was heavily pregnant, gave Amelia a big hug and looked into her eyes with a kindly expression that portrayed all the words that she wanted to say about the loss of Amelia's baby, and her horrific time at the Factory. Little Rowland Davies, who had been a toddler on the *Rajah*, was now six and proudly told Amelia that he was having a baby brother or sister. The Reverend asked them which church they would prefer to be wed in. They had no preference as John had been a regular at most of the Anglican churches close by, so the Reverend said that he would choose one based on the availability, being so close to Christmas. First, they would have to wait until the approval from the Lieutenant-Governor was officially proclaimed and published in the newspaper.

The Reverend told John that the new bishop, Bishop Nixon, the first bishop for Van Diemen's Land, had arrived in the colony in June and had been to visit him and expressed some interest in establishing a college for the wealthy landowners and merchant's sons, similar to the public schools in England. The Reverend had told him about *Vron* and said that he might be interested in looking at it on his next visit. John said that he would be very welcome.

They then made a very quick stop to see Jarvis at *Brickendon* who was ecstatic at the news, and to see Amelia again. John asked if Jarvis would be his best man and Jarvis' lip quivered as he said yes. He told Amelia that Georgina Gatehouse who had been with her on the *Rajah*, had recently married William Grubb. They were both working at the *Woolmers* estate.

Then it was time to get back to *Vron*.

They arrived as the sun was setting, and as they came up the pathway a small greeting party came out to meet them. Cook had tears streaming down her face and Amy and Jess came out along with some of the male workers. They all cheered as Amelia climbed down from the carriage.

There were hugs all around and then they all left John, Amelia and Cook alone to talk.

Cook almost jumped for joy when she heard the news about the wedding. She cried again when she saw Amelia's poor hands, all red and cracked, and took in her stick thin figure.

"It's all right lassie, we'll have you all better and plump as a pudding before you know it."

John was expecting Amelia to move back into her old room in the women's quarters but after dinner she went straight to his room. They were both exhausted.

The narrow bed was a bit squashy with them both on it.

"We're going to have get a bigger bed I think," John laughed. He saw that poor Amelia was almost asleep already, so he helped her out of her clothes and into a soft new nightgown that Mary Beswick had sent in one of her packages. He told her he was going to bring a mattress in so that he could sleep next to her, but she was fast asleep before he left the room.

Over the next few weeks there were many discussions about what they would do once they were married. Neither were keen on making big changes in their lives after being separated for a year and a half, and *Vron*, and the people there, felt like family, and they both felt that was what they needed to have around them.

One big thing that John did, which he had been thinking about for some time, was to purchase his own sturdy brougham carriage and two beautiful horses chosen for him by John McKenzie, who knew exactly what to look for. John had been savings his wages from *Vron* since he received his Ticket-of-leave and having nothing much to spend it on had accumulated almost three years of wages. The carriage and horses took a fair chunk, but there was still plenty for him to buy a decent house and land when he and Amelia were ready. The trustees were happy for him to utilise the *Vron* stables and carriage house, and he paid one of the stable boys a small stipend to care for his horses when they were not needed for the *Vron* horses.

The brougham was very practical for the climate in Van Diemen's Land, having an enclosed cabin, so that those not engaged in driving the carriage were able to sit in comfort out of the elements. There was also plenty of room to carry supplies.

The trustees were keen to know what John's plans where now he was to be a married man. They certainly didn't want to lose the only person who knew the *Vron* house so well. They knew that they could rely on him to speak in a knowledgeable manner to buyers when they came to view the estate. John's accent and demeanour helped the potential buyers to see the estate as suitable for the upper crust, and hopefully to get the best price. Now that the depression seemed to be easing, they were hoping for a sale before too long.

They increased John's wage by a quarter, which they needn't have done, as he and Amelia had already decided that until they had to, they would stay living, and working at *Vron.* The trustees were even happy to pay Amelia a small maid's salary as an enticement for John to stay.

With the help of some of the workers, John moved one of the larger beds from a guest room in the main house, which was no mean feat, as it was on the top floor and was made of solid oak. But once it was situated in John's room and Amelia had made some decorative touches, it felt like their first home. They still ate in the main dining room in the men's quarters with all the workers, and of an evening they would adjourn to the library, which was still mostly intact, and Cook would sometimes join them, as would Mr Dryden on the rare nights that he stayed at *Vron.*

John asked Mr Dryden about his farm and how he managed the commute to and from his work at *Vron.* Mr Dryden said that it wasn't too onerous, less than an hour's drive to and fro, and the benefits of having his own dwelling and seeing his wife every night, outweighed the effort of travelling each day. He told John that there was still land available at the village adjoining *Vron,* now called Little Hampton, and also at Oaks, the *Quamby* estate and Carrick that were all close by. Oaks was on the other side of the Liffey river, so would take longer to get to than Carrick, and *Quamby* was closer to Westbury. But now that they had the brougham, no-where was too far.

*Quamby* was the estate of the Dry family. Richard Dry had recently passed away and the estate had transferred to his son, also Richard, who was only 28 years old, and now one of the wealthiest landowners in the area. The *Quamby* house was even more stunning than *Vron*, and almost at the same standard at the Archer's estates. Old Mr Dry had often sidled up to John at parties and other events and tried to poach him from the Walker's.

On 15 November 1843, the *Cornwall Chronicle* included the news that:

> *In accordance with the Act of Council 6th Victoria, No. 18, I hereby give notice that His Excellency the lieutenant-Governor has been pleased to approve of the solemnization of matrimony between the under-mentioned parties: William Open, per Bardaster, in the Police, and Margaret Clarke, per Rajah, in assigned service, Campbell Town. John Harris, per York 2, holding a ticket of leave, and Amelia Laing, per Rajah, Factory, Launceston.*

John and Amelia saw the Reverend Davies the following Sunday at Longford and the Reverend advised then that he had been able to book them in on 18 December at Westbury. The Reverend Bishton would be pleased to marry them after the normal Sunday service.

It was a hot summer's day in Westbury when John Harris and Amelia Laing were married by the Reverend Bishton at St Andrew's Anglican church at Westbury. The new church had only formally been opened the year before and was quite beautiful. John remembered the many Sundays that he had watched the church slowly being built while attending services across the road in the Police office. He also remembered the many times that he and Elizabeth had attended services there. He felt like visiting Elizabeth's grave while he was there but decided that today wasn't the day.

Amelia looked stunning in a beautiful blue dress adorned with cream lace, that Mary Beswick and her ladies had quickly put together. Amelia had lost so much weight from the first time that Mary had measured her up when she had first arrived in the colony, that at the first fitting the dress had to be unpicked and resewn so that it fit her and didn't hang off her limply. The sleeves dropped off Amelia's shoulders in the modern style and beautifully showed off her elegant shoulders and long neck. Cook arranged Amelia's hair in an elegant up-style with a blue bow to match the dress, and Mary Beswick had loaned her a pearl necklace and earrings.

At 36 and 29, John and Amelia were finally getting married for the first time. Oh, what a life they had both led, that had finally brought them to this happy day.

A small celebration was held back at *Vron,* where Cook and the girls had decorated the dining area with lace tablecloths, candles, and native flowers. There was a delicious spread set out for everyone and a substantial amount of both Irish whiskey and Scottish whisky took centre stage, as well as *Vron* cider that had started production again that year. As the sun went down, the predominantly Irish attendees brought out their fiddles and the dancing started. Amelia led the crowd in several beautiful songs and hymns, which many said was the highlight of the day. Thankfully her voice had not been affected by her ill treatment at the Factory. And after almost eight weeks of recovering from her imprisonment where she had been very quiet and contemplative, on this, her wedding day, Amelia's naturally joyful and high-spirited nature came out once again.

Chapter Twenty Four
# *1844 -Vron*

*T*he beginning of 1844 was one of the worst that the workers at *Vron* had experienced. The drought continued and the crops failed to thrive. With no crops, the livestock risked starvation and had to be sold at bargain prices. However, the trustee's kept all the workers on who had been there when they took over, or who had started since, because their wages only ate into Mr Walker's potential sale profits, not their own. Every week the newspapers reported another wealthy landowner who had gone under, along with many of the small crop farmers and merchants.

However, all was not completely bleak. It was being reported that items that had previously needed to be imported from England or other countries, were starting to be produced in the colony. An article in the *Launceston Examiner* reported:

> *COLONIAL PRODUCTS - We have seen a sample of the colonial glue prepared by Mr. Thomas Button, whlch, uri account of its quality, must soon supersede that imported from Britain. Mr. Button is also about to commence a blacking manufactory; and there can be no doubt that many articles might be prepared in the island superior in quality to those drawn from other countries, and at a less price. It is the interest of all to encourage the consumption of the products of domestic industry. English tallow candles are no longer in demand; a cheaper and better article is supplied on the spot. Sydney cloth is fast*

*superseding British superfine, and refined sugar can be obtained from New South Wales which is preferred to East London loaves. Mr. A. Anderson lately imported from Sydney some prepared brown sugar, technically termed "pieces" superior in grain, colour, and strength to West India samples, which cost much less than the latter; and 'the soap manufactured in New South Wales is preferred to Hawes best London. We hope a proportionate share of attention will soon be devoted in this colony to the manufacture of articles which can be produced at less cost here than we are compelled to pay for them when imported.*

John turned 37 on the first of April and that week news that he was recommended for a Conditional Pardon was posted in the newspaper. Once that came through, he would be a free man, free to do anything but return to England. But that was certainly not something that he was interested in doing. Having now been in Van Diemen's Land for almost 12 years, this was now his home.

Amelia turned 30 on 29 April and for both birthdays a special cake was made by Cook. In her whole life, thought Amelia, this is the very first time that I have actually felt like celebrating my life. Things seemed somehow different now, ever since she had left the Factory and received the marriage approval. She felt like she had grown 20 years in the past two. The Factory had broken her in a way that the neither the Edinburgh slums, the British prisons nor transportation could. Now, safe at *Vron*, with people who cared about her she finally felt some kind of peace and stability in her life for the first time.

It wasn't long after their birthdays that Amelia was able to share with John the exciting news that she was again with child. And now this time they would both be able to nurture and protect it.

They were excited to share their news with the Reverend and Mrs Davies, the following Sunday. The Reverend's much anticipated and very impressive new church, Christ Church at Longford, was moving ahead well with the new building set to be opened by the new Bishop for Tasmania, Bishop Nixon, later in the year.

After church they went for tea and a visit to the Davies' home, next to the church. Mrs Davies told them to call her Maria from now on, as she considered them to be friends. She knew of their friendship with the Beswick's and was excited to tell them that her father William Lyttleton had served in the 73rd Regiment with Mary Beswick's legendary father Sandy McKenzie. They had even been in Ceylon together during the war, which was where Maria had been born as her mother had accompanied her husband. Maria was almost five when they left Ceylon and said that she still vaguely remembered the heat and the monkeys and the delicious yellow bananas.

Amelia and John told them the news of the new baby, and both Maria and the Reverend gave Amelia a hug, and Maria gave her a kiss on her cheek. She then called for young Rowland to join them.

Rowland ran in to tell his mother something exciting that he had just seen in the garden. He was now a boy of seven and seemed so much older than the little boy who Amelia had met running around on the *Rajah*. Maria heard her baby daughter stirring in the next room and went to get her. Amelia marvelled at the beautiful baby girl and hugged her close. Oh, how she missed her

Emily. She smelled baby Maria's tiny head, and the intoxicating scent of a clean baby made an involuntary tear fall from her eye. Maria reached in to take the baby thinking that it was too early and had upset Amelia, but Amelia hushed her away with a smile, brushing the tear away.

"It's all right, Maria, soon I'll have my own beautiful babe to cuddle."

Maria leaned in close, "And I will have another around the same time as you," she looked at Amelia with wide eyes then gave a little smile.

"Really!" said Amelia, "well you have been busy." They both giggled.

"Why yes, doesn't the Lord work in strange ways. For years after we had Rowland, nothing, and now two babes in a year!"

Amelia realised how much Maria and the Reverend Davies had nurtured her since the first day that she met them on the *Rajah*. Maria had never judged her and, being two years younger than Amelia, she almost felt like a sister.

"Did you know that Mary Beswick has also just had another daughter, little Jane was born last September," said Amelia.

"Well then, I'm sure that we will all be able to find some time to play babies together," said Maria cheerfully.

"She's also got Thomas, who's now five and Margaret who's four to keep Rowland company, and even better, Mary Ann who is now nine to keep an eye on them all," said Amelia.

The Reverend Davies was also equally comfortable in John's presence. Being only two years older than John, it often seemed like they were brothers. Amelia looked over and they were deep in conversation.

"Would you like to see my latest watercolours?" said Maria, to which Amelia eagerly agreed. How on earth Maria found time to paint as well as look after a rambunctious little boy, a new baby and one on the way, as well as all the parishioners, she didn't know. It all seemed exhausting to Amelia. Maria's paintings reflected the woman herself, light and beautiful and peaceful.

How extraordinary, thought Amelia; three years ago she was mucking out pig styes and then languishing in prisons and now she was looking at watercolour paintings with the daughter of a magistrate, niece of one of the most successful landowners and wife of the most beloved Reverend. And she was married to a tall, dark, and handsome man who was kind and gentle, but strong and protective and could easily pass as a member of the aristocracy. And she had Cook, dear, wonderful Cook. If Maria was her new sister, then Cook was like a kind Aunt that she'd never had but had always needed. On that day Amelia felt the luckiest that she ever had. But then, she thought, she'd made her own luck. She wondered how her old friend Maggie from Edinburgh was faring. She'd never believe Amelia's story!

On the way back to *Vron*, John told Amelia that the Reverend had told him that Bishop Nixon was now very interested in *Vron* as the site for his 'Christ College' that he had been planning since he arrived in Van Diemen's land in July last year. The previous Lieutenant Governor, Sir John Franklin, had envisaged for over five years a college in Van Diemen's Land to replicate as closely as possible, a college such as those in the Universities of Oxford and Cambridge in England. The first sites were chosen in Hobart, and before she left which was around the same time that Bishop

Nixon arrived, Mrs Franklin's gifted a large tract of land near her Hobart Museum for the purpose. But despite a lot of talking and planning nothing had come to fruition, mostly due to a lack of funding during the past few years of the depression.

After two visits to *Vron*, Bishop Nixon now thought that it was the perfect spot for the new college, wishing for a more rural location where the temptations of a town would not be readily available to the scholars.

Just as it was starting to look like winter was coming to an end Bishop Nixon arrived with the Reverend Davies, a Mr John Gell and the trustees of *Vron* to discuss the terms of the sale. This was to be a stay of several days for the Bishop and Mr Gell, so John, Amelia, Cook and the girls had been busy preparing the house for their stay. This was no small job because the main rooms had been closed up for several years now, and all needed to be dusted, cleaned and readied for the visitors.

Bishop Francis Nixon was a charming and very good-looking man, with large kind eyes, and dark ringlets flopping over his ears. He had spent some time already with John and the trustees on his previous visits and was kind and respectful of Amelia and the other staff. He was a few years older than John and the Reverend Davies and had been educated at Oxford before he was ordained in 1828 at the age of 25. He became the first Anglican Bishop when he arrived in Van Diemen's Land in 1843, which was much needed as the church had greatly expanded since the Reverend Davies had arrived in 1830 and then later, after his visit to England, on the *Rajah* with Amelia.

Bishop Nixon had been the chaplain to the Archbishop of Canterbury for four years until 1842 and knew Lambeth Palace like the back of his hand. He had spent several hours reminiscing with John, on a previous visit to *Vron*, about the Palace and Archbishop Howley, who was still there. Even Nigel was still there and the Bishop was able to tell John that Nigel and his family were all well. John made a mental note to write to Nigel soon to tell him of his adventures in Van Diemen's Land.

The Bishop had been married twice. He had two daughters, Harriet and Frances, with his first wife who had sadly died giving birth to a son, who also died. He then married Anna in 1836, and they had a son, Charles, who died aged 3, a daughter Mary who was four when they arrived in Van Diemen's Land, a son Francis, who was two and Anna had recently given birth to a son they named George.

Later when Amelia had time to talk with the Bishop alone she shared her tale about her darling Emily. The Bishop told her that he too had lost several children, not only Charles, but two others who died not long after birth and then in the worst possible tragedy, his beautiful Frances, aged 10, had died on the journey out from England. So much sadness and loss. They prayed together.

The Bishop then told her of a terrible story that he had recently read in the Launceston Advertiser where a poor woman had finally been able to send for her child from the Orphan's School and when the child arrived she was overjoyed. However, she had not seen the child for many years and then another woman who had been at the Factory more recently said to her 'why that's not your child, that's_____ child,' naming the father, who was then sent for. He immediately acknowledged the child as his own and the child was not sent back but retained by the father. The poor mother again requested the Orphan School authorities to send her child to her but again the child who was sent was not her child. Their Reverend had to intervene and finally they sent her own child.

"What a disgusting and abhorrent chain of events!" said the Bishop, "no one should have to go through that!"

The Bishop was a staunch opponent of transportation and even more so after hearing stories such as Amelia's about the terrible Factory and hearing what the Reverend Davies, also an opponent, had to say. He upheld his journey on the *Rajah* as an example of how a rag tag bunch of underprivileged women could all find peace and goodness with a bit of nurturing and the acceptance of the Lord.

The Bishop had brought Mr John Gell with him. Mr Gell was the same age as Maria Davies, two years younger than Amelia. After graduating at Trinity College, Cambridge he had sailed for Van Diemen's Land, recommended to be head of the first institution of higher education under Sir John Franklin's government. Gell's original mind, natural spirits and equable temperament made him immediately a friend of the Franklins, with whom he stayed on his arrival in March 1840. He had many plans for the school that he envisaged as a stronghold of learning and a school for Christian gentlemen. But bitter conflict between the various religious denominations for government funds and the economic depression had stifled many of his plans.

He had finally opened the Queen's School in Macquarie Street, Hobart as an interim measure. He was then bitterly disappointed when in November 1840 the foundation stone of Franklin's envisaged Christ College was laid and overturned the same night. Now finally Bishop Nixon had arrived, and things seemed to be moving and Gell might get the College that he dreamed of. He was very impressed by everything about the *Vron* estate and agreed with the Bishop that it seemed the perfect place for the College.

Maria had told Amelia that it was rumoured that Mr Gell had been very friendly with Sir John Franklin's daughter Eleanor, while the Franklin's were in Van Diemen's Land, however he remained a single man.

After two days at *Vron* where the Bishop and Mr Gell got to know everything about the house and the estate, and dined on the most succulent delicacies that Cook and the girls could muster, an agreement was decided.

On the last day of August 1844, Bishop Nixon signed the papers to purchase from Mr W.G. Walker, 700 acres and the mansion at *Vron* to establish a college and a township, which he declared was to now be known as Bishopsbourne, previously Little Hampton, or the *Vron* village. The Bishop had no interest in farming pursuits and instructed the former trustee's to continue, now for the Bishop, with their pursuit of someone to purchase or lease all of the pastures and cropping lands.

All the buildings would be retained as would the gardens. Eventually the Bishop would like to see a cricket field and other sporting areas established.

John, Amelia, Cook and the others were all very excited about the development but were unsure what would happen to them all once the College was established and Mr Gell took over.

That evening the trustee's called a special meeting over dinner with John and Cook. Jarvis arrived not long before dinner to the delight of the others who hadn't seen him for a few weeks. Amelia, as John's wife, also attended. Mr Gleadow announced that as part of the sale, Mr Walker wanted to thank his loyal staff by making provision for John, Jarvis and Cook with a grant of land, suitable for a home and small crop farm, at the newly named Bishopsbourne village, right next to *Vron*. The new landowners sat around the kitchen after dinner and over cups of tea discussed what this might all mean for them. Jarvis said that he was very happy at *Brickendon* but was glad to have somewhere familiar to retire to when the time came. Cook said that she had no intention of leaving *Vron* unless they wanted to kick her out, and John jumped in quickly and said that after the last couple of nights meals, he was sure that wouldn't be the case.

John and Amelia went to bed that night with their heads in a spin. So much change in such a short time. And for Amelia, being heavy with child, made the questions about their future all the more scary.

The Bishop and Mr Gell called John in for tea on the last morning or their visit.

"John," said the Bishop, "I'd like to put a proposal forward to you. Now I know that you are probably eager to take up that land in the village and get a house organised for you and Amelia, but please listen to what I have to propose first."

John nodded, intrigued that the Bishop was offering him a proposal.

"Now, no one knows this place better than you, well maybe Mr Jarvis, but he is happy at *Brickendon*. I need a man to act as caretaker for the soon to be College, that would be a similar job to what you are doing now. And more importantly I need someone who knows the library, and who better than a man trained in the library of Lambeth Palace, what?" He gave John a broad smile, which John returned.

"Look, one day we might appoint someone from England to the job of librarian, but at present, you know everything about the library and the books that it currently contains, you know how to catalogue, and you come with excellent credentials from the Mechanics Institute and my dear friend the Reverend Davies. Soon we will be moving the libraries of the current Queens College and books from other places here to Episcopal House (my new name for this mansion), and I will need you to take care of them appropriately. Can you do that?"

John nodded, a little dazed at the proposal.

"Naturally we will need to reconsider your current wages. I know what the trustees were paying you, but with a child on the way, I think double might be the right amount, would that be suitable for you."

Again, John nodded, unsure of what to say, this was all too good.

"Now, we understand that you and Mrs Harris, the delightful Amelia, are currently using the rooms that were previously used by the butler and Mr Dryden, as well as your own. We would be happy for you to continue this situation, until such time as you have built your own house in the village. We are about to offer Cook to stay on and also take the two girls on assignment as well, and depending on enrolments we may need more kitchen hands and maids, although the staff and scholars will be required to attend to their own rooms and clothing. The other staff involved in the livestock and crops will only be staying until such time as Mr Gleadow can find a buyer or lessee for the land, their quarters will then be refurbished for the scholars until such time as I can build a second building, in a similar style as this house for that purpose, which will be starting immediately. The groom, farrier and stable hands will stay, and we will be keeping the coaches and buggies, but we will be closing the cider mill," he took a breath and a long sip of his tea that was going cold, "we will keep on a few general hands to manage the yards, the dairy and the pigs, and for maintenance work. Eventually we will need them to build the sports fields. Mr Dryden has said that he will find suitable men from the village so there will be no need to house them. Oh, and while we are on that subject, from now on you will only be required to work from Monday to Friday, and only on-call at other times to manage any emergencies that may arise at the house. Once the College opens there may be a need every now and then for you to work in the library on Saturdays, but never on Sundays, naturally."

John nodded again, and then a wide grin grew on his face. He rose and moved across to where the Bishop was sitting and extended his hand, which the Bishop took.

"Your Excellency, I would be honoured to serve on at this estate. I have much enjoyed my time here and would be very pleased to continue on the terms you propose."

"Well," said the Bishop, "that's settled. Welcome to the staff of Christ College," he pumped John's hand. "Now you will report directly to Mr Gell here, who will on his return to Hobart be making immediate arrangements for his move here to the College. Have you picked your room yet, John?"

"Yes, your Grace, I'll show Mr Harris directly after this meeting. Mr Harris, I will be deferring to you on all matters regarding the house and grounds for some time if you will indulge me. I will be very busy making the arrangements for the College and the scholars."

John nodded his understanding.

"Now," said the Bishop, "it is quite all right for you to take time to attend to your own needs when you are not directly needed at the College, by that I mean arrangements for building your own house, although you and Amelia are welcome to stay here for as long as you want, although things might get difficult once the young one arrives."

Cook was the next one to enter as John left the room with a broad smile and a skip in his step.

Amelia was eagerly waiting for him in the kitchen and the girls were also there, he hastened her into the sitting room that had been Jarvis's room. As he explained their new situation, she too was at first quite shocked and then so happy and excited and relieved that she needed to sit down.

"So, do you think we should build a house in the village, my love?" she asked.

"I do," said John, "but there doesn't seem to be any rush and I know nothing about building a house, so we will have to make lots of enquiries, and until then we can all just stay here, you, me and little John isn't it?" he leaned over a patted her belly with a wink.

"Or little Amelia," she said with a smile.

As the morning went on and more of the staff spoke to the Bishop, the estate was abuzz with excitement at the new changes.

The Bishop and Mr Gell left in the early afternoon and things went back to normal, except they weren't. There was still a lot of uncertainty about when things would happen, but the staff all settled back into maintenance mode, and quietly got on with life.

## Chapter Twenty Five
# *1844 - Bishopsbourne*

*A*t Little Hampton, the former *Vron* village, the citizens were getting used to the idea of having a fancy College next to them, and to the change of name. The blocks reserved for the Harris's and for Cook and Jarvis were next to each other and close to families who they already knew from church. John started the first enquiries about how to design and build a suitable house. Cook and Jarvis were both happy to have their land kept vacant until such time as they wanted to use them.

Over the years John had come to know many of the local families and knew at least by sight all the families at the newly named Bishopsbourne village. He also knew quite a lot of families from around the other areas where he went to church. He was glad that he had spread himself around the various services and befriended both the Reverend Davies and Bishton, and since she'd been his wife Amelia had also been pleased to meet many of them too.

1844 had been a strange one for Amelia. Her life had been in such a whirlwind of survival for so long that, until she had become heavy with the child inside her, she had felt a bit restless. She really didn't have a purpose at *Vron*, now officially named Episcopal House, but *Vron* stuck. She was now just John's wife. Which she was very happy about and was excited for the rest of their lives together, particularly now that it seemed that good fortune had blessed them so well. But she still had no purpose.

She kept herself busy, helping John with the house and helping Cook and the girls, but she had been thinking for a while that she'd really like to get back into singing, even if it was just hymns at church. And she had really enjoyed teaching the children on the *Rajah* and the Walker's children at *Vron*. Maybe, she thought, once the baby was born, she would find that her purpose was just to be a good mother and to protect this little one, as she'd been unable to protect little Emily.

Not long after Bishop Nixon and Mr Gell left, the Reverend Davies arrived at *Vron* one morning (no-one could really get their heads around the new name, Episcopal House) and over a cup of tea and cake told the staff that the bishop wanted a chapel built at Bishopsbourne right away. The bishop wanted to make sure that there was a suitable chapel close to the College before he started looking for students, as this would be a vital consideration in their family's decision the enrol them. The Reverend had come to meet with the builders and asked if John would like to join him and maybe discuss his own building needs. He had engaged Henry Conway, a Launceston architect, to design the chapel, as he had also drafted the changes to Christ Church at Longford. He suggested that John might like to talk with Conway as well.

The block reserved for the chapel was right in the centre of the village. The bishop had contracted a local man to build the church. William Webb had started a building company and had many projects on the go around the area. John had met William Webb and his wife Maria first at Westbury and later at Longford. The Webb's were an older couple in their late 50's who had recently built a large house in the village, and an impressive building that they hoped to have approved as a tavern, the first for the village. Mr Webb had come to Van Diemen's Land as a convict four years before John and was assigned to Maria Davies' father Captain William Lyttleton. The captain thought so highly of him that he sponsored Maria and their children to come out to the colony to join William. They had arrived in 1833.

Mr Webb had also been given a life sentence, like John, so it had taken him a while to gain his freedom, but he had finally received a Free Pardon in 1843. Before this, and as a Ticket-of-leave holder he had been very busy. He had first run the punt service across the South Esk river at Longford and he had also operated a carrier service from Longford. He had come to Little Hampton, now Bishopsbourne, in only the past year. Their three eldest daughters were already married, but son John, 22, and daughter Sarah, 18, lived with them.

The three men stood around discussing the burgeoning village and the new College, the new arrangements at *Vron*, and the soon to be built chapel, that the Reverend told them was to be called The Church of the Holy Nativity. After the Reverend had finished talking with Mr Conway and Mr Webb about the church, Mr Webb invited them to have a look at his new proposed tavern.

Inside the large, whitewashed stone building was an impressive bar with stools and several tables and chairs. He had already brewed his first batch of ale, said Mr Webb proudly, as well as some cider which the women preferred, and was cheaper to make, he said with a wink. He had not yet got into spirits and due to the delicate nature of its production, he thought that he might buy that, rather than make it, at least for a while. There was so much competition around with the different whiskies in the colony, he didn't want to step on anybody's toes. Maybe he could hold a whiskey competition, he said wistfully. He was still looking for a decent cook as he intended to provide meals for locals and travellers. He asked John with a wink if Cook would be available. John laughed and said he didn't think so as she'd just been offered a fairly lucrative offer to stay on and run the kitchen for the new College.

"Oh well, maybe she'd share some of her recipes then, I have heard the men talk of her fruitcake like the angels made it."

William asked if John had a builder yet, to which John replied that he didn't. He then told John that he was already contracted to build several houses in the village and John was welcome to go and look at some of the houses currently being built. They wandered around the village and saw Mr Webb's men hard at work building around the village. After further discussion it was agreed that John would trust Mr Webb with building his and Amelia's home as well.

After they left the village John invited Mr Conway back to *Vron* for advice on the house that he wanted to build. Cook quickly threw together a tasty meal and sat with them as John, Amelia and Mr Conway discussed the possibilities.

Everyone at *Vron* were very pleased to hear in September that William Webb's petition to open *The Bush Inn* had been approved. Although the teetotaller brigade didn't approve of the decision, most did agree that a tavern would be a good addition to the village and provide another place for the community to get together. Mr Webb was also busy turning the huge pastureland behind the tavern into stock yards for use by the local farmers and creating a charming park with seats and tables under some of the huge trees next to the tavern.

It was with much excitement and anticipation on the sixth of October that Bishop Nixon opened the new Christ Church at

Longford, as the Davies' both beamed on proudly. The Church was still not completely finished as the Reverend would like it. A tower was still to be built, and there had been much disappointment when the stained-glass windows had turned up with cracks in them, but it was time that the building was opened for services.

Amelia and John wore their wedding outfits for the day which also included another much-anticipated event. Thomas Reibey III was to receive Holy Orders. He would be the first person to be ordained in Van Diemen's Land.

Thomas Reibey had inherited the beautiful and expansive *Entally* estate, between Carrick and Launceston, in 1843 on the death of his father. A year later, aged just 22, he was pestering the bishop to ordain him as he felt his calling in life was to work as a minister. He stressed to the bishop that he required no remuneration for his work and would be putting a lot of his own money into opening new Anglican chapels and schools. The bishop had finally agreed and ordained him as a special Minister as he was still too young to be properly ordained.

Maria Davies told Amelia, Cook, Mary Beswick and her sisters who were there for the day, that the situation was made more interesting because a minister was required to have a degree and although Thomas had been to Oxford he had never received his degree, and word was that while growing up at *Entally* he had much preferred to run around and play with the native children than participate in his school work. But then, he was an incredibly wealthy man, and the church could certainly do with an injection of funds. Maria only hoped that he was in it for the right reasons and not on a whim.

Despite the intrigue, a wonderful day was had by all, with tables and refreshments set up in the church yard and even a band playing. The Harris and Beswick group were honoured when the new Reverend Reibey's young wife Catherine came over to their table to greet them and introduced herself simply as 'Katey'. Katey had recently turned 21 and not long arrived in Van Diemen's Land. Her father had been one of Thomas' tutors at Oxford and was now the Mayor of Inveresk, just outside of Edinburgh in Scotland. For someone who had grown up with such privilege, Katey seemed to be a lovely, friendly, and bonnie lass who talked easily with everyone at the celebration. Maria noted to Amelia that it seemed so far that she would make a wonderful minister's wife.

Again, Amelia felt she had to shake herself. Less than four years ago she had been scrounging her next meal in the poverty-stricken streets of Edinburgh and now here she was in her finery, drinking tea with a mayor's daughter. What an extraordinary place this was, she thought. Like a world turned upside down, but in such a wonderful way.

The following day Bishop Nixon laid the foundation stone for the new chapel called The Church of the Holy Nativity or just Christ College Church at Bishopsbourne, and it seemed that all the village turned out for the event, as well as many from the surrounding areas. The Church had a bell attached. It was a ship's bell and inscribed with the date, 1836. It was gifted by villager George Skarden, who had used it at his property to call people to worship at services previously conducted at his house. He also presented an impressive wrought iron pulpit.

The Webb's took great advantage of the gathering, setting up tables outside their tavern and bringing jugs of ale, cider, and lemonade out for the attendee's. There was a small band playing and at one point Mr Webb asked Amelia if she'd like to sing, as he had heard of her prowess, but she declined, indicating the now enormous size of her belly.

"I dinna want to bring the child on now Mr Webb, that would cause a commotion," she said, and they both laughed.

Mr Webb's tavern had become quite the meeting place and on the second of November the Ticket-of-leave muster was held there, with all the Ticket-of-leave holders in the area required to attend and provide information of their current dwelling place and employment. Ever the businessman, Mr Webb admitted to John that his hospitality during the opening of the chapel was a marketing technique, as he hoped that all the attendee's would go away and extol the virtues of his establishment to all their friends and family. Maria and son John had been busy putting the finishing touches together for the boarding house, next to the inn, where overnight and short-term tenants would be welcomed.

A couple of weeks later, John and Amelia were in the village checking on the progress of their house. So far only the foundations had been set out and the areas set aside for the home gardens, dairy and chicken runs. The house design that they had chosen was cozy but allowed for expansion of their family. There would be a cooling veranda along the front and sides. The front door would open onto a small parlour with a large sitting room off to the right and a large dining room behind that. The kitchen would be behind the dining room but detached from the house for safety. It was going to include all the modern equipment, which was good thought Amelia, because she would need all the help that she could, as cooking was not her best talent. But it was one of John's passions and he had arranged for the kind of kitchen that he had seen in some of the newer homes he had been in, including the Webb's.

At the back of the house was to be a laundry and washroom, close to the well, currently being dug, and again with all the modern conveniences. John and Amelia's bedroom was to the left of the parlour with large windows to look out to the front and side of the house, where John was going to create a beautiful sitting area in the garden under the one large tree on their block, and lots of room for the children to run around. Two large bedrooms were located behind John and Amelia's to be filled eventually with children, and a smaller guest room behind the parlour. And something that made her most excited; as well as a coach-house and stable and a garden shed, John was building another large room separate but close to the house, that could be used as either a school room, or a music room or for whatever purpose they decided to put it to. It was to have veranda's all around with wide eaves to keep it cool in summer and a central fireplace to keep it warm in winter. And the privy was positioned between the two buildings, but at a suitable distance, making it convenient for all.

Back at *Vron*, Amy's beau Oliver who was hoping to be kept on as a general hand, had made the most beautiful crib for the new baby, and there was a little ceremony as he showed it off to John and Amelia, complete with exquisitely embroidered linens made by Jess, with some help from Amy and Cook. Amelia cried when she saw the crib and thought of the drawers full of beautiful baby cloths waiting in their room. It was all so different to her last experience. This time she was surrounded by love.

Vron

The first weeks of November where hot and sticky and everyone was feeling it, but more-so Amelia in her enlarged state. Most afternoons were spent on the veranda to catch whatever breezes came along, with a cold lemonade and a wet towel to cool off.

With the help of Cook, who knew everyone, Amelia had engaged the services of a woman from the village who had acted as midwife to many of the locals over the past 20 years. A room was ready in the women's quarters for the birth.

Amelia was awoken one night feeling the same pains that she had felt with Emily. Knowing how long things took, she got out of bed so as not to disturb John, made a cup of tea, and went to sit in the library, taking towels in case her waters broke like the last time. She spent the next few hours, until dawn broke, walking around the library, stopping for a rest in between contractions. When John found her side of the bed empty, he came rushing into the library while she was mid contraction and almost had a heart attack. He came over and patted her on the shoulder looking very concerned until she said everything was fine and things seemed normal. Still, he hurried off to get Cook. Once Cook saw Amelia squatting down and holding onto a chair during a contraction, she yelled out for one of the men to get a buggy and go and fetch the midwife. She then helped John to lead Amelia down to the woman's quarters and the birthing room.

Things happened quickly once the midwife arrived and within the next hour a fine, chubby baby boy had been delivered, Amelia had been attended to and popped into bed with a cup of tea and biscuits, and her new son, wrapped in swaddling cloths was handed to his father.

John was overjoyed as he held his son in his arms. The baby was long and had a small covering of dark hair like his fathers, and even in squishy baby form, they could see that he would have a fine, slender nose like his own. John Harris Jnr, and actually the third John Harris in his line, was born on the 22nd of November 1844, surrounded by love.

Less than four weeks after little Johnny's birth, the house was thrown into chaos when a huge auction was held on site to dispose of as much of the estate as possible that was not needed for the new school. The auction started early, with many buggies and carriages arriving from dawn, and carried on all morning. There was a break at 11am where refreshments were served. Cook and the girls had been run off their feet getting the refreshments organised, having not needed to do any entertaining for some time, and John and the men were kept busy with the extra horses and carrying the various items out to the veranda where the auction was held.

The advertisement for the day stated:

> The whole of the ELEGANT and MODERN HOUSEHOLD FURNITURE, comprising every requisite for the residence of a family of respectability, amongst which are drawing and dining room suits, in rosewood and mahogany, consisting of couches, sofas, chairs; loo, card, sofa, chess, coffee, and pembroke tables; brussels, carpets and rugs, fenders and fire-irons, mahogany pedestal sideboards, winged bookcases, with and without secretaires, dining tables, chimney glasses and ornaments, window curtains, lamps, chandeliers, paintings, mahogany four-post, French, tent and iron bedsteads and bedding, mahogany

*wardrobes, chests drawers, wash-stands, and other chamber furniture, etc.*

*Also*

*One hundred head of CATTLE, all in the highest possible condition, consisting of – WORKING BULLOCKS, not to be surpassed in the island, DAIRY COWS, of the most valuable description, Well-bred HEIFFERS, and powerful STEERS fit for the yoke, Five hundred FAT SHEEP, in lots to suit purchasers, A number of most useful horses, broken in to saddle, carriage, cart and plough, A very handsome chariot and harness, with a pair of excellent horses well matched, an open carriage and set of harness, a large quantity of farming implements, consisting of carts, drays, wagons, ploughs, harrows, rollers, thrashing and winnowing machines, cider mill etc.*

*An extensive assortment of dairy utensils, blacksmiths' tools, forcing pump, etc.*

John noted with interest that William Hartnoll, who had extensive farming interests near *Vron* purchased most of the livestock and stayed after the auction to talk with the trustees. William was married to the Webb's oldest daughter Eliza and had come out as a convict in 1826. William was a year older than John and the two men were on friendly terms, however William's interests, like his father-in-law's, tended more towards business, rather than intellect. William and Eliza had a son Henry aged five, Willy aged three and Eliza was due to have another any day.

John wasn't surprised when a few months later the bishop sent word that all the farming lands on the estate where to be leased to William Hartnoll for ten years. The remaining farm workers, not chosen to stay and maintain the home, were also transferred to Mr Hartnoll.

The Hartnoll's lived at Longford, where William had a very successful butchering business, employing several man and apprentices. He had farming interests all over the area. The Harris's would see them at church and when they came to visit their parents at Bishopsbourne.

1844 rolled into 1845. Amelia and John, along with the Beswick's, Cook, Jarvis and several others attended a quiet Christmas luncheon at the Davies' home after the morning service at Longford. Maria was very heavy with child and ready to give birth, so all the women had arranged for the food which they either bought with them or prepared at the Davies home. Old Thomas Brennan attended the service for the first time in a long time and greatly enjoyed the luncheon. John was amazed at how sharp he still was, discussing farming with some of the younger men.

A small Hogmanay celebration was held at the village, organised by Cook, Amelia, and some of the other Scottish villagers. Everybody was happy to participate and went from door to door offering gifts and sharing drinks and laughs with their neighbours. The Webb's then put on a meal of roast meats and sweets for the whole village, and even arranged for a Scottish trio for the night for a little dancing. He winked at Amelia and said that she should get up and sing, but having little Johnny strapped to her chest and asleep prevented her from doing so. She did vow that she would start her singing again in some way in the new year.

## Chapter Twenty Six
# *1845 – Expanding population*

*T*he Harris's and the workers at *Vron* had started to attend

services at the new Church of the Holy Nativity at Bishopsbourne village, but John, Amelia and Cook also regularly attended the Reverend Davies' services at Longford.

They arrived on Sunday the 12th of January for the morning service to find that Maria was in full labour. The Reverend told Amelia that it might be a good idea if she went to attend on Maria, as the labour had been long and hard, and the midwife was a new one and not known to Maria. The Reverend nervously continued with his preparations for the service, which was about to begin, encouraging the small choir to sing louder to drown out the sounds of poor Maria's moans and screams.

Amelia burst into Maria's bedroom to a terrible sight. The poor woman looked grey and was very pale and clammy. The room was already stiflingly hot, and Amelia first threw open all the windows. The midwife looked ancient and didn't seem to be helping poor Maria at all, rather she was sitting in a dark corner muttering to herself.

Amelia had little Johnny strapped to her chest as usual, and he was still sleeping which freed up both of Amelia's arms to help Maria.

"Oh Emma," gasped Maria in little more than a whisper, "the midwife that we had arranged, who the Archer's recommended as their family midwife, was taken ill, and the one who we had last time is visiting family in Hobart for the festive season. I don't think granny over there knows what she's doing, and something isn't right, Emma, it feels all wrong. The doctor is on his way, but he's coming from Launceston."

"Dinna you worry my friend," said Amelia, "I'll help you now. I've seen many a birth in the Factory and helped with some, we'll get this wee one out of you no bother. I'm just going to have to have a look, my dearest and see what is going on with baby." Maria waved her arm wearily as if she had given up all care.

She was lying on the bed across several towels, but it seemed that her waters were yet to break. Amelia had a look to see if she could see the head. What she saw struck her with fear. There between Maria's legs was a small round bottom, poking out about an inch.

Amelia wished with all of her might that Cook or one of the girls were with her now, or especially the midwife from Bishopsbourne who had so ably assisted her birthing Johnny, although that was a simple birth compared to this. But Cook and the girls had decided to stay at home and attend the village service after such a hectic past month.

"Look here ye old cailleach," she whispered through her teeth in anger at the old woman in the corner, "the bairn is coming out bottom first, are ye going to help this woman or not?"

The old woman appeared to wake from her reverie and stumbled over to the bed.

"I've seen this before," said Amelia quietly to herself. "Right Maria, on yer feet, I need you to stand up, the midwife here will hold you up but I need you to stand and push with all of your might once you're up." Maria looked for all the world as if she was about to pass out, but Amelia had also seen this many times before in the Factory. "Come on woman, get on with you, this baby isn't getting out by itself, you need to wake up now and get this baby out," Amelia's voice had taken on an urgent tone.

Maria was helped to the end of the bed where the midwife held her as she leaned slightly over the bed. The contractions, which had all but stopped while she was laying on her back, suddenly started again with a vengeance, "That's it, that's it my love, push, push that baby out."

Amelia gently held the baby's bottom as it inched slowly out, and then in a big gush the waters broke and splashed onto the floor. The tiny body slithered out a little more. Maria was wracked with another big contraction and suddenly a little leg came free and waved around in the air. Amelia quickly held it to prevent any injury and then just as quickly the other leg popped out. The baby now hung from its mother with only it's head still un-birthed.

"She's almost out now Maria," said Amelia, knowing that the next part was the most dangerous.

Annie and the other nurses at the Factory made sure that some of the mothers were called in to assist with the births, knowing that when they went off to their assignments and later as citizens, any skills in this remote colony would be much needed, and skills at birthing would help to ensure the next generation were born safe and healthy. Amelia had seen a breach birth a few times, and all had been successful under the experienced guidance of the nurses at the Factory, but at the same time Annie had told the women that if not done correctly a breach birth could result in terrible injuries or even death to the newborn and possibly also the mother. It was with this fear that Amelia went into the next part of the birth.

Maria was now calm and her breathing had slowed, "Is she out yet," she whispered having picked up from Amelia's last words that she had another daughter.

"Nay, not yet," said Amelia as she gently lowered the body from her grasp and then, holding her breath let the body hang free. Just as it was supposed to do Amelia saw the tiny body start to turn with the force of gravity into the best position for the head to be born without injury. She prayed so hard that what she was doing was correct. The hymns from the church could be heard on the breeze and the world seemed to stand still as the baby did its thing as naturally as the sun shone.

Maria was suddenly wracked with another huge contraction and Amelia told her that it was time to push now with all her might. She held the baby's tiny torso, cradling its little belly with its arms and legs hanging down, and holding it at what she thought was the right angle for the head to be born safely. As Maria pushed with all her might Amelia lifted the tiny body as the head emerged and its tiny face pushed itself out. Finally, the baby was born.

Amelia grasped the child, who was not yet breathing and started to rub her little back vigorously with her right hand. Mucus ran from the baby's nose and mouth. Amelia turned her onto her back and wiped it away and then started to massage the tiny arms and legs, giving the little one small taps on its bottom. Finally, after what seemed like an eternity but was really less than a minute, the tiny body shook, gave a huge inhalation and then let out a God almighty howl.

Shakily, Amelia handed the baby to Maria who was now lying back on the bed. The midwife finally sprang into action and went to the end of the bed to attend to the afterbirth.

Amelia, who had been squatting on her haunches, fell back onto her bottom, her legs out straight, leaning against the chest of drawers. She then realised that her dear little Johnny was still fast asleep across her chest and had been throughout the whole saga. She stroked the top of his soft head and kissed him, breathing in his baby scent. Just as she did that, he opened his eyes, screwing them up against the offending light, pushed his little legs and arms hard against his bindings, and let out his own howl. Lunch time thought Amelia.

And that was how the Reverend and the doctor found them, sitting in the bedroom, the old crone cleaning up having delivered the afterbirth, and Maria nursing her new daughter on the bed and Amelia nursing Johnny on the floor.

The men's eyes were wide with fear and anticipation as they tentatively entered the room, not knowing what the outcome was going to be.

The Reverend rushed over to his wife and took her and the new baby into a warm embrace, "This one was harder than the others, Rowland. I might not be here except for Emma." The Reverend looked horrified at Amelia.

"Ah it's all good, Reverend, all of the prayers obviously worked," she smiled wearily.

An hour or so later, the doctor had examined both mother and baby and deemed them both to be fit and healthy. However, he fell short of praising Amelia's efforts, it would not do to acknowledge any skills acquired at the Factory. He stayed for a cup of tea and cake with the Reverend and was then on his way.

Amelia cleaned herself up and borrowed a petticoat from Maria to wear over her wrapper, worn daily now to aid her with breastfeeding Johnny. Her own petticoat was now being scrubbed by one of Maria's maids. The children ran freely around the table where the adults sat taking tea and relaxing after such an eventful morning, Rowland, now eight, kept a watchful eye on his two-year-old sister Maria. Little Maria was obsessed with tiny Johnny and kept pestering Amelia to touch or hold him.

"You've got your own baby sister now, lamb," said the Reverend.

Later as the Harris's were preparing to leave, Maria arrived on the veranda, freshly washed, her hair done, and in a clean dress, looking like she'd barely raised a sweat instead of being awake in agony all night. Amelia looked on admiringly. What a sturdy woman, she thought.

The Reverend held her arm as she descended the steps elegantly with the new baby on her other arm, and little Maria clambering around her feet, Rowland trying in vain to keep her away.

"Emma," said Maria, "before you go, the Reverend and I have something to ask you." Amelia was intrigued.

"We have decided, if you are agreeable, to name this child after you, she will be Emma Lyttleton Davies." Amelia's eyes opened wide with shock.

"Look, I have a few Emma's in my family, and I am acknowledging my family with her middle name as well, but if this child can grow up to be half as kind and strong and resilient as you then the Reverend and I will be well pleased. And if not for you she may not be here. So do you approve?"

Amelia burst into tears of happiness and went over to hug Maria, as well as she could with both of them holding babies. John looked on with pride and happiness, so pleased that everyone else could see what an admirable woman that his Amelia was.

The house at Bishopsbourne progressed slowly. There were many other people building houses and places of business at the time and the demand for skilled workers outweighed the amount available. While convict labour could sometimes be obtained for public or community works, private buildings had to wait for tradesmen to be available. And Mr Webb would not employ just any tradesmen, he only wanted those who had come recommended and whose work he had seen. There were plenty of out of work Ticket-of-leave or free settlers willing to have a go at various trades, many with limited skills or experience. Several ramshackle dwellings with leaking roofs or walls that had fallen in stood as a warning to others.

Amelia received her Ticket-of leave around the same time as she realised that she was again with child. Although her sentence was for seven years it was usual for Tickets-of-leave to be issued after four years for those who had not re-offended in the colony. Hers had been delayed slightly due to her absence without leave and pregnancy offences. Now, being assigned to her husband, there would not be much of a change to her situation, except that she now needed to attend Ticket-of-leave musters every year which were now being held conveniently at the Webb's, Bush Inn.

Johnny was still a tiny babe in arms when the new child started to make its presence known, and as Johnny was becoming increasingly wriggly in his swaddling harness, she was being kicked from outside and in.

The Webb's youngest daughter Sarah, who was yet to marry, had become a frequent and welcome visitor at *Vron*. At 19, she appreciated some time away from her parents and would often come for meals and was learning to knit and crochet with Jess. She was also handy to have around as she loved to play with little Johnny and would look after him so that Amelia could help with the house and yard work. This had become more important to Amelia that year because she needed to learn how to manage her own house, having had limited experience in her younger years.

Even though there were far less people to feed, and the house was now all but stripped of its furnishings, meaning less to take care of inside the house, the work in the kitchen, the chicken coop, the dairy, and the stables went on. And after mid-year constant deliveries were being received as supplies for the College started coming in.

John had purchased a small buggy and another horse at the *Vron* auction, and Amelia had taken a liking to helping in the stable with the grooming. She found that she had an affinity with the animals, and she could indulge in her love of singing with them, as it appeared to calm them, as it did her, and the baby she carried. She practiced all her old Gaelic songs from Scotland, and all the new songs and hymns she had learned. Sometimes when she was feeling naughty, she would throw in some of the bawdy lines from her days in Edinburgh, much to the stable hands delight. But now, as a mother and wife to a respectable man, she knew she had to mostly leave that life behind. John did catch her, though, one afternoon, singing one of her tamer ditties, and she caught him leaning against the stable door and grinning at her words. She loved him even more in that moment, silhouetted against the glowing autumn sun, letting her be herself and loving her for it.

The buggy was convenient as it could be quickly organised with just one horse and travelled faster than the carriage, although it provided no protection from the weather. With the baby and another on the way, instead of walking to the village, it was easier and less taxing to take the buggy.

As they had previously discussed, Maria Davies had set about organising a children's playgroup for the new mothers in the area. Once every month the mothers who could be spared from any home or work requirements, gathered at the church hall at Longford on Sunday afternoon. The men would go off for bible studies with the Reverend, or to the local tavern to discuss farming and other business. It was an interesting mix of women, free settlers, and Ticket-of-leave mothers and sometimes the wealthy landowners and merchants who did not turn their nose up at those in lesser circumstances. The parishioners soon learned that most of the Anglican ministers where loyal supporters of the convicts and strong opponents of transportation and the convict system.

On this particular spring afternoon, the flowers were blooming, and a gentle breeze blew through the trees, cooling the air. The women sat under the shade of the trees outside the hall, on chairs or picnic blankets. Maria nursed little Emma while her little Maria ran around with the other children. Little Johnny was now sitting up and grabbing for anything put near him and the children delighted in finding him items to explore. Amelia had to remind them not to give him gum nuts and leaves as they went straight into his mouth. He relished the cake and soft fruits that they gave him and munched on them happily. How delightful, she thought, to not have to worry about him weaning and to let him explore foods, although her heart gave a thump when she saw him doing so, a reminder of all the times she had tried to stop Emily from looking like she was weaning.

Everyone had told her that it was impossible to fall with child again while you were still nursing one, but Amelia had certainly proven that to be incorrect. It was starting to get difficult to carry Johnny who was getting bigger and had started to crawl, with her belly starting to protrude again.

Mary Beswick was there with Thomas, six, Margaret, four and Jane almost two. She was also heavy with child again and due any day. The other women said that she probably should have stayed at home, but she laughed and said what better company could she be in than all of them especially Emma! The story of baby Emma's birth had been told several times.

Katey Reibey was also in attendance, although there were no children for her yet, she revelled in cuddling the babies to give their mothers a break, and with so many around there was always one needing a cuddle.

Mary Beswick's sisters, Margaret Kerr and Elizabeth Emery were also there. Ann Kerr was now eight, James seven, William four and Jane would be two in three months, on Christmas day. Elizabeth had three-year-old George, with golden curls just like his mother, who was running around with the others. Dear old Margaret Beswick, Thomas' mother, was also there and provided another welcome lap for baby cuddling. She was still as sharp as a tack and participated in the women's conversations easily.

Eliza Hartnoll, who lived near the Davies' was also in attendance with Henry seven, Willy four and Alfie who was a month younger than Johnny. She had just discovered that she was again with child as well and hoped for a girl this time. Eliza had also still been nursing when she fell again, which completely dispelled the women's belief that nursing prevented conception.

Mary Beswick's eldest daughter Mary Ann, now twelve, was a godsend and ran around after the smaller children, along with Mary's youngest sister Ann who was fifteen. Ann was engaged to be married to her brother-in-law, George Emery the following January. They had met at the same time as her sister Elizabeth had met her husband, John Emery. Elizabeth and John were married in 1840 and Ann had been pestering her father and older sisters since she was 14 to be allowed to marry George. George, as well as her family, had definitely wanted to wait until she was older, but her firebrand nature convinced them to allow her an earlier than usual marriage. Her father, Thomas Brennan, laughed that her nature had to do with the fiery red hair that she had been the only child to be blessed with. He would miss her greatly when she left the McKenzie farm to start her own family, although she had been spending most nights at her sister Elizabeth's house lately, where he suspected there were less rules.

After Mary's sisters had left and while Margaret Beswick was having a comfort break, she confided in Amelia and Maria that things weren't going so well at the McKenzie farm, as it was still known. At first, they had been able to ride out the worst of the economic crisis, due mainly to the alternative businesses that the family had going, namely the dressmaking and boot-making businesses, but as the tide had turned throughout the colony there were less and less customers for their gowns and finely made footwear. And now with the drought setting in and another year of failed or almost failed crops, things were getting quite lean. Still, they were doing better than most and shouldn't complain, she said.

Eventually the children became too much for Mary Ann to manage and she wandered up to find her stepfather to take them home. He had been having a great time talking with John and the Reverend, three men with similar interests. The Reverend Reibey had joined them at first, but being so much younger, they quickly saw his interest in their conversation wane, and he eventually took his leave and joined some of the younger gentlemen, as well as some of the older farmers that included Thomas Brennan, in talks about farming and sports. Sport was his favourite topic, apart from his burgeoning ministry.

One of the topics of conversation, between the Reverend, Thomas, and John, was the current unrest about the treatment of the aborigines at Flinders Island. Since Governor Arthur had ordered them to be rounded up and taken to the Flinders Island Protectorate in 1830, it was assumed that they were all being well taken care of by the government and afforded the same dignities and legalities as the rest of the colony. Granted things had changed in the past fifteen years with the newer generation, many of whom were born in the colony, demanding their legal rights and being far more aware of justice and equality. There was even growing discord about transportation and the whole convict system. Having not been subjected to attacks from aborigines for so long, many had forgotten the ire that many settlers had had towards them, and many only remembered the friendships that had developed before the Black Line took them away. Years later, the darker complexions of some of the colony's children, and the way that some of the aborigines had settled into life working for colonists or even being married to colonists prior to 1830, further softened the hearts of the people towards them.

Naturally there was still discrimination as John had witnessed first-hand once, when visiting John McKenzie's hotel in Launceston. John had already met Johnny Mac's good friend John Rose, whose father, David Rose had served with Johnny Mac's father Sandy McKenzie in the 73rd Regiment and was responsible for Sandy's original land grant. John was the heir to the very successful *Corra Lynn* property, near the McKenzie farm at Paterson's Plains, which he ran with his cousin Alexander Rose. John's mother had been an aboriginal woman of the Ben Lomond tribe in the mountains near Launceston.

While John dressed and spoke as well as any wealthy Englishman, having been schooled by a private tutor, and his skin was caramel rather than black, he still looked distinctly native. Darker skinned people were not unknown in the colony with many emancipists and settlers having workers or even children who were born with native blood, and there were several African and African American people living around Launceston as well. Richard White, known as 'Black Dick' or 'Dicky' was born in America but travelled to England where he was charged with highway robbery in 1797. Like so many ex-convicts, back in the olden days he received a land grant in Launceston and opened the first hotel in 1814. He had been a mentor to Johnny Mac and had become incredibly successful in the colony. He had only just married again at the age of 73 and was still going strong.

However, on the day that John was at the *Scottish Chief's* having a drink with Johnny Mac and John Rose, a group of men came into the hotel and immediately started to be rude to John Rose. When Johnny Mac took them to task, they demanded that John Rose leave the hotel as they would not drink with 'darkies'. Johnny Mac, being a large man, gave then short shrift and poor John Rose was terribly embarrassed and told the other men that it happened all the time.

It was with shock and horror, in many circles, that they had recently read that Robinson's protectorate was anything but, and that the people had been living in a state of utter wretchedness and depravity, despite extensive funds being passed to Robinson for their care. The newspaper report stated that "*The miserable broken-hearted creatures struggled on in discomfort and sickness. Many perished in the bush, where mismanagement and unkindness had induced them to remain until too weak to move.*" Robinson had since moved on to Port Philip and was now the Chief Protector of Aborigines there, but the report demanded that an investigation be made into the whole protectorate system.

John shared the latest goings on from the Mechanic's Institute. He had attended a very interesting lecture in May called 'the Diffusion of Knowledge.' The lecturer, a Dr Paton, talked about how in this new modern age, knowledge was beginning to be more and more open to the masses, whereas in the past it was thought by those in power that a little knowledge was a dangerous thing, and it was best to keep the general population ignorant. How amazing it was that science was advancing at such a rapid rate that such things as the printing press were now so advanced that news could quickly be spread far and wide, and how man had been able to decipher the ancient hieroglyphics and discover ancient knowledge that had been hidden for centuries. Tasks that would once have taken months or even years, could now be accomplished far quicker. Take, for example, the time it now took to travel to and from England, less than three months and getting shorter and shorter all the time.

Mary Ann broke their musing with a pleading voice to Thomas to take the children home. Thomas reluctantly agreed. He found his time with John Harris to be very stimulating and actively sought out times when they could see each other. He didn't tell John or the Reverend of the troubles that he had been having with the farm and businesses. However, that should all be over soon, he hoped, and his father-in-law was sure that the drought would turn soon and all would be well.

After the Beswick's left, Amelia was left with Maria Davies and Katey Reibey. One of Maria's maids had come to get little Maria and Rowland had gone off to play inside. Katey turned to Amelia, "Mrs Harris," she started.

"No, no, lass, it's Emma please!" said Amelia.

"All right then Emma," said Katey tentatively, "you said that you're from Edinburgh, and I grew up there, but I know that you came here as a convict," she paused, looking timidly to make sure that she was not causing offence. Seeing none she went on, "I want to be a good minister's wife, Emma, but I know little about poverty or the harsh side of life, and if I am to be a good minister's wife I need to know about these things," she paused again, checking Amelia's response, "could you, would you, tell me a bit about where you grew up and what brought you here?" She took a breath of relief that she had finished her question, which had been so difficult to ask.

"Of course I can, lass, how long have you got?" Amelia let out a laugh, and the others followed nervously.

Over the next hour Amelia regaled both Katey and Maria with the story of her life, her happy but destitute upbringing in Fife, the attempts of the local pimps to recruit her when she started to bloom, her escape with the others to Stirling and then to Edinburgh, and her desperate eight years spent trying to survive on the streets. She didn't leave out any of the details either, telling them about singing for coins, poor Maggie, dying slowly of the clap, and even about the merchant boy and the pig stye, and her several offences and time in prison. The story culminated with her meeting Maria Davies on the *Rajah*, and the start of her new life.

Maria didn't know any of the details of Amelia's past life and when she had finished her story, both women sat with their mouths slightly open. Neither had much idea about the deprivations that the poor in Britain lived under.

"And as you can now see, lass, it's only a matter of time and place and circumstances that makes any of us differ from each other. Under it all we are all the same, a little good and a little bad, hopefully more of the good though," she smiled wistfully, "but desperate times change how a person reacts, and sometimes more of the bad has to come out for them to survive. But never judge a person on what they had to do to survive, as that was only them at that particular time and place."

Katey jumped up with a tear in her eye and hugged Amelia, to which Amelia blushed profusely. She had felt embarrassed to share her story, but also compelled to help these influential women to learn about the side of life that they had vowed to help and support.

"Nay," laughed Amelia, "that be enough of that. But if you've got a little whisky lying around, I wouldn't say no to a small dram, after sharing that story." Maria motioned for Katey to go inside the house as there was a bottle and glasses on the sideboard. The women sipped on the strong liquid and watched as the afternoon started to cast shadows across the lawn.

The men eventually returned, and it was time to leave. Hands were shaken and hugs were exchanged. Amelia told Katey to come and visit her at *Vron* any time that she wished to discuss anything, her door was always open. Katey gave her a hug again and a deep smile of appreciation.

A week later Mary Beswick gave birth to another daughter who she named Louisa, Amelia was glad that she held on for that extra week and Amelia didn't have to help to deliver another baby at the Davies' house.

Finally, in November and in time for Johnny's first birthday the Harrls's home was ready. Many trips had been made to Launceston to collect furniture and items for the house in the past few months. Rugs, curtains, and linens as well as other assorted household items had been ordered from the Beswick's friend Mr Avery Stodges who was a very wealthy merchant in Sydney and imported items from all over the world. Mary told Amelia that Mr Stodge's wife had been like her second mother when she was a baby in Sydney, and her mother was on her own with two small children while the legendary Sandy McKenzie served in the Army in Ceylon. All the items arrived in perfect condition and were exactly what John and Amelia were after.

John had purchased two excellent milking cows, an assortment of chickens and a stout pig from the *Vron* auction and the animals had been happily living in their new accommodations for a month before the family moved in. There was already a small orchard that had an established apple tree and a native lemon tree, but at the recommendation of Maria Webb, who knew everything about growing food, Amelia had also planted several stone fruit trees and berry bushes. The kitchen garden was already going along splendidly as it had also been planted the year before and had already delivered a season of produce. There was also a large potato and pumpkin plot that was also producing already.

When the house was completed, William Webb proudly gave the Harris's, with Cook and Jarvis in tow, a grand tour of the home, pointing out all the features, which he had personally checked himself. That year he had built 12 houses in the village as well as extensions to the *Bush Inn*, which was proving to be one of the most profitable in northern Van Diemen's Land.

On the day that they moved in John moved his boxes of books which he had been gifted from Mr Walker, as well as many that he had since purchased himself, and arranged them in his new floor to ceiling bookcase, designed to his specifications, in the sitting room. The room had a large window that looked out onto the front yard, and a beautiful fireplace for winter. Two new leather easy chairs were arranged with a small table between them, so that John and Amelia could enjoy each other's company, to read or chat, or enjoy refreshments. There was also a low couch suitable for seating three that could be used either by visitors or eventually children.

As Amelia was heavy with child and due at any time, Cook was invited and agreed to come and live with them for a while to help Amelia and keep her company. Jess and Amy said that they were quite capable of cooking for themselves, and the workers left at *Vron*, and nothing more exciting was due to happen for months, when the College staff would start arriving.

Although the Christmas celebrations were held at *Vron* which was easiest for all their friends, which now included all the *Vron* workers, in the afternoon the attendee's all travelled the short distance to the new Harris home where pudding were served, thanks to Cook and John, and the men played an impromptu game of cricket in the yard. The ensuing cheers and laughter elicited some interest from the neighbouring homes and soon the Harris' yard was full of neighbours playing cricket, ladies on the veranda relaxing and children running around. Johnny toddled around happily, holding the hand of one of the older children for security.

Vron

## Chapter Twenty Seven
# *1846 – Christ College*

*L*ittle Tommy Harris was born on 14 January with very little fuss. Amelia started having pains as she went to bed and Tommy was there for breakfast the next morning, with Amelia getting up to help with the toast. Cook chastised her terribly, but the birth had been easy, and she felt amazing with all the baby weight gone. She'd sleep later in the day, she told John and Cook, and they could look after Johnny, who was now running around everywhere and getting up to mischief.

Ann Brennan and George Emery were married on 28 January by the Reverend Davies at Longford. John and Amelia went for the service but as Amelia was still tender from the birth, they didn't go to the McKenzie farm for the celebrations. The service was beautiful. It was another hot, dry, day and the bride wore a dress made by her older sisters that had the new fashionable dropped shoulders, showing off Ann's beautiful creamy shoulders and decolletage. She carried a matching parasol to shade her face from the harsh sun. Her hair, in all its fiery auburn glory cascaded down her back like a river of fire. It was the first time that Amelia had seen Ann dressed up because she was a bit of a tomboy and was usually gambolling around with the children in sturdy drill outfits, with her hair scrabbled into a (usually dirty) bun on top of her head. George tended to be the same and after the service they raced out of the church and kissed each other boldly in front of everyone before being chased by the children around the church yard.

Ann's father Thomas Brennan was now 79 and only just starting to slow down in body and mind. This was the first time he'd had to attend a major event without his beloved Ann, and he knew how much she would have loved to see her youngest child, and her namesake, on her wedding day. His older daughter Elizabeth and stepdaughters Mary and Margaret gathered around to support him throughout the day.

Ann's brothers, Johnny Mac and the extraordinarily handsome, blonde haired, blue eyed, William Brennan caused much of a stir amongst the young ladies attending the service. Some had come along just to see the two men, who were two of the most eligible bachelors in the north of the colony. But Johnny Mac, at 36, was married to his hotels and horse-racing interests and William at 28 was terribly shy and preferred his own company and that of the farm animals. Word was that he was looking at work in the burgeoning mining industry. Many hearts would be broken.

The Reverend Davies had recently shared with John that there was currently a lot of conflict going on in the colony with regards to the schools and the church. It was a requirement of the clergy to encourage the prospering of their own religion, no matter what that religion was, and it had been usual for the various churches to open schools at or near their churches and to provide religious studies in their own denomination, as part of the curriculum. However, the government provided more funding to schools of the Anglican faith, and this angered those of other religions, of which there were many; the Methodists, Lutheran's, Roman Catholics, and a small smattering of Jews, to name but a few. Families from other churches were angry that their children were not getting the same education and perceived privileges.

To make matters worse there was also conflict within each denomination. The Reverend had come under fire over the past year as he had taken a strong interest in the schools that he had opened, some eleven at last count, and he made sure that at each school he knew every student and their circumstances, ensuring that the church helped when they could if they found a child in need. He also made regular visits to the houses of families who were not sending their children to school to lecture them on the importance of schooling and attending services. This did not sit well with many of the families in the communities he attended. Many were ex-convicts from very poor backgrounds. At home in Britain school was only for the gentry and the rich, and children stayed at home and helped with the house, the farm, and the younger children. For many, church was not a priority and some even told him that they didn't believe in God, much to the Reverend's chagrin. Maria tried hard to explain to him why these people felt the way they did, her understanding expanded by Amelia's recent talk.

In the end, some communities banded together and banned the Reverend from harassing them, as they stated, and brought charges against him. Although the charges did not stick, he had to end his interference in the lives of the children and try by other means to support them through the church's philanthropy and charity. It was agreed that for schools in the colony to receive government funding, they would have to teach a secular curriculum and only those students whose parents wished it would receive religious education.

On the opposite scale, wealthy parents in the colony only wanted their sons to attend schools where their chosen faith was highly valued. So far, John Gell, who was to run the new Christ College had avoided being ordained, but in 1845 his Queen's School in Hobart was dropped from government funding and soon closed.

At the bishop's urging, Gell was ordained a minister and started work at St John the Baptist church in Goulburn Street, Hobart, while he continued the planning for Christ College at Bishopsbourne.

Throughout 1845 and into 1846 both Bishop Nixon and the now Reverend Gell visited *Episcopal House* (*Vron*), many times, and deliveries continually arrived of furniture and supplies for the College. The Reverend Gell, a single man yet to turn 30 moved into *Episcopal House* early in the year to make sure that everything was ready for the College's opening, scheduled for October. Cook received three new house maids and three new kitchen maids, who arrived mid-March.

John was kept busy maintaining the library that kept growing. Items kept arriving and included many books donated by the Reverend Thornton and other British clergy, the Reverend Gell's own library, books donated or lent by the Reverend's Davies and Marriott (who was opening a church at Paterson's Plains), and the Diocesan Clergy Library provided by the Associates of the late Dr Bray of London.

It was around this time that John received his Conditional Pardon. He was now a free man in all respects, except that he could not return to England. That suited him fine. Van Dieman's Land was now his home and was where he wanted to raise his children. John had to pinch himself sometimes to believe that he was so lucky. Now approaching his 40th year, it had taken him a while, but he was so very happy that he now had a beautiful wife and two delightful sons. His circumstances, that had seemed so dire for so long, had certainly changed since he met Amelia, and he would be forever grateful for what she had given him. He had to admit that they did make an odd couple. Even though he came from humble circumstances he was very thoughtful and refined and had been easily accepted into intellectual society, if not as an equal, at least as a friend and colleague. Amelia was fun and loving and made everyone feel happy and comfortable around her, her rolling Scottish brogue aiding in that regard. She loved her family and friends fiercely and she showed them that every day. While she loved to dance and sing and throw down a dram of whisky, she was equally happy sitting quietly with John playing a board game or reading a book. They were perfectly suited; perfect opposites that made a perfect whole.

Cook had enjoyed her time living with the Harris's immensely and had been travelling to and from their home since February with John. The house was so close to *Vron* that in the good weather they would walk, but in poor weather they would take the buggy or carriage. Cook had a few brief discussions with John and Amelia about maybe building a small cottage on her block, that was right next to theirs, and then she could be closer to help Amelia and watch the two boys, who she felt were like her own grandchildren. John and Amelia said that they would be delighted for her to do that. First, though, she needed to see how intense her new role running the house at the College would be.

Amelia had so far been quite capable of managing most of the household needs, but with two small boys she struggled to take care of the animals and the gardens. Lila, a girl from one of the village farms was hired to take care of milking and caring for the cows, tending the garden, and collecting the produce. Amelia was also teaching her to read and write and Lila demanded that

Amelia reduce her pay to account for the tuition. Amelia put that small amount away in a tin, to give to Lila later on one day. Her older brother Lance was employed as a stable-hand and to maintain the carriage and buggy. Although Amelia had offered, he had not yet been interested in learning his letters.

The *Bush Inn* had become the place for the small community of Bishopsbourne to congregate during the warmer months, and on Sunday's Mr Webb commenced selling roast luncheons that were served under the trees in his little park. Amelia had started to lead the hymns at the new chapel, with John and Cook taming the little boys, and Mr Webb asked if she would provide some songs over his Sunday lunch service. She agreed heartily and the entertainment, with Amelia accompanied by two of the local men on instruments, became very popular. As more staff started to arrive at *Vron*, Cook had to go back to oversee the Sunday meals, but Johnny and Tommy were ably managed by John and by Sarah Webb.

The Reibey's were at the luncheon one afternoon when Katey told Amelia that they now had an organ at their church. When Thomas had first started his ministry there was no church in Carrick, so he held his services in a blacksmith's shop. In 1845 he moved his church services to a brick schoolhouse on his *Entally* estate and had just finished renovating it into a church at a personal cost of several hundred pounds, including the organ. Amelia had heard that Katey played the organ beautifully with her little dog Toby under her feet, delighting everyone. Amelia made a note to get over to Carrick as soon as she could.

Always on the lookout for new business ideas, Mr Webb found out that many in the colony had a love of the English tradition of the fox hunt, particularly the wealthy men. He started a hunting club out of the stables in the stock-yards next to the *Bush Inn* which was immediately embraced on a regular basis by Richard Dry of the *Quamby* estate who, at 31 and unmarried, was always looking for exciting activities to keep him interested. William Field, aged 30, also attended, along with his younger brothers Thomas and John. William had inherited the massive *Enfield* estate near Bishopsbourne. Thomas lived at the beautiful *Westfield* homestead at Westbury which his father had almost completed but had died before it was finished. Their father had been known as the Cattle King of Van Diemen's Land and owned more land and cattle than anyone in the colony. They supplied most of the beef that the government purchased and had therefore ridden out the economic crisis.

Another regular attendee was the young Reverend Thomas Reibey, who had to try and keep his interest a secret from the bishop.

To start with, various breeds of dog were used for the hunt until suitable setters could be brought out from England, and rather than foxes, the men chased deer and kangaroos. The catch of the day was often donated to the *Bush Inn* and the local community happily gathered for a free meal of venison or kangaroo stew, thus ensuring that complaints about the sport, which could sometimes disturb the normal peace of the village, were kept to a minimum.

The hunting club complimented the horse racing which had become a regular activity at William Field's racecourse, which he had built in 1844, half a mile from Little Hampton/ Bishopsbourne. That year a horse race with a prize value of 300 pounds a side, was wagered between Richard Dry's colt and William Field's filly, both 3 years old, and run three times around the course. William Dry's colt won. Johhny Mac and William Brennan were frequent attendees at the races and would always visit the Harris's while in the area.

Bishop Nixon had been very busy further expanding the superior education of boys in the colony, not just at Bishopsbourne. Two grammar schools were opened, the Launceston Church Grammar School in May was followed by the Hutchins School in Hobart in August and then Christ College in October.

John, Cook and the others had been kept very busy all year preparing for the opening. By opening day, the College had 20 pupils, all housed in the new dormitories renovated from the workers quarters, plus the Reverend Gell as warden, three clerical fellows, three lay fellows who were candidates for holy orders, six scholars and a bursar, as well as John in the library and the house staff. Once again *Vron*, or *Episcopal House*, was bustling.

Old Sammy appeared every now and then to tend to the rose gardens, which had become beautiful and very impressive, even though the bishop had employed two new gardeners. When John saw him he'd take a cup of tea or a lemonade out to him and the two men would sit and discuss horticulture. The Reverend Davies once caught them together and spent the afternoon happily talking about plants and flowers. He was also very interested in plants, having brought a number of specimens with him on the *Rajah* and was a member of the Launceston Horticulture Society.

On the College opening day numerous people attended from throughout the colony with Bishop Nixon declaring that the intention of the institution was *"to be a stronghold of learning and a school for Christian gentlemen"*. On the same day the bishop also laid the foundation stone for the extensions, a second double storey residence having the same tall gables as the *Vron* mansion, with a small octagonal tower at one end.

*The Examiner* newspaper reported on the 3rd of October 1846:

> *The Opening of Christ's College.*
>
> *On Thursday, 1st. October, the College at Bishopsbourne was opened. There were about 100 persons present and the ceremonies performed were interesting to all who delight in anticipations of the future importance of this institution. At 11o'clock morning prayers were read. A procession was then formed to proceed to the laying of the foundation stone of the new building in the following order, two and two. The Archdeacon and clergy present (we believe six but neither of the Launceston ministers were there). The Rural Dean and the College Trustees. The Warden, fellows, scholars and other students of the College, amounting we believe, to about 25. While they laid the stone, a psalm was read.*
>
> *An excellent collation was prepared to which the visitors did ample justice; next to this principle attraction was the library which contained some 3,000 volumes.*
>
> *The 20 pupils walked in their gowns and caps, the College costume, suggestive of school reminiscences of a pleasing and hopeful character.*

While the Reverend Davies and other clerics were having their own problems in the colony, Bishop Nixon was also having problems with the Lieutenant-Governor, Sir John Eardley-Wilmot, who had taken over from Sir John Franklin not long after the bishop arrived. The government had in its employ many convict chaplains who were vested with providing ministry to the convicts. They had been appointed by the government and Bishop Nixon found them very wanting as far as their Anglican values, experience, and commitment to the ministry. He refused to ordain, licence, or have any official responsibility for them, as he had no control over their employment or the quality of their work. He was also very outspoken in his condemnation of the whole convict system which further angered the Governor who was a strong believer in the convict system of justice. The situation became so dire that Bishop Nixon ended up travelling back to England to enlist the support of the government and the Archbishop of Canterbury. He left not long after Christ College opened.

Meanwhile many others in Van Diemen's Land were also becoming outspoken and condemned the convict system, which they said was cruel and outdated. The Reverend Davies was very outspoken, as was the Reverend Marriot, who had recently opened the first Anglican church at Paterson's Plains, which the Beswick's were very happy about. They did still intend to attend services at Longford though, as all their friends met there and keeping in touch was very important to them.

John Jackson, who was married to the Walker's eldest daughter Marianne, had recently returned to Van Diemen's Land. They had gone to England, where he was eventually exonerated for any wrongdoing in South Australia and had recently been working is Sydney on the census. He came back to Launceston invigorated with information about the anti-transportation movement that was spreading across Australia, and the pleas of the people for some form of self-government, the system of having to defer to England for every decision caused much angst amongst the wealthy landowners and merchants as well as the emancipist and free-settler community. The most prominent members of the community, including the clergy who had been submitting article after article to the newspapers about the evils of transportation and the convict system, urged Jackson to take on the role of their Agent to the government in England, which he readily agreed to and set off on his mission of representation. He was buoyed on by the fact Governor FitzRoy of New South Wales was supportive of an end to transportation and in a despatch to England suggested the need for a 'central intercolonial authority'. Self-governance seemed to be just around the corner.

Vron

Vron

Chapter Twenty Eight

# *1847 – 1848*
# *Freedom*

*I*n April 1847 the seemingly indefatigable Margaret Beswick,

Thomas's delightful mother, died at the McKenzie farm where she had lived for thirteen years. She had taken a fall outside of the house while chasing after her beloved grandchildren, not that anyone blamed the young-uns. The doctor said that she had broken her hip and a few days later, after much laudanum, she passed away peacefully, aged 77, surrounded by her many loved ones.

Her funeral was held at the new St Peter's church at Paterson's Plains with the Reverend Marriot presiding. Mrs Beswick had made a name for herself with kind acts amongst the community and within the church and the mourners spilled out around the new churchyard.

It was with a lot of interest that the Harris's learned that young George Walker had purchased land at Bishopsbourne. George was now 23 years old. It was Amelia who almost bumped into him while purchasing supplies at the village grocer. Although it had been four years since they had seen each other they recognised each other straight away.

"Miss Emma!" George cried out happily. Emma had Tommy in his wrap, trying to escape, and Johnny trying to escape and run out into the road. George told her quickly where he was living, and Amelia invited him to come to her house that evening for dinner.

Over dinner that night George told them that he had been quite sickly up at Forth, where his parents were now settled, and had decided to move further south. He had no interest in the logging industry that his father and brothers had moved into. He had very fond memories of his time at *Vron* and had been very sad to have to leave it. John remembered how George had always been more thoughtful and studious than the others. He preferred to be out in nature or reading a book to tearing around with the others. John invited him to come and visit the new College and he could see Cook and visit the new library, and both he and Amelia told him that he was always welcome at their house.

George told Amelia that he was very sorry for everything that had happened once they got to Forth and admitted that he and his siblings contributed to the disharmony in the house. But it had been very difficult for them all to suddenly go from extreme wealth to almost poverty. His mother and poor Miss Lemaire couldn't cope. Miss Lemaire had sadly passed away not long after they settled at Forth, just as things were starting to look up again for the family. Mr Walker found a new lady's companion, this time a practical and congenial older Scottish woman, much like Cook, and Mrs Walker had then perked up, thankfully.

Poor Mrs Walker, thought Amelia, even coming from such a privileged background she had known so much unhappiness in her life.

At Maria Davies mother's group at the end of May everyone was very excited to meet the gorgeous Sarah Emery, the first child to Ann and George. The tiny baby looked just like her mother with a light covering of bright red hair and red eyebrows. Ann told everyone that so far, she was a very placid baby, thankfully. Ann was still only 17 and full of energy. They were living with her sister Elizabeth, and George's brother John, while the men completed George and Ann's house, which was close to their own. Elizabeth was thankful for the help, as young George now six, Martha three and John two, needed a lot of attention. Elizabeth was also heavy with child again, and due over winter.

While baby Sarah was happily sleeping on Kate Reibey's lap, Ann raced off into the church yard with the loud gaggle of children, leading them in chasing and hiding games. All the other mothers agreed that they wished they were 17 again and full of all that energy.

One afternoon in July, John came racing up the path from *Vron*, through the terrible sleet that had been pouring down all day and came to an abrupt stop right outside the house. He whistled for Lance to come and get the horse and buggy, something he never did, considering it very bad manners.

Amelia saw all of this, from where she was sitting in the front room looking out of the window, in the front of the fire, while the two little boys played with their toy horses. Tommy at 18 months was babbling away, using new words every day, and Johnny at two and a half liked to baby him. Tommy yelled at him and told him "No! I not baby!" Sibling rivalry, said the older women, the burden of having children so close in age. Amelia didn't really want to admit that she was fairly sure that she was with child again.

John raced around the back and she could hear him stripping off his wet coat and boots in the washing area before coming into the house in his socks. He quickly appeared in the sitting room with a newspaper in his hand, almost hopping with excitement.

Amelia wearily stood up to greet him and then looked on with interest as she saw he had something monumental to say.

"Amelia, Amelia, guess what? You have been granted a Certificate of Freedom!"

"Oh my," said Amelia not quite believing it. Although having been sentenced to 7 years in 1841 she was due for it.

"You can also return to England if you ever wanted to!"

"Not without you, ya oaf!" she laughed and gave him a big hug. Having been given a life sentence, John's Conditional Pardon did not allow him to return to England, ever.

"Oh well that's good," said Amelia, "one less thing to worry about."

There was much discontent amongst the citizens of Van Diemen's Land, about what was being decided for them by the government. A proposal had been put forward that all the convicts left in New South Wales be sent to Van Diemen's Land, when they were receiving large numbers of convicts from England already. There were few assignments for them because the depression meant that landowners couldn't afford to pay and house them like they used to. Under the proposal some of the worst bushrangers that the Lieutenant Governor had sent to New South Wales for better security and to get them out of Van Diemen's Land would be returning. Mr Webb's *Bush Inn* had become a meeting place for concerned citizens and meetings were regularly held where petitions were written to be taken to the Lieutenant Governor to express the community's concerns.

Vron

In the middle of November as Amelia was again getting heavy with child and not looking forward to another summer baby, a messenger arrived at the house. As she went out to collect the letter or parcel, she made a mental note to not have relations around Easter time anymore. It was way too hot to be this big and to nurse a newborn.

The messenger gave her the letter and accepted a coin and was on his way. Amelia stood out in the yard to open the letter, as she had been pursued by her two little boys, who were much easier to manage in the large expanse of the yard where they could run and tumble around freely.

She tore open the letter and read the contents.

> "Dearest Emma,
>
> I unfortunately write with the very saddest of news. I wanted to let you and John and some of our other closest friends know quickly as the news will travel soon on the rumour mill.
>
> Our dearest darling Ann was taken ill with this wretched influenza last week and sadly, although she put up a brave fight, she passed on to Gods' care on Tuesday.
>
> Ann and George had recently moved into their home next to Elizabeth and John, and Ann had stayed there, away from the rest of the family, during her illness. As I write this letter dear George is also suffering, but his fever has broken, and we are hopeful that he will recover soon. Baby Ann is with Elizabeth who I also need to tell you was delivered of another baby boy only a week ago. She has

*named him William. It is a blessing really because she is now able to feed little Ann as well as tiny William.*

*Please do not rush over as we are all deeply in mourning, Father more than anything. Ann was such a bright light in all our lives and losing her hurts even more than losing mother, if that is at all possible.*

*The funeral will be held at Longford, as Father would like the Reverend Davies to perform the service, and have dear Ann buried at Christ Church. We all love that church and the Reverend.*

*I am sorry to deliver such terrible news Emma. I hope that you and the boys are well and pray that you remain so.*

*I shall send further word of when the funeral will be.*

*Your loving friend*

*Mary Beswick"*

Amelia dropped the letter, burst into tears and fell to her knees. The boys seeing this came running across to her.

"Mammie, mammie why are you crying?" asked Johnny patting her on the shoulder. Tommy stuck his thumb in his mouth, as he tended to do when he needed comfort, and looked at her sadly with his big blue eyes.

"Mammie just got some very sad news is all boys, I'm all right." She got up and brushed down her skirts and led the boys inside. She really needed a cup of tea.

Not Ann, of all people, not Ann. Ann was the brightest girl in the whole district. She stood out because of her bright red hair and her incredibly outgoing personality. She was larger than life! And only 18 years old. And with her little miniature, baby Sarah, only six months old. Oh, why was life so cruel?

There had been a terrible influenza epidemic that had spread through northern Van Diemen's Land over the past few months. It had interrupted important events and meetings with so many sick in bed with it. A whole new industry had sprung up with men coming to the villages to sell their 'cures' which the doctors said was little more that sly grog. So far Bishopsbourne had been spared the worst of it. Amelia decided that she and the boys would stay away from events for the time being, to try and avoid them getting sick as well. She couldn't bear to lose another child, after Emily.

Bushrangers were still a problem in Van Diemen's Land, with homes, businesses and travellers regularly being robbed and attacked. News arrived in the village that Hugh Glacken, a notorious bushranger had been hanged in Launceston in November. Glacken received the death sentence after he robbed and seriously assaulted Thomas Powell, Richard Dry's overseer at *Quamby*. The Reverend Reibey's father had attested to Glacken's good behaviour while he was working for him at *Entally* and was responsible for him getting his Ticket-of-leave in 1836. He had then turned to a life of crime.

As it got closer to the next baby being born Cook came more and more frequently to the house. Her work at *Episcopal House* was getting busier and busier and she had to admit that she no longer enjoyed it. She was lonely without John and Jarvis living there and the staff at the College were all 'hoity-toity men' as she described them. She loved the Reverend Gell. As a young single man, he would often come and chat with Cook and the girls, and even take tea and biscuits with them in the kitchen, but most of the others, including the pupils, the wealthy sons of the colony, could be quite rude and looked down their nose at the staff. Except John of course, he had been accepted as one of them, goodness knows he looked and sounded like one of them.

And she wasn't getting any younger. Cook would be 60 in a couple of years and was starting to feel like it was time to slow down a bit. She certainly couldn't be bothered anymore with everything that went along with managing a large kitchen and house. She'd miss the maids, but they had become her subordinates not her friends, so the relationship was different.

After the tragic news of Ann Emery's death, Amelia had confined herself and the boys to the house, fearing that the dreaded influenza would get them too. She wasn't even happy about John going to the College, but the only option would have been for him to stay there and not come home, and that was not an option she could live with. She still needed to see him every night and feel him against her every night. Poor Lila and Lance were not even allowed near the house.

"Only until this influenza has gone," she said trying to sound cheery as she waved at them across the yard as they got on with their chores.

Cook was the only one allowed to visit, because Amelia said that she would go mad without seeing her. But when Cook saw what chaos the little boys were causing Amelia, she went back to the College and turned in her resignation that day. She went back to the Harris's home that night and told them what she had done and that she would be ever so grateful if she could stay in their guest room for the time being, until she could arrange for her own house to be built next door. She had more than enough money put away from all her years of working and barely spending a penny, so she would not be a burden on them.

Amelia jumped up and threw her arms around Cook, bursting into tears. John also came over and hugged Cook and they both said how very welcome that she was. Cook had become the mother that they no longer had, but that they both needed, so much.

On the 22nd of February, after a very quiet Christmas and New Years period, little David Harris was born with even less fuss than the other two. There was not even time for the midwife to arrive before he was there. Amelia was in the best of spirits, having been able to rest so well for the last part of her confinement as Cook so ably entertained the children and had taken over cooking all the meals, much to John, and Amelia's relief. John would cook as often as he could, but he was often home after the boys needed to be fed, and he left too early to get the bread started of a morning. There had been many interesting meals in the house before Cook moved in. A few times they had needed to wander down and seek a decent meal at the *Bush Inn* after another of Amelia's disasters. They all laughed about it though. "At least I can sing!" she laughed at them when they teased her. And that she could.

Amelia had a very good reason to cease her quarantine at home as John Webb was set to marry his sweetheart Jane Lyall on the

4<sup>th</sup> of May. She started to step out again in April, hoping that the influenza had abated enough to be safe.

Everyone was very happy to see the Harris's back again at services, both at Longford and at Bishopsbourne. Amelia started leading the hymns at both churches, and after the service at the Church of the Holy Nativity she would again sing at the *Bush Inn*, Cook taking the two little boys back to the house for the afternoon and John caring for tiny David until he needed to be fed.

Cook had chosen a very small and simple cottage for her purposes, and it was positioned just past the Harris's beautiful yard and outside sitting area near the big gum tree. She asked if rather than making her own if she could share in the Harris's kitchen garden, dairy and chicken yard.

Mr Webb was taking some time to start the house because there was much building activity going on, and once again he was having trouble finding good tradesman. But the Harris's did not care at all as they were happy for Cook to stay with them forever if she wanted to. They would just add on to their own house, John said, if they were blessed with more young ones. Amelia cringed a little. Four babies in a little over six years had all but worn her out and she remembered her vow and told John that they would have to go back to their 'other' ways of showing their love to each other for a while. John, having not even thought about those other ways for nearly six years remembered them with glee and was almost pleased that they could not do the usual thing for a while.

In 1848 the young Reverend Reibey and William Field founded a racing club and racecourse at Carrick, not far from the Reibey's

*Entally* estate. Thomas gifted a racecourse south of a property called *The Moat* where the first races at Carrick were held. The Moat had originally been owned by Mrs Walker's parents, the Fletcher's, before the Walkers' moved to Van Diemen's Land. The racecourse soon became known as the best in Tasmania, as Van Diemen's Land was starting to be called more frequently.

John Webb and Jane Lyall's wedding was truly something to behold. Mr Webb had erected a massive pergola to the side of the *Bush Inn* and it was adorned with lanterns and more flowers than Amelia had ever seen. The ceremony was held at the Church of the Holy Nativity with the Reverend Gell presiding and the huge crowd then moved to the pergola for a sumptuous meal and dancing into the wee hours. Many people chose to stay for the night and there were tents erected all over the stock yards area, as well as many people being billeted to homes in the village. It reminded John of the halcyon days at *Vron*.

During the night, Mr Webb stood up and announced that as a wedding gift he was handing over the *Bush Inn* to his only son John. John, 26, had been working side by side with his father for many years and knew everything about the business.

The bride's parents had a very similar start to their life in Van Diemen's Land as the Webb's. Jane's father, Robert Lyall, a butcher from the East End of London, was convicted and sent to the colony, and luckily was assigned to Richard Dry senior, who owned land at Adelphi and the *Quamby* estate. Mr Dry supported Mr Lyall in bringing out his wife and two daughters in 1835. Robert and Margaret Lyall were a few years older than John, in their mid-40's. As a Ticket-of-leave holder Robert had run the Mailstop Inn at Westbury and received a government contract to supply meat and produce to the government outpost at

Westbury. In 1843 Robert won the licence for the *Westbury Inn* and the family had been getting richer every year.

With both children familiar with the hotel industry and having their parents to mentor them, John and Jane were off to a good start.

In June Mary Beswick added another daughter to her brood. This child she named Sarah. The Beswick's now had five children aged 9 and under as well as Mary Ann who was now 15. As the winter was especially bad with snow and storms almost every day, the Harris's and Beswick's were unable to see each other for many months.

The Webb's turned it on again for a winter wedding this time when Sarah Webb married Thomas Lawson on the 3$^{rd}$ of August. This time the celebrations were held inside the *Bush Inn* with fewer attendees, but it was a beautiful night by candle and lantern light and the food was delicious. Thomas came from another hotelier family, his father having the licence for *The Plough Inn* in Launceston. He had promised the licence to Thomas once he was old enough, so Sarah would be running a hotel as well as her brother John. Maria, one of the older Webb daughters, was also running a hotel, the *Berridale Inn*, with her husband William Saltmarsh at Longford. William Saltmarsh's father was a close friend of Thomas Brennan as they had come across from Norfolk Island together in the 1810's.

It seemed that every hotelier in the north was at the wedding. Johnny Mac and his entourage of friends was also there, as he was good friends with Thomas's father Richard. He stayed at the Harris's home on the night of the wedding, and John gave him a tour of the College the next morning. They laughed that Johnny

Mac had no use for the College as it seemed that he would never get married or have children, it was the bachelor life for him! John told him not to be too sure as he had thought the same until Amelia stumbled into his life.

The Lawson wedding was the last service that the Reverend Gell conducted. He had decided to return to England and was succeeded by the Reverend Frederick Cox. Cook told Amelia that the poor Reverend had been like a love-sick puppy the whole time he was at the College. Having no-one else to confide in he had spoken to Cook and told her that while living at Government House in Hobart with Sir John and Lady Franklin, he had fallen madly in love with Eleanor, Sir John's daughter with his first wife who had died young. All he wanted to do was to be with Eleanor, but he had felt obliged to do the best he could to make the Franklin's dream of superior education in Van Diemen's Land, come to fruition first. Now with the three schools running, he had asked and been approved to go home.

By 1848 the College was running exactly as it had been envisioned. There was daily morning and evening chapel, communal dinner was held in the main dining hall with a high table. There was now a college football and cricket ground and a college cricket club. The members had formed themselves into a senior common room, like that of an Oxford or Cambridge college.

In his farewell address the Reverend Gell announced that he would fund the Gell scholarship at Christ College for settlers of all denominations. The college staff presented him with a service of communion plate.

Two weeks after the Lawson wedding, the Reverend Davies, who was one of the trustees of the College stopped in for an impromptu visit and visited John in the library. He seemed rather stern and asked John if he could send a messenger to Amelia and have lunch with them at the Harris house. They shared a buggy across to the house because as usual the weather was inclement. They could smell the aroma of cooking coming from the house as they got closer. Cook would have been making something special for the Reverend.

"I'm afraid," said the Reverend, "that after my news we may not feel like eating," he looked sadly at the assembled trio. "Little Sarah Emery died just a few days ago."

Amelia and Cook both drew their breath in shock. Oh no! Little Sarah was only a baby. She had just started toddling. Poor George, to not only lose his beautiful wife, but to also lose his darling daughter!

The Reverend told them that George and Sarah had only recently moved into their own house on the same property as John and Elizabeth Emery. Sarah had succumbed to a chest infection and had just never rallied despite the administrations of everyone who had been summoned to help, including the doctor from Longford.

When Maria Davies started the mother's group up again once winter broke in September, everyone felt the presence of two beautiful angels watching over them. Two beautiful souls who should have been there with them.

## Chapter Twenty Nine
# *1849 – 1850*
# *Life goes on*

*J*arvis visited the Harris's regularly and would usually stay the night in the Harris's second bedroom. Little David was still in with his parents and the two boys shared a room.

Jarvis enjoyed playing backgammon and cards with his best friends and having a few whiskeys. Sometimes they would all go for a luncheon at the *Bush Inn* or attend one of the sports matches that were now held every weekend in the warmer months. Jarvis had become particularly fond of the hunting and although he felt he was too old to participate in the hunt he would assist in setting out the scent trails and revel with the others at the end of the hunt if it had been a good day.

Often John and Amelia would hear Cook and Jarvis talking well into the night after they had gone to bed.

During one visit Jarvis shared some sad information about some of Amelia's shipmates from the *Rajah*. He heard often about Maggie Miller who had been assigned to *Brickendon* when he first started working there. Maggie had been a model prisoner on the *Rajah* and her assignment at *Brickendon* reflected the regard she was held in. Jarvis said that she was a lovely girl while at *Brickendon* and everyone was surprised when she became involved with one of the rougher men from a neighbouring farm.

Sadly, it seems that she was being abused, turned to the drink and had been in and out of the Female Factory.

"I wonder if the Reverend could do anything to help her?" said Amelia.

"He's already aware of the situation, and sadly she won't accept any help," sighed Jarvis.

Amelia was very sad for Maggie. She thought that Maggie would be the one to have a wonderful life here in the colony. She was a good person and didn't deserve the life she had got. She had also found out that Maggie Speirs who was so much fun while they were in prison in England and on the *Rajah* and who helped her so much during her first stint at the Female Factory, had recently died aged just 33. They said her death was caused by her heavy drinking. She'd been married after she'd left the Factory and had two sons. But she kept getting into trouble. Amelia wondered what had happened to her boys.

And poor simple old Sarah Woodhouse had also recently died, although she had apparently spent several years with a kindly family in Hobart before she died in the hospital, they said of old age.

She wondered how the other women had fared. Perhaps she should try and contact some of them. She had written several letters to her friend Margaret in Edinburgh, but never received a reply. Maybe it was easier to just try to forget that part of her life.

Maria Davies' mother's group was more popular than ever and there were now two distinct groups of women. There were the younger mothers in their teens and twenties, who Katey Reibey mostly sat with. Sadly, at 25 and having now been married for over 6 years it seemed that children were not going to happen for the Reibey's. Still, Katey came to the mother's group and cuddled all the babies and never once complained about her lot. She was far too busy doing good works in the community and supporting the Reverend in his church work. It certainly seemed that the bishop had been right in ordaining him because he had done so much for the community. He was tireless in his efforts and he and Katey were friends to everyone, convict, emancipist, and free settler. It was said that he had been in trouble with the bishop a few times due to his unorthodox love of all things sporting, and he was partial to a little gambling and drinking, but he was still a young man and his good works more than made up for his little indiscretions.

Then there were the older mothers, all in their 30's now, of which Amelia, Maria Davies, Mary Beswick and Mr Webb's daughter Eliza Hartnoll belonged. Between them they had Johnny and Tommy Harris, aged four and three and baby David; Maria and Emma Davies, aged six and four, as well as Rowland now 12; Margaret, Jane and Louisa Beswick, aged eight, five and four, as well as Thomas 10 and baby Sarah, being cuddled by the mothers; and Henry, William, Mary, Alfred and Emma Hartnoll, nine, seven, six, four and two, and baby Priscilla in the lap cuddling group.

Mary Beswick's eldest daughter, Mary Ann Peck, now 16, was spending her time with either the younger mother's or the other single girls who, if allowed, would sit in the church yard after services and converse, at a safe distance, with all the single men, or go to watch the cricket at a safe distance from their parents. Mary Beswick kept a close eye on her eldest daughter and would call her back to the mother's group if she thought she was getting too forward with any of the men.

That left Rowland Davies now 12 and Thomas Beswick, no longer Tommy now he was 10, and Henry Hartnoll, nine, to wrangle the younger children in their group.

The seven little girls, ably lead by eight-year-old Margaret Beswick played babies with their dolls and had tea parties with the toys they had brought along. Every now and then they would get an energy spurt and chase each other around the grounds.

The three older boys arranged themselves and the four younger boys into two teams and usually played tug-of-war, chasey or cricket. But today Thomas had brought knucklebones that his grandfather had polished up for him and taught him how to play. The mothers watched on smiling as the group of boys sat listening intently to Thomas as he explained the game. But before too long they had grown bored and were off racing around the grounds laughing and yelling at each other.

These days were truly blissful, with the sky above them as blue as anything they had seen, with soft puffy clouds quickly floating past, and a gentle breeze every now and then blowing the delicious scent of eucalyptus through the air. The women could almost count on one hand the days they had had like this back home in Britain. In the colony, strangers who they would have never even met back at home, had become friends, and with so many having no extended family in the colony, those friends had become family.

Amelia was so proud and happy of the wonderful 'family' that she had made for herself here in Van Diemen's Land. She had to pinch herself sometimes that it was all real. She had certainly been through hell to get here, but now she was reaping the rewards of her dreams and her careful planning. It was so good to finally be here.

John ran into one of his old acquaintances one Sunday at Longford. James Ashton who went by the name 'Golden' had been assigned to Thomas Reibey's father at *Entally* when John first met him in 1839. They would run into each other at the stables of the various houses that they had delivered Mr Reibey and Mr Walker to, back in the olden days. Golden had once told him that his family had been gypsies and travelled around with a circus in England, which was where he had learned his horse-riding skills.

John had lost touch with him since they both got their Tickets-of-leave but the two men greeted each other warmly, both a world away from where they were 10 years ago. Golden excitedly told John that he was about to purchase a circus troupe from Thomas Mollar who had been touring it around the Hobart area.

"I've got me some big plans for this circus John, mark my words," said Golden. John had to lean down to talk to him as Golden was barely five foot tall. He asked John if he'd like to have lunch at the *Berridale Inn*. After checking that Amelia and the boys were happy at the mother's group, John spent a very interesting afternoon talking with Golden about his plans for the circus.

"John, I think this circus is going to be big. It is currently the most popular entertainment in Van Diemen's Land, apart from the horses and the sports of course. But the theatre offerings have been woeful to be honest, and the majority of people here want something exciting, not some snobby opera or play," remembering who he was with he checked himself, "of course those who are interested in the more intellectual pursuits should have something of interest too."

John laughed. "Golden! Old man. I may sound like a hoity toity and work at the College, but I come from humble beginnings too as you well know, and my wife Amelia and I would love to see a circus. They sound very exciting. I do remember seeing clowns, and fire breathers and stilt walkers at the Lambeth Gardens in London, but that was a long time ago now, but I very much enjoyed the colours and the pageantry and the joy they gave," he took a long sip of his tea remembering the old days back at home. No, he corrected himself, his old home. Van Diemen's Land was now his home.

"Well, I'll be sending some tickets your way John as soon as we are up and running in Launceston. I have a feeling that they will still be talking about this circus in a hundred years time!"

Around Christmas time Amelia realised that she was with child again. She estimated that this child would be born in the middle of the following year at which time Johnny would be five and a half, Tommy four and a half and David two and a half. She secretly hoped this time for a little girl, someone to give her company into her old age. It was with much happiness that Maria Davies confided that she also thought that she was with child again. How exciting for them to have babies again at the same time. "This time", laughed Amelia, "I'll be staying away from ye around the birthing time." It was funny to think that Amelia had delivered two more babies since her little namesake Emma was born.

Having Cook living with them had been wonderful for the Harris's. Her cottage had been completed months beforehand, and while she had added furniture and decorations to her liking, everyone preferred her staying in the Harris home. It just seemed practical over the cold winter months, and then when the weather got warmer, she just didn't bother to move into the cottage. The cottage was getting very good use though. Over winter with three small, energetic boys to entertain, Cook would often break up the long days by taking them all over to the cottage for a few hours so that Amelia could have a rest, or Cook would sometimes go over and spend some time there reading or knitting and enjoying the peace. She said, though, that after years of living around lots of people that too much time on her own drove her batty and she needed to have the routine of the kitchen and the cooking, and playing with the little boys, to keep her sane!

Young Lance was still employed in the stables, and Johnny and Tommy would go there when the weather allowed and help him with his work. They both loved the horses and Lance would pop them on the back of the quieter ones and lead them around the yard.

Lila had since married a young butcher, who was working in the village, but she would still come every morning to milk the cow, and tend the chickens, leaving the fresh milk and eggs outside of the back door. Sometimes she would enjoy a cup of tea with Cook if she was already up and about, which she usually was, as the bread did not make itself, she often said if reprimanded by Amelia for being up so early.

An interesting development that year had been that Jarvis had quietly started to invite Cook on outings. Just the two of them. They had attended regatta's, the circus, and the Olympic Theatre in Launceston already, travelling in Jarvis's new and impressive carriage, which he drove himself in good weather or hired a man in poor weather. They would usually stay at Johnny's Mac's hotel where Cook said they were made to feel like royalty.

Cook had even gone with Amelia for her annual dress fitting visit to the McKenzie farm that year. Amelia had been going there every year, ordering any new items that the family needed, when hand-me-downs had fallen apart, or Johnny outgrew his clothes. Amelia would usually measure up the boys and John, who needed to regularly update his work clothing, and Mary and the ladies would make all the items to order. Amelia would go by herself while Cook minded the boys. She had learned to drive the buggy well and enjoyed the time out in the open countryside by herself and the day out with Mary and the ladies. She could also look at the fabrics on offer and look at the new magazines from England and Paris, that Mary and Thomas subscribed to. New boots were also usually needed for the boys, who outgrew them or destroyed them very quickly. Again, Thomas would make the little boots to order based on measurements.

But this year Cook decided to come too. The boys were left with Lila who was happy to supplement her income for the day, although when they got back that afternoon, she was very happy to hand them back over.

Cook ordered two evening dresses in the latest fashion, "For the theatre you know, lassie, you can't look dowdy for the theatre," and three new day dresses in soft cotton, with patterns, suitable for daytime outings. This was all very different to how Amelia had always seen her, in her sturdy brown or navy drill dresses with her cotton apron over the top. Amelia liked the change.

Vron

At the beginning of 1850 everyone was talking about what was being called the Gold Rush in far off California. Apparently so much gold had been discovered in this far off place that men from all corners of the world were travelling daily to a town called San Fransisco, where everyone could make their fortune. A newspaper report said that there were often up to 300 ships at anchor off the coast. John and Amelia marvelled at what this must look like, having seen the port in England with a few hulks and a few ships, even that looked busy.

John told Amelia that Mr Webb's son-in-law William Saltmarsh had left for California, leaving Maria to run the *Berridale Inn* on her own. The couple, in their 30's had not been blessed with children, so Maria had to rely on paid workers to support her. She had run into problems as the licence was due for renewal and the magistrate would not let Maria renew it on behalf of her husband. The legal wrangling continued for the poor woman.

The weather was poor that year and over winter the Harris family only ventured out to the village and to the Church of the Holy Nativity for services. There were now too many little ones to try to wrangle in the bad weather on the journey to Longford. This sadly meant that they missed out on seeing their friends who lived over that way. Still, as the years went by, they became more and more part of the community at Bishopsbourne.

Amelia had told everyone that after this baby was born that she was going to start classes for the young ones, just the children around Johnny and Tommy's ages, from her schoolroom that had lain dormant since they moved into their house. It had been used several times for dinners and family events where they needed more room than in their house, but it was yet to be used for the purpose for which it was built.

Jarvis came every second weekend, and either took Cook away for the weekend, or stayed at the Harris home. It had been more of the later in the past month with the weather so bad. He arrived in May to let them know that Maria Davies had been delivered of another daughter, this one who she named Mary.

The anti-transportation and self-government supporters continued their agitation with regular meetings held at the *Bush Inn.* In a very interesting turn of events, it was announced that Queen Victoria had signed a document that provided some separation of government for New South Wales and the newly renamed Victoria which was previously called Port Phillip. The Governor was to have a lot more power to make decisions and laws rather than always having to defer to England. This move was celebrated in Van Diemen's Land, however as it was still a penal colony, there was little chance that England would give up any control soon. It was also announced that convicts would start being sent to Western Australia, which it was hoped would alleviate some of the pressure in Van Diemen's Land.

Amelia and John always welcomed the visits from Jarvis as he always had the most interesting pieces of information. By July Amelia was very heavy with child and not coping as well as she had with the others. Cook had decided as soon as the weather had turned that there would be no more overnight outings for her until the new baby had arrived and Amelia was coping by herself. This family was her priority, as much as she enjoyed her visits to the theatre and what not. She had to admit that she very much enjoyed Jarvis's attentions, which, while they started off in a brotherly way, had now developed into something very different. On their last trip he had even reached over and held her hand as they travelled to Launceston. She knew that she had blushed like a ripe beetroot, but she had to admit that it felt very nice.

After the children had gone to bed on this particular night Jarvis asked Amelia if she remembered Georgiana Gatehouse from the *Rajah*? Amelia said that she did, and also that Jarvis had once told her that Georgiana was assigned to *Woolmers.* Jarvis said that Georgiana had married another man assigned to *Woolmers* called William Grubb in 1843. Both of them were considered to be the finest workers on the estate and William had, earlier this year, received an award for being the best employee. The couple had bought a house near the estate and were very happy. However, another worker from the estate had obviously been harbouring a lust for Georgiana and had broken into their house, tried to rape poor Georgiana and then stabbed her in the leg and arm as she tried to ward off his attack. Luckily, he was interrupted in his murderous attempt by a carter who had been making deliveries and had heard her screams. Henry Hart had been arrested for the vicious crime and had been sentenced to death.

Although the Harris's had been lucky during their time in Van Diemen's Land, it could still be a wild and dangerous place to live. The notorious bushranger James Hollway had been hanged the previous year in Hobart following a rampage through the district that included a robbery where the wife was badly assaulted.

Word came from the Beswick's as winter settled in, that dear old Thomas Brennan had died on the 30th of June. Like Thomas's dear mother Margaret who they had lost three years before, Thomas had seemed somehow larger than life. Until the very end, at the age of 84, he was still doing most of the management of all the farms and properties owned by him and inherited by his stepdaughter Mary. Thankfully he hadn't needed to manage the farms left to Mary Ann Peck, as her uncle's had said that they would do that after poor Jeremiah Peck's early demise.

But Amelia and John had heard Thomas grumbling every now and then that he was too old for so much work. Sadly, Thomas Beswick did not seem to have the talent for farm management, although his shoe-making business was doing well.

As Amelia was very close to having the baby it was decided that the family would not attend Mr Brennan's funeral, as it was also very poor weather, and the funeral was being held all the way over at Paterson's Plains.

Beautiful little Amelia Harris was born on the 12th of July 1850. Amelia had been complaining of severe back pain for several weeks beforehand and when the midwife examined her after her waters broke it was found that the baby was lying with her back along her mother's back. This presentation often meant that labour was prolonged and more painful than usual as the baby was not in the most ideal position to slither out.

The birth pains started before dawn had broken and by mid-afternoon Amelia was a seething, howling mess of pain. Cook summoned Lila to come and take the boys over to the cottage and not to bring them back to the house as they had all become quite distressed seeing their mother in such pain. John had been sent to work, hastened out the door after breakfast by Cook who promised to come and get him once the baby was born. But hearing nothing, he had hurried home early to find chaos.

Vron

Poor Amelia laboured throughout the night. Cook and John took turns rubbing her back, helping her to walk around the house and running food out to the boys and Lila, none of whom could sleep from the worry. As dawn broke, Lance arrived to tend the horses and John was just about to send him in the fast buggy to get the doctor from Longford, when they both heard one long piercing scream followed by silence. The men both looked at each other in terror and stayed that way unable to move for a few seconds, until the air was rent with the first cries of a newborn baby. Thankfully, the cry sounded healthy and robust.

John raced back into the house and into the bedroom, to see his beloved lying on the bed with her head propped up on pillows nursing a new baby.

"Is she all right? Are they all right?" He gasped.

"Yes laddie, they are both fine, ye have a lovely daughter," said an exhausted looking Cook.

John gave Amelia a kiss on her cheek. She looked as she must feel after not sleeping for over 24 hours and having been in such pain for so long. He kissed the tiny baby on the top of her head and was then shooed out of the room by Cook and the midwife.

After everything was cleaned up and Amelia and the baby given a bill of good health from the midwife, Cook brought Amelia some tea and toast with jam and tried to get her to sleep but buoyed with adrenalin Amelia found that impossible. For the rest of the morning the family all gathered in the bedroom to see the new baby, their first sister, who immediately became "Little Emma."

As the weather finally started to turn, John received advice from the College warden, the Reverend Windsor, who had replaced the previous Reverend in 1849, that the Reverend Davies had been appointed as the Archdeacon of Launceston. This was very exciting news. Their friend the Reverend Davies had done so much good work, and it was so nice to see him being rewarded. They guessed that the news would mean that the Reverend and Maria would be moving to Launceston. But John and Amelia had already concluded that the Bishopsbourne church and village had become their community. While they would still visit the Beswick's and the Davies' when they could, they would try to spend more time near home. As the family expanded it grew more onerous to travel around.

Amelia told John that she might start a mother's group here in Bishopsbourne in a similar manner to Maria's group at Longford. There were certainly enough mothers and children around. And she also intended to start her classes in the new year.

In September the weather finally broke and they had decided to make a final trip to Longford to see the Reverend's last service in the church that he had built, but that week John received word that the service was suspended due to ill health in the family. Apparently, there was an outbreak of illness in the Longford community and little Maria Davies had fallen ill.

They were all devastated the following week when word came that Maria, aged six, had died.

Amelia left everything, and with tiny Emma strapped to her chest she took the fast buggy over to Longford to comfort her long-time friend.

Maria was stoic in her grief, as Amelia suspected that she might be. The two women sat with their thoughts, nursing their newborns. Amelia lay with Maria at night when the grief took her, and she cried into her pillow until she fell asleep. Reminders of Maria were everywhere. Her doll house, her 'babies,' her tea-set. Four-year-old Emma was confused and kept asking where "Mia" was. Maria had been her idol, and she had followed her around everywhere. Rowland came and checked on his mother frequently and took Emma off to play. He hadn't needed to do so for so many years as Emma had been Maria's constant shadow.

Oh, why was life so cruel, thought Amelia. She didn't even try to ask the Reverend the meaning of it all, and he luckily didn't offer any good words from the Lord, because Amelia didn't think she could stand it. Her beautiful Emily, little Sarah Emery, and now little Maria so full of life and love. All taken before their lives could even start.

The funeral was well attended and became the poor Reverend's final service. John, Cook and the boys came across for it, and brought Lance who drove the fast buggy home so that Amelia could travel back in the carriage with her family.

The Harris's hugged their four children closer over the next few weeks, feeling the harshness and vulnerability of life too much.

Vron

## Chapter Thirty
# *1851 – Lost and found*

$\mathcal{E}$arly in the new year Amelia wandered up to the new
Bishopsbourne Post Office with Emma strapped to her chest, wriggling like a possum in a hessian bag. She was proving to be a feisty one, this girl-child named after her. She had much more gumption already, at six months, than little Emily or any of the boys had at that age.

William Hartnoll had recently purchased the Post Office licence and he, Eliza and their brood had moved into the village. Eliza was happy to be so close to her brother John and their parents, as well as the Harris's and other families they had become close to.

Amelia was pleased to only need to go on a quick walk to post her letters, rather than having to drive to Longford or Westbury.

She entered the lovely new post office that smelled like fresh white-wash and approached the counter. The man behind the counter turned around and Amelia had the oddest sensation. She could swear that she had seen him before, and that she knew him well. The man noticed her staring at him.

"Hello Miss, is there something I can help ye with?" he said in a broad Scottish brogue.

"Oh, umm, hello Sir, I am Mrs Harris, Mrs Amelia Harris, my husband and I live down the road past the tavern. We, um, know the Hartnoll's very well," she was grasping at straws trying to wrack her memory about where she knew him from.

"Sir, I feel like we might know each other," she started. Little Emma's arms had escaped their binding's, and she was reaching out to the man babbling "Dadda, Dadda." How embarrassing, thought Amelia.

"Well, Mrs Harris, I'm not sure where we would have met as I've been down in Hobart since I arrived in the colony near on seventeen years ago now, and my wife and I only just arrived here in this lovely village in the last month."

"Oh, that would be why I haven't seen you yet as I haven't been to the post office yet, but I'm sure that I know you, that we've met. Did you come from Fife at all, or Edinburgh? Stirling even?"

"Why no lass, I was born and bred in Glasgow, and lived there until the law saw fit to send me out here," he gave a light-hearted but embarrassed chuckle. No one really wanted to talk to a stranger about their conviction.

Amelia finished her business while Emma continued to reach out and call the man 'Dadda.'

"Thank you so much Mr……." she said

"Smith. It's Mr Smith, James to my friends, and hopefully we become that now we are living here in the village."

"Yes, thankyou Mr Smith, er James, very kind of you, and I hope so too. You said you are here with your wife. Do you have any children? Only I am going to start a small school at my house for the younger ones soon, I have three young boys at home who need to start their schooling."

"Nay, Mrs Harris, my Lettie and I have not been blessed, but I'm sure that she would love to meet you. Maybe at services?"

"Oh yes, of course, I am usually there so long as the weather allows."

Amelia took her leave and wandered off down the road back to her house. It wasn't a long walk, but she was terribly distracted by Mr Smith, there was just something about him that she could not pinpoint.

She walked in the back door, unstrapping Emma as she came in, as the infant continued to struggle for her freedom, and it was time for her lunch.

As she entered the kitchen she looked up and saw Cook who was kneading the bread dough.

Amelia took one look at her and almost fainted. Then she did fall into a chair that was against the wall.

"Ere, lassie, are you all right girl?" said Cook, rushing over to check her. "You're no in the way again are you, lassie? It's no been seven months yet."

"No!" said Amelia, "I hope not!"

Cook went back to her kneading. Amelia looked thoughtfully at her.

"Cook, you said your boy was called Jimmy, wasn't it?"

"Aye, lass that was a long time ago I told ye that story. Ye've got a good memory, I'll give you. Yes, my little Jimmy, I miss him every day."

"And your name was Alice? It wasn't Alice Smith, was it?"

Cook stopped her kneading and looked up at Amelia.

"Why are you saying this lass?" she asked with concern.

"Oh Cook," Amelia rushed over and took Cook's shoulders in her hands, looking right into her eyes, "I don't want to upset you, and I could be entirely wrong, but if your Jimmy was a Smith then I think I may have just met him. It didn't occur to me when I was at the post office but looking at you as I walked in, well this man could be a younger you!"

Cook was the one who then staggered over and fell into the chair.

"My Jimmy? My dear little Jimmy?"

Amelia told her the whole story. Once she was finished, they looked at each other and then tried to figure out what to do. Cook wanted to rush up to the post office straight away, but Amelia told her that might upset Jimmy/James. What if it wasn't her Jimmy. And he was working. She couldn't interrupt his work with such a big announcement.

They finally decided that Amelia would go and speak to Eliza Hartnoll at her house. She was overdue to see Eliza anyway. Eliza would know what to do. Maybe Mr Hartnoll could arrange a meeting without giving too much away just in case it wasn't Cook's Jimmy at all.

"Yes, yes, but go now lass, because I won't be able to stop myself going up there, now I know," said Cook, now in a fluster.

Amelia quickly fed her daughter who was luckily not a fussy baby, and left Cook with Emma and the boys while she took the buggy to the Hartnoll's house. She probably could have walked but the buggy was quicker.

Arriving at their impressive new house, she didn't have time to knock on the door before Eliza opened it and almost threw herself at Amelia.

"Oh Emma, hello, I'm so glad to see you. Please come in, come in, it feels like ages since we saw each other properly."

It was true. The Hartnoll's had only recently moved to the village, and Amelia had not been to Longford since little Maria's funeral, before Christmas. Amelia looked around at the beautiful home.

"Oh Eliza, this is lovely. I knew that you'd build something beautiful."

"Oh this," said Eliza swishing her hand, "it's nice. It serves its purpose. Come in, have some tea. I heard you might start a school? I would love for Alfie to attend. The two older boys have a tutor who comes to the house, but the work is too hard for Alfie, and he's seven now."

They settled in for their tea and it was all Amelia could do to stop herself from blurting out her news. Finally, she had the chance and told Eliza everything.

"Oh, goodness," said Eliza, "we must consult with William. He will know the best way to go about this. Oh, how delightful if this is true."

Amelia and Cook told John the news when he got home from the College, and he was as excited as they were. How wonderful for any of them to find a link with their past, to find a beloved family member. He hoped that the reunion, if it was true, would be a happy one.

Eliza arrived early the next morning with her own little Emma who was four. Big Emma went straight to play on the rug with baby Emma, and the three women talked.

"So, William has arranged to have lunch under the trees at the *Bush Inn* with James. Some pretence about discussing work issues. So, if you could walk past around that time Cook will be able to see if she thinks that he is her Jimmy. Then if he is, William will look after the post office for the afternoon while they get reacquainted. If Cook doesn't think so or is unsure, then William said that he will introduce you to James and explain what we suspect and then you can talk it over to see if it is Jimmy or not."

"What a brilliant idea!" said Amelia.

Cook was terribly nervous all morning. She told Amelia that she wanted to wear one of her old work dresses and aprons with a bonnet, rather than one of her new colourful dresses, because Jimmy would be more likely to recognise her in work clothes.

"Oh, Emma, it were a long time ago. He were only 11 years old, Emma, and I were only a young woman. What if we don't recognise each other?"

"Well, Cook, I recognised him because he looks a lot like you!"

Finally, the time arrived, and the two women made their way up to the Inn. Lila had been convinced to stay for a couple of hours and watch the children, so that the two women could have some peace and privacy while on their emotional endeavour.

As they approached the Inn, they could see William Hartnoll sitting at a table with another man. There were several other tables with two or three people at each, enjoying the summer air. They couldn't see James well as they approached as he was side on to them, but as they approached the Inn, William called out to them.

"Mrs Harris, Cook, how pleasant to see you both," he called out.

The two women turned to face the men and Cook got her first good look at James. Immediately she knew it was her Jimmy, even after all these years. Her lip trembled and she grabbed Amelia's arm.

The two men stood to greet the women and Cook and Amelia could see the look of confusion on Jimmy's face. Sensing his confusion, Cook untied her bonnet and took it off, holding it is her right hand. She then looked up at Jimmy.

Suddenly realising what was happening, James lifted his arm up as if to reach out to Cook.

"Mammie?" he said quietly, looking at Cook searchingly.

"Jimmy?" said Cook. They both took a step towards each other and then suddenly they were in each other's arms.

The two onlookers looked on with love and happiness, and a little embarrassment to be watching such a personal moment.

They finally released each other and then all the questions came pouring out.

William told James about his arrangement so that James did not have to go back to work, and Amelia told Cook that she would pop in to visit John and Sarah Webb. She might give them a hand in the Inn if they were busy. She had often done so on the afternoons when she was singing.

Vron

It was a couple of hours later and the shadows had started getting longer when Amelia emerged from the Inn, feeling quite accomplished as she had washed a huge number of dishes as well as cutting up a huge pile of vegetables in preparation for the dinner service. She shielded her eyes from the sun as she walked out into the yard and saw that Cook and James were still talking and had been joined by a pretty, young woman in a pretty house dress of pink with grey trimming. Her hair shone golden in the fading sun and Amelia could hear the sweetness of her giggle at something that one of the others had said.

They all stood as Amelia approached.

"Ah Mrs Harris, please meet my wife Lettie, she saw us sitting here as she came to bring me my afternoon tea, and joined us," said James happily.

Lettie bobbed a courtesy to Amelia, who held out her hand to her.

"There's no need for that Lettie, if I may call you Lettie. I am Amelia or Emma is what everyone calls me, and it seems that we are all now family," they all giggled.

"Emma, would you be all right to get the dinner started if I just pop over with James and Lettie to see their new house? Mr Webb built their house as well. It's just down the road past the Jamieson's house."

"Yes of course," said Amelia, "Are you all right to get back home."

"I'll escort my mother back home," said James proudly puffing out his chest a little.

What a wonderful thing, thought Amelia. What a wonderful day.

Amelia did what she could with dinner, which was not very much, some lamb chops and some vegetables in the oven that she hoped she didn't ruin. Lila had left as soon as she'd got home and the little boys and baby Emma were out of sorts, having missed their mother while she was out.

John arrived home as it was starting to get dark, and Amelia rushed out to greet him to tell him everything that had happened. He was very excited and happy for Cook.

Not long after John arrived home, Cook arrived as well, escorted by her son. John invited James inside and offered him a whisky, and they sat for a short while before James needed to return home. It was arranged that he would come for Sunday luncheon, as Jarvis would also be there for the weekend, and everyone knew that he would be ecstatic about the reunion.

As usual it was then chaos in the house as the children were still out of sorts and demanding attention. The adults quickly saw to the children, fed them, washed them, and saw them all off to bed. John read the boys a story which was quicker than usual as he was very keen to find out the news of the day.

As it was a warm night they took their tea out to the veranda, where the yard and gardens were muted by the moonlight, and a gentle breeze wafted through the big gum tree. The glow from the lanterns inside the other houses cast a fairytale like appeared across the village.

Cook told them that Jimmy had recognised her straight away. Her face was embedded in his memory, he told her. He had not had a great time of it after Cook had been arrested. He never blamed her for the arrest. He knew that she was trying to help them both to survive. Jimmy had been put in the orphan's workhouse and had a terrible time, until he was finally old enough to be sent out to work. As luck would have it, he was sent to work for a factory owner in Glasgow, which was a fate worse than death for most poor people. Long hours, in harsh conditions, working for a pittance that just kept them alive, most died young. But the manager of the factory noticed that Jimmy had a talent for numbers and took him under his wing in the office. He taught him to read and write, which Jimmy picked up quickly, and Jimmy was put to work with the other clerks.

On his one day off each week, the manager would take Jimmy with him to the cock fights, where Jimmy kept track of the bets. Over the years this led Jimmy to get to know various characters from the underworld of Glasgow who dealt in all kinds of interesting trades.

He started working for a fence, and soon left the factory and was able to get a small room for himself in the city, near where he was working. He was only 20 years old when he was caught trying to sell stolen goods and sentenced to life, to be served in the colony. He had arrived in Van Diemen's Land nine years after his mother. At first, he was sent to Port Arthur where he was put to work building ships with all the other men who were not immediately assigned. By that time, assignment was all but over, and male convicts needed to have very special skills to be employed by one of the settlers.

Finally, after advocating for himself for years, he was able to convince his captors that he had skills that could be of use outside of the prison. An emancipist who was starting an importing business asked to take him on trial, and James Smith became a clerk again, working in the office of the merchant for several years. During that time, he befriended many of the townspeople and purchased a small cottage. He was then lucky enough to pick up a job at the newly opened Hobart post office, where he learned everything about the trade, working for the Postmaster Mr Collicott. By then he had been granted his Conditional Pardon and had married a lovely young girl who he had met at church.

Lettie was working as a maid for one of the wealthy exclusive families. Lettie had been orphaned young, and while living on the streets, trying to survive, she, like Cook, had been charged with stealing a loaf of bread so that she didn't starve. She was only fourteen when she had come out to Van Diemen's Land in 1840, the year before Amelia.

However, Lettie had spent months at Millbank prison before she was sent to a ship, and in that time, she had been severely abused by the guards who had not only used her for themselves but had hired her to men outside the prison who would come in to have their way with the young and pretty girls.

Amelia was aghast that this had been happening, and around the same time as she was in prison, but she knew that Millbank did not follow Mrs Fry's teachings and she remembered what the women from there looked like on the *Rajah*, when Amelia had first arrived.

It appeared that her treatment had wide repercussions and she suffered terrible nightmares and so far, had been unable to fall with child. James had told his mother all of this before Lettie arrived, and as soon as she met her Cook gave the girl a big bear hug. This was to be her new daughter!

James had received the offer from Mr Hartnoll a few months ago and it seemed like a good idea for the couple to move north, away from reminders of their time as convicts and start afresh. So far,

Vron

they loved the village and everyone they had met. Mr Hartnoll was a fair and decent employer, and he and Eliza had taken the young couple under their wing, helping them to find their block of land and build their cottage.

When Jarvis came on Saturday, he was ecstatic to find that Cook, who he now called Alice, had found her long lost son. It was so heartening when a story like this happened. There were so many sad stories of people in the colony trying to find loved ones back in Britain, only to find that they had died either over there or here in the colony. Or of people finding their loved ones in a terrible state, physically or mentally. Not everyone had a great time in the colony, and there was a lot of poverty since the depression. Lots of people turned to drink and to crime, and things did not end so well for them.

For Alice to find her son, happy and thriving was a true blessing. Perhaps all those prayers every Sunday had worked.

## Chapter Thirty One
# *1851 – Changing times*

*J*arvis also had some news for his friends. It was now 10 years since he had left *Vron* to work at *Brickendon*, he had just turned 60 and he had enough money to retire, or at least to stop working full time. He wanted to build a house on his block of land, and he had been talking to John and William Webb about doing some work at the Inn and the Hunting Club.

The young Reverend Reibey had arranged to import three breeding couples of prize setters from the late Sir Eardley-Wilmot's kennel. Jarvis had taken a strong interest in the hunting dogs and the Reverend intended to entrust them to Jarvis's care, his land being so much closer to the Club. He would need to build a kennel and suitable birthing area, as well as train the pups to follow a scent. In return the Reverend would give Jarvis a percentage of the winnings from the dogs hunting endeavours and pay for their upkeep. Several years ago, the Hunting Club had released deer into a fenced area near Bishopsbourne, that was still heavily treed, which was to become a secure hunting area. However, they had bred like rabbits and were now in proliferation. Unfortunately, many had escaped their bondage in the secured area and gone on to destroy crops and gardens. Some were killed by feral dogs that were also a problem in the bush, but the farmers welcomed the Hunting Club helping to eradicate the problem deer, as well as the feral dogs if they saw them, from the surrounding areas.

The Reverend had a wily pet deer who he kept at his expansive estate, and was sometimes allowed inside the house, much to the worker's disdain. The Reverend would lead his unusual companion around to lay scent trails for the hunt. Katey told the women that she didn't think it was sporting and if only the poor thing knew that it was setting up its fellow creatures for murder. Still the men enjoyed the hunt, and the farmers welcomed them.

Cook and the Harris's were very happy to hear of this turn of events. Jarvis had been a father figure to John ever since he arrived in the colony almost 20 years ago, and now at 44, John was very happy that his children would grow up with an extended family, just like he had, with his grandparents.

Jarvis would tender his resignation the following week but did not intend finishing up until his house was ready for occupation, which would be later in the year. The Webb's builders were still always busy as the village and the surrounding towns kept expanding.

The village increased tenfold in February when the first interstate cricket match was played at the Bishopsbourne College oval between Tasmania (which Van Diemen's Land was now often being called) and Victoria. William Field, now 35, played in the Tasmanian team. William had married his wife Sarah in 1839, but sadly, like the Reibey's they had not been blessed with children.

It seemed that every wealthy landowner in the north of the colony was there. The Reverend Reibey and William Field's brothers had arranged catering for the day, provided by the Webbs. There were marquee's set up for those who had purchased a ticket and delicious food and wine overflowed. Food and drink stands were set up for the rest of the crowd, and the Webb's had set up a chair hire booth.

There was a band that played before the match, and between innings, as well as providing entertainment for several hours afterwards. Everyone was dressed in their finery, which John thought was magnificent to see in the colony. It almost remined him of the Lambeth Gardens. Amelia said that it reminded her of watching the whore's parading their wares in Edinburgh. They really did have a different upbringing, laughed John.

At the end of April Mary Beswick gave birth to her ninth child, a daughter who they named Charlotte. Because the Harris's had not been able to see the Beswick's as frequently as they used to when they all attended the Reverend Davies services at Longford, towards the end of May, and before the weather turned again, they made the trek across to Paterson's Plains for a day with the Beswick's.

The journey over had been just as bad as Amelia had imagined that it would be. John drove the carriage and Amelia and Cook took turns sitting with him up front to escape the chaos inside. Her three boys now aged seven, five and three were incapable of sitting still. Johnny was able to sit quietly if one of the adults was reading to him or teaching him his lessons and would get angry at the other two with their noise and rough and tumble play. Tommy and David were just wild, they had obviously taken after her wild Scottish ancestors, rather than John's quiet, sedate ones. Luckily Amelia didn't mind getting out into the yard with them, and Lance was very good with them, letting them help in the stables and then running around with them in the yard, but they were impossible in enclosed spaces, which was why they had been sticking to the village. It was all they could do to remain reasonably quiet in church services, but as soon as the door opened, they were off racing out to the yard with the other rowdy boys. A carriage trip was Amelia's worst nightmare.

They finally pulled onto the path that led to the McKenzie farm. They hadn't been there for over a year, and they immediately noticed the difference. There was no farm activity going on at all, whereas once the farm had been a hive of activity. Like everywhere else most of the pastures were now fallow with dust kicking up with the wind, but even the home yard looked quite barren and unkempt, and they noticed broken fences along the path.

As they came up the path the Beswick's came out of their house and onto the veranda to greet the Harris's. Thomas at 45 was starting to look his age, and Mary, holding tiny Charlotte, at 38, was starting to look worn out from her many births. Standing beside her parents was lovely Mary Ann, now 18, and running around them and bursting out onto the path were Tommy 12, Margaret 10, Jane eight, Louisa six, and Sarah three.

Amelia could hear them from far down the path. Funny how the giggles and gaggles of girls seemed to carry so much further and was equally as annoying as the fights and chaos the boys created.

The boys tumbled out of the carriage as soon as it pulled up and were thankfully all taken away quickly to play in the yard by the girls.

"Tommy, Margaret, you keep an eye on those little ones," called Mary with a look of exhaustion on her face, "please, please come inside, it's been forever since we saw you," she said as she ushered the Harris's and Cook inside.

A soft rug was set out in the sitting room for little Emma to play on, with a box of baby toys at the ready.

"Mary Ann can you please get the refreshments, Charlotte needs feeding again." Mary fell into a chair and quickly pulled Charlotte, who was fussing, to her breast. The men had gone out into the yard to talk, or to watch the children, or to ponder life. Amelia didn't care, so long as there was some quiet.

"Well Emma, that were a wonderful trip, weren't it?" Cook looked sideways at Amelia and they both burst out laughing. They told Mary what a terrible time they had with the boys and Mary sympathised with them, saying that her life was much the same, and some of her she-devils definitely had some of the Scots in them as well. Tommy and Margaret had quietened down now they were older, and they were both at school a lot of the time, but Jane and Louisa were hard to manage, and they made little Sarah wild as well, although toddlers were wild anyway.

"Tell me about it," said Amelia, "my Tommy and David never stop."

"I tell you Emma, if it wasn't for my Mary Ann, I'd be lost, she holds this house together," a tear sprung to Mary's eye.

The poor woman, though Amelia, this was not like Mary Beswick at all.

Over the morning Cook and Amelia realised that there did not appear to be any workers at the farm or the house. Mary Ann served refreshments and Mary ushered Cook and Amelia into the kitchen where the four women prepared the luncheon together.

The sun had come out and was casting a slight warmth, so lunch was served in the yard so that the children could be released as soon as their parents allowed, and the adults could sit and linger over their meal.

Later as the women were cleaning up, and Mary Ann had left them, Amelia said quietly to Mary, "Have you no help at the moment Mary?"

"No," said Mary in a forthright manner, "there's no money for help. The farms are all but finished, we can't get them to produce anything anymore, and the businesses are not going very well either. Thomas has no mind for the business side of things. Oh, he's brilliant with his ideas, and his patterns and he can make the best pair of boots in the colony, but he has no idea how to make money. And now with father gone, there's no-one to help him," She stopped and looked at Cook and Amelia, who were now staring at her.

"And," she went on, "I cannot possibly run mothers' business as well as care for all of these children, and look, they just keep coming," she motioned to little Charlotte asleep in her crib in the sitting room. "The government stopped buying our clothing once the Factory was producing adequate supplies, so all that was left for us was the gowns and reticules and parasols for the ladies, but as you know the market for that has dwindled significantly." She waved her hand in the air in a show of resolve. What could be done. It was what it was.

"Oh Mary," said Amelia, "I didn't know that things had got this bad. What will you do?"

"Well, Thomas has been talking about selling the farms. We have a lot and none of them are doing anything. William moved to The Springs after father died, but he is now talking about moving to the mines. I'm sorry to say but my sister Elizabeth's husband has made some comments that The Springs should have gone to Elizabeth and not to William, as Elizabeth was my stepfathers only blood child. But father promised The Springs to William for all his hard work on the farm for so many years and he always treated us all the same. And then there are the Peck's!" Now she sounded exasperated.

"My first husband, Mary Ann's father, has quite an extensive family here in the colony, and ever since he died, they have been adamant that they would manage all of Jeremiah's land and not hand it over to Thomas to manage. In hindsight it seems that they were right. Mary Ann owns a lovely piece of land over near *Quamby*, not far from you actually and she will probably move there once she marries but heaven forbid that happens soon, I need her here so badly!"

"Oh Mary, I had no idea," said Amelia. She gave Mary a big hug as they made tea together.

"Thomas has dearly missed John, and the Reverend Davies. He reads the newspapers avidly now that he's not so consumed with his patterns. He's always telling me this bit and that bit and saying to me 'Oh I must discuss this with John next time I see him,' but I can see, Emma that he has lost his spark. He feels responsible for our downturn of fortune but doesn't know how to fix it."

Amelia thought for a while.

"Mary, let me talk to John, not now but later. I'll see if he has any ideas to help your situation. He knows so many influential people now, one of them might be able to help, or know what can be done."

They left the McKenzie farm, mid-afternoon for the long drive back to Bishopsbourne. Amelia sat up front with John, hoping to talk to him about the Beswick's situation, but the wind was quite fierce all the way home and made conversation too difficult. Amelia looked back in through the carriage window several times and could see that thankfully Cook was snoozing with Emma asleep across her lap, and the three boys slept or played quietly, obviously worn out.

Amelia finally got to talk to John about what Mary had told her, and John was a little shocked, as Thomas had said nothing to him about any problems. He had only told him that things were going well with the business, even if the farm had yet to revive again. John said that he would ask around and see what advice some of the more successful men could give to Thomas.

The news over winter was full of stories about 'The Great Exhibition' or the 'Crystal Palace Exhibition', that was being held in Hyde Park in London from May to October. France had held similar exhibitions in Paris, the last in 1849, and England was eager to make theirs better.

John told Amelia that the event was organised by Prince Albert, the husband of Queen Victoria and Henry Cole, who was a great inventor and known as the creator of Christmas cards that were now quite familiar, even in the colony, and sent to loved ones before Christmas.

The Great Exhibition was to be a platform for countries from around the world to display their achievements. Britain also sought to provide the world with the hope of a better future. Britain hoped to show that technology, particularly its own, was the key to a better future.

It was made all the more exciting because The Reverend Davies was part of *The Royal Society* committee who had organised a Van Diemen's Land exhibit for the exhibition, and he had been telling them all about it since the previous year. 80 packages arrived in London for the exhibition from Van Diemen's Land as opposed to only 12 from New South Wales and 29 from South Australia who were in the midst of heavy recruitment for settlers at the time.

The Reverend had proudly showed John an excerpt from a popular *Guide to the Great Exhibition* which noted that the:

> *"Vandiemonian display is most satisfactorily abundant in its ocular evidences of civilization. Their cloths, preserved meats (beef-steak to wit! [Mrs Adcock's second hit]), enamelled hides and excellent furniture, almost equalling our own for make and taste of execution, are triumphant proof of the progress of knowledge and industry over brute force and self-contented un-intellectuality"*

Mrs Adcock was the illiterate wife of a Hobart butcher and had entered her two tins of preserved meats, which seemed a mundane offering but was touted by a London journalist who saw them as promising Australia's capacity to boost the livelihood of British workers, and her produce won further praise from others.

Another journalist seemed to have captured the sentiments of a lot of the current generation in Van Diemen's Land when he wrote about the aboriginals:

> *In our forty years' possession of that settlement we have utterly destroyed them, by as atrocious a series of oppressions as ever were perpetrated by the unscrupulous strong upon the defenceless feeble. Yet these poor people*

*had tastes and industry too. Their bread appears to be worth reviving as a new truffle for soup by the gourmands of Hobart Town. The specimen of the root exhibited weighs 14lb. They obtained a brilliant shell necklace by soaking and rubbing off the cuticle, and gaining various tints by hot decoctions of herbs. They procured paint by burning iron ore and reducing it to powder by grindstones. They converted sea-shells and sea-weeds into convenient water-vessels; they wove baskets' and they constructed boats with safe catamarans. All these things are exhibited. Surely, then, the men whom their greedy supplanters admit to have done this, and whom the least possible pains ever bestowed upon them proved to be capable of much more, ought not to have been hunted down, as we know they were, and then almost inveigled to be shut up in an island too small for even the few remaining.* (*The Courier* 3 September 1851, p. 3, quoting from *The Illustrated London News* 24 May 1851)

Oh, how John would have loved to have gone to see this Great Exhibition. Hyde Park had been one of the most beautiful places that he had enjoyed walking through as a young man. He could imagine this 'crystal palace' in his mind. How wonderful it must look. But even if he could afford to, he was still never allowed to go back to England again.

Another item that consumed the news was what they were calling the 'Gold Rush' in New South Wales and Victoria. In June the papers were reporting that gold had been found near Orange in New South Wales. The man who found it had been to the California goldfields around the time that William Saltmarsh has also gone over there. He had learned new gold prospecting techniques called panning and cradling. Over the rest of the year the gold rush spread to many other parts of New South Wales.

In July Victoria's first gold rush began when gold was found at a place called Clunes. By August it had spread to a place nearby called Buninyong and by early September to the nearby goldfield known as Yuille's Diggings, and in November Bendigo Creek. It seemed that the country was just full of gold for the taking, it was literally just running down the creeks, and men were making their fortunes overnight.

As the rush grew, people left their homes to join the quest, and it became noticeable as the Harris's heard of this man and that man and sometimes whole families up and leaving for the mainland. It was an excellent opportunity for men who had little more than chain-gang and labouring experience to make something of themselves. For years they had been trying to eke out an existence for themselves and their families in what had been for many years an unproductive land. Life was good for the wealthy and those who worked for them, but not for many others.

Things were slowly changing on the question of transportation. The Launceston Association for the Cessation of the Transportation of Convicts included many prominent men in the north including the Archer brothers, Richard Dry, John Jackson and most of the clergy including the now Archdeacon Davies. They sent letters to the chief magistrates, colonial secretaries and legislative councils of the Australian colonies and New Zealand.

There was sufficient response to encourage the Launceston association to expand its aims into a national movement and the Australasian Anti-Transportation League was formed.

The members pledged not to employ any person arriving under sentence of transportation for crimes committed in Europe. The League expanded that sentiment with a symbol of nationhood, the Australasian Anti-Transportation League banner. The banner was hand sewn in silk by the women of Launceston and was unfurled for the first time at the inauguration of the League at the Queen's Theatre in Melbourne on the 1st of February 1851. It had the Union Flag in the canton, and a broad deep blue field with four stars displaying the Southern Cross. On the upper border in gold were the words 'Australasian Anti-Transportation League'; in the lower margin, 'Established 1851'. Since then, the banner had been copied, manufactured in bunting, displayed at rallies, flown from mastheads, and observed on ships as far afield as the United States. Many houses in Van Diemen's Land, especially in the north around Launceston now displayed the banner. By December five of the colonies were united under the symbol of the Southern Cross. It seemed that it would only be a matter of time before the convict system ceased for good.

## Chapter Thirty Two
# *1852 - A Summer Wedding*

*W*hile all the excitement was in the air about the Exhibition

and the gold rushes and the Anti-Transportation League, Jarvis and Cook announced one Sunday afternoon as they, the Harris's and James and Lettie Smith, were strolling from church to the Inn, that they were to be married.

It was no surprise to most people and certainly not to the Harris's. They had watched the relationship evolve over many years. But it was when Jarvis started to call Cook, Alice, that they knew things had changed.

Jarvis's house was just about finished. From the Harris's veranda, Jarvis's house could clearly be seen, looking past the big gum in the yard and then past Cook's cottage, which was little more than a playhouse for the children nowadays.

The kennel had been built, which Amelia called 'Hound Hall,' as it was very spacious and elaborate for "a lot of rowdy dogs," she said. Jarvis had created his house in much the same style as the Harris's but with fewer bedrooms, having only two, one for him and one for his beloved Alice. Cook explained to Amelia that having lived alone for so long he didn't want to thrust her into his bedroom, but the intention was for them to sleep as man and wife, but for Cook to have her own space if she needed it. How thoughtful, thought Amelia, just like Jarvis.

The room that they saved on bedrooms, they increased in the size of their sitting and dining areas. Jarvis said that the way that the Harris family kept expanding they would need an extension to be able to seat them all for dinner eventually. This way Jarvis would have the type of long table that he had for so long waited on, and he would have the comfortable leather lounge chairs that he so admired for many years. Behind the house was a small abode suitable for a maid to live in, because Jarvis said that his Alice deserved someone to look after her after all her years looking after others. Cook said there'd be nothing for a maid to do because she wasn't giving up her cooking. But, when Jarvis reminded her that she would still be needed at the Harris's house with their growing brood, as Amelia was again with child, she agreed that a maid could keep their house, while Cook was over with the Harris's who she loved as her own. Then there was also James and Lettie. It would be nice to have someone to cook them a meal when they had the two young ones over for lunch or dinner, that way they could spend their time with their loved ones.

"And we're not getting any younger, Alice," said Jarvis in all seriousness, "we will need someone to care for us as we get older. That is what we have worked hard for all these years."

Cook agreed to employ a maid, but not a live in one. She'd find one of the young ladies from the village. There were plenty of unmarried daughters looking to learn and to make their own money.

Every now and then old Sammy would appear in the Harris's garden, tending the flowers or pruning the bushes. He still frequented his *Vron*, as he still called it, but had been shoo-ed away by the head gardener a few times. When he saw that

Jarvis's house was being built, he appointed himself as the official gardener and dropped a garden plan to Amelia one afternoon. Cook and Jarvis quite liked the plan and left a note for Sammy to go ahead, and just tell them how much he needed for supplies. The garden already looked magnificent before the house was finished. Jarvis knew that Sammy was not charging him as much as the supplies he was using were worth and had no idea where the man got his supplies from, but there were obviously people in the area who took care of Sammy, as he took care of their gardens.

Sammy did not drink liquor and would rarely accept gifts. The two things he would accept were scented soap and chocolate. Both were odd items for a man such as Sammy, but no one asked him why they were his requests, they just kept a supply for him and gave them to him when they saw him. Cook and Amelia giggled at the vision of weather-beaten old Sammy, who usually looked moth-eaten, lounging in a fancy tub of hot water washing himself with the scented soap and eating the chocolates.

The wedding, which Cook and Jarvis had wanted to hold in April, had to be brought forward to the end of February when the doctor declared that Amelia was more advanced than she had thought, and the next baby would be due in early April.

Alice and Bartholomew Jarvis were married on Saturday the 14th of February 1852 at the Church of the Holy Nativity at Bishopsbourne by Archdeacon Davies, who could not stop beaming as he read the service. While Jarvis knew people from all over the north, he had lived for 16 years in the area now known as Bishopsbourne and 10 years at *Brickendon* near Longford, so most of his favourite people lived around these areas. Still, people came from Launceston, including the Davies'; and the Beswick's came from Paterson's Plains.

The reception was held at the *Bush Inn*, with everyone seated under the big gum trees at long tables adorned with flowers that old Sammy had brought from various gardens around the area. nannies were hired for the day and all the children were taken down to the Harris's farm and entertained in the schoolroom (that was still yet to be used) and Cook's cottage. The adults enjoyed a delicious luncheon with plenty of ale and cider flowing. Dancing followed with the music provided by a string quartet made up of students from the College, which had a brilliant music program.

The music and sedate dancing were not really Amelia's thing, and she figured that it wouldn't be Cook's either. Amelia much preferred the energetic folk songs, but it was lovely to see Cook and Jarvis taking a gentle spin around the dancefloor, an area that had been cleared and compacted for just such an occasion.

There was no dancing for Amelia, as she could feel the baby pressing down low in her abdomen and was not keen on it coming early. If she was honest, this time it was getting hard to even walk, and when she did it was with a waddle like a duck. The boys laughed at her, to which she gave them a mock scowl.

Her plans to run a school room had not come to fruition in the past year when she promised herself that she would start. But no sooner was she over one birth and stopped feeding one baby when it seemed another was on the way, and she just didn't have the energy to organise a workspace as well as wrangle four children.

After the party was over everyone gathered on the road to wave farewell to Mr and Mrs Jarvis as they left in their carriage for Launceston. Although Jarvis's finances did not stretch to a European honeymoon, they were travelling by ship to Sydney for two weeks. It would be their first journey on a ship since they came across from England over twenty-five years before. Obviously, Cook's experience had been very different to Jarvis's, who travelled with the wealthy Walkers in First Class, but they were both interested to see how sea travel had changed and to do it this time in style. And they had both heard so much about Sydney that they wanted to see it all for themselves. Amelia was so excited to hear about their travels but also feared how she would cope on her own with the children.

Amelia spent the afternoon sitting under the big tree with Mary Beswick and her daughter Mary Ann Peck, Lettie Smith, Maria Davies, Eliza Hartnoll and Katey Reibey.

It was interesting to see the different groups of children now. There were the older boys sitting together under the veranda discussing important boy things. Rowland Davies was now 15 and was joined by Tom Beswick, 13 and Henry Hartnoll, 15. Hanging on the peripheral was 11-year-old Billy Hartnoll.

Then there was the gaggle of girls: Emma Davies, seven, Margaret Beswick 11 and Louisa Beswick seven, where organising the smaller girls into a pretend school and taking them through various activities. Their charges, who were not as cooperative as the older girls wanted them to be and included little Emma Harris who, at 18 months, was toddling around, Mary Davies, two, Sarah Beswick, three and Emma Hartnoll, six.

And then, as they had seen them do before, Amelia and Mary noticed that John, now seven and little Jane Beswick, now eight, were playing off by themselves. They had wandered off and were sitting on the veranda of Cook's cottage just chatting quietly. They were both two thoughtful and quiet children as compared to the rest. John, like his father, was happiest with his head in a book, or out in the garden. Jane was much the same and had taught herself to read with only her older siblings showing her how, and she loved to tend the kitchen garden and bring in the vegetables and flowers when they were ready.

Mary and Amelia looked at each other.

"Are you thinking what I'm thinking?" said Amelia.

"That those two will marry one day?" said Mary with a giggle, cuddling little Charlotte close.

Amelia slapped her leg and let out a laugh, "No Mary lass, but I hope that will be true. But I was thinking how I wish they were all as quiet and easy as those two!" They all laughed.

Oh, who knew what the future would hold? They had all seen so many changes to the world already. What would happen in the coming years? What would the world look like for their children in another 20 years?

All Amelia knew was that she was happy. Her life had so far turned out to be much more than she had ever thought that it could be. Whatever the future held, she was looking forward to seeing it all unfold.

Vron

The last ship to bring convicts to Van Diemen's Land, the *St Vincent*, left London on the 28th of December 1852 and arrived with 241 male convicts on the 26th of May 1853. Although convicts were still sent to the fledgling Western Australia until 1868, the Association had won its fight for Van Diemen's Land.

# *Epilogue*

There are parts of this story that are true according to records and research, and parts where I have had to fill in the gaps to make a realistic and interesting story and paint a picture of life during the early years of Australia.

The information below has been gleaned from the snippets of information.

### John and Amelia Harris

The Harris's second daughter Sarah was born on the 1st of April 1852 and their last child Solomon was born on the 10th of March 1855, completing their little family with four boys and two girls. None of their children, except little Emily, predeceased them.

In 1871, when Amelia was 57, there was a notice in the newspaper that John had posted to say that "CAUTION — The public are hereby cautioned against harbouring or giving credit to my wife Emma Harris, as I will not be responsible for any debts contracted by her, she having left her home without provocation. JOHN HARRIS, Carrick"

From the facts it could be deduced that towards the end of her life Amelia fell into some kind of mental health crisis, maybe as we know now and acknowledge nowadays, trauma related. It was common for ex-convicts to have mental health problems which they self-medicated with alcohol, which then got them into trouble with their partners, neighbours, or the law. We don't know if this is what happened to Amelia, but in 1871 things were not well between John and Amelia. Some records imply that their youngest son, Solomon, was sent to live in Victoria when he was a child. His older sister Emma moved to Victoria at some time after she married in 1877, when Solomon would have been 12. This could also point to troubles at home. Both Emma and Solomon lived in Victoria in their adult years.

On the 8th of August 1884, the *Launceston Examiner* reported that John Harris had died on the 6th of August at the residence of his son-in-law at *Entally*. At the time he must have been living with daughter Emma and her husband Henry Smith. Reports note that he died of senility, aged 77. *Entally* might not necessarily mean the estate of the Reibey's but could be the surrounding area. When John died, Thomas Reibey III had already been the Premier of Tasmania and was at that time the Speaker of the House. John Harris was buried at St Andrews church at Carrick, the church that was built by Thomas Reibey III during his young days as a new Reverend, and his tombstone was erected by his youngest son, Solomon, who was living in Victoria.

Amelia died as Emma Harris on the 20th of February 1891 of senility, or decay of nature as they called it, at the Invalid Depot, Launceston, aged 77. Her funeral was held at Carrick, but a tombstone cannot be found. Amelia dying at the Invalid Depot may mean that she was estranged from her family, but this is unknown.

### John Harris Jnr

John Harris, aged 20 and Jane Beswick, aged 21 were married at St Andrew's church at Carrick on the 10<sup>th</sup> of August 1864 by the Reverend Alfred Mace. It seems that the couple spent some time living at Jane's parents farm at Paterson's Plains. John was recorded as being a farmer in the Westbury district, and the young Harris family continued to live in that district until at least 1877, by which time eleven children had been born to them. John Thomas Ebenezer in 1865, James David in 1867, Mary Jane in 1870, George Alfred 'Solomon' in 1872, Emma Ada (the authors Great Grandmother) in 1874, Margaret Ann in 1876, William Henry Samuel in 1879, Alfred Arthur in 1883, Frances Sarah Louise in 1884 and Emily Jane Winifred in 1886. All their children lived into old age. A well-presented man, John Harris earned the nick name 'London Johnny,' and the photos are attributed to being him.

The family moved around the general Launceston area with John recorded as a labourer in 1867 but by 1874 they were living at *The Moat* where John is recorded as being the farm overseer.

*The Moat* was a property near Carrick, which it seems was originally owned by the Fletcher's who were Mrs Jane Walker's parents (Walker who built *Vron*). The first racecourse in Van Diemen's Land was built at *The Moat* which is between Carrick and Bishopsbourne and close to the village of Oaks. The Reverend Reibey and the Field brothers built the racecourse south of Bishopsbourne, which is discussed in the story. The Carrick Racing Club, another racecourse, was formed in 1848 and was called "the best in Tasmania" by author Hugh Munro Hull in 1859. The Carrick Plate, run annually from 1849 to 1913 was the oldest horse race in Australia. The racecourse still operates today in 2024.

Many of the workers from the Reibey's estate, *Entally*, built houses around the Carrick area. Many of the original houses still stand and are occupied. It could be that John also worked at *Entally*, as so many did.

John Harris's grandson John Victor Withers (the author's grandfather) married Mary Ethel Mace in 1938. We know that the Mace's were a prominent horse racing family in the Launceston area, especially in the late 1800's and early 1900's. It may be from this horse racing association that the families were affiliated.

When Jane died on the 8th of December 1913, at the age of 70, it seems that they were living at Turners Marsh, which is north of Launceston, and the funeral, held in Launceston, left from their son Solomon's house. Son's Solomon and William were butchers in Launceston. Jane was buried at the Carr Villa Memorial Park, Kings Meadows, Launceston. When John died in 1919, aged 74 he was also recorded as being resident at Turner's Marsh and was buried with his wife.

To the left is a photo of their tombstone and above is a photo attributed to being Jane.

### Thomas Harris

Thomas Harris was born on the 13<sup>th</sup> of August 1846. He married Mary Bailey in 1875 at the Princess Square Congregational Church, Launceston, when he was 29 and she was 24.

They had eight children, four boys and five girls between 1876 and 1891. May, born in 1879, died as a baby. Their daughter Gertrude died in 1893, aged only 10.

Mary died on the 7<sup>th</sup> of Jul 1897 aged 46 and then daughter Ellen died in 1898 aged just 22. Poor Thomas must have been grief stricken. He was left with four sons aged between 9 and 21, and daughter Ivy aged just 6.

Thomas went on to marry Mary Robertson two years later when he was 53 and she was 49. They had no children together.

Son, George who was born in 1880 died in France, aged 37, on the 3$^{rd}$ of May 1917 during WW1. He was with the 15$^{th}$ Battalion at the Dardanelles, and would have been there on 25 April, ANZAC Day. On 30 April 1915 he received a bullet through his right knee. After treatment he was sent back to the front, this time with the 11th Reinforcements, 23$^{rd}$ Battalion in Belgium, where he was sadly killed. He is buried at the Villers-Bretonneux Memorial in France.

Thomas died on the 26$^{th}$ of Jul 1923, aged 77, at his son Arthur's residence at Inveresk, a suburb of Launceston. He is buried at the Carr Villa Memorial Park.

Thomas William born in 1876 lived to age 65 in 1941, Arthur born in 1885 lived to age 49 in 1934, Thomas John (who must have been known as John) was born in 1888 and lived to age 71 in 1959 and Ivy who was born in 1891 lived to age 80 in 1971.

**David Harris**

David Harris was born on the 2$^{nd}$ of February 1848. He married Margaret Imrie in 1875 when he was 27 and she was 21. It seems that they didn't have any children. There are several David Harris's who lived in the area at the time, but none can be confirmed as this David. David may have died on 1 Apr 1901 aged 53, but this is not confirmed.

## Emma Harris

Emma Harris, who is recorded as both Emma and Amelia (as was her mother), was born on the 12th of July 1850.

She married Henry Smith at Westbury on the 31st of May 1877 when he was 24 and she was 27. They had eight children, six daughters and two sons, all of whom lived to adulthood.

Eldest daughter Mary, who had married George Russell in 1906 and had a daughter Jean, died in 1908 aged 31. She was living in Burnie.

In 1891 the family were living at *Entally*, when son Henry was born. Before 1914 Emma and Henry moved to Victoria and lived at South Yarra. We know this because their son's Henry and John listed their addresses in Melbourne and living with their parents on enlistment in the Army.

Son John, born in 1894 was killed in France on the 21st of August 1918, during WW1 aged 24. He was with the 14th Battalion. On enlistment in 1916 he was noted as being a baker and was single. He is buried at the Daours Communal Cemetery, at the Somme in France, Plot 5, Row B, Grave 22. Son Henry, born in 1891 also went to WW1 but came home. He died in Mildura in 1937 aged 46.

Henry died in Melbourne in 1930 aged 77 and Emma died in Melbourne on the 23rd of December 1945 aged 95. She is buried at the Coburg Pine Ridge Cemetery, Grave 1133.

Their five daughters all lived to an old age, with four of them living in Melbourne and one in Sydney.

## Sarah Harris

Sarah Harris was born on the 19th of April 1852. Sarah married Alfred Aram in about 1877 when she was 25 and he was 39.

They had eight children, three daughters and five sons. They all lived into old age except George who died in 1907 aged 26 when a horse accidentally fell on him and Arthur who died in 1923, aged 40.

Sarah sadly died at Launceston on the 7th of September 1893 aged just 41, when their eldest, Minnie was 15 and youngest Elizabeth, just 2.

Alfred died in 1933 at Perth, Tasmania, aged 95.

## Solomon Harris

Solomon Harris was born on the 10th of March 1855. In 1882 Solomon Harris, aged 27, married Rosetta Sparkes at Kew in Victoria. It's not known why he moved to Victoria, but his sister Emma was living there, and it is possible he moved there when he was quite young. They had five daughters and one son. Son Claud served  in the Army during WW1 from 1916 to 1920 as an ambulance driver with the 10th Field Ambulance, came home and lived to an old age.

Rosetta died on the 15th of December 1939 and Solomon died in Berwick, Victoria in

1942. The photos are attributed to being Solomon and Rosetta.

**Kezia Hayter and Captain Charles Ferguson**

In 1842 Charles left Van Diemen's land on his ship the *Rajah*, and left Kezia to attend to her prison work. But after becoming disillusioned, she resigned and became the governess for William Archer's children at *Brickendon* where she waited for Charles to return.

Charles married Kezia Elizabeth Hayter on the 1st of July 1843 in Saint Andrews Presbyterian Church, Hobart, and they both left on the *Rajah* on the 10th of August. Between 1843 and 1851 the couple travelled the world on the *Rajah*, and their son George was born in Hobart in 1846 during a brief stop there.

In 1851 Charles, then 38, became the Harbour Master for Geelong near Melbourne, and then the Harbour Master for Williamstown. Charles and Kezia settled at Williamstown. Charles became Victoria's first Chief Harbour Master in February 1852. Ferguson Street in Williamstown was named in his honour. In the same year he began to perform the duties of both a Police Magistrate and a Water Police Magistrate for Williamstown.

In April 1853 Kezia gave birth to their third child, Sophie at Williamstown.

Captain Charles Ferguson was very active within the Williamstown community. In 1855 he was made Chairman of the Committee for founding the Fire Brigade service. In the same year, he was responsible for raising the first volunteer force, Volunteer Marine Artillery at the time of the Crimean War.

Kezia Ferguson was a member of the Williamstown Ladies Benevolent Society. The organisation was formed in 1856 and was supported on a voluntary basis. In the same year Captain and Mrs. Ferguson's fourth child, Alice Ferguson was born in Williamstown. In the year that followed, 1857, another daughter, Edith Ferguson was born in August. Two years later John Franklin Ferguson was born in April 1859 when Kezia was 41. Sadly, two months later, in June, Alice Ferguson died aged just 3 years.

In 1861 George Ferguson, aged fifteen years took a keen interest in military matters, joining the Williamstown Volunteer Rifles as a private. Captain and Mrs. Ferguson's fifth child, Wallace Ferguson was born in April of the same year. Sadly, baby Wallace died in December the same year, aged 8 months.

The Cecil Street Sunday School was opened on the 29th of August 1865. Captain Ferguson was the first superintendent, and the roll contained the names of 17 teachers and 130 scholars.

After a long and honourable career in the Government Service of Victoria, Captain Charles Ferguson died in London on December 1868, while visiting Great Britain on sick leave, and was buried in London Cemetery.

In 1882 Kezia, her son George and daughter Sophie moved to Adelaide, South Australia. Kezia died on 30 December 1885 in Adelaide and was buried in the Cheltenham Cemetery.

### William and Jane Walker and family

William Gwillim Walker and his wife Jane lived in the Forth area where William died in 1852 and Jane died there in 1867 aged 73.

Their daughter Marianne and her husband John Jackson led a busy life, with John holding many prominent roles in the colony in both Van Diemen's land, Adelaide, Sydney, and Melbourne. On retirement John and Marianne returned to England where John died at Ealing in 1885 at the age of 76. Marianne was to live for a further five years in England till her death in 1890 and is also buried there.

Henry Walker farmed in the area near *Vron* and he married and had two children before being killed in an accident at Mount Bischoff in 1876 when he was 38. He was riding on one of the trucks on the tramway to Emu Bay, when a sudden jolt threw him off, and some of the iron with which the truck was loaded fell on him. He fell ten to fifteen feet, and was insensible for a short time, dying two days later.

George Walker was married in 1864 aged 39, to Emma Wilkinson the daughter of Frederick Wilkinson who was the Government Medical Officer at Latrobe. Another daughter of Frederick Wilkinson, Louisa, married Alfred Walker, George's younger brother. It is believed that George Walker mostly worked as a farmer, firstly at Bishopsbourne and later in the Forth region near his parents. George died at the early age of 43 years the result of a heart condition. His death notice reads-

> *George died on the night of the 29th. November 1867 of Mount Eric River, Forth. Aged 43 – disease of the heart of long standing, deeply deplored by a large circle of friends.*

Edwin married Alice Brown, who was the daughter of one of their neighbours at Forth, and they had a large family with ten children who lived into adulthood. In 1862 Edwin and his family sailed to New Zealand and took up land on the South Island and by 1865 had purchased a 20,000 acre property called *View Hill*, and he had 13,000 sheep. They later moved to the North Island near Cambridge where he continued farming. Edwin died suddenly in a draper shop on the 7th of February 1898 in Auckland aged 71.

He is buried in the Hautapu Cemetery near Cambridge in the same plot as his son Ralph.

Alfred married Louisa Wilkinson and they farmed around Forth. In August 1877 Alfred was declared insolvent and then the following month four of their children died within a week of each other, the result of diphtheria, which was rampant in the area at the time. Their children who died were Rhoda aged 9, George 5, Nellie, and her twin brother Alfred, both 3. Two other children would also die at a young age, Louis, their eldest son born 1867 died in 1891 aged 24. Their youngest daughter, Jean also died while relatively young, aged 39 years. After his insolvency Alfred is noted as being a storekeeper. Alfred died in 1881 leaving his wife Louisa to rear the remaining six children out of the total family of 10. He was aged 51 years.

Adelaide found her way to Melbourne at a young age, where she married John Benn in 1852, when she was 21. John became a prominent businessman. They had no children. John died in 1895 leaving Adelaide a very wealthy woman. She died in England in 1900 aged 69.

There is little information to be found about Rhoda. When John Benn, Adelaide's husband, died in 1895, he left 6,000 pounds to be invested for her.

Rebecca who was known as Emma, married Ralph Brown who was a Wesleyan Minister. They lived in Tasmania, South Australia, and Victoria. They had six children, one who died as a baby, but the others lived into adulthood. Ralph died in 1903 aged 60 and 'Emma' died in 1929 aged 94.

### Alice 'Cook' Jarvis

Cook is a fictional character, as are her son James and his wife Lettie. She represents many of the women who were sent out to Van Diemen's Land as convicts.

### Bartholomew Jarvis

Jarvis is also a fictional character. He represents the men who chose to move to Van Diemen's Land as free settlers to make a better life.

### Sammy Cox

Sammy Cox was a real person. He claimed to have been born Samuel Emanuel Jervis in 1773 in England and spent time on his uncle's ship after his father died, then jumped ship in 1789 near the Tamar heads and lived with the local aboriginals for twenty-six years. This would have him resident in Tasmania years before the first recorded settlement, in 1803 on the Derwent River, and before even the existence of Bass Strait was proved by George Bass and Matthew Flinders. In 1814 he met and was befriended by the Cox family, residents near Hadspen, and took the family's surname.

He ended up working as a gardener and spent about 50 years living in a cottage at *The Moat*, near Carrick. Cox died in the Launceston insane asylum in 1891 claiming to be 117 years old. His story has been widely reported and the dining room of the Carrick Hotel is named after him. His story has been called into doubt, with historian Dr Andrew Piper describing the story as a tall tale constructed by Cox. While writing about Cox, Thomas Monds, who had befriended and assisted him, also expressed doubt as to the story's veracity.

## Rowland and Maria Davies

Rowland became Archdeacon of Launceston in 1850, and two years later became Vicar at St David's in Hobart. He was instrumental in the establishment of Christ College, becoming a trustee in 1845 and an honorary fellow in 1856. He was an inspector of schools at Longford and became a trustee of the Hutchins School in 1853. Rowland was appointed Archdeacon of Hobart in November 1854. In 1862, he was commissioned as chaplain to the colony's volunteer force and attached to the Second Rifles, Southern Division. The appointment made him the first military chaplain to the Australian colonies' fledgling military forces.

A keen horticulturist, Rowland introduced many plants into Tasmania. He was elected president of the Launceston Horticultural Society, of which he is regarded a 'guiding spirit'.

Rowland retired in September 1866 on a government pension. He died in Hobart in 1880 aged 75. Maria died in Hobart in 1902 aged 86.

Their son Rowland was sent to England for his education and returned to Tasmania in 1859. He married Martha Pitt in 1875 and died on 11 July 1881 aged 43. After his death a selection from his literary productions was published, under the editorship of his English tutor.

Emma Davies married Frederick Mace in 1875 when she was 30 and he was 28. They had five children between 1877 and 1887. Eldest son, Frederick died at a young age, only 19, but the others lived into adulthood. Frederick had been born in Sydney but at the age of 9 his parents had died, and he was put into the care of his Aunt Sarah and her husband the Reverend Cox in Hobart. He went to the Hutchins School and then his aunt and uncle took him to England for his education. He returned to Tasmania where he learned farming from an uncle and became a wealthy landowner. He became a Senior Justice of the Peace in 1873 and a coroner in 1883. By 1883 they were living in the property *Malunnah* at Orford.

Emma's son Cyril served in WW1, enlisting when he was 28 in 1915, he served as a driver until 1919, at the end of the war.

Emma died in Hobert in 1927 aged 82 and Frederick died in 1931 aged 84. Frederick was a prolific diary writer which he kept from 1918. A Facebook page records his diary *"Frederick Mace Esq. 100 Years to the Day."*

### Mary and Thomas Beswick

Little Louisa Beswick died during a scarlet fever epidemic in 1853, aged just 9. Mary and Thomas' last child Samuel was born in 1854 when Mary was 41. She'd had ten children in 21 years.

It seems that Thomas Beswick had been under financial strain for some time and in 1854 he transferred the ownership of the farm at Paterson's Plains into the trust of his youngest brother Samuel Beswick, who was a successful tailor in London. He must have been desperate and thought that a brother, who he had not seen since 1823 when Thomas was 18 and Samuel was 11, could save the family's inheritance. A second trustee was a farmer called William Hill. The trust stipulated that the trustees or others appointed by Thomas Beswick had right of succession to the use of the property after the death of Thomas and Mary in such a way that their children and the heirs of Thomas would have full rights to benefit from it, but Mary's daughter from her first marriage, Mary Ann Peck, could only benefit during her life time and as

Thomas allowed in any deed or in his will. Thomas could direct how the benefits would be shared but not in any way that allowed Mary Ann Peck to gain a share that might be inherited.

This may have been because Mary Ann was already inheriting land from her father Jeremiah Peck, or it could have been due to concerns about her new husband. Mary Ann married Martin Hardy on 28 October 1854 and the Hardy's moved to *Quamby* near Oaks.

Samuel Beswick arrived in Tasmania with his wife and daughter shortly afterwards. They might have lived at Paterson's Plains for a short time, but they were soon established at Cressy. Samuel's daughter, Charlotte, married Charles Duncan Robertson at Carrick in 1857. Samuel may have been a farmer or a storekeeper.

Mary and Thomas Beswick moved to the Oaks/Quamby area not long after the Hardy's and Thomas took up farming at a very inhospitable time perhaps trying to fix his terrible financial situation. By then the properties were all heavily mortgaged and his property in Bathurst St, Launceston was also mortgaged. There were other mortgages in 1859 and 1861 and in 1866 he was forced to sell everything. According to the deed of the 15th of November 1866 the only bidder at a public auction was John Williott (who had also bought a property from Thomas in 1860). The sale realized 700 pounds from which he repaid 600 pounds in loans and 27 pounds in interest. The land at Adelphi comprised 112 acres out of 500 acres granted originally in 1837 to Richard Dry. It was adjoining land occupied by John Rose and land occupied by James Haydock Reibey and part of the Adelphi estate. The Rose and Reibey families both owned land near the Paterson's Plains farm and John Rose's father had been

Alexander McKenzie's captain in the 73$^{rd}$ Regiment and had helped him to secure the land.

Son Thomas married Catherine Peever in 1862, and their first two children were born at Paterson's Plains. Jane, who married John Harris also lived there for a time after their marriage in 1864.

In the meantime, the Hardy's had nine children, Mary Ann giving birth to a son in 1855, twin girls in 1856, a daughter in 1858, and four sons in 1859, 1860, 1863 and 1865. They then moved to Scottsdale in 1865.

In Scottsdale, new land was being opened up in an area that had been completely unknown while settlement had extended around Launceston and along the Northwest Coast over the preceding fifty years. An explorer, James Scott, found the fertile land in 1852 in what had been thought to be mountainous, uninhabitable terrain. When the Hardy's moved there in 1865 it was described in *The Examiner*:

> *In the township at Scottsdale we saw numerous cosy, neat cottages with their fruit trees and flower gardens in front. There are five or six hundred inhabitants. There is a schoolmaster under a Board of Education, a chapel, the post-office and a corn mill is just being completed. There is neither police station nor public house but the people appear to get on harmoniously without them.*

Tragically, Martin hung himself on the 7$^{th}$ of January 1868, and then poor Mary Ann gave birth to a daughter who she named Rosetta on the 28$^{th}$ of May 1868.

Thomas, having lost all his wife and children's inheritance, moved to Scottsdale with Mary to support poor Mary Ann. They were followed by Thomas and his wife Catherine with their three little ones, and Charlotte aged 18 was married to Alexander James in Scottsdale the same year.

Son Thomas soon established the Dogwood Tavern in 1869, the first in Scottsdale and went on to breed and race horses, and later ran a coach service between Scottsdale and Launceston, which was later run by his youngest brother Samuel.

At some time after they moved to Scottsdale, Thomas Snr became estranged from his family. Perhaps he ran away in shame which is very sad. Thomas died in the Port Sorrell district `on or about' the 16th of January 1877, aged 72. His death was reported for registration by the Coroner at Torquay (now East Devonport) on 23rd of January. He was described as a labourer, and it appears that he died alone and was found dead some days later in circumstances that required a coroner's court to record a finding.

In 1878 Mary Beswick, aged 64, married Richard Fuller, 65, at Launceston. It seems that they lived in Launceston, where Richard died in 1884, at their home in Wellington St, aged 71. Mary died two years later at Ringarooma, near Scottsdale, where she had no doubt gone to live with her children. She was 72 years old.

### Thomas Reibey III and his wife Catherine (Katey)

Thomas took two years away from his ministry in 1853, honouring a promise that he had made to his wife to return to England after ten years of marriage. Whilst in England, he received an honorary MA Lambeth Degree from the Archbishop of Canterbury.

In May 1856, Thomas was appointed Archdeacon of Launceston, and held this position for thirteen years. In his role as Archdeacon, Thomas hosted the Duke of Edinburgh's visit to Northern Tasmania. On the 17th of January 1868, the Duke and Thomas attended a luncheon at *Woolmers Estate*, Longford.

Scandal was common in the 1860's, and Thomas was no exception to this. He was accused of 'diverting a lady's affection' in 1868, and unsuccessfully sued his accuser, Mr Bloomfield, for libel in 1870. With the ensuing scandal he resigned from the Anglican ministry and retired to private life at *Entally*. In his defence, an anonymous writer wrote to the Mercury stating, '..*those who have known Archdeacon Reibey the longest...cannot bring themselves to credit the evil things laid to his charge....from his early manhood to his mature age, he has been a benefactor, and a self-denying faithful servant of the church to an extent unequalled by any other man in Tasmania, or probably in any other of the Colonies; and we have already seen that during the same time he has been a kind and respected landlord, a good and honoured master, a trusted and faithful friend*'. Due to the erupting scandal, Thomas withdrew his financial support for the building of the Anglican Church at Hadspen. The church became known as 'the Reibey Ruin' and was left unfinished for over 100 years.

Thomas's friends persuaded him to return to public life by entering politics. A vacancy had occurred in the constituency of Westbury in 1874. Thomas won the election with a resounding victory, and thus, his political career was born. Thomas was the sitting member for the constituency of Westbury from 1874 until his retirement from politics in 1903. During his entire political career, only two candidates ever stood against him in the State elections. During Thomas's time in politics, he had a progressive public works policy, including the purchase of the privately-owned railways.

Thomas was Premier of Tasmania for a year from July 1876 - August 1877. In December 1878, he was both the leader of the opposition and Colonial Secretary until October 1879. In 1887 - 1891, Thomas was elected Speaker of the Tasmanian House of Assembly.  It was said, *'Few prominent public men are more widely known and respected than the Honorable Thomas Reibey, the "Squire of Entally", who, after a long political career, now wears the role of Speaker of the House of Assembly'*.

Thomas had, on several occasions, been offered a knighthood but had refused this honour.

Following Thomas's retirement from politics in 1903, he confined his interests to country pursuits for the remainder of his life. On the 24th of October of that year, Thomas was made a Justice of the Peace at an Executive Council Meeting in Hobart. In addition, as President of the Northern Agricultural Society, he worked to improve agriculture in Northern Tasmania.

Catherine died in 1896 aged 73 and on the 10th of February 1912, Thomas died at *Entally*. His body lay in the *Entally* Chapel until the burial, where he was buried beside his wife Catherine, behind the half-finished Anglican Church in Hadspen. There were no children of the marriage. Thomas left *Entally* Estate to his nephew, Thomas Reibey Arthur.

*Entally* Estate is open to the public in 2024 on weekends, where the buildings and gardens have been kept in their original state. It can be hired as a wedding or event venue.

**Bishop Francis Nixon**

During almost twenty years in Van Diemen's Land, Francis Nixon was active in many aspects of life over and above his pastoral duties, especially in matters of education, convict transportation and theology. This resulted in many disputes with both fellow clergy and the official establishment. Although compromise was normally reached, he returned to England during 1846-48 because of a clash with Lieutenant-Governor Eardley-Wilmot over state interference in affairs over which Nixon claimed episcopal authority.

Due to his ill health, the family returned to England permanently in 1862. Nixon resigned his bishopric in 1863 and was given the living of Bolton Percy, Yorkshire. His health did not, however, improve, and he retired to his villa at Vignolo, Italy, in 1866. Here in 1868 his wife Anna Maria died. Two years later Francis married Flora Muller (known as Agnes) with whom he had two more sons. He died on 7 April 1879 and was buried in the British Cemetery at Stresa.

Nixon was a keen sketcher and painter in watercolours, using his drawings to record his travels around his colonial diocese. This included the whole of the Tasmanian mainland, the Bass Strait Islands, including King Island and the Furneaux Group, as well as Norfolk Island, to which he made a formal two-month visitation in 1851. He went to Melbourne several times and to Sydney for seven weeks in January-February 1844 and in 1850, sketching everywhere. His Cruise of the Beacon: A Narrative of a Visit to the Islands of Bass Strait (London 1854), published as a record of one of his northern Tasmanian journeys, contains ten illustrations after his original sketches (now in the Anglican Diocesan Archives, Hobart).

RC Carpenter's photograph of Bishop Nixon, 1840s (ALMFA, SLT)

### Reverend John Gell

John Gell was still only 33 when he left Van Diemen's Land in 1848 to return home to England. In 1849 he married Eleanor, Sir John Franklin's only child by his first marriage to Eleanor Porden. John had met her in Tasmania. He obtained a curacy at St John's, Notting Hill. In 1852 he joined the Canterbury Association and was appointed bishop-designate of its settlement in New Zealand, but the appointment lapsed when the proposed see was not created. At this time the friendship he had previously enjoyed with Lady Jane Franklin deteriorated as Eleanors's claims to her rightful inheritance from her mother's estate were waived when Lady Franklin used the money to pay for an extensive quest for Sir John Franklin's lost Arctic expedition, during which he lost his life. He died on 12 March 1898 in London, having had three sons and four daughters.

## Christ College

By 1854 Christ College was in serious debt, despite the Warden reporting that there were 39 students, with more expected, the College was full, and he was planning new buildings. In 1856 Bishop Nixon ordered an inquiry into the College that recommended the appointment of trustee's and the closing of the college at Bishopsbourne.

Christ College opened again in Hobart in 1879 but was again closed in 1891 due to finances. It was reopened in 1912 for higher school education in conjunction with the Hutchins School. There have been many iterations of the college and in 2024 it is still operating at Sandy Bay, Hobart, as part of the University of Tasmania and is known as the oldest tertiary institution in Australia. Picture below of *Vron* and Christ College.

**William and Maria Webb**

The Webb's *Bush Inn* had always been the venue to host community activities, and after William retired and passed the Inn to his son John, he continued to be more and more involved in community issues. In 1853 he was appointed to the Longford Road District Trust, which raised road taxes and determined the priorities for expenditure in the district. He was re-elected in 1854 and 1857. In 1854 he was on the committee of the Little Hampton Ploughing Association, which met regularly at the Bush Inn.

He continued with his interests in all areas of farming and agriculture and owned many properties into the 1860's. Maria died in 1860, aged 73. In 1862 William moved to his daughter Mary Dodery's house at Longford and lived there until he died in 1868, aged 76.

**John and Jane Webb**

John and Jane had one son, John, who was born in 1849 and two daughters. They ran the *Bush Inn*. John was also the Treasurer of the Little Hampton Ploughing Association. In 2024 ploughing matches are still held in this area. He owned several farms and houses in the area. Sadly, John died of a stroke, aged just 34 in 1857. Jane moved to Longford and leased all the farms and properties.

**William and Eliza Hartnoll**

Eliza gave birth to a son named Alfred in 1853, but he died soon after birth.

William relinquished his job as the Postmaster at Bishopsbourne in 1853. He was also operating the stockyards as well as a store at Bishopsbourne and had numerous properties in the north. In 1853 he cashed in all his assets and William and Eliza left for England in January 1854. Their eldest son, Henry was already in England and their second son, William stayed behind. Their daughter Lydia was born in 1854. They returned to Tasmania in 1864, with William bringing some prize horses and sheep with him.

William purchased a property at Evandale and the family lived at the residence called *Leighton*. He was a very successful businessman. William died in 1887 aged 81. Eliza died of heart disease in 1890 aged 71.

**The Archers – *Woolmers* and *Brickendon***

In 2024 the Archer's estates of *Woolmers* and *Brickendon* are still owned by the Archer family and are listed as World Heritage Sites. They are both open to the public with *Brickendon* having a

Historic Farm Village and Heritage Gardens and either the Historic cottages or the Farm cottages where guests can stay. *Woolmers* offers guided tours of the estate, there is a restaurant/cafe and guests can stay in one of the cottages.

## James Henry 'Golden' Ashton

Golden Ashton was assigned to the Reibeys at *Entally,* where he worked as a servant from 1839 to 1842. He founded the Ashton Circus in 1850, having purchased it from a Thomas Mollar in Hobart. Ashton's Circus (currently operating as Circus Joseph Ashton) is the longest surviving circus in Australia, pre-dating most other circuses in the English-speaking world. The circus operated as the Royal Amphitheatre or Royal Circus.

When Ashton passed away in 1889, his son Fred, then 22, inherited the circus. The circus continues to be handed down throughout the family, and today is run by the 6th generation of Ashtons - Michelle & Joseph with their sons Jordon & Merrick.

## The Rajah Quilt

The *Rajah quilt* is one of Australia's most important textiles, and a major focus of the National Gallery's textiles collection. While it is a work of great documentary importance in Australia's history, it is also an extraordinary work of art; a product of beauty from the hands of many women who, while in the most abject circumstances, were able to work together to produce something of hope.

Its story is one of hope and persistence and has been a central subject of study into colonial life since its rediscovery in 1987.

From the quilt's 2815 pieces, we can see a cross-section of contemporary textile technology of the period, its patterns, printing techniques and design influences. While we do not know the women who worked on it, we can see there was a considerable variation in their skills. Among the women on that voyage of the *Rajah* were 15 whose occupations were listed as tailoring or needlework. However, there are small bloodstains still on the quilt—probably from the pricked fingers of some of the less-skilled workers.

At some stage after its arrival in Tasmania the quilt was returned to England, to be presented to Elizabeth Fry. Whether she knew of it before her death four years after its completion, we do not know. Its life and ownership during the following 147 years remains to be revealed.

One of the many improvements the Society implemented was to offer prisoners useful tasks, such as needlecraft, to keep them occupied during their incarceration. The Society donated sewing supplies, including tape, 10 yards of fabric, four balls of white cotton sewing thread, a ball each of black, red and blue thread, black wool, 24 hanks of coloured thread, a thimble, 100 needles, threads, pins, scissors and two pounds of patchwork pieces (or almost ten metres of fabric).

These provisions were carried by the 180 women prisoners on board the *Rajah* as it set sail from Woolwich, England on 5 April 1841, bound for Van Diemen's Land. When the *Rajah* arrived in Hobart on 19 July 1841, these supplies had been turned into the inscribed patchwork, embroidered and appliquéd coverlet now known as *The Rajah quilt*. It was presented to the Lieutenant-Governor's wife, Lady Jane Franklin, as tangible evidence of the cooperative work that could be achieved under such circumstances.

A project of this size and technical complexity—the quilt measures 325 x 337 cm—would have been the result of skilled labour and planned direction. It seems such a task may have been assumed by a free passenger on board the *Rajah* for this journey—Miss Kezia Hayter, from the Millbank Penitentiary. On the recommendation of Elizabeth Fry, Hayter had been sent to assist Lady Franklin in the formation of the Tasmanian Ladies' Society for the Reformation of Female Prisoners. Her instigation, supervision and completion of the quilt was a clear demonstration of the success of the shipboard project.

Textile arts and industry have held societies together for millennia, providing for our needs and stimulating the growth of industry and technology. Despite their fragility, textiles endure because they can be remade with inherited and remembered skills.

*The Rajah quilt* has miraculously endured the ravages of time and physical decay to provide us with a tangible link to this country's fragile early society and the women who transcended their conditions to work together in the service of art.

https://nga.gov.au/stories-ideas/the-rajah-quilt-1841/

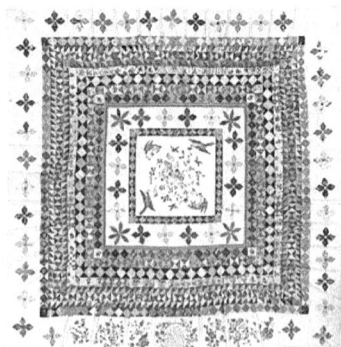

# *Afterword*

I wrote and published my first book, Paterson's Plains in 2023. It is a fictional story, based on facts about my ancestors Alexander 'Sandy' McKenzie, who was a soldier with the 73rd Regiment and Ann Clark who came to Sydney as a convict in 1810.

I enjoyed the writing experience so much that I decided to go back into my family history research notes and see who else had an interesting story that I could write about. Of course, that was like trying to pick a needle out of a haystack because there are so many interesting stories to be told, so I guess I won't run out of subject matter quickly.

I chose Amelia Laing because I knew that she had come out on the *Rajah* in 1841 and soon discovered the significance of the *Rajah* quilt. I was also drawn to the story of the matron Kezia Hayter and Mrs Fry's ladies who helping the female convicts at that time. There was lots of information available about the journey and some of the people who were onboard. It was then very interesting researching all about Edinburgh and Scotland at that time, as well as the prison's the convicts were sent to. I also found out so much about what happened during the journey. My first story started as Ann arrived in Sydney and I hadn't researched the convict ships yet.

I wrote Amelia's story up to when she arrived in Launceston before I even started doing my research on John. As happens, something was compelling me to get the story on paper.

I knew absolutely nothing about John Harris. Gradually, I put the small snippets of information that I had together. I already had a photo attributed to being John's son, and a story from a descendant that noted that he was known as London Johnny due to his dapper dress and bearing. I knew John came from an area right near the Lambeth Palace, and so John's story just came tumbling out. I really enjoyed researching London at that time, and the Vauxhall Gardens and the royals.

I was trying to figure out how John and Amelia would have met, when I discovered that they were both assigned to William Walker at the same time. My journey then began to research the details of life in the Launceston area at the time, and the lives of those who lived there.

The story of little Emily's death at the nursery at the Launceston Female Factory was difficult to write, but this story needs to be told because there were hundreds of little souls who never made it out of there. While the colony provided a wonderful land of opportunity for so many, those who came as convicts first had to survive the cruelties of the convict system.

I hope that I have done justice to the people whose stories are told in this book.

# Chapter Notes

There are parts of this story that are true according to records and research, and there are parts where I have had to fill in the gaps to make a realistic and interesting story and paint a picture of life during the early years of Australia.

**Chapter One – 1832 - Lambeth**

John's date of birth and where he grew up are true. Where John and his parents worked is made up, however, for people of humble means who lived in that area, the choices would have been to run or work in a shop, work at one of the many factories, work in the Palace or in the wealthier homes, or turn to crime, which had started to encroach into the area as it became more urban. Given where John turns up later in the story and the story passed on by descendants about his son, who was known as London Johnny due to his good looks and bearing, I felt that the career path that I wrote for John was not too farfetched. The dates of his parents passing are true.

**Chapter Two – 1827 - The Palace**

The story of John working at Lambeth Palace is made up. The information about Archbishop Howley and King George IV is true. The Coronation and the opening of Pall Mall were very interesting to research.

**Chapter Three – 1832 - Sentenced to Life**

The story behind John's arrest is made up, but the facts behind his sentencing are true. The story about his time on the hulk is as true as I could find.  There has been a lot written about the hulks, so I was interested to find that they worked on the shore and attended lessons on the hulks of an evening. John was on the hulk *Leviathan* and travelled on the *York* and his convict number was 1463. The story of the *York*'s journey, while made up, is based on the documents that can be found regarding the journey, as well as research on other convict journeys around the same time.

The story of John at the Launceston gaol and on the road gangs in made up but is typical of what happened to most of the convicts on arrival. The story of Mr Walker choosing John is made up, however he must have had some talents to be chosen to go to such a prestigious estate as *Vron*. It may not have been as a footman, he may have simply been a common labourer, but later, after *Vron* is sold, John is still noted as being there, and there must have been a reason, so this is my interpretation of why.

Jarvis, as much as we grow to love him, is a made-up character.

## Chapter Four – 1839 - Edinburgh

While the details of Amelia's story have been made up, the dates, times and places in this chapter are accurate. Amelia was born in Fife and at some time after she became an adult, she made her way to Edinburgh. It is true that Amelia (and I) are descendants of the Gillespie family and that there is still a stained-glass window dedicated to The Reverend George Gillespie at the 'Old Kirk' at Kirkaldy. How Amelia, and her friends made their living is made up, however the story is typical for women of humble means at that time and place. The names of places in Stirling and Edinburgh are real, and some still exist. The dates and details of all her arrests are real. I found descriptions of the conditions in the Bridewell and the prison system in Scotland during my research. They were treated a lot better than in England.

### Chapter Five – 1839 - A Grand Plan

The details in this chapter are made up, but the dates and the details of Amelia's crimes are all true. I thought that there had to be a reason why a woman in her mid-twenties, who had never committed a crime previously, suddenly went on a crime spree. It was then that I started to read that at the time lots of people in Britain were doing the same thing. They were living in such abject poverty with no way of getting out of it, and they heard stories of this magnificent new land of opportunity. Whereas the government had previously sold the story that the colony was a terrible place to go to, after so many years the stories coming back were quite the opposite. People who had lived in poverty and travelled to the colony as convicts, were coming back to visit Britain as wealthy landowners or merchants. It must have seemed like a legitimate way out of their dire situations for many Brits.

### Chapter Six – 1840 - England bound

While all the dates and places are true the story in this chapter is made up. However, prisoners were kept in Scotland until they were called forward to London, usually just shortly before a ship carrying female prisoners was due to leave for the colony. England didn't want to have to pay for their keep for any longer than necessary. The other women in prison with Amelia are real, and they all travelled with her on the *Rajah* to Van Diemen's Land. Details about them were found in various documents, the best being *Patchwork Prisoners* by Trudy Cowley and Dianne Snowden, which has an incredibly detailed account of the facts behind the journey of the *Rajah* and was an invaluable source of information for this book.

Matron Kezia Hayter was very real. The details of the women's journey to the *Rajah* and their days waiting for the voyage to start, was put together from several accounts of such journeys at the time. Doctor James Donovan was the Ship's Surgeon. Mrs Fry and her Religious Society of Friends were very real and made an incredible difference to the lives of female convicts for many years. The items given to the convicts by Mrs Fry and her ladies are true. Amelia's convict number was 229, and the tin tickets on red ribbon are true. An excellent account of this and other convict women's journeys is found in the book *The Tin Ticket* by Deborah J. Swiss.

## Chapter Seven – 1841 - The High Seas

The Reverend Rowland Davies, with his wife Maria and young son Rowland were on the *Rajah*. There has been a lot written about the journey and Miss Hayter and the Davies' part in treating the women fairly and with dignity. There were 10 children onboard, and I used the story of Amelia being put in charge of the children to explain how she later got to *Vron*. The story about the romance between Miss Hayter and Captain Ferguson is true. Most of the stories onboard are true and were found in other documents and accounts of the journey; the women were separated into messes, the chapel services that the Reverend held, the women sewing with Miss Hayter to put together the famous *Rajah* quilt and the visits along the way to tropical ports is all true.

## Chapter Eight – 1841 - Van Diemen's Land

The details about the end of the journey were imagined after reading many accounts of such journey's arriving at Hobart at the time. Poor Sarah Parfitt was the only person to die on the journey. Details of their wait in the harbour are true, including the visit by Sir John and Lady Franklin, where Lady Franklin was presented with the famous quilt.

The details of the journey to Launceston are made up as I was unable to find much information about that, but I read lots of accounts of other ships that sailed into Launceston at the time, which is where I got my descriptions from.

The details of the Launceston Female Factory and the convict system at the time are true. It must have been a terrible shock for the women after being so well treated for months on the *Rajah*.

**Chapter Nine – 1833 - *Vron***

The story about *Vron* and the Walker family is mostly true, including their background and how they came to Van Diemen's Land. The farm was managed by Mr Dryden. The description of the *Vron* mansion and the expansive estate is true. It was one of the largest estates in Van Diemen's Land.

The journey to *Vron* is made up but the descriptions of the area at the time are real. The descriptions of *Vron*, while made up, were developed in my head after extensive research into the estate at the time, including several pictures that are still available. Cook is a made-up character, but all the workers are typical of convicts, Ticket-of leave and free settlers working in Van Diemen's Land at the time.

Old Sammy Cox was a real person, and his story can be found within the bibliography.

Miss Lemaire and Nanny are made-up characters, but the Walker's would certainly have had a lady's maid, a governess and a nanny. I have created these characters as they could not be found in the records that I found.

The Walker's holding church services at *Vron* is true. This was in the very early days in the area before people like the Reverend's Davies and Reibey built their many churches and schools. St John's church in Launceston is real and can be visited in 2024. It is still impressive.

### Chapter Ten – 1833 - Launceston

The descriptions of the journey to Launceston and the town itself are accurate. Sparky tells John a story of his first assignment, and it is true that not all convicts had a great time, and some masters were cruel. Mr Walker was a magistrate. It is unknown if he had a town house in Launceston, but it seems likely as his work would have meant that he had to spend a lot of time there.

Thomas Beswick the bootmaker is a real person, and he is a character in my first book Paterson's Plains, which gives a full account of his time as a convict and Ticket-of-leave man and his marriage to Mary Peck (McKenzie). They are also my ancestors.

The places of knowledge in Launceston that are mentioned, were real.

### Chapter Eleven – 1833 - History

The wedding of Marianne Walker to John Jackson is real, as is the story of the Walker's history.

### Chapter Twelve – 1835 - Love blossoms

The stories about the other wealthy landowners in the area are true. The first stone was laid for the church at Westbury in 1836. King William died in 1837 and Queen Victoria's Coronation was held in 1838. Henry Walker came home from England and his 21$^{st}$ birthday was held at *Vron*.  The events that led to the depression are real, it was a difficult time across the whole of the colony. The story of a romance between John and Nanny Elizabeth was made up to explain why a man of John's calibre did not have an interest in women until he met Amelia, when he was 34. Elizabeth's story is made up.

### Chapter Thirteen – 1839 - The Beginning of the End

The story of the Jackson's is real and William Walker's business interests. The winding down of the Walker's interest really happened. The economic downturn in 1840 really happened. The death of Nanny is made up. John getting his Ticket-of-leave happened. Miss Lemaire's stroke is made up but the downfall of the Walker's really happened around that time.

### Chapter Fourteen – 1841 - New beginnings

Amelia was chosen to work at *Vron* in 1841, how that happened is uncertain and this part of the story is made up. But it is odd that Mr Walker was taking on new workers at a time when things were winding down at *Vron*. There must have been a good reason. The Beswick's are real, but how they met Amelia is made up.  We know that their daughter Jane married John and Amelia's eldest son John, but how they met and how close their friendship was, is imagined. Mary's mother Ann had died in a tragic fire in July of 1841. The ages of the Walker children are all accurate for the time.

### Chapter Fifteen – 1841 - Work to do

This chapter is all fictional, except the children's ages are correct.

## Chapter Sixteen – 1841 - Love

The names of the Reverend's at Westbury and Longford are correct. The developing relationship between John and Amelia is made up but it certainly happened around this time. This story tumbled out and it was only after I'd finished writing it that I checked the accuracy of the Auroa Australis being visible at that time and was shocked to find that it would have been.

## Chapter Seventeen – 1841 - Shocking news

It was around this time that Mr Walker had to relinquish *Vron* to trustee's and he and the family left to move to Forth. It is unknown what happened to the staff at *Vron*, including Amelia, except we know that John stayed.

## Chapter Eighteen – 1841 - the Frogmore adventure

It is unknown if Amelia left with the Walker's, or what happened to the Walker's at Frogmore where they first moved to. It is true that Amelia was charged with being absent from her place of assignment and sentenced to six weeks at the Launceston Female Factory in 1841. The descriptions of life inside the Factory are accurate for the time. The story about John and Amelia's fear of her getting pregnant were very real fears, the punishment for such a misdemeanour is accurate as written in the story.

## Chapter Nineteen – 1842 - Consequences

The operations at *Vron* and the visit to *Brickendon* are made up, but Miss Hayter was there at the time, and so where the women from the *Rajah*. Kezia Hayter's disillusionment at the time was true. Amelia would have found out that she was pregnant around this time.

## Chapter Twenty – 1842 - The Factory

Mr Swanston and Gleadow were the trustees of *Vron.* The circumstances of Amelia being caught are unknown but could well have happened as they did in the story. The description of life in The Factory is accurate, from the accounts that can be found about that time. Hannah Perry from the *Rajah* was in The Factory at the same time as Amelia, and she was also pregnant. The story about what happens in the Nursery and afterwards is accurate according to accounts that can be found, but the details are made up.

Little Emily Harris was born on the 19th of July 1842 at the Launceston Female Factory.

## Chapter Twenty One – 1842 - The Nursery

The description of life in the nursery is accurate according to accounts that can be found but the story and the details are made up. The other women from the *Rajah* who are mentioned did come into the nursery while Amelia was there. The story that the nurse tells the women about what it was like when the colony first started was true. The riot at The Factory really happened in October 1822. Records show that there were 44 children in the Nursery over Christmas 1842. It is true that epidemics and illnesses broke out frequently in the Nursery and the death rate was very high. Little John Perry died in the Nursery, aged 10 months. There was a fire at The Factory in February 1843.

Kezia Hayter and Captain Ferguson were married in Hobart in July 1843 and left Hobart on the *Rajah* the following month.

The women having to leave their babies once they were weaned to serve their six-month sentence in hard labour was true, and the fact that many babies died soon after is also true.

## Chapter Twenty Two – 1842 - A tragic loss

It's not known if Mr Dryden came back to *Vron*. The Launceston Mechanic's Institute and the other societies for learning were real. John McKenzie owned hotels in the area, and one was the *Scottish Chiefs* in Launceston. The ages and dates of birth for the Beswick children is real. Amelia's petition for a marriage licence, while she was at The Factory in April 1843 was denied. The Jackson's returned to Launceston in May 1843. Little Emily sadly died at The Nursery on 21 May 1843 and Amelia had to serve out her sentence, and it is true that it is was very common for the babies to die soon after their mothers were taken away, and this was attributed to heartbreak.

## Chapter Twenty Three – 1843 – The Journey Home

This chapter is all made up as I tried to imagine how a woman must have been feeling after 18 months locked up at The Factory. Jane Beswick was born in 1843. Convicts did have to wait until their marriage approved was promulgated in the newspaper following approval from the Lieutenant-Governor of the colony. The land available at the time was true. The excerpt from the *Cornwall Chronicle* is real. John and Amelia were married in the church at Westbury by the Reverend Bishton on the 18th of December 1843.

## Chapter Twenty Four – 1844 – The Journey Home

The excerpt from the newspaper is real. The Reverend Davies' church at Longford was opened by Bishop Nixon in 1844. The dates of birth and ages of the Davies' children is real. Maria Davies was a watercolour artist, and her works are still displayed at the Anglican Diocesan Registry, Hobart. Bishop Nixon was showing an interest in *Vron* for his college in 1844 and would have visited there several times. Bishop Nixon's backstory is true. The story about the poor woman being sent the wrong child from the Orphan's School, twice, is real, and was reported in the newspapers. The clergy were staunch opponents of the convict system and transportation. The Reverend Gell's back story is true, as is the story of the beginnings of the college in Hobart.

It is not known what work that John did at the college, but it is known that he was still there long after the college opened. Mr Walker leaving land to John and the others is made up, however this was not unusual for employers to do for valued employees at the time.

**Chapter Twenty Five – 1844 – Bishopsbourne**

Bishop Nixon named the area, previously known as Little Hampton, or *Vron*, Bishopsbourne. The mansion was renamed *Episcopal House*. The Bishop built a church at Bishopsbourne that he called the Church of the Holy Nativity. William Webb owned lots of land and properties in the area and had recently built the *Bush Inn*. He was also building many of the houses in the area. His backstory is also true, that he was at first assigned as a convict to Maria Davies' father, Captain Lyttleton, who sponsored Maria and the children to come to the colony to join William. Henry Conway was a popular architect and he had designed the church at Longford.

Christ Church at Longford was opened by Bishop Nixon in October 1844, and the young wealthy landowner Thomas Reibey the Third, was ordained under special considerations on the day. Thomas Reibey III backstory is true, and he was married to Catherine, known as Katey, whose backstory is also true. The details of the laying of the foundation stone for the church at Bishopsbourne is true, as is the donation of the ship's bell.

John Harris junior was born on the 22nd of November 1844. The details about the auction at *Vron* in December are true. William Hartnoll, William Webb's son-in-law, purchased most of the livestock and took over a lease of the pasture lands on the estate.

**Chapter Twenty Six – 1845 – Bishopsbourne**

Maria Davies gave birth to a daughter that she called Emma on the 12th of January 1845. That she was named after Amelia 'Emma' Harris is made up, but could that possibly have happened? Maybe.

Amelia received her Ticket-of-leave in 1845 and she was pregnant again already. While the mother's group at Longford is made up, the ages of all the children mentioned is true. It is true that the Beswick's were starting to feel some financial strain at the time, as were so many in the area at the same time.

The story about how people thought about the Aboriginal Protectorate is true and was published in the newspaper. It is true that John Rose was a wealthy landowner and was the son of Sandy McKenzie's friend David Rose who had been his Captain in the 73rd Regiment. John's mother was an Aboriginal woman, who sadly died young. Richard White or 'Black Dick' was a real and prominent character in Launceston at the time.

The lecture called *The Diffusion of Knowledge* is real and shows that even back then, people were interested in how knowledge was starting to spread with the advent of technology, such as printing and the quicker passage of information.

It is unknown if John and Amelia lived at Bishopsbourne village, but records of the time have them at *Vron*. Mr Avery Stodges was a made-up character in my first book *Paterson's Plains*.

### Chapter Twenty Seven – 1846 – Christ College

Thomas Harris was born on the 14th of January 1846. Ann Brennan and George Emery were married on the 28th of January. The story that the Reverend Davies tells John about the conflict in the church and the Reverend's problems at the time, is real. The story about John Gell being ordained to run the college is true. John received his Conditional Pardon in 1846.

The story about the Reibey's new church at Carrick is true and Katey did play the organ with her little dog Toby at her feet. William Webb started a hunting club, and Richard Fry, the Field brothers, and Thomas Reibey were real wealthy landowners and were very involved in the hunting club, horse racing, and other interests in the area.

Bishop Nixon was opening other schools at the time. The Reverend Davies was a member of the Launceston Horticulture Society. The details of the opening of Christ College on the 3rd of October 1846 is true. Bishop Nixon was having troubles with Lieutenant-Governor Sir John Eardley-Wilmot and travelled back to England to try and sort it out.

The Reverend Marriot opened the first church at Paterson's Plains in 1846. John Jackson's involvement with representing the members of the anti-transportation movement and advocating for self-government is all true.

## Chapter Twenty Eight – 1847 - 1848 – Freedom

Margaret Beswick died in April 1847. George Walker came to farm the land back at Bishopsbourne. Sarah Emery was born in 1847. Amelia was granted her Certificate of Freedom at this time. Things were heating up with the anti-transportation movement after the government stopped sending convicts to New South Wales. Van Diemen's Land struggled to be able to sustain all the convicts being send to the island.

Ann Brennan died of influenza in 1847 aged only 18. Bushrangers were still a problem in the area. David Harris was born on the 22$^{nd}$ of February 1848. John Webb married Jane Lyall on the 4$^{th}$ of May and William did declare that he was passing the *Bush Inn* on to his son to run.

The Reverend Reibey and William Field opened a racing club and racecourse at Carrick in 1848. Jane Lyall's parent's backstory is real. Sarah Beswick was born in 1848. Sarah Webb married Thomas Lawson on the 3$^{rd}$ of August and his backstory is true. The Reverend Gell returned to England in 1848. Little Sarah Emery sadly died in 1848.

## Chapter Twenty Nine – 1849 - 1850 – Life goes on

The information about the other women from the *Rajah* are true. The Reverend Reibey was a very well-loved member of the community and the Reibey's did not have any children. The ages of all the children are again true. The story of Golden Ashton is true and the family circus still operates in 2024. The Olympic theatre was the place to go in Launceston.

The information about the Gold Rush in California is true and William Saltmarsh did go over there leaving his wife Maria to run his hotel. The anti-transportation and self-government supporters continued their agitation with regular meetings held at the Bush Inn and all across the area. Thomas Brennan died in 1850.

Amelia Harris was born in 1850, known, like her mother, as both Amelia and Emma. Maria Davies sadly died in 1850 and the Reverend Davies was appointed Archdeacon of Launceston.

## Chapter Thirty – 1851 – Lost and found

William Hartnoll became the postmaster at Bishopsbourne in 1851. The rest of this chapter is made-up, but there are stories where people did find their loved ones in the colony, but they were rare.

## Chapter Thirty One – 1851 – Hard times

The story about the Reverend Reibey importing Irish Setters is true, as is the story of how deer that were introduced by the settlers became rampant in the area, and still are in 2024. The first interstate cricket match was held at Bishopsbourne between Tasmania and Victoria and William Field played.

Charlotte Beswick was born in 1851. The ages of the children are correct and the Beswick's were having increasing financial trouble.

The Great Exhibition happened in London as described and Van Diemen's Land sent the largest number of exhibits from Australia. The Reverend Davies was part of the committee.

The Gold Rush had started in New South Wales and soon in Victoria, and many men and families raced across the ocean to get there and make their fortunes. Some did, but most didn't.

The Launceston Association for the Cessation of the Transportation of Convicts was getting more and more momentum, and most of the wealthy landowners and clergy were a part of the push. The banner that the Association created in 1851 is noted as being the precursor of the Australian flag as we know it today.

**Chapter Thirty One – 1852 – A Summer Wedding**

This chapter is all made-up, but the ages of all the children are correct.

The last convict ship arrived in Van Diemen's land in May 1853. Amelia and John saw the end of transportation to Van Diemen's Land.

The name of Van Diemen's Land was officially changed to Tasmania in 1856.

# Acknowledgements

I want to first acknowledge the authors whose work that I referred to when writing this book. Your works have made it possible for this story to come together:

*Patchwork Prisoners,* by Trudy Cowley and Dianne Snowden, was an invaluable non-fiction resource, and although Hope Adams book *Dangerous Women* is a fictional account of the Rajah's journey it still contained invaluable descriptions. *The Tin Ticket* by Deborah J. Swiss provided excellent details about how the convict women were treated and the journeys.

Ivan Badcock's incredible *History Over Dinner* website and blog, provided so many details about *Vron*, Christ Church, Bishopsbourne and the people who lived there at the time of this story.

The work of John Watts in his books, *Robert Lyall, The King of Westbury* and *Legacy of a Norfolk Plains convict* was invaluable. I met John on a Facebook page and purchased these books that include the extensive research that he has done into the Lyall and Webb families.

The work and guidance that I have humbly received from David Beswick. David is also a descendant of Thomas Beswick. David has had an illustrious career, a mixture of ministry in the church and academic work in psychology and education. He is a retired minister in the Uniting Church in Australia, and Professor Emeritus at the University of Melbourne where he has an honorary appointment as Principal Fellow in the Melbourne Graduate School of Education, and as a Fellow of St. Hilda's

College. David has done extensive research into the Beswick family and thank goodness put it all on a public website where I found this amazing information. Thank you so much David for www.beswick.info, another invaluable resource. I have had the pleasure of connecting with David in 2024. He has read my first book Paterson's Plains and provided some lovely feedback and will be one of the first who I send a signed copy of this one to.

I'd also like the thank my wonderful advance readers for their proof-reading and advice about the story. My dear friend and fellow author, Sara Powter, whose books on colonial Australia first inspired me to write. Carmel Excell-Cole, who read my first book and was so amazing at picking up the errors in the first publication, she is now on my list, and will also be helping me with research for my next book, about German ancestors. Rebekah Robinson, whose cover designs are truly beautiful, you just 'get it'. And the others who I let read the draft copy before it's sent for publication, as there are always tweaks to be made. Your input is vital and very much appreciated.

# About the Author

Facebook: Lee Boehm – Author

Instagram: Lee_Boehm_Author

Lee Boehm was born in Melbourne and raised near the beach in Adelaide. After leaving school she joined the Army where she served as a clerk until after her three children were born. She then started a career with the Australian Public Service and served in many roles over more than 20 years.

In 2024, Lee has three adult children and three grandchildren, located across Queensland and New South Wales, and travels to new destinations to live every three years with her beloved husband who is still a serving member of the Australian Army.

As well as writing, Lee enjoys researching family history, making photo-books, reading, watching movies and series of many genres, and the company of her German shepherd dog and Siamese cat.

Lee's first book Paterson's Plains was published in September 2023.

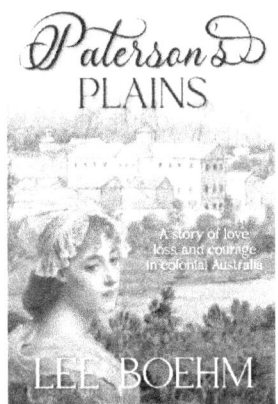

Born in Liverpool Ann Clark resorts to theft to save her father's life but finds herself on the other side of the world at the Parramatta Gaol.

Private Alexander 'Sandy' McKenzie from the Scottish Highlands is a career soldier who finds himself in Sydney with his Commanding Officer and now Colonial Governor Lachlan Macquarie. Thinking that love had passed him by he falls for the pregnant convict girl who catches his eye in the grounds of Parramatta Gaol.

And so begins a saga that takes the reader to Sydney, Newcastle and Launceston from 1810 until 1839 as the story of Ann and her children comes to life. This is a story of love, loss and courage during the forming of a Nation.

Read about the incredible lives of everyday people who happened to live at the same time as many of Australia's prominent historical characters. Their story is interwoven with those already well known in Australian history.

Available from Amazon via Kindle Direct Publishing.

# Bibliography

I wasn't sure whether to include a bibliography with this book. The reason that it is included is because I know that this book might inspire other descendants to explore their family history, so a list of resources that I used will hopefully be useful for others.

While I tried to include everything that I read that contributed to the book, I am sure that there is more that I have left out in the mad chaos of research and writing.

Watts, John. *Robert Lyall, The King of Westbury* and *Legacy of a Norfolk Plains convict*

Cowley, Trudy and Snowden, Dianne, *Patchwork Prisoners: The Rajah Quilt and the Women who Made it*, Research Tasmania, 2013

Adams, Hope, *Dangerous Women*, Penguin Books Limited, 2021

Swiss, Deborah J, *The Tin Ticket: The Heroic Journey of Australia's Convict Women*, Berkley Books, 2010

https://beswick.info/
The website of David Beswick. Extensive research into the Beswick family.

https://www.kirkcaldyoldkirktrust.org.uk/Index.asp?MainID=25672#HistoryGeoGill
Kirkcaldy Old Kirk Trust – stained glass window of George Gillespie

https://freepages.rootsweb.com/~dferguson/genealogy/Capt.Ferguson/CKFerguson.htm
Captain Charles Ferguson, family history.

https://brickendon.com.au/about/
Brickendon Estate, World Heritage Site, Longford, Tasmania

https://www.woolmers.com.au/
Woolmers Estate, World Heritage Site

https://www.ourtasmania.com.au/launceston/carrick.html
Carrick, Tasmania

https://researchoutput.csu.edu.au/ws/portalfiles/portal/20273002/44842_44340postpub.pdf
Flogging Parson? Australian Anglican Clergymen, the Magistracy, and Convicts (1788 – 1850)

https://www.churchesoftasmania.com/2021/08/no-985-patterson-plains-st-peters.html
St Peter's Anglican Church, Paterson's Plain's and Reverend Marriot

https://eprints.utas.edu.au/16445/1/butler-secondary-ed-tas-1917.pdf
The Foundation of Public Institutions for Secondary Education in Tasmania

Alan Dyer Books, Field brothers
https://www.alandyerbooks.com/20-field-bros-cattle-kings-in-kentish-1840-1940/

Maria Lyttleton Davies, biography, Design and Art Australia.
https://www.daao.org.au/bio/version_history/maria-lyttleton/biography/?p=1

Van Diemen's Land at the Great Exhibition of 1851
https://eprints.utas.edu.au/41081/1/04%20Roe.pdf

The Australasian Anti-Transportation League Flag (1851), Australian National Flag Association (ANFA)
https://www.anfa-national.org.au/australian-red-ensign/first-union-flag/anti-transportation-flag/#:~:text=This%20flag%2C%20featuring%20a%20golden,to%20Australia%20and%20New%20Zealand

Australian Anti-Transportation League 1851 – Australian Flag
https://australianaflags.com.au/flags/australasian-anti-transportation-league/

Federation of Australia: Part 1 1840 – 1879
https://mhnsw.au/guides/federation-australia-1840-1879/

Title (aph.gov.au) John West and anti-transportation

Facebook page – Australian Historical Dance

https://www.tasfhs.org/downloads/Volume17Number3_1996.pdf
Dicky White

https://www.daao.org.au/bio/francis-russell-nixon/biography/
Bishop Franis Nixon biography

https://eprints.utas.edu.au/18612/1/UA17.pdf
Christ College Index: University of Tasmania.

Christ College Library pamphlet (utas.edu.au)
Christ College Library pamphlet

https://adb.anu.edu.au/biography/gell-john-philip-2087
Biography – John Philip Gell – Australian Dictionary of Biography

https://Monissa.com/hotels
Hotels in Launceston to 1900

https://media.onthemarket.com/properties/3796887/doc_0_0.pdf
Possibly the original Vron

https://candicehern.com/regency-world/glossary/
Regency Glossary

https://researchmgt.monash.edu/ws/portalfiles/portal/9389250/2009_Kippen_convictnursery.pdf
The convict nursey at the Cascades Female Factory

https://archivesandheritageblog.libraries.tas.gov.au/sewing-for-freedom-clothes-production-at-the-cascades-female-factory/
Sewing for freedom – clothes production at the Cascades Female Factory

https://resources.christchurchlongford.com.au/Church%20Booklet%20c.1960.pdf
A Short Account of Christ Church, Longford

https://ipc2009.popconf.org/papers/91837 – Scarlet fever, measles and flu outbreak 1852

https://en.wikipedia.org/wiki/History_of_Tasmania
History of Tasmania - Wikipedia

https://www.utas.edu.au/tasmanian-companion/biogs/E000092b.htm
Companion to Tasmanian History – Beswick Family

C:\Users\leewi\Downloads\Launceston-Thematic-History-Report.pdf
Launceston Heritage Study, Stage 1: Thematic History, July 2002

https://www.ourtasmania.com.au/tas-history-church.html
Tasmania: Historic Churches and Church Architecture

https://gutenberg.net.au/ebooks14/1401091h.html
Sketch of the History of Van Diemen's Land - 1832

https://eprints.utas.edu.au/14281/1/1966_Howeler-
Coy_Food_and_drink_Tasmania.pdf
AN ACCOUNT OF FOOD AND DRINK IN TASMANIA. 1800-1900.

https://bpb-ap-
se2.wpmucdn.com/blog.une.edu.au/dist/a/1415/files/2022/11/JACH22-2020-
Piper.pdf
The dregs of a criminal population: Impression Bay and the origins of Tasmania's
residential charitable system, c. 1839-1857

https://tasmaniantimes.com/2020/08/matthew-forster-biography/
The assignment and the probation system

https://www.ourtasmania.com.au/launceston/carrick.html
https://historyoverdinner.com/sammy-cox/
Sammy Cox

https://historyoverdinner.com/bishopsbourne-chronology/
Bishopsbourne - Chronology

https://historyoverdinner.com/bishopsbourne-william-webb-family/
William Webb and Family

Bishopsbourne Relics of Christ College – History Over Dinner
Bishopsbourne relics of Chris College

https://historyoverdinner.com/christs-college-bishopsbourne/
Vron after 1844

https://www.examiner.com.au/story/6653930/nixons-grand-bucolic-plan/
Sketch of Christ College

https://journals.openedition.org/abe/5887
Scottish networks and their buildings in Can Diemen's Land

https://janeaustensworld.com/2008/01/24/footmen-male-servants-in-the-regency-
era/
Footmen: Male servants in the Regency era

https://adb.anu.edu.au/biography/jackson-john-alexander-2265?fbclid=IwAR1lhWWPzA1ZL1O7AI86fPzeDQmGUeddjLM8oxvo3cgfJRRqt81BqFmHCaw

https://historyoverdinner.com/an-e-s-a-bank-notable/

Biography – John Alexander Jackson

https://eprints.qut.edu.au/121495/1/Heather_Clarke_Thesis.pdf

Dancing on convict ships

https://www.utas.edu.au/library/companion_to_tasmanian_history/C/Convicts.htm#:~:text=Between%201803%20and%201853%20approximately,transported%20from%20other%20British%20colonies.

The Companion to Australian History - Convicts

https://historyoverdinner.com/william-gwillim-walker-family-vron-property/

William Gwillim Walker and family – Vron property

https://vauxhallhistory.org/vauxhall-gardens-madame-georgina/

Vhttps://en.wikipedia.org/wiki/Vauxhall_Gardens

https://vauxhallhistory.org/vauxhall-gardens

https://www.regencyhistory.net/2019/03/vauxhall-gardens-finding-your-way-around.html

https://www.regencyhistory.net/2019/01/vauxhall-gardens-in-regency.html

https://www.google.com/maps/place/Vauxhall+Pleasure+Gardens/@51.4874385,-0.1209093,15z/data=!4m6!3m5!1s0x487604ec69963e8b:0x936642d303ece8e6!8m2!3d51.4874385!4d-0.1209093!16zL20vMDZtNGZn?entry=ttu

Vauxhall Gardens

https://en.wikipedia.org/wiki/Lambeth

http://partletontree.com/EarlyLambeth.htm

Lambeth

https://libraries.tas.gov.au/family-history/convicts-in-van-diemens-land-now-tasmania/?fbclid=IwAR39okuCk5m9AiADDaJjUaiYu3SKWkuDzk2qacBqxiBh7iyxWeL3g2q7UQw

Convicts in Van Diemen's Land – Interactive Map

https://librariestas.ent.sirsidynix.net.au/client/en_AU/names/search/detailnonmodal/ent:$002f$002fNAME_INDEXES$002f0$002fNAME_INDEXES:1399418/one?qu=harris&qf=NI_SHIP_FACET%09Ship%09York%20(2)%09York%20(2)&fbclid=IwAR0b8dW7dWPJf4b6Tc9-biL9Sz_q-2lLa3g16KVjC1_prMJFZM3pn4_O4Jg
https://stors.tas.gov.au/CON31-1-20$init=CON31-1-20P181?fbclid=IwAR2F7Bo2zGDBuxOe6PeXqaN8Yf8nW8otx1TpLhWbYmTOncD56Ohl
XHPcVsE
John Harris Convict records

https://www.discovertasmania.com.au/things-to-do/heritage-and-history/brickendon-and-woolmers-estates/
Brickendon and Woolmers Estate

https://adb.anu.edu.au/biography/davies-robert-rowland-1962
Biography – Robert Rowland Davies

https://www.femaleconvicts.org.au/convict-institutions/children/infant-mortality
Female Convicts Research Centre – Infant Mortality

https://www.narryna.com.au/narryna-blog/2021/3/23/the-crime-of-pregnancy
The Crime of Pregnancy

https://www.femaleconvicts.org.au/pre-transportation/the-prisons/scottish-prisons
Female Convicts, Scottish Prisons

http://www.vam.ac.uk/content/journals/research-journal/issue-01/doing-time-patchwork-as-a-tool-of-social-rehabilitiation-in-british-prisons/
Doing time: Patchwork as a tool of social rehabilitation in British Prisons

https://femaleconvicts.org.au/docs/seminars/TrudyCowley_Self-HarmByFemaleConvicts.pdf
Self Harm by Female Convicts

https://tasmanianbibliophileatlarge.wordpress.com/2021/05/25/dangerous-women-by-hope-adams/
Dangerous Women by Hope Adams - article

https://ewh.org.uk/learning/historical-maps/
Edinburgh – historical maps

https://www.euppublishing.com/userimages/ContentEditor/1439825554690/A%20History%20of%20Drinking%20Sample.pdf
A History of Drinking

https://archive.org/details/englishandscotti01chiluoft/page/4/mode/2up
English and Scottish popular ballads

https://genealogical.com/store/the-people-of-perth-and-kinross-1800-1850-2/
The people of Perth and Kinross

https://www.culturepk.org.uk/wp-content/uploads/2017/11/Kinross-shire-through-the-Archive-Guide.pdf
Kinross shire through the archive guide

https://www.electricscotland.com/history/australia/scotaus3.htm
Large scale emigration to Australia after 1832

Scottish Slang 1.0 (The Ultimate Guide to Help You Blend in North of the Border) - Highland Titles
Scottish Slang

https://www.portrait.gov.au/magazines/60/material-culture#:~:text=The%20Rajah%20was%20your%20garden,member%20of%20its%20human%20cargo.
Rajah Quilt – National Portrait Gallery

https://convictrecords.com.au/ships/rajah/voyages/463?page=2
Rajah Convict Ship

https://discovery.nationalarchives.gov.uk/details/r/C4106884
Medical journal of the Rajah

https://www.quakersaustralia.info/Stitches/rajah-quilt
The Rajah Quilt

https://www.researchtasmania.com.au/rajah-biographies/
Rajah biographies

http://researchtasmania.com/wp-content/uploads/2017/05/LAING_Amelia.pdf
Amelia Laing

https://sevenlittleaustralians.com/product/my-name-is-lizzie-flynn-a-story-of-the-rajah-quilt/
Link to purchase - My Name is Lizzie Flynn : A Story of the Rajah Quilt, by Clare Saxby and Lizzie Newcomb

C:\Users\leewi\Downloads\Rural-Launceston-heritage.pdf
Rural Launceston Heritage Study

https://femaleconvicts.org.au/docs/seminars/IreneSchaffer_FromFingertinker.pdf
Irene Schaffer - From Finger tinker to the First Woman Horse Trainer in Van Diemen's Land.1805-1849. Mary Bowater Convict & Landholder

https://www.tasfhs.org/downloads/Volume27Number3_2006.pdf
Tasmanian Ancestry, Tasmania Family History Society Inc, Volume 27 Number 3 – December 2006

https://monissa.com/hotels/category/when/
Launceston Hotels

https://sparc.utas.edu.au/index.php/watercolour-of-christs-college-at-bishopbourne
Painting of Christ College

https://www.churchesoftasmania.com/2019/02/no-354-christ-college-and-its-chapel-at.html
Chris College information and paintings